Praise for Carlyn Greenwald's

DIRECTOR'S CUT

"With Greenwald in the director's chair, one-of-a-kind voice and sharp Hollywood detail light up this fun and passionate romance. Val and Maeve's relationship is at once resonant with meaningful questions and utterly charming. Vivid, steamy, and smart, *Director's Cut* is a rom-com to remember."

— Emily Wibberley and Austin Siegemund-Broka,
authors of *The Breakup Tour*

"Carlyn Greenwald has done it again! With glossy prose and shining voice, Greenwald has crafted a captivating love letter to both the power of film as well as our most transformative relationships. Driven by a sweeping, swoony (and steamy!) romance, and decorated with enough film references to delight any cinephile, *Director's Cut* will have you glued to your seat. Pass the popcorn."

— Becky Chalsen, author of *Kismet*

"Witty, horny, and told with poignant authenticity, *Director's Cut* puts queer love center frame. The vulnerability of Val's experience is delivered through a thoughtful lens, and Greenwald manages to blend the larger-than-life Hollywood setting with a beautifully grounded and relatable love story. I cried, laughed, and yearned—this book has it all." —Rebekah Faubion, author

Carlyn Greenwald

DIRECTOR'S CUT

Carlyn Greenwald writes romantic and thrilling page-turners for teens and adults. A film school graduate and former Hollywood lackey, she now works in publishing. She resides in Los Angeles, mourning ArcLight Cinemas and soaking in the sun with her dogs.

Also by Carlyn Greenwald

Sizzle Reel

DIRECTOR'S CUT

DIRECTOR'S CUT

Carlyn Greenwald

Vintage Books
A Division of Penguin Random House LLC
New York

A VINTAGE BOOKS ORIGINAL 2024

Copyright © 2024 by Carlyn Greenwald

All rights reserved. Published in the United States by Vintage Books,
a division of Penguin Random House LLC, New York, and distributed
in Canada by Penguin Random House Canada Limited, Toronto.

Vintage and colophon are registered trademarks of
Penguin Random House LLC.

Library of Congress Cataloging-in-Publication Data
Names: Greenwald, Carlyn, [date] author.
Title: Director's Cut : a novel / Carlyn Greenwald.
Description: First edition. | New York : Vintage Books,
a division of Penguin Random House LLC, 2024.
Identifiers: LCCN 2023048822 (print) | LCCN 2023048823 (ebook)
Subjects: GSAFD: Novels.
Classification: LCC PS3607.R46813 D57 2024 (print) |
LCC PS3607.R46813 (ebook) | DDC 813/.6—dc23
LC record available at https://lccn.loc.gov/2023048822
LC ebook record available at https://lccn.loc.gov/2023048823

Vintage Books Trade Paperback ISBN: 978-0-593-46822-7
eBook ISBN: 978-0-593-46821-0

Book design by Steven Walker

vintagebooks.com

Printed in the United States of America
10 9 8 7 6 5 4 3 2 1

To Introverts with Hip Problems. Kate, Taylor,
and Will, wouldn't have gotten here without you.

DIRECTOR'S CUT

CHAPTER ONE

I need a drink.

A Pellegrino sweats on my makeup artist June's vanity. It falls somewhere in the corner of my vision; June and the understood *Stay still* form a brick wall between me and even pretending to placate the dryness in my mouth. They'd offered me a laundry list of nonalcoholic drinks when my manager, Trish, and I first walked into the *Late Late Show with Winston Gray*, everything but what I need. I consider asking the intern with the infected nose ring for a glass of wine, to see if she'd bend the rules, but I don't. I sit, and the wisps of June's eyeshadow brush ghost featherlight across my skin.

I've never needed alcohol to get through an interview before. I've certainly *enjoyed* it, maybe even used it as a crutch once everyone got talking, but it's never been on my mind like this before. That said, I've never done an interview where I've talked about my directing before. It's never mattered like this.

June pulls away. "Gonna set you and you're good to go." She glances down at her phone. "And right on time."

In other words, T minus five before I'm on with Winston.

"You're promoting TV today, right?" June asks, her back facing the mirror.

"Yeah, *Strange Prey*'s second-season opener."

It was one of the first things Trish booked me when I signed with her, one of those *pick any random thing you'd love to do* bucket list items. An experiment. What Trish calls an excuse to own my narrative. I thought being out would be no big deal, that *that* was going to be me owning my narrative. When I reshuffled my team, that I'd get more opportunities that aligned with my values, my creativity and passions. A few new types of opportunities and I truly thought everything would change for the better. But then the media branded me as only one thing. I tried to deal for a while, but I could handle being taken even less seriously than before I came out for only so long. I disappeared from the public eye not even a month after throwing myself into the spotlight. Focused on the work. No press. I acted and directed and ended up finishing my PhD all while sustaining myself off delivery groceries and forcing my friends to meet at someone's house.

While productive, it wasn't healthy. Over the past month, I've reentered public places for the sake of my social life. Trish insisted press was the next step. I'm back, and the layers of makeup and hair spray feel heavy and unfamiliar on my skin. I haven't given an interview in front of a camera since the *Goodbye, Richard!* promo last spring, and something that used to be second nature now feels terrifyingly foreign.

Trish won't say it, but I can also read between the lines: I'm promoting this episode, but Hollywood is watching me. Gay actress Valeria Sullivan is a commodity worth investing in, but is director Valeria Sullivan? *Oakley in Flames,* my directorial debut, and its upcoming tour around the festival circuit hinges on how I do tonight.

June sprays my face as my heartbeat picks up. She smiles, gloss shimmering on her lips. "Beautiful."

Nothing else. June stands up, her fingers ghosting my shoulder in a moment of assurance. Then she disappears, and a curly-haired guy mics me up. Another leads me to the side of the stage. Trish is nowhere in sight. She insisted when we signed that she'd be different from my helicopter parent manager, Steven, that I'd have the freedom to say and do what I wanted. That she trusted me. And, yes, originally I hadn't felt I needed her here, and she'd come only because we both decided why not, but my skin crawls when I can't find her. I know all the interview questions, but I can't shake an almost superstitious dread that I *need* to see her before I go on. Like I've given her the key to my brain and just remembered the lock was there.

But there's Winston Gray onstage, saying, "Valeria Sullivan!" to a roar of applause.

The mic is attached to the lapel of my blazer, so I can't give myself a pep talk under my breath. That this will go well and I'll get my career—the career I want—back on track. Instead, I walk out with my best fake smile and the assurance that none of the bright, grinning faces in the audience or those watching this while falling asleep in their living rooms will be able to see my shaking hands or hear my hammering heart.

Valeria Sullivan, whoever the fuck that is, is back.

Winston is one of those hosts whose best feature is his grin. Nothing else about him is memorable. He's white, maybe midforties, wears generic suits, has a flat California accent, and can't even claim an embarrassing laugh as a trademark. We've met once before, when I hosted *SNL* some years back and he was still a cast member.

"Valeria, it's so good to see you again," he says, making easy eye contact. His caramel-brown eyes sparkle in the harsh stage lighting; his handshake is firm.

I wish I remembered more about him from our time together in New York. But as a reckless closeted lesbian, I was too busy floating on cloud nine because the writers wrote me sketches where I got to make out with female cast members. As *jokes,* but sometimes jokes and costumes and *wink wink, nudge nudge* can be water in an oasis of fame and closeted queerness.

"So great to see you too," I say, wondering what he remembers about me that I can't recall.

I take my seat. He's got a more modern setup than most talk show sets, dark blue leather couches for both of us instead of the host behind a desk. He's one of those trendy hosts, and he's given me, Trish, and my publicist, Frankie, a list of bits we could do, ranging from video games to a version of Russian roulette where I take shots of condiments. It all feels a little like I signed up for *All That* or some shit. I believe my exact words to Trish were *I'd gladly live through the homophobia of the nineties if it meant just doing a normal fucking Rosie O'Donnell interview.*

So, yeah, I opted for just the interview, and I can see the disappointment in Winston's eyes as he adjusts his legs before speaking.

"Love the suit, by the way." He doesn't sound quite as smarmy as Hannibal Lecter did saying that line, but it's still an early curveball. It's too close to the lesbian-fashion comments for my comfort.

"Thank you. I don't know what my stylist is doing, but she needs a raise. People have been noticing so much more lately."

Winston gives a polite laugh, but the audience seems to genuinely enjoy that one. I can't really make out faces given how brightly lit the studio is, but the audience seems to be enjoying themselves. I relax my shoulders, letting that sink in. There aren't any comments I have to avoid, truths I have to skirt anymore. This should be—and can be—easier than before. I want people like me to feel seen by me.

"So, coming back to the promo circuit, you're bringing something a little different here, aren't you?" Winston says. "How has switching hats affected you? Do you think you're a better director because of your experience acting?"

It's a standard actor/director question, and one for which I've been studying countless answers from actor/directors. "I don't think I necessarily am, especially when it comes to directing for TV. I have more experience with the ins and outs of features, so I actually had a ton to learn from the actors, who've become experts in their own rights about TV as a medium."

He snakes the ball as I take a breath. "You think it's that different, even with a streaming show like *Stranger Prey*?"

I dig my nail into my side, knowing it's obscured from cameras. Interviewers are just a part of the process. I let my thoughts go and try to answer his question directly. "The scripts and my ultimate vision don't differ much from what I would do for a feature, which is amazing. I think I just wanted to not feel like I was barging onto Justin and Pete's scene like I knew everything. I suppose *that's* what I took from being an actor, knowing most of us don't thrive under a patronizing director."

"Do you see yourself as a natural leader?"

The wording throws me, seconds ticking as I scramble for puzzle pieces, baking in the lights. Then, thank god, I remember. "Somehow, yes."

"You told me that you've almost unwittingly found yourself in a leadership role with your family."

I take a sip of the water they provide on set before answering. My response is one of those anecdotes that cracked up all my friends, and the moment I told Trish, she said it was time to incorporate it into the late-night circuit.

"Yeah. So I'm Jewish on my mom's side, and she's one of five kids, so holidays like Passover were these huge family affairs for me growing up. I'm the second oldest of the cousins and started the, shall we say, rainbow train."

This gets a laugh from the audience, who must be a little queer if they're laughing at that.

"I come out to my larger family at twenty, and my mom warns me before Passover, saying, 'Val, sweetie, you know everyone's just curious. They're just gonna be *curious*.' Which, if you know, you know."

The audience laughs as I give a shrug, quick to keep the story focused. It's not that I'm unwilling to talk about being gay. It's an integral part of my life. But I want to decide when it comes up.

"And I'm a bookish college student on spring break," I continue, "that's the absolute last thing I want to answer, so I decide I'm gonna buy weed to take the edge off."

The audience rumbles in laughter.

"I'm sitting through Passover, and I'm blazed out of my mind. Definitely took too much. To the point where I don't even really remember who talked to me or what happened during the seder. Just that maror and haroseth have never tasted that good before."

Winston, who I *think* is Jewish, laughs especially hard at that.

"God, that is saying something," Winston says.

"Yeah." I sit up straighter, rub my hands together. "So the next year my cousin Eric pulls me aside before seder starts. He's maybe seventeen at the time. He takes me into our grandma's bathroom, and goes, 'Can I have some of your weed?' And, of course, I'm like 'Hell no.' I'm pretty dumb, but I'm not *give a minor marijuana* dumb. But this kid looks me right in the eye and goes, 'I'm gay too, and the only way I'm getting through this seder is high.' And—" I throw up my hands, getting into the dramatics a bit. "I give him one of my edibles, and we have a great time. I *have to* support the community. A couple more years pass of us secretly doing this. At this point,

I'm twenty-five, working in Hollywood, should probably know better. But my teenage cousin *Kenny* pulls me aside—not Eric, mind you, who's now twenty-one—and says, 'Hey I'm gay, can I get the weed?' And I'm thinking I already gave Eric the edibles, and what kind of cousin would I be if I didn't also give Kenny some? So the duo became a trio."

"You became the family drug dealer?" Winston says, holding back a laugh.

I grin and shrug. "I guess I did."

"So what happened? Did a family member catch you, or how did it stop?"

I smile; now for the punch line. "Oh, no, it's still going on. I prepared my grandma for this, said I was going to tell this story on the air, and all she said was 'That's fine, it's not like you need your brain for acting.'"

The room roars in laughter and *OHHHH*s.

"Which, usually is pretty fair," I continue, resisting the urge to bite my newly manicured nails. "But I gotta teach a guest semester at USC in a few weeks, so godspeed to me and the administration."

The guest-teaching was another one of those *anything you want to try* requests from Trish. She said she would've secured it regardless of the fact that I finished my PhD a few months ago, but I still get a little flame of pride in my chest knowing that even if I weren't famous, I'd still be qualified to teach the course. I couldn't get a real adjunct professor job without more experience, but close. Another opportunity where I'm not my face, my body, my sexuality.

Now, to get deeper into academia with Winston.

"It sounds like your sexuality has been a big part of your life for a while, then. Were all your family surprised when you came out publicly last year?" Winston asks.

For a moment, I'm in my first dissertation defense again, getting my oral presentation notes out of order. The interview is supposed to go *directing, Passover anecdote, USC, end.* I only agreed to tell the drug story that makes me look like a clown knowing that we'd be focusing on my academics. That we'd end on a serious note. Under the armor of the black suit, I'm sweating. On camera, I adjust the way my legs are crossed.

"Not really. My family's known for years and knew why I wasn't out to the public. There wasn't really anything new to ask."

The fluttering panic drives nervous energy through me. I want to look everywhere but at Winston, so I keep my eyes locked on him. I watch the way his lips turn, how tightly he's holding his hands in his lap, looking for clues, anything to guess what he's thinking right now, where he's going.

Still, I try to course-correct as smoothly as I can. "At this point, I find exploring sexuality comes more naturally from behind the camera—"

"Not even why you chose to come out when you did?"

I know somewhere behind me, there's a countdown clock that will end this interview, but only Winston knows what it says. And as I process that question, each second in silence a second that some asshole body language expert will rip me to shreds for, every muscle in my body aches to turn around to see that forbidden clock.

"It was the right time," I answer before I can think anymore. "Which was a theme I wanted to explore with this episode—"

Then Winston smiles. But it's a pinch before the burn regardless. "No person who prompted it?"

Person who prompted it. No, no one's asked this before. They're too polite to. But the words flood into my head like I've rehearsed this one to death. Her name is Luna. She's a sweet, oh-so-talented young cinematographer who reminded me there was cerebral connection in my vapid world, who was so tortured under the weight of what society had drilled into her, who still got up and made herself happy through the tearstains. Who—just like every other closeted Hollywood girl who's ended up in my bed over the past seven years—I'd never out in a million years.

And I don't know what comes over me, but it feels a hell of a lot better than the squirming panic. If he's going to keep fucking interrupting, I can play too. I smirk.

"You really want me to name names, don't you? You want to imagine it was some costar whose name you can use for clickbait? You don't have to be so coy."

I wait for him to back down, ignoring the burning embarrassment that's fallen over my skin. But all he does is shrug.

"Well, will you?" He says it with a laugh. "People were really shipping you and Phoebe Wittmore during the *Goodbye, Richard!* junkets."

Of course they were. That was the last junket I did before coming out of the closet last year, where my anxiety was so bad that I could barely eat or sleep and existed in a perpetual state of nearly blacking out between the carousel of interviews; where every brush of Phoebe's shoulder against mine reminded me of the mediocre "experimental" sex we *had* indeed had; where I still laughed and flirted and charmed her because even if she was straight, she was the person I knew. In those junkets where one wrong word could out me, I took whatever comforting presences I could.

I laugh, despite the fact that my insides are melting as fast as my sweat-slicked skin. "Are you gonna bust out the real people fanfic next?"

The laughter is getting thinner and thinner. Winston, in fact, is the only one who's laughing in any meaningful way. "Man, testy. And they say the best time in a celebrity's life is *after* they come out of the closet."

I can't see Trish. I can't see Trish, and it's a good thing. Because when I stand up and walk out opposite the way I came on, I only make it behind the curtain because I don't see anyone's faces. My ears are ringing, my insides are as liquid as the tears in my eyes. I only take in one thing.

There were thirty seconds left in the interview, and I just walked off.

Trish finds me within seconds—but they feel like hours. She grabs me like a summer breeze, whisking me out with barely a touch on my shoulder. A tinted-window Escalade picked me up for the interview this afternoon, but Trish leads us to her midnight-black BMW. She blasts the air-conditioning against the lingering furnace of LA August. Winston's studio's in Downtown LA, one of the few places in this sprawling town that captures heat the way New York City does. I take a seat in her cushy white leather, acutely aware of how my neck sticks to it. As I undo my hair from the updo my stylist could barely create with my growing-out pixie cut, Trish turns the knob on her radio and backs her car out of a parking spot.

"I'm not mad at you," Trish says, slicing through the silence. "I know you said Steven was pretty harsh about missteps. This isn't a misstep. At least, I don't see it that way. I'm on your side."

I snort. "You're my manager. You have to be."

"As a *lesbian woman,* I was horrified on your behalf."

It's a brief, but familiar, spark of comfort, one I've felt since I connected with powerhouse Trish: queer woman topping Hollywood best-of-business lists that are otherwise stuffed with lukewarm straight people, and then landed her as my manager. It's a start.

"You know doing interviews with people like us aren't going to get me trending."

"And I don't particularly care about that."

We merge onto the 101. It's so late that there isn't any traffic.

"You were off before the interview even started. I can't imagine you'd have flipped out otherwise, not with your poise. So, what's on your mind?"

"He was supposed to be interviewing me about my directing and teaching. He couldn't even stick to it for two questions."

Trish frowns. "Val—"

"I was an idiot to think that I could change that. People only want me if I'm a *gay* actress."

"And you knew you'd be wading back into the bullshit. I know we didn't expect it to hit like *this*, but it's just nonsense we have to deal with to get to the art. You've always wanted to act and direct. Remember? You told me that when we first signed. You were so excited to make art without having to justify your identity or views. We're almost there."

"Do you really, truly think, even if *Oakley* sells, that I'll ever direct another feature? Would anyone buy one if I'm not acting in it?"

"You know I can't predict the market that way."

"But you've seen a hell of a lot of actors try to break into directing. You've seen what kind of folks make more than one film." I squeeze my hands together. "Do you think I'm one of them?"

Trish is silent—painfully silent—for a long time. Enough time for a lump to migrate up my throat. "If you woke up tomorrow and could only act, would you quit Hollywood?"

If I woke up tomorrow and all I could ever do was sift through scripts hoping for one written with empathy for people like me, hoping I'd get paired with a director who was organized, talented, and kind, and then throwing myself through the press ringer after being cornered into another obtuse lesbian role and only talk about that—yeah, I know the answer to that.

"No." Panic beats its wings in my stomach. "But what choice do I have? What else would I do?"

Trish doesn't have an answer.

CHAPTER TWO

Trish and I slowly ease back into normal conversation as we get closer to my home in Hollywood Hills. Yes, I'm that asshole who lives in Hollywood Hills. I've wanted the *BoJack Horseman* view ever since I binged the show and like fifty pounds of Wendy's in the months post-failed PhD and failed engagement with Emily. At least I *think* that's where I got the idea to move here from. Truthfully, all I remember about that time period was sobbing into my older sister Gwyn's shirt and asking if I was Mr. Peanutbutter or Diane. Gwyn told me I was the worst parts of both.

"You have anyone waiting for you at home? Anyone who could keep you company tonight?" Trish asks.

The farther I get from DTLA, the stronger the humiliation becomes. I know industry people deal with Actresses Gone Too Far all the time, but it feels like I've failed. I've been doing interviews for years. If I'd just stayed for another thirty seconds, there wouldn't be headlines circulating. In an industry where being dramatic and unprofessional is nothing to write home about, I fucked up *so* badly that I'll be a talking point. And I'm supposed to *teach* next week. There won't be publicists and fixers in academia; my head's already spinning thinking of it. If I can't even do what I've been doing successfully for years, I cringe to consider how disastrous returning to teaching is going to be.

"I guess there's Gwyn," I say.

It's so late that it's more than a safe bet to say that my older sister by five years has commuted back from Beverly Hills, where she works as a GI doctor for old celebrities/old rich Jewish people. You know, the type who like asking her if she has enough time to mother her kids while she's got a finger up their asses.

"You wanna call her?"

It's almost midnight, so I opt for a *you up* text that I regret the wording of immediately.

But, within seconds, Gwyn's name lights up on my phone.

"Are you having a flare-up?" she asks *right outta the gate.* Even though Trish is focused on her throwback disco music, I cross my arms self-consciously.

"Why would I call you at midnight over a flare-up?"

Short and skinny: if you were born ten weeks early in the nineties, you were at high risk of exposure to necrotizing enterocolitis. Some premature babies took antibiotics and had no damage. Some, like me, required major surgery to remove entire sections of viscera. It was a harrowing experience for my parents, and they never got therapy for it, but I've managed to survive with minimal but constant bodily inadequacies. A near constant stream of probiotics and IBS that supposedly only flares up when I'm stressed. Which would be cool if I wasn't stressed 24-7.

"Because that's all you ever text me about. Why? Is there something else up?"

My phone chimes, a text from Charlie. Charlie has been a weird, fluctuating presence in my life since we were in high school, including him being my Hollywood beard up until a year ago. Everyone loved the fact that we were "high school sweethearts," still together after we'd both made it in acting. We were nearly inseparable when he starred in *Oakley in Flames*, but I haven't heard much from him since we wrapped. I think he's having a life crisis over the fact that, at twenty-nine, he's too old to be a twink. I hate to admit it, but he's been one of the last friends to be fully reintegrated into my daily life after I hid away post coming-out.

On the phone to Gwyn, I sigh. "The interview I just did went shitty, and I was hoping for some company."

There's a pause that's a lot longer than I need it to be. "Have you eaten today?"

I resist the urge to roll my eyes; she's such a fucking mom. "No. I had a photo shoot earlier."

Another text from Charlie. I swipe it away and highly consider hanging up this call as my stomach tightens from post-interview stress. I'm not sure I could articulate the black hole of emotion I'm feeling right now if Gwyn asked me about it.

I needed to come out last year. At first, I thought it was even going well, that I could hire Trish and be my authentic self and reinvent myself properly with *Oakley in Flames*. But once postproduction ended, I realized that that media quiet I thought I was experiencing was just reality in waiting. Every interview I attended, whether it was trade cover stories, podcasts, or the silly Instagram AMAs I'd do when bored, the same questions would pour in. *How long have you been gay? What made you come out now? Are you wearing that because you're out? What lucky woman are you dating?* I tried to swallow it and answer the questions quickly and blandly.

But after my answers were out in the world, I'd get another round of interviews and they'd *keep asking them*. Even while promoting acting roles that weren't even gay, I'd get the questions. I'd get them at charity events, at Hollywood parties, while stopped on the street.

I started only receiving scripts for roles featuring Character Name (late twenties, lesbian). Not complex lesbian roles either; raunchy sidekicks, tragic historical love interests who end up dead, action heroes where the character description in the script is the only place you'd even know they were queer. Decidedly less complex, emotional roles than my work before, all I'm sure because some executive said this movie needed *authenticity*. It was as if nothing I could ever say, no matter how insightful or impassioned I was, could compare to my sexuality or what I hoped to explore creatively. By the time I saw an *SNL* sketch teasing the photo I took to come out, I . . . well, I had no choice but to disappear.

Tonight has only solidified it.

I have to face the writing on the wall: even if the TV directing gig has aligned more with my passions in years, it's misery to keep going like this. Even if we fix the PR fallout of the interview. That uncertainty wraps itself into my aching guts. I *know* I haven't had a bad flare-up in years, but the possibility of one does enough damage.

I take a deep breath. Will the pain away.

"Val?" Gwyn's voice sounds far away. It's the tone she uses when she's scared I'm going to react a certain way. "Why don't you order a pizza and I'll drive over, okay? Get Domino's like you like." She audibly exhales. "We can give the twins the leftovers tomorrow."

It gets me to smile for what feels like the first time in hours. "Half cheese, half pepperoni and jalapeño?"

"Yeah, perfect."

"I'll get those lava cakes too, for good measure. The twins love them."

"God, no! *You* don't have to deal with them."

"Eh, just give them heroin after. They'll be fine."

"Don't have kids."

No amount of joking quite softens the sting of Gwyn's joke.

My parents have been fine with my being gay since I came out ten years ago, but they're still, like, boomers. Their pity looks might as well weigh fifty pounds per eye per parent. *Oh, our poor homosexual daughter! Nearly thirty and the last person she dated was a twenty-four-year-old camera PA. How's she ever going to find a wife and give Lily and Oscar cousins?*

The worst part is I'm starting to *buy it*. I haven't slept with anyone since Luna in July of *last year* because of some delusional idea that I want sex to mean something. It's only a matter of time before I go all U-Haul, yet LA has been a desolate landscape of club bathroom hookups and straight girls having short dyed hair and septum piercings like that isn't supposed to *mean something* for me. I can't even find a *girlfriend*, let alone someone to enter into heteronormative familial bliss with.

"Fuck you," I say, not quite a joke enough.

Another text from Charlie.

"I'll text you when I leave." She hangs up first, just in time for Trish to pull off the freeway and cruise into the obnoxiously narrow streets of my neighborhood. It's moments like this, when I'm woozy and mildly exhausted by my lifestyle, that I tell myself I'm going to move to Palos Verdes and live in an isolated cliffside manor until the ocean swallows it because of climate change. That *BoJack* view isn't worth it. Paparazzi slink around the streets as often as raccoons do. And even though the paparazzi aren't going to steal my twelve-pound dog, it's not ideal. In fact, I'd take an invasion of Los Angeles coyotes if it'd mean knowing I could walk Eustace around my neighborhood in pajamas without being photographed.

Trish parks outside my house, killing her headlights. For a moment, she just stares at me in silence. Mulling over her words.

"Does acting still bring you the joy it did when you first started?" she asks. "Creative work in general?"

The answer threatens to take my breath away. "I hope."

She nods slowly. "Let's follow through on the projects we already booked and keep the meetings we set, okay? We tried to rebrand you, and it didn't stick. So catch your breath, and we can try again."

"Okay."

"And don't assume *Oakley* is dead just because it's a long shot on the festival circuit." She smiles. "You're talented, Val. That's worth fighting for. I wish you'd see that."

We exchange hugs, I thank her for the ride, and I step off into the rapidly cooling night. Eustace comes bounding up to me as soon as I open my front door, jumping on my legs and licking my formerly sweaty shins. He's a Chihuahua mix, so he doesn't get much higher than that. I call Gwyn back, figuring it'll be faster than texting.

"I'm in," I say.

"Okay, I'm headed to my car."

I scoop up Eustace and walk to the living room/kitchen, knocking lights on as I go.

"Perfect."

And then, in the millisecond after I flip the light switch, I see the figure sitting on my couch. I scream and fall into straight-up deer-in-headlights mode.

"Val?" Gwyn still says over the phone. "Is everything okay? Jesus, do I—?"

"It's Charlie," I say, my tone flat.

Yeah, there's fucking Charlie Durst, just sitting on my couch in a *Star Trek* T-shirt, shorts, and sandals. His phone is in his hand, and he has a giant grin on his face like it's normal to break into someone's house. He reaches into his pocket and pulls out a *garage door opener*.

"I forgot to give this back to you, so perfect timing!" he says, smile still on his face, like he's genuinely thrilled to see me.

Eustace wrestles out of my arms and goes to lick Charlie.

"Oh," Gwyn says on the phone. "Is he staying over?"

I look at Charlie, narrowing my eyes. "Are you staying here tonight?"

Charlie's grin slides into a soft frown. "I was hoping . . . ?"

"Yeah," I say into the phone.

"Forget the pizza," Gwyn says. "I'll call you tomorrow."

And then she *hangs up on me*. The twisting pain of anxiety is stabbing into my insides relentlessly. I shove the phone into my back pocket to avoid throwing it against a wall. My gaze falls to Charlie.

"So you were going to get pizza?" he asks. "I can order if you want . . ."

Gwyn's never been Charlie's biggest fan. The dude *is* kind of a dumbass, but I'm a dumbass too. I've never gotten Gwyn to admit it, but I think she's still angry about Charlie enabling my beard thing. That, or she's mad about a very specific incident involving Charlie at a holiday party in the last five years. Regardless, it's not a *good* reason.

I want to call my sister back and demand she explain why she abandoned me. I want alcohol, for the second time today. But instead I walk over to the couch, drop onto it, and say, "I'm going through a crisis too."

He moves to right above my head. Lets Eustace go and starts stroking my hair. "We can talk about it tonight."

Just like that, that boob has weaseled his way into staying the night. One way to fulfill Trish's ask that I not be alone.

A year and a half ago, a woman would've been occupying the space Charlie is in now. And now I can't even masturbate.

I'm pretty sure Charlie has about 7 percent body fat, so I'm actually quite surprised by what he ends up ordering from Domino's when I tell him the toppings I like and then leave him to his own devices. But there his beautiful self is, carefully selecting a chicken wing from the tin foil container like he's trying to find the one with the highest protein value.

"I don't get why that interview ended you, though," Charlie says once he finally chooses a wing.

I dip a slice of pizza into ranch. "All people care about is that I'm pretty and gay. Even during an interview that was exclusively about my directing. Hollywood's never going to see anything else about me."

"I don't think that's necessarily true. Most people can't even remember an actor's worst interview. You can always change the way you're perceived by the public with a great enough future performance."

I sigh, dread creeping back in. "Maybe I'm just tired, then. I don't think I can wait to see if the universe changes its mind."

"Well . . . that sucks." He pauses. "Is there anything you're looking forward to?"

I search my brain as I chew. Even back to the seconds before the interview went sour. "I mean, there's the guest-teaching gig."

Something possibly even more intellectual and not about my sexuality than directing. It's the perfect way to catch my breath, as Trish said.

"There ya go! That'll at least be a different pace. Flex a different muscle."

Even though Charlie regularly calls me while reading his weekly scripts for the *Star Trek* reboot he's on to ask questions like "Do humans breathe nitrogen?," he's picked up on my academic spouting a decent amount, down to the minuscule details of my failed dissertation that I explained to him when we lived in a shitty apartment together four years ago. The warmth prickling at my chest is an old but familiar sensation.

"Yeah, it will be." A sprinkle of lightness hits me as I let the thought wander. "They're letting me teach a real course. The kind of class I would've led given my specialization in pop music history. The co-professor they assigned me has been hands off and let me design the course. Maybe it will be good for me."

Charlie smiles, waving his pizza around. "Yeah, fuck Winston Gray. That sounds so fun."

I sigh, a twist of guilt running through me as I consider the crust of the slice of pizza I just finished. "If I'm even still good."

He looks up at me and shakes his head. "Hey, look, I'm not saying switch careers, but don't lie to yourself. You're great."

"Even though I haven't taught since I was a TA in postgrad?"

"Well, sure, but they're not measuring you up to a regular adjunct. Do you think any of the celebrities who taught at USC could *actually* teach?"

"No comment," I say.

I need to focus. Charlie asked if I think the institution thinks I can teach.

I hadn't considered it. Does USC think I'm not going to be taking this position seriously? The *Dr. Valeria B. Sullivan* on all my bills is fucking real. I legitimately am qualified for this job, barring some years of teaching experience other candidates would have. I know they assigned me a more seasoned faculty member and a TA to assist with running class and grading papers, but the other professor is just there as a formality. They let me make the syllabus and everything.

That couldn't have just been celebrity placating, could it? I don't need a whole new set of people thinking I'm a joke.

"Charlie, do you think they think I'm not qualified for this?" I ask. The salt from the wings is starting to coat my mouth rather than actually taste good.

He studies me. I set down another slice.

"No offense, but if I wasn't your best friend—"

"You're my best friend?"

"*Best friend*, I'd assume you were dumb." He pauses, as if waiting for me to throw the still-full-and-pointy lava cake box at him. "It's just the curse of being blond and beautiful. Not to mention there's video footage of you dropping yogurt on Oscar's head and then licking it off him."

"Dude, there's no blond-and-beautiful oppression. You're the first canonically gay Captain Kirk because of that."

Something soft passes through Charlie's expression, but it's gone so fast I can almost convince myself I'm just falling into a salt, fat, and sugar coma. "It's more about the documented dumbassery part," he says.

A mental note: next time Trish wants me on a late-night show that *does* serve you wine beforehand, stop offering up terrible home videos Gwyn has taken of me and her children and start offering to teach Baudrillard. "Is that seriously my brand other than gay?"

"Yeah, but don't change it. It makes you seem approachable."

I throw my hands up. "This co-professor must think I'm an idiot!"

Charlie picks up his phone. "Wouldn't he have to read your dissertation to work with you? I mean, if anyone thinks you're at least a smart idiot, it's him."

"Her."

I don't know why I bother correcting him. I flip open the lava cake box.

"Her." Charlie pauses again. "What's her name?"

"Maeve Arko."

I only remember that because my mom asked the other day and then made a point to tell me the last name is Jewish. As if that's going to affect how well we work together.

Charlie looks to his phone, his eyes lighting up a moment before he looks back at me. "Also, not to be that guy, since I am second-billed in your movie, but have there been any updates on Sundance?"

All it takes is the mention of Sundance to tighten my stomach. The first of many festivals that *Oakley* won't get into. Not to mention it's one of my least favorite festivals because of the altitude, which makes my usual press anxiety even worse than usual—

I rub my arms. "We find out in November."

He quirks an eyebrow. "You don't seem excited."

I stab at the lava cake. Use the extra few seconds chewing and swallowing to think of the right words. The cake tastes vaguely like Oreos, and suddenly I understand why my niblings love this thing so much.

"There's no reason to get our hopes up."

Charlie gives me a weak smile. "I may be biased, but *I* hope *Oakley in Flames* gets in. We need a win."

I'm moments from asking about Maeve Arko again. But then I see it: Charlie's lips have been turned down over neutral the whole night. "What did you lose?"

I have a feeling before he says it, my stomach twisting as the seconds wash by.

"*Star Trek* got canceled, even with the great ratings and reception."

The lump clinging to my throat is a familiar pain. This business is all about rejection and having your dreams cut off. Even in our positions, with fairly consistent jobs and teams that find us genuinely great projects, there's so little guarantee. And I *loved* Charlie in that *Star Trek* role. It was one of those roles he slipped into like a glove. Even his press interviews about the show were some of his best work.

But he keeps going.

"And I . . ." He squeezes his eyes shut. "I—I've been an idiot. I didn't invest well. I have back payments on my house that I was gonna pay off with the check from *Star Trek*'s new season. I've already sold all my assets to get the Feds off my back, but I can hardly afford to live in a shithole motel for a week—"

My first instinct is to slide the other lava cake over to Charlie. The second is to pull him into a hug. He shudders a little in my arms, but no tears.

"Hey, hey, you can stay here for a couple of weeks until your manager gets you a new gig. It's okay."

He mutters "Thank you" into my skin as I eye the Domino's on the table.

Another reminder of how fleeting our careers are. As much as I don't have a good feeling about Hollywood, the scarier thing remains that I don't *know* what's going to happen after it. Twenty-four hours ago, I was a respected actress and up-and-coming director with a teaching side gig. Now I'm a PR disaster with a brief stint as a professor.

Hopefully it'll go better than the interview.

CHAPTER THREE

Charlie settles into my house that week, and the two of us end up spending a lot of time cooking together and commiserating over our prospects in Hollywood. He even manages to help me pick out a first-day outfit and accompanies me to my stylist to shorten my sides again. The class I'm teaching meets at 2:00 p.m., but I've been asked to meet Maeve Arko and our TA at one thirty. Even given all my preparation, I'm incredibly nervous, and I find myself cursing my ridiculous taste (and Charlie) as I adjust the lay of the blazer on my pinstripe suit. It should be fine—*I look amazing in this,* and we found a blouse that doesn't show off my tits—but I swear I can feel the Tom Ford label digging into my back.

Not that I'm the only bitch at this school clacking from Parking Lot D to the cinema school in 85mm Louboutin pumps. In fact, I find myself hyperfixated on the brands I see as I pass. Jimmy Choo, Valentino, Tom Ford, Gucci, all slid onto lithe bodies that have yet another label slapped onto their backpacks, Greek letters on their shirts.

Then I step into the courtyard of the School of Cinematic Arts. It's the most beautiful spot at USC, illuminated in the last-week-of-

August LA sun. The set of buildings are all modeled off a classic Paramount-type studio lot, soft cream stone layered upon rust-colored paint and pueblo-chic red-tile roofs. I force myself not to stop at a rather impressive fountain, perfect red and yellow flowers planted around the edges and a shining statue of some kind of cinema man in the middle. And suddenly the sorority girls I was vibing with so much are gone.

The students here are all scraggly beards and beanies. Industry people who don't have the money to clean up yet. These people also *stare* at me. I tug at the collar of my shirt as I locate an elevator. Everyone is gazing at me in an unnervingly specific way. Not like people on the street, who squint at me like I may or may not be someone they knew in high school. These kids *scrutinize* me, as if trying to remember if they enjoyed my filmography enough to approach me.

I enter the main building and press the elevator button for the fourth floor, forcing a deep breath as the inside stays empty. Then footsteps sound, and a guy darts into the closing doors. He's glistening with sweat and brushes his jet-black hair off his dark brown skin. He's probably in his thirties but has a baby face and, maybe it's the heels, but I can't help but notice how awkward it feels to look down at him when we make eye contact.

"Oh my god, you're Valeria Sullivan," he says. His voice is gravely.

We hit the second floor, no stops. I can't even get my lips to stop trembling as I smile. "Yeah."

Third floor. We stop, doors open, but there's no one there. I press the CLOSE button. The guy is still staring. My first instinct is to look down at my chest; given the way he's looking at me, I'm starting to worry I've had a nip slip.

But my shirt is still perfect. I make eye contact again when I look up. He flusters right along with me, but my blush is now visible.

"I'm so sorry," he says. "Shit. Oh my god, I'm your—I'm your TA."

Oh.

Oh, fuck.

He holds out a hand. "I'm Ty Dhillon. Should've opened with that."

We shake hands. Now if I could just get my heart to stop racing. His palm is sweaty. Or maybe it's mine. Either way, we pull out of the handshake quickly.

"I can take you to Dr. Arko's office."

A twinge hits my chest. When I was a TA, even in England, I called the professors I worked with by their first names. How hardcore is Maeve Arko that she's making her TA use her title and her last name?

"That'd be great."

We step off the elevator. I can still hear the clack of my shoes, despite the carpeting. Ty's brown eyes slide down to them, then swiftly, perhaps automatically, slide up my outfit. It's not sexual necessarily, but there's a feeling I always get with these things. You can tell which fans spend their nights adoring gifsets on social media during convention meet and greets.

"You look great," he says. Bingo. He frowns, pauses. "Like, chic."

I swallow a snort of laughter, but a smile still creeps across my face. "Thank you."

My gaze falls on his outfit. It's a surfer-brand T-shirt, cargo shorts, and sandals. Like the worst straight-California-boy outfit in existence. "You too." My lukewarm comment still seems to fluster him.

Finally, we reach an office door with MAEVE ARKO, ASSISTANT PROFESSOR written in clean letters. Ty knocks before stepping inside.

"I'm sure *you* don't have to knock," Ty says as he opens the door.

Just like that, there's Dr. Maeve Arko, in a navy pantsuit with a floral patterned blouse underneath. One of her hands is wrapped around a pair of Beats as the other closes a laptop with a single finger. Her nails are red.

And here's the problem. I didn't look her up before. In fact, the only thing I knew about her going into this was her name and that she got her PhD in Queer New Wave cinema from Berkeley. But I didn't, you know, look up what year she graduated. Because I can't imagine it was more than three years ago. Considering she's already a tenure-track professor, she must be a providential combination of hypercompetent and lucky.

Oh, and Maeve Arko is fucking hot. Big, expressive brown eyes, an elegant narrow nose, sharp cheekbones and jawline. Shaped brows that look almost natural. A pink swath across Cupid's bow lips, dark brown chin-length hair that falls in waves, like she runs her hands through it all day.

Let me formally apologize to every person I've judged for staring at me like a clown.

Maeve gets up from her desk and shakes my hand. "So nice to meet you, Valeria."

Her voice has a slight timbre, like it'd dip deeper with certain inflections. I'm fucked.

I'm . . . also fucked because she doesn't actually sound happy to meet me. I cannot look to check my blouse again. My jaw's clenching. I need to unclench it. "I go by Val."

She offers me a brief, curt smile. The office is pretty minimalist, set up almost like a therapist's office—her desk, bookshelves filled to the brim, a brown couch, and one chair by the window. She lingers near her desk, and Ty darts for the additional chair. I go for the couch.

"Thank you for agreeing to help me out," I say. Is my voice cracking, or do I always sound this high-pitched?

She straightens some papers, gazes away from me. "Of course.

I've never had a co-professor before, so it'll be new for both of us. You can call me Maeve."

My eyes fall on the papers. I catch the word *syllabus* on one. Should I have brought my own copy?

"Oh, I've taught before," I say. "I think you'll be pleasantly surprised."

She still doesn't look up. "Still, it's been a while. It'll be good to keep the pressure off you for the first couple of sessions. Like we talked about."

My insides melt. Not in a good way. "What do you mean? Aren't you just helping with the administrative portion? Feel free to sit in . . ."

Finally, she locks eyes with me. Yes, her eyes are expressive. And she's not happy right now. "I emailed you the updated syllabus this week. We talked about co-teaching. We're each handling a part of the lecture."

I find myself glancing at Ty, whose own gaze rests heavily on a piece of art on the wall. The email account Maeve has been corresponding with is usually filtered through Trish's assistant. Trish says my teaching is part of my professional business, so it should go to a professional email. Trish said she and her assistant would send them to me. My mind's been so occupied by the TV directing and the Winston interview that the idea of these emails didn't even cross my mind. I haven't checked it in weeks.

And they were apparently *important emails*. Shit.

"That email must be having problems," I blurt out. "Let's use my personal one for class."

She raises her brows. "On the syllabus too?"

Probably going to regret it, but . . . "I'll tell the class."

"Okay. What email?" She clicks a pen, writes down my email on two packets, and hands one to me.

Maeve's handwriting is beautiful. I shouldn't be feeling this hot just from seeing my name in those slanted lines of hers.

The heat only continues to rise as I look over the syllabus. My original syllabus was focused on cult classics and analyzing both successes and failures in the musical genre: *Les Misérables, Chicago, Little Shop of Horrors, The Phantom of the Opera, The Rocky Horror Picture Show, Mamma Mia!, Rocketman,* and the like. But this syllabus has dared to remove *Cats* and put in *Carousel* and *West Side Story* (1961).

"I see there are . . . other changes," I say. My legs are starting to cramp up.

"Again, we talked about this. We agreed there should be some cornerstone pieces for deeper analysis along with the more pulpy, modern pieces that have less complex styles."

I *mean*, at least she kept *Little Shop, Chicago,* and *Rocketman,* but—?

"Okay," I say. "We can . . . see what happens after the first class."

I cross my legs.

Her gaze slips right off my face, down to my shoes.

Down to that flash of a red sole. Her eyes shine in recognition.

She doesn't look pleased.

I was supposed to go to the classroom early to prep and get in the teaching mindset. At least, that's what I tell myself when I bid Maeve and Ty goodbye and head over to a screening room across the court-yard at my assigned building, SCI. My stomachache is back, but my head's swimming so much that I can't even feel it. I can't focus on one train of thought, when teaching theory, my memories of guest appearances and Q&A's I've done at this school, and embarrassment over the way Maeve looked at me are all swirling in my head. Especially the Maeve thing, which I can still see in vivid Technicolor: the break in eye contact, the pulsing tightness of her jaw, locked in annoyance.

No one's looked at me that way since my dissertation got rejected.

As I step into my classroom, I identify all the basic classroom shit. Thank god. I've been having stress nightmares that none of it would be here. But the room has a projector and forty empty chairs facing a table, and a couple of chairs in the front for me and—and Maeve, I guess. Does she really plan to co-teach with me? Who made these fucking arrangements without telling me? I mean, she seemed *very* poised about this. It's not like I would've been opposed per se, it's just that I prepared this entire class under the assumption that I'd be giving all the lectures. It's like being on a set with a writer-director who keeps changing the lines I spent weeks considering and memorizing. Like, I get it, I'm part of a team and shit changes, but I'm not trained in improv. If I have any chance of making this class a success, I sure as hell can't start by looking like a huge fucking clown.

One hand stays on my racing heart as I open my laptop and scan my email. Hundreds of unopened emails, including, fuck, the correspondence between Maeve and "me." Including an updated syllabus, and *I'll intro you and go over class logistics, you take the first basic term lecture, and I'll pick up the slack. No one wants to work hard first class, so don't stress.*

I'm filled with a new bout of self-loathing. This has escalated to a huge, months-long problem that will mess up at least the first class but possibly the next month, but it's also something I could've caught up on in *one night.* I wouldn't have looked like such an asshat in front of Maeve if I had even considered prepping for class today instead of picking out a good outfit. It's downright *embarrassing*. What professor, guest or not, doesn't check their emails before class starts?

I massage my temple as my head starts to ache. If Maeve can be this nice to Trish's assistant posing as me, maybe there's hope. If not, Trish's assistant can just teach this class and I'll go walk into the sea. I shake the frustration out of my body and look at my phone, about to call Trish. But no. I can do this. My antiperspirant is working; I'm a literal expert in music pop culture studies. I'm just teaching eighteen- to twenty-two-year-olds basic film theory and making them watch bad musicals. I have at least twenty-five minutes to catch up as best I can. I scan the syllabus.

So we're doing *West Side Story* for our first film. I don't know why my argument for *The Sound of Music* was rejected, but okay. I know that one. Natalie Wood played a Puerto Rican woman, it won a record number of Oscars, and was a product of its time? Was that the point we were making? It definitely aged worse than *The Sound of Music*.

I flip over to my PowerPoint. Yeah, okay, it'd be easy enough to insert examples from *West Side Story* into the vocab.

The first student rolls in right as I click into my presentation. I can't help but check my phone; twenty minutes early, here even before Maeve and Ty.

Nice to know students are eager, but I don't need to be cramming with an audience. While I panic over the PowerPoint, I find myself trying to avoid staring at her. She's got an Aang sticker from *Avatar: The Last Airbender* on her laptop over the Apple logo. It's a cool *fuck corporations* vibe. Groups of other students filter into the classroom soon after, grabbing seats and chatting with one another. One particular clump of blond, tan young men actually talk *about* taking a class with me as I stand at the front of the classroom. Others throw their gazes toward me and let them cook. Something I'm pretty used to at press events, premieres, those sorts of things. But I remember teaching back at King's College, how students would hardly lay an eye on me. Where my words meant more to them than the body I said those words in. I shiver, searching for Maeve and her very particular academic scrutiny. Even that feels better than being exposed under the students' gaze. It's intense enough that I can't cram anymore.

I don't know what game Maeve is playing, but she slides in a few minutes before class starts, leaves Ty among the students, and approaches me. No laptop, just her irritatingly good looks and presumably years of film theory studies. Kids smile and call out to her as she passes. They share snippets about their projects, ask her opinions on films, which she responds to with a clipped *Didn't see* or *Worth a watch.* Still, the students lap up her sparse thoughts like gospel. I find myself taking my own seat as she reaches the front of the room. I know how to work a photo shoot, interview, or red carpet, but there's something magical about how Maeve approaches a classroom.

"Congrats to everyone for surviving the Hunger Games of registering for this class," Maeve says during her welcome speech. "Now, if you're not going to put in the work, feel free to walk out now in front of Professor Sullivan here."

The class chuckles a bit. I just squirm; I know I know the answer to this somewhere in the back of my mind, but I can't remember if most professors are called professor even if they're doctors, or whether she should've called me Dr. Sullivan.

And suddenly Maeve's lecture stops. Maeve's lecture stops, and her gaze falls on me. I spring out of my seat and move to the front of the room. My hands are shaking. Fuck, it's like the Oscars but I think I have like thirty times more minutes to fill. Is this why I never did theater?

"I have to guess at least some of you fought for entry into this class because you fucking love musicals, so for you, I'm—"

I glance at Maeve. She looks unhappy. Was I not supposed to swear?

"Professor Sullivan. I got my history BA from Oxford University and went on to almost get my PhD from King's College before manic-depressively falling into an acting career."

The students laugh. Mental health jokes work. Good. I get Gen Z.

"I now juggle my time between acting, producing, directing, and being my sister's unpaid nanny."

I get another few chuckles, despite how *not funny* that was. I switch slides. Please tell me we're just going into it. If they want more useless snippets of my bio, they can ask me after class. I guess. Should I have put in precautionary measures in case of stalkers?

"So yeah, sorry, we're gonna start diving into material now," I say. I glance at my computer screen. I've never wanted a laser pointer so badly in my life. "Movie musicals have pretty much been married to the film genre since film incorporated sound, with *The Jazz Singer* in 1927. Like all Hollywood trends, there were attempts to mimic the success of that film, all mediocre and forgotten by historians except for suckers like Professor Arko." The class laughs. Really laughs, there.

I glance at Maeve. Her arms are crossed now. My face burns, but hopefully I'm wearing enough foundation to hide my blush.

"By the second half of the twentieth century, what had become a Hollywood cookie-cutter genre had to adapt to a rapidly changing audience and society. Influences from audience taste to the whims of Hollywood businessmen created starkly different products, to the point where we could see an adaptation of the same show from the eighties and today and the experiences will inevitably be miles apart.

The process of adapting a musical is often more complex and difficult than making a normal movie. In this class we're going to focus on major movie musicals of the past sixty years, both successes and failures, and discuss what techniques were used."

I flip to the vocabulary slide. My body clenches, but I resist the urge to look to Maeve for approval. This isn't some ego-driven Hollywood shit. I can do this all on my own. I'm not being funny enough, but the lecture is completely passable.

"And the biggest question we'll wrestle with for every film we discuss revolves around diegesis."

A cacophony of keyboard clicks sounds through the room. The noise brings back a familiar feeling somewhere deep in my bones. It takes me back to when I was a wholly different person, freezing my ass off in England, losing sleep over disappointing my parents by getting a humanities PhD, returning home to a fiancée who sometimes wouldn't kiss me if I was too tired to go to the archives with her.

"In a musical, songs are either diegetic or non-diegetic." Said that in the wrong order. "But the effect of diegesis can be seen in any movie, really. Take a montage where some hack director decides to play 'We Are the Champions' over his generic sports drama. That song is non-diegetic. The fabled basketball team isn't actually hearing hours upon hours of the same Queen song."

The class chuckles again.

"It's there on a meta level to form the movie itself. But then take the 'Can't Hurry Love' scene in *Bad Times at the El Royale*. Cynthia Erivo plays an actual singer who sings actual songs that the other characters in the movie can hear. Music in that film is diegetic."

I flip to my *diegesis-music* slide. "When it comes to musicals, it's mostly established that songs are non-diegetic. They serve as something more symbolic. Audiences are forced to suspend their disbelief. Exceptions being, of course, actual music performances in shows. The operas in *Phantom of the Opera* or cabaret numbers in *Cabaret*. In a theater setting, where drama is larger than life anyway, it's had a history of success. But with movies, which, over the past several decades, have trended toward realism, it becomes harder and harder to just buy that people are singing about their feelings. Thus, every movie musical filmmaker has to decide how they're going to address music diegesis. Will songs really be sung in their movie universe; will they not exist for the characters, only for the audience; or will it be a mixture of the two? Which brings us to our first case study . . ."

I click my tongue. Switch the slide.

Aaaand it still says *The Sound of Music*. My hand migrates to my neck.

I finally glance over at Maeve. She's got a heavy frown on her face. Like I did this to personally humiliate her.

"That's a clip we'll look at if we have time," I say, flipping back to the diegesis slide. A quick scan around the room establishes that no one noticed. I pull my hand from my neck. "We're actually focusing on the 1961 classic *West Side Story* to start."

It's fine, we'll just not have a slide for that. I wonder why Maeve and Trish's assistant established the syllabus but didn't change my slide, but go figure. I do the rest of the lecture as planned. By the time I get to the end, about half an hour later, my blood's buzzing. I'm still on edge, but something about this almost feels good. Familiar. The good parts of England, the parts that filled my well when Emily stole from it.

Maeve returns to the front of the classroom when I finish speaking.

"Does anyone have any final questions before the screening?" Maeve asks.

One of the blond guys raises his hand. She calls him Trevor.

"Yeah," he says, leaning his elbow on the desk. "Can we talk to Valeria—Professor Sullivan, like, one-on-one?"

I know this Trevor dude is my student, but my insides quiver a little when that's the first question he asks. It just feels very straight-man-in-a-club from my own undergrad days.

Maeve still has that frown on her face as she glances at me. "She can be met with by appointment only, and given what I'm sure is her busy schedule, don't expect for her to become your mentor. I'll be holding regular office hours for any class-related questions."

"But what if we have industry-specific questions?" Trevor asks. "I mean, aren't we paying for the industry access as much as the theory?"

My stomach gets hot. *By appointment only?* What's she going on about? I literally cleared my schedule so I'd have two whole days dedicated to this, and my life every other day of the week is pretty much going to be me hanging out with Charlie and reading potential scripts. I *made* time for stuff like office hours. In fact, I'd happily set this guy straight about the outsize expectations in the industry.

"I can—" I say.

Maeve puts a hand on my shoulder. The move is unexpected, her grip strangely firm, and I swear the impact of her bare hand on my clothed shoulder is akin to being pushed off a cliff. Stomach free fall and everything. "Any industry insight you need can be found through appointments." She drops her hand. "We're grateful that Professor Sullivan is doing this. There's no need to be demanding."

The class goes dead silent. I look to Ty, who nods along.

Is Maeve seriously going on this power trip right now? I can hold office hours and handle whatever stupid entitled questions these kids have for me. It's what I do every day in my normal life anyway.

These kids already feel miles away from me and we're in the same room. What's the point of doing this if I don't get to actually interact with my students in a meaningful way?

Then Maeve starts the screening. She nods to Ty and motions for me to follow her. I do, heading out of the classroom and back into the echoes of the stone-floor hallway on the first floor. It's quiet with just the three of us out here. She stares at me for a long moment, posture tight.

"Look, Valeria—"

I hate how my heart jolts hearing her say my name.

"I appreciate what you're doing with the office hours thing, but stick to what we outlined. We've dealt with celebrity guest professors before, and this is the best way to handle it. How to get the best results possible."

I raise my chin. "You do realize you've been corresponding with my manager this whole time, right? She told me that you approved my syllabus and you'd be helping with logistics. I'm sorry if something got lost in translation. Can we at least—?"

Maeve's jaw clenches, a little spark in her own eyes. She smooths out her wrinkleless blazer, says, "Then talk to your manager," before returning to the classroom.

Yeah, this is not the self-esteem bump I had envisioned.

CHAPTER FOUR

"Why can't you just order clothes online?" Charlie asks as he jumps out of my car the next morning.

This trip is the result of a long, overcalculated decision Charlie and I made last night. When I talked to Trish after leaving USC, the conversation boiled down to one thing: if I wanted Maeve to respect me as a (temporary) academic, I had to act worthy of respect. Which meant taking responsibility for not preparing for the class and looking the part. The humbling was surprisingly easy to swallow—I *had* fumbled the first class—but the clothing was surprisingly harder. Yes, I did notice Maeve judging the expensive shoes. Maybe even making the connection that I picked out the expensive outfit instead of reading my emails. Trish agreed—perhaps a more affordable wardrobe would take the heat off me. But that meant going to a *mall*. As in, a public place, which, depending on how close it was to my house, could be crawling with paparazzi.

So, Charlie and I came up with a solution. We're going to Torrance, otherwise known as the most unremarkable suburb next to the town with the best beaches in LA. It's also dominated by a giant half-outdoor shopping center, and it's our best bet for actually braving a mall while not getting recognized.

"It'll be quicker to just grab everything I need," I say. I smile at him. "Plus, even with you staying at my house, we have a lot of hang time to make up for."

I click the SEND button on an email to Maeve and roll back up the sleeve on the Blink-182 crop tee I selected from my normal-person clothing. My collection turned out to contain an embarrassingly high amount of Dodgers merch; one of said Dodgers caps is currently on Charlie's head. Hoodies are my usual regular-person outside clothing, but with it pushing ninety in the first week of September, it's not happening. I'm gonna try not to think about how Maeve and I are going to discuss my syllabus tomorrow after my disastrous first impression.

"And since this is us hanging, try to look a little happier," I say as Charlie holds the door open for me, his Nebraska transplant parents having thoroughly imbued him with Midwest hospitality.

The burst of cool—no, freezing—air in Nordstrom almost makes me regret not wearing a hoodie. But one glance around at the countless makeup stations, gleaming stone floors, and the abundance of white light and I'm sweating again.

Charlie looks over at me and rubs my shoulder. "Breathe, Val. We're not *that* important compared to the people of Sunnydale's shopping needs."

My breathing softens at Charlie's sweet little *Buffy* joke (the show was primarily filmed in Torrance). "You're right."

Still, I take Charlie's hand as I aim us into the main area of the mall. My heart jolts as I do it; it's so automatic a gesture to do with him as a friend, but being out in public gives it a whole other connotation. It's like, we are going to be perceived as a man and a woman together, and any tiny sign that we're affectionate or comfortable

makes the average person think we're a het couple. All it would take
would be me grabbing Charlie's hand like this to make a stranger
think we're going to go home and fuck. Both our queer identities
erased—just like that. It makes me queasy.

Still, I keep holding his hand until we're out of Nordstrom. Whatever Charlie and my sexualities, we've always been physically affectionate, holding hands through those early days of opening emails
from reps to see if we got nothing parts. We fit together naturally,
and if he's not bothered, I'm not either.

His gaze slides across the stores lining the three-plus levels of the
mall. "Do you think they have your favorite store here?"

"Gonna give it a solid *no* that they have a Cupid's Closet . . ."

I realize a second too late that that's the kind of joke I have with
Mason Wu, my very gay *Goodbye, Richard!* director, who likes
hijacking press interviews by jokingly asking me what porn I recommend to people.

Charlie lets go of my hand to give me a dismissive wave as he
bites back a laugh. "No, *Hot Topic,* you horny dolt."

As if it's haunting me, at that moment we pass by a Hot Topic a
floor above us. Charlie spots it at the same time. "I haven't stepped
foot in a Hot Topic since studded belts were a necessity."

Charlie laughs. "You say that as if MCR isn't back together and
you couldn't have gone there yesterday."

Which—*fine,* is correct. But I still get full-body shivers thinking
about what kind of a surly Hot Topic asshole I was as a teenager.
Sure, I can turn it into a joke I tell friends and cute girls, but I was
not pleasant to be around when I frequented that cursed store. I
don't want to know what kind of Past Me spirit would possess me if
I went back there and put on red jeans, an MCR tee, a studded belt,
and wrist warmers.

"It's not gonna happen," I say. We're so close to Zara. So close to getting in and out of this mall. To shed the half-assed attempt at a new endeavor the first class was. I *do* want to give this job my all, to impress Maeve. I'm not only going to do it, I'm going to pass with *flying colors.*

"You know what your two favorite stores have in common, though?" he asks, raising his eyebrows as he says it, which worries me.

The Zara sign is in sight. "What?"

"Leather collars."

The joke makes me feel like I've been punted back in time across this very mall and I'm now standing with teenager Charlie. He was the guy in every class we shared together who would, without fear or shame, tell sexual jokes in class right to the teachers. Kids in our school started calling the red-faced squirming that teachers did after one of his jokes Charlie's Principle. As in *Mr. Cockburn was afflicted with Charlie's Principle in APES fourth period.* Mason can be crass, but I've awakened Charlie, and he's so much worse than she is.

Good thing I've been around him long enough to be immune to Charlie's Principle. "You know I can't wear one of those."

"We find you a designer one and you'd one *hundred* percent do it. You're too goth not to." Charlie grins. "Sorry, you're getting one for your birthday."

And there it is again. The ubiquity by which Charlie and I talk about *designer.* I can still remember so clearly the way my mom's face lit up when my dad bought her a single Chanel bag for their ten-year anniversary. Designer used to be rare, aspirational, an indulgence to celebrate accomplishments and milestones. Maybe it means nothing that something special has become routine, but I find myself glancing around the mall searching for those high-end labels. Feeling embarrassment at the looking itself when I don't see them.

We enter Zara right around then, ending the conversation.

Charlie claps his hands together as I scan the store. They're still halfway between seasons, getting rid of summer looks and transitioning into fall. And, considering we're in LA, they know to keep the light linen out. The store is pretty crowded for a weekday, but mostly filled with South Bay moms. Athleta clings to Pilates-sculpted bodies, designer bags from Nordstrom Rack hang off perfectly tan shoulders, AirPods play in their ears as they purse their lips looking at dresses. One dubiously not-in-school youth is searching through graphic tees. Since we're in LA, my first instinct is to guess up-and-coming child actor.

Overall, though, no one's looking at the two blond idiots in the matching backward Dodgers hats. My gaze falls on a pair of lilac ankle pants and a matching blazer. Fluttering fills my chest, that specific chemical hit shopping has always brought me, even back in my Hot Topic days. Relief that I don't hate everything in the store slides in soon after.

"Aren't ankle dress pants the equivalent of capris for the modern age?" Charlie asks.

I resist shooting him a good-natured eye roll. "It's a summer look. Besides, with a great pair of shoes, they really get to speak."

One summer suit, one fall suit, and a couple of blouses in now. Running my hand along the fabric, searching for loose threads, I wonder if Maeve's felt the way I do right now, surrounded by these signs, feeling the texture of this material. Or if it's just another chore for her.

I grab the lilac blazer and pants, drape them over my shoulder, and head to another blazer display. Once I pick out one more set, we'll be done.

I reach for the tweed.

"Isn't tweed *too* professor?" Charlie comments, pulling his lips in.

So at this point, Charlie and Trish know this look is all manufactured. But I hadn't even considered the fact that anyone else could be perceiving my clothing that way. My first instinct, which is usually the one not doused in anxiety, was that this looked professional. Like something Maeve would wear for its plainness. But maybe I'm past the point where plainness works.

I let my fingertips brush against the scratchy fabric. "Maybe I should just get a neutral one."

Charlie reaches out and grabs a brown blazer with some ruching detail on the sides. "Nah, you don't want to look like your manager or agent. Brown is warm, approachable. Fall."

God, I love Charlie sometimes. A true-blue jock boy who knows about fashion. I missed the rhythm we settle into together. I know it's only been a year since we filmed *Oakley* together, but it feels like it's been so much longer. "Yeah, you're right. Maybe I'll get a couple of skirts as well."

"And don't you have to get non-designer shoes too?" Charlie asks. "To *truly* convince the ornery, hot professor you're a regular ole person?"

He knocks my hip as he speaks, nearly knocking me into one of the blazer mannequins. I *just* manage to catch my footing, leaving my cheeks red as he observes my reaction.

"And shoes, I guess," I mumble. I glance at a couple of pairs of stilettos lining a shelf nearby.

Charlie stands next to me, following my gaze. His mouth turns up. "You know, *that* heel height isn't a neutral power-bitch look."

I shoot him a quizzical look. "What do you even mean by that?"

"Professors wear flats. If they do wear heels, it's because they're short. Which . . ."

Which, I'm five foot eight.

Charlie leans into me, wiggling like a puppy. "All I'm saying is I *think* you're thinking more about how good you'd look in your normal-people outfits and less about being professorial."

Well, fuck, *am I*? Am I still in Hollywood mode, aiming for the "sexy Halloween" version of professor? I pause to chew on the thought, but it fades. Isn't that the whole point of buying clothes: to look good? That can't be inherently bad. What is he getting at?

I pull off my hat and run my fingers through my hair. "I can wear whatever shoe I want, Charlie. There aren't any rules."

"Then get unsexy loafers."

Charlie picks up a random pair of loafers with the kind of sharp cruelty Rachel Berry's high school torturers had when they doused her in red slushie. I know I wouldn't even have worn them when I was working the receptionist job at my parents' dental office, the job that made me want to claw my eyes out.

A beat of silence passes. "No."

I move to a display of ankle boots, Charlie following me like the frat boy poltergeist he is. There's a simple pair of black leather ankle boots with side elastic goring and three-inch heels that could work. Red lining sends a pang through me. The Joker Donna Louboutin ankle boots I bought myself for my birthday a few years ago look like chic circus tents, and I can't wear them to elevate these basic linen—

"Charlie, am I a vapid prick?" I ask as I grab the Zara boots.

Charlie grabs the boots off me in one hand, the loafers in his other hand. His hands have disappeared into both shoes, making him look like a cartoon character. "Yeah, but you've been this way since you were eighteen."

What he's saying, even though he's definitely insulting me, is pretty funny. I'm overthinking this. My designer clothing wasn't appropriate for the academic workplace, and all I'm doing is complying with an unsaid dress code. Maybe this says something about how disconnected from reality I've gotten, but there's always room to reconnect. And if Maeve thinks I'm unable to teach because I wear heels to work, then that's *her* misogynistic problem.

"I could say something similar about you," I reply, keeping a straight face, if only to make sure this conversation doesn't get derailed.

I look down at his shoe hands, then back at him. I try—god, I try—but soon I'm laughing with him. He wraps his shoe hands around me, allowing me to catch my breath in his chest. I touch his wrist, giving him a silent thank-you.

When we pull away, he shoves both shoes back into my hands. Charlie then proceeds to pluck a basic pair of white pumps off a stand. "You know what'd really complete this professor look?" He bites on his bottom lip the exact same way he does in modeling shoots. "A long necklace that dips below your cleavage. A *little* sex appeal to go with killing your next lecture. Maybe Maeve will even fall in love."

My ears go hot as a piece instantly comes to mind. I have a vintage costume necklace from my paternal grandma that wouldn't go against the academic dress code. Maeve couldn't ignore that. I can see it, watching those brown eyes travel down my chest . . .

"I'm not going to seduce Maeve!" I snap.

I say it a *little* too loud, causing several necks to whip our way. I freeze like a deer in headlights. But none of them approach.

No, not none of them. The youth browsing the graphic tees squints and starts moving toward Charlie and me. I thought I could cope with this, but my chest tightens like it's about to burst.

To make matters worse, she comes right up to me. My breath catches in my throat.

"I like your shirt," she says. "Where's it from?"

Instead of *Are you Valeria Sullivan I saw your last movie your coming-out post was so brave do you date men though.*

My muscles loosen, but I still can't grab a breath to speak.

Charlie smiles. "Hot Topic."

My phone goes off with an email notification. As the girl goes away, satisfied, I read it. Maeve's replied to my email.

> I have 30 minutes before our next class. My office.
> - sent from my iPhone

The worst part of it isn't even the flippant way she's addressing me. It's the fact that I continue to walk through that mall goofing around with Charlie and all the while I can't get the image of Maeve seeing me with that necklace disappearing down my blazer out of my head. It's giving a whole new meaning to *fuck Maeve Arko* that I'm not willing to think too hard about.

It's definitely more of a "feeling good in my Zara suit" than anything about my teaching, but I'm actually optimistic going in to meet with Maeve before the second week of class. Thirty minutes. There's also a certain change in the air as I enter her office. Unlike Ty, I have no interest in knocking. I'd imagine it's illegal to be touching yourself in your office in a school anyway.

"Morning, Maeve," I say, sliding on my best pleasant-but-not-too-eager smile.

She's got a blouse-skirt getup today. Just a button lower than I was expecting, but the tightening in my gut isn't going to distract me. And—fuck you, Charlie—high heels despite *her* being about my height. She keeps her expression neutral, hands folded together on the desk between us, even as she gives me a once-over. My heartbeat picks up.

"So, what did you want to talk about?" she asks.

I pull a syllabus still sitting on her desk over to the space between us. She watches my hands as I move. "I don't understand why we switched *The Sound of Music* for *West Side Story,* and I'd love it if we could actually go down the list to explain the changes . . ."

It's like I'm acting. A little distance, hold on to the core emotion the character is feeling. This is my class. Hell, even if it's *our* class, I'm not going to be treated like a first-year grad student because I haven't been in this grind as long as she has. *I* wrote a fucking dissertation on twentieth-century music and pop culture. I'm here to impart my *expertise* to these students, and no way in hell is she going to stand in my way.

Maeve folds her fingers tighter. She has these really delicate hands: slim fingers, nails that come to a perfect stop before they reach her skin, which looks soft—like she moisturizes often. "I figured we were introducing cult classics and specifically working with stage adaptations. *West Side Story* would be more familiar."

"They're not necessarily adaptations." I point to a spot on the syllabus. "You let me keep *Rocketman.*"

"I think it serves a different purpose and expands on the jukebox musical."

I scan the list again. "Okay, then why have two movies dealing with Oscar bait? I put *Tenacious D* there on purpose."

"You wanted to show a success and a failure, right? *Les Mis* wasn't an Oscar darling, but *La La Land* was. And *Tenacious D* is barely worthy of being called a movie."

"It's an actual *cult classic* of the modern age. Do you think *Rocky Horror* has any value as a film? Of course not. But I'd rather talk about a complete flop that has music that's endured enough to still be on tour. It's a different conversation than establishing two musicals that were made for the Oscars. I live and breathe the Oscars; it's really not that profound. We can study *Les Mis,* and I can show clips of *La La Land* to show a contrast in one class."

Maeve takes a deep breath. Her hands unclasp, just enough to lightly slap the wood. "Look, you can combine the two into one Oscars-bait lecture. That's fine. But I *refuse* to be a part of a class that shows a film that has an entire scene of Jack Black getting an erection. We can show a bad movie if it's at least *trying* to be a good movie."

I have to stop, even though I have a response to that one on my lips. Maeve Arko, whose dissertation—which I have now read—was about analyzing voyeuristic violence versus liberation as violence in early nineties American art house queer film, *actually* watched *Tenacious D.* It sparks something inside me. "You really saw *Tenacious D*?"

She looks away a moment, blinking rapidly. "I'm not putting it on in my class."

So much for Maeve having an open mind about the movie selection. "I need one ridiculously bad film to work with."

"Isn't *Mamma Mia!* bad enough?"

I have to win something on this syllabus. Even if she's right about *Tenacious D.* "*Cats.* The one from 2019. I want that on the syllabus instead of *In the Heights.*" I pause. "That or *Dear Evan Hansen.*"

Maeve looks up at me like she's gone through a lifetime of not experiencing religious blasphemy—until now. "People pay money to attend this school."

Five minutes until class starts.

"Look, *Cats* would provide a ton of material for the students to analyze for final papers. I want them to have a wide range of different topics and angles to talk about. If we just do classic adaptations or relatively okay adaptations or Oscar-winning adaptations, the papers are all going to come out the same. We're trying to pick unconventional movies so they can pick different things out. *In the Heights* was great, but it didn't do anything new filmmaking-wise.

Cats tried to fucking take a movie that was only going to be good as an animated film and make it live action to bring in bucks from stars' faces only for it to go completely and utterly wrong. Even *Dear Evan Hansen* showcases the Icarian results of hoping an out-of-context Tony performance will trump the needs of casting in film. There's so much to dig into with both of them, and the students will be more engaged."

For a moment, Maeve is silent. Her hands have retracted to her lap, out of my view. Her jaw is tensed, but there's a certain unsureness in her eyes. She's still refusing to make eye contact with me. And she's almost tucked in, making me realize I've leaned forward while talking. I scoot backward, my back pressing against the wood of the chair. She reaches out to turn the syllabus to her, a pinch of a frown on her lips.

"We're not doing *Cats*. Do you want to switch out *Mamma Mia!* for *Rock of Ages* to work with the rock musical?"

It's been so long since I've had this searing burn of anger inside of me. It feels like an old feeling dug up from somewhere in the past, when Steven was representing me and explained really obvious themes in movies I was doing when I mentioned a role was difficult to crack. I'm being spoken to like I'm a child instead of an actual published scholar of the genre *and* someone with years of practical experience in the art we're discussing. I didn't study this shit for nearly ten years to be told I'm doing it wrong by someone with the exact same fucking degree as me.

"Is this my class or not?" I snap. I wait a few seconds, hands clenched in my lap as we wait to see if this wave curls and crashes down on us.

"I don't think you get this," she says, voice even. Like she's heard this exact blowup a million times. "I already wrote out my lectures based on the syllabus I was under the impression *you* created. Ty and I worked out his section outlines so they'd be ready so he can focus on his *full student course load and research.* Even if the students don't care what movies they have to find on streaming platforms at a moment's notice, we aren't flexible on the teaching side. We don't have *time* to change anything."

There's no winning with someone who's already ended the argument. Less than five minutes, and we still have to make the walk to class.

I push out of my seat, my arguments spent. "Fine."

I step out of the room before she can say anything else. The burning has shifted into something with more teeth, an edge of uncertainty to it. But it doesn't do much to stop me.

The declaration of war is very simple. Twenty-three words.

"Hey, guys, there's an adjustment to the syllabus," I say as I start the lecture, just barely avoiding sending a smirk in Maeve's direction. "I will be holding office hours on Wednesdays twelve to two in Professor Arko's office."

The look of utter panic and anger on Maeve's face says she gets it. Game on.

CHAPTER FIVE

Naturally, my first office hours visitor the next day is Trevor, the guy who seemed to think access to me was included in his tuition. This guy swaggers in—I don't think I've ever seen anything like it. He doesn't even sit down. Just leans over the desk and shakes my hand. The whole thing feels like the hundreds of interactions I've had in my seven years in Hollywood, so I take it with a relaxed smile. I can't wait for Maeve to see how good I am with the student interactions when she takes her space back.

"Trevor Lewis," he says, maintaining uncomfortably intense eye contact.

Now, all my USC knowledge might come from Luna; Luna's partner, Romy; and Steven's old assistant, Wyatt, but this guy seems very business school. I'm curious to see if I'm right.

"Valeria," I say. I'd been going back and forth on it—was my full name *too* associated with Hollywood?—but ultimately I figure it's professional without being standoffish. Plus, it *is* pretty. Sometimes I wish I'd picked a stage name so I didn't feel so disconnected from my full name. Time to reinvent it along with myself.

He takes a seat, leaning back in the couch. Major manspreading.

"Yeah, I could never get into *Goodbye, Richard!,* too preachy, but *Stroke* and *Needlepoint* are amazing. Effervescent performances."

Translation: *Your most popular movie is too feminist for me, and I just described your performances in your most depressing/harrowing movies as vivacious.*

"Thanks," I say. "What'd ya need from me?"

He asks how common it is to get famous and if I think it was because of my looks, my talent, or because I knew someone. His enthusiasm wanes as I tell him it was pure luck. As if a guy like him doesn't make his own luck.

Once he leaves, another guy comes in. He's got honey-brown hair instead of blond but is otherwise alarmingly similar to Trevor. I can only hope he'll be a little better.

"I'm Jamie," he says, just as confidently as Trevor before him.

This one takes a seat, *then* offers to shake my hand.

"I wanna be an actor," Jamie says. "But I don't know if I could do the nude stuff like you did in *Needlepoint.* I mean, that's like, tits and snatch just . . . available. I mean, do you think about that? Is it weirder because you're gay? I'm gay too."

Is this guy talking about *my nude scenes* during professor office hours? My disaster interview with Winston was tamer than this, for god's sake.

"And I just—dude." He's still going, and I pray the color of my face has remained constant. "I think about girls jacking off to me and it's like . . . it's weird."

I pause, look over at him. His face is expectant, like he asked something completely on topic and reasonable. I'm not going to impress Maeve talking to students about nudity in commercial film. We're not even talking about musicals.

"Someone will inevitably leak your nudes if you get famous enough, so if you believe in the art, might as well get ahead of the curve," I reply. "But you also have every right to do as much or as little nudity as you want."

He squints at me. "Can I not do it if I wanna be on premium cable, though?"

I give a tight smile. *I* can't even get a premium-cable starring role without the guarantee of simulated sex and/or nudity. And that was before I started only getting the shitty scripts. "Sure."

And, thankfully, that's all he wants. I take a deep breath, drum my fingers on my thigh, trying to telegraph how offended I am by his questions. This is fine, though. I've heard worse. Hell, it's all over my social media. I can handle this, even if I have to clutch one hand around the other one to stop it from shaking. *Someone* will want to talk about the class. I won't let this escalate to anywhere near where I was at the Winston interview.

My next visitor is a girl named Ginger, who starts by asking how I balanced academia and acting (I didn't) and ends with asking if I'd show her reel to my manager (no). She walks away looking downtrodden even after managing to get an answer to her question about MLA format.

At least one question was about school. It's a start.

The students keep pouring in.

They mostly don't ask about class. Each missed shot feels like I've added a new brick onto my shoulders.

Before I know it, I have only five minutes before Maeve will be in.

I place a hand on my chest, willing my heartbeat to slow down. Not only am *I* starting to forget what last class's lectures were about, but the past two hours were a trial. I don't feel as panicked as I did that night in Winston's studio, but I still feel like I'm scrambling to return to reality, to remember what I'm supposed to be doing. I try to calm down. There will be more office hours, more chances to impress Maeve. I'll just give her the raw statistics on how many students came in. I can tell Charlie all the stories when I get home.

I glance at the door. No one else. I run a hand through my hair. Whether I'm primping myself for Maeve or calming my nerves, who knows. Then a student walks in. The girl with the *Avatar: The Last Airbender* sticker. She's tentative, sticking to the doorframe before I offer her a smile. No handshake. She just sets down a small notebook and a pen after she takes a seat.

"So I know Professor Arko has office hours after this, but I was wondering if we could talk about last week's lesson," she says.

"Of course," I say, surprised by the jolt as my heart lifts. "What's your name, sweetie?"

The girl blushes as I blanch about using such a condescending name replacement. "Cory."

"Cory," I repeat. Half for me, half because I read somewhere that it makes people feel like you care about what they're going to say. Which, for the first time today, I do. "What's up?"

She tucks a dark brown hair behind her ear. "So, did we ever come to a consensus about 'Cabaret' being diegetic or non-diegetic? I mean, are we really supposed to believe that Sally just knows a song to perform that's a metaphor for knowing a fellow showgirl who died? Like, was Elsie real? And if Elsie *was* real, doesn't that break the film's entire thesis about only having diegetic music?"

I shift in my seat—*Maeve's seat,* mind racing. It's a good racing, though, like my body feels after a solid workout. "Well, I'll leave that up to your interpretation. Would you have an easier time believing that Sally is finding meaning in 'Cabaret,' a song that just happens to exist in this universe, or that the filmmakers blundered their vision?"

"I mean, it's— I don't know how they could be so careful and miss that."

I fold my hands together on the desk. "Well, think about it in terms of what emotional beat is happening at that point. When you watch the scene, is Sally straight up talking about her feelings, or does it feel more grounded than that? Do you see Sally as the type of character who is so in touch with her feelings that we'd put a non-diegetic song into the movie?"

Cory rubs her eyebrow. The door opens, but I focus on her. "I guess it could be simpler than that. Sally's just going through an emotional moment singing a song. It starts off as a performance, but you see it shift into Sally singing her feelings out. But you're right, she wouldn't have the words. She's a performer. She borrows from others. Even about something as personal as her friend's death."

As relief floods her face, I find myself smiling. I'm actually doing it, being a professor. It's simultaneously a familiar feeing and a thrilling new one.

I still have no idea what I'm going to do after this class, but for the first time since this class started, I'm starting to feel *good* being here. Like I'm objectively making an impact on these young filmmakers' lives based entirely on the knowledge I give them, how I help them think through something. Maybe I could actually do this beyond this class.

"There we go," I say. "Is this for the reflection paper?"

"Nah," she says, closing her notebook. "I did that on 'Tomorrow Belongs to Me.' This is midterm prep."

I raise my eyebrows. "Preparing early." As in, we're only on week two. Granted, I don't remember when the midterm is, so maybe this isn't that outrageous. We hold eye contact a moment, as if neither of us is sure whether this interaction is over. But as pathetic as this sounds, the minutes we spent together have been transformative. Like I've finally realized I'm in this ecosystem I really do love and I want to know everything about everyone in it. "What do you study?"

"Animation," she says.

It's real enthusiasm that comes out of her mouth. And it works better than the strong shot of espresso I took this morning. "That's so cool! What sort of movies would you want to make?"

She shrugs. "I'm not sure yet, but something more Don Bluth than Sony."

I laugh. "I don't think anyone wants to work for Sony."

Despite the fact that Trish insists Sony would be a huge payday. That my three-year-old niblings would *love* the movies even if the critics didn't. Going back to Hollywood is bad enough; I can't even consider going back for *that* kind of Hollywood.

"Have you done any voice acting?" Cory asks me.

"Not yet, but there are a couple of projects my team is making me look at. I wouldn't be opposed to an animated role, but who knows."

It's around then that I look past Cory and notice Maeve standing by the doorway. She doesn't look particularly *happy,* but I'm tempted to say she's neutral as she watches us, hands in her pockets, leaning against the wall. I'd call the pose *greaser in a movie* if not for the, dare I say, softness in her mouth and eyes.

"Is it time?" I ask. I touch the desk for my phone, but it's not there.

"Yeah, but take your time," Maeve says. Maybe it's Cory's presence, but Maeve's tone is much softer than usual.

Cory picks up her notebook and stands. "I'm done." She looks to me. "Thank you, Professor Sullivan."

The name sends a shiver down my spine.

Cory exits unceremoniously, leaving me to collect my sparse items off Maeve's desk.

"No, you can sit a minute," Maeve says. "No one ever comes right at the beginning."

Something about the way she says it makes me think it's not a suggestion. Time to see if this week's gamble was worth it.

Maeve takes a seat on the couch across from me, crossing her legs like a perfect lady. I get a weird, pervading thought as I wait for her to speak. Is she queer? I know she did a dissertation on queer cinema, but there are always allies who do shit like that. I swore I'd just automatically clocked her as queer, but suddenly I'm not sure why I thought that. Especially not in her look today: blouse, pencil skirt, and heels. She could just be femme, but something is making me uneasy. Like I need her to just bring up her sexuality to ease my nerves. Nerves that . . . I don't need to think longer about why they're there. What *that* kind of interest in her implies.

"What's up?" I ask, my voice going a little higher than it has in any other encounter I've had today. Fuck that, whatever gay evolutionary tic it is.

"Did the students stay on topic?" she asks.

She recrosses her legs and I hyperfocus on her face. My gay lizard brain is thinking *She could accidentally flash you,* and I can't get it to move on from that thought. My stomach knots.

"They . . ." I pull my lips into a thin line. If I want to get on a better standing with her, the last thing I should do is lie. "They had a lot of strange questions about my acting career and breaking into the industry and work-life balance. A couple of bizarre gay comments, but nothing too bad. Then Cory—"

She bristles. "Tell me no one asked who you're dating."

If I wasn't red before, I'm definitely visibly red now. I eye the door beyond Maeve, wishing I could head that way. This is so deeply embarrassing; even as I told Trish about all the gay questions I'd get, I never told her about the encounters on the street that made me feel so small. And it's not what we need to focus on when my interaction with Cory was so good, when I've had this moment of clarity about teaching. But somehow the words spill out of my mouth.

"Uh, no, not that. Just some kid asking if I feel uncomfortable at the thought of straight dudes jacking it to my naked body in films."

We're in a school office, and now I've made Maeve Arko think about men masturbating and me naked on film. Great. Yes, this is *exactly* how I need this conversation to go.

Maeve full on *scowls.* "Give me a name so I can ban them from your office hours."

The heat of the moment simmers off with that comment. *Banned* from office hours? God, that confirms it. I've failed. She doesn't think I can do it. As if people haven't been sending me lewd comments since *Goodbye, Richard!* Now they mostly say some variation on *man-hating dyke.* I can handle some dumb kid pouring his insecurities onto a perceived authority figure. "It's okay. Cory—"

"No, it's not. This is not even in the *realm* of normal or okay." Her face gets red as she speaks. "How would you feel if I told you one of my students asked me if I'd ever encountered a certain sexual situation? This is a *school.*"

My segue into Cory falls away as I process what Maeve is saying. It's like every biological process in my body has just stopped. My mind goes blank. And then it hits me all at once—*no one* has ever taken anything I've said this seriously. No one's called it harassment.

Is she right?

"Listen," she says, the color fading from her cheeks, "you can keep your office hours, but that student can only speak to me."

I exhale. "Deal." My heart's still thudding in my chest, I realize. Slow off the comedown, but I can't believe how much lighter my muscles feel in general. "And for the record, it wasn't a complete failure. Cory had some great questions about *Cabaret,* and we came up with a solid direction for her midterm topic."

"You're a lot more relaxed one-on-one," Maeve observes. "You should bring that to your lecturing. It's not a one-woman show when the classes are under forty students. They need to be engaged to learn. You can cut down your material to the meat if you can avoid the tangents too. They're writing down everything you say, so it's best to not overwhelm them with anything more than a few jokes here and there."

She can't just give a compliment, can she? "Thanks for the feedback," I say, deadpan.

Her posture returns to perfect, jaw tight in further scrutiny. "Why did you want this job?"

I rub my arms, considering my options. Out of every answer to this question I could give, I keep coming back to the truth. The truth sounds absolutely batshit, but we've opened up so far when I've chosen honesty. "I've always loved teaching and entertainment theory. This class was my first opportunity to really show people that I can do it, even after taking years off to be in Hollywood."

I study Maeve's facial expressions the way I'd study a scene partner. Her breath hitches, which causes a slight twitch in her chest. She eyes me, her gaze not quite scanning me so much as barreling into me, like there's more to the words I said. Then she slowly exhales, with an unmistakable snort. The whole thing is topped off by her crossing her arms, looking at me the way I was looking at those ridiculous students an hour ago.

"I see," she finally says. "We have midterms to plan tomorrow. Ty wanted you to come, but I told him you'd be busy."

"I'll be there," I say before she can say no.

She recrosses her legs one more time as I grab my bag and head to the door. She's mocking me. Still, I can't help but watch, acutely aware that she's watching me too.

CHAPTER SIX

Ty's the one who sends me the location for my meeting the next day. It's a café called Literatea and sits on the southeast side of campus, a quadrant I've never been to. It's tucked into the largest library on campus, a behemoth of red brick stacked amid dozens of classical arches. East Coast style in USC's red and (sort of, not really) yellow.

The café itself is unassuming, marked by a small sign off a court-yard lined in baby palm trees, buzzed grass, and redbrick walkways. The students passing through this area feel, for lack of a better word, more normal than the glitzy Greek students around the Tutor Campus Center or the rumpled film students by the cinematic arts build-ings. They're baby-faced, weighed down by backpacks and laptop cases, and often decked out in USC apparel I recognize from the gift set the university sent to me before I started.

I open the heavy brown doors into the café, only to find it barely fits fifteen patrons inside. Midcentury faded red-and-yellow cush-ioned chairs and tiny octangular wooden tables line the two walls to the right and left. Ty and Maeve are already seated on the left side, an artistic pile of leather-bound books stacked up in an alcove behind them. Only Ty smiles and waves me over.

"Great to see you two," I say, my unnecessary friendly instinct kicking in before I can stop myself.

"Same," Ty says. "We figured you'd want to sit with your back to the crowd."

I resist the urge to paw at my throat as Maeve shoots Ty the sharpest look before saying, "I don't think the Philosophy Department is going to bother you."

Once I take my seat, Maeve pushes an iced coffee over to me. It's a kind gesture to have taken note of my coffee order, which means it was probably Ty's idea. Even if it was full of poison, though, I know I'd still drink it to not seem high maintenance to Maeve. But it's just coffee. I'd put in some oat milk, but I don't want to be the first one to get up. Not with Maeve peering my way as she takes a sip of her own blond drink.

"We're going to be sticking to the department-wide standard for a four-hundred-level class, which will be five short essay questions on a take-home midterm," Maeve says.

"So no Scantron?" Ty asks.

"If we're going to test them on key terms and plot beats, the course isn't doing what it set out to do. Convenience for us shouldn't ever trump what students get out of the class." Maeve's gaze flits up to me. "You have time for that, right?"

I had time to come here and be patronized, so . . . "When's the midterm?"

"October seventh."

So, five weeks from now. It's somewhat of a relief that we're still weeks away. "I'll be there to grade every paper." I punctuate my words with a wry smile.

Maeve cocks her head ever so slightly. "Have you graded subjective material before?"

No. "Yeah."

"Let's get to the essay questions," Ty says. He looks to Maeve, a soft pleading expression. "By then, we'll have had lectures on *West Side Story* through *Chicago*. Do we want to give them a theory question?"

"Might as well have one," Maeve replies. "Start them off with a question that could help them navigate the rest of the exam. Let's have them describe what diegesis is and how it informs the narrative in any of the films discussed in the first half of the semester."

"Perfect."

"From there, they can continue to reference diegesis, but the goal would be to encourage them to incorporate other structures and lenses."

Maeve and Ty fall into a perfectly synched tennis volley of pedagogy. It's not exactly like the conversation is in a language I don't understand, but the rust isn't brushing off as quickly as I would've liked. Right as I'm processing the real-world implications of one piece of their exchange, they've moved onto the next. The only real, real thing grounding me is Ty listing off the number of questions as they set them in stone. One, two, three—each number a burst of relief. I find myself tapping the underside of the table as they're said out loud.

I can't sit here like this. I have the skill set for this; they're just using fancy words to come up with essay questions. I think back to Cory asking about how emotion informed the need for reality in a musical. What sort of question would she be excited to answer?

"What if we do one specifically for *Rocky Horror*?" I blurt out. "They can analyze the callbacks."

While Ty's eyes light up right away, Maeve rubs her chin.

"That could be—" Ty says.

"Would every callback work?" Maeve interrupts. The cutting tone of her voice softens as she turns to her TA. "Sorry, Ty."

He shrugs, and Maeve goes on.

"Some of the callbacks are only one line of dialogue. Wouldn't you want to encourage students to pick a bigger chunk to analyze? Would you give any guidelines to encourage robust analysis? We don't need to see students arguing for two paragraphs that the live audience says 'say it' during 'Sweet Transvestite' just because Rocky is hot."

What is she trying to say? If a student did that, then clearly they didn't answer the question well. What is she even critiquing? "Sure, I guess we could spell that out in the question! But isn't that implied?" There is so much more I could say about the richness of theme that can be derived from those callbacks, but I can't keep my thoughts straight.

Maeve glances at Ty. "It's also very specific. We're prioritizing one movie."

I've been inching out of Maeve's space for the past half hour; it's time to break that habit. I lean forward, maintain eye contact with her the way I do with difficult directors trying to intimidate me. I almost miss that dynamic; at least I know how to deal with those egos. "What's wrong with that? We'll have eight movies and only five questions, so there's no need to be egalitarian about it. All you'd have to do is mention callbacks in class."

Maeve raises her brows. "I'm going to do it?"

Why does she keep needling me? I hold my hands at my side, resisting the urge to slap them on the table and spill our drinks.

"Whatever, I will." I exhale. "Again, I'm sorry about the syllabus and the first class, but I don't know where you've gotten this impression that I'm not putting in the work. I've been showing up and teaching the lectures I've prepared each week. Who else would've been doing it?"

Maeve sucks on her teeth, as if whatever she wants to say is too embarrassing to be said out loud.

And, despite her really shitty reaction, that shame does crash over me.

My manager and her assistant. The same people who corresponded with Maeve at the beginning of the year.

I let the shame hit me, then float away. Out of the corner of my eye, I see Ty fidgeting. But I look back at Maeve, giving her the full force of my eye contact. "I promise you I'm doing the work."

She stands up.

"Where are you going?" I ask, the indignation slipping into my tone.

Ty's gaze flits between us.

"We decided on our five questions, and I have an appointment at an archive in Hollywood in thirty minutes." She looks to Ty. "And you have class after this, right?"

Ty nods. "Dixon's seminar."

Maeve looks over to me and shrugs. "There ya go." She collects her items quickly but hesitates as her fingers wrap around her sweating tea container. "You really want to take charge of this class?"

Embarrassment slaps me again. This sounds like a trick question, like she'll berate me for my answer no matter what it is. Still . . .

"Yes."

"Well, if you want to do it without training wheels, I have to turn in a big conference proposal and some paperwork for a research grant over the next two weeks."

No way. My heart thrums.

"There are a lot of responsibilities I'm taking on for you behind the scenes right now. So why don't you meet with Ty tomorrow in order to work out how you'll handle the *Rocky Horror* and *Little Shop* weeks together? If I'm done early, I'll happily take a back seat to see how you do *Little Shop*."

Oh, of course.

Cold fear stabs through me. Tomorrow I have back-to-back meetings with producers for some movie Trish wants me in next year, plus I promised Charlie I'd help him do self-tapes. This is going to be more of a circus than a press tour.

But like hell does Maeve get to know that.

I smile through the sweat pooling in my lower back. "Sounds great."

Maeve smiles. "Can't wait to see what your lessons look like."

When I ask Ty if he'll meet me on the Warner Bros. lot in Burbank, his reply is quite literally just "🎬🎬🎬🎬🎬🎬🎬." Which, I'll admit, I think about far more than I need to while I sit through three hours of morning meetings with two independent WB-first-look sets of producers. One is for the animated movie I mentioned to Cory, which I'm still not convinced isn't going to get 3 percent on Rotten Tomatoes. They've handed me the script, and it's kind of baking on a table in the outdoor seating section of the commissary. There's something deeply ironic about fame. When I was starting out, I was only big enough for indie movies drawn from the blood of starving filmmakers. In the middle of an A-list career, I was given everything—the searing indies, blockbusters, and prestige dramas I want along with the kind of movies that these studios vomit out for profit. Then they all got filtered through my sexuality, including the two meetings today. Lesbian detective and lesbian rabbit. The only good things I have I got through Mason, one indie she's doing and *Goodbye, Richard! 2* next fall. It only confirms that nagging worry I've had since the interview, that studio executives haven't changed their narrow scope of me even with the directing credit. It's like a weight hung on my heart.

Trish texts me when I'm waiting for him. How's everything?

I could break my thumbs texting her the whole truth: I'm three of six meetings in today and already overwhelmed, and I have a lot to say. Still, I decide a *Good!* will suffice. Just at that moment, Ty comes bounding in, a WB-stamped iced coffee in his hands. He slides right into my table.

"Whew," he says, shaking his hands a bit. "This place is so cool."

I not-so-discreetly turn over my script, so Ty's innocence can be protected. He doesn't have to know just how not cool this place is. "Glad you're enjoying it. Have you not been here before?"

I got Ty a guest pass today by claiming he was my personal assistant, but nonindustry people have often gone through a tour or two of the studio lots.

"Not yet," he says. "My work sends me to archives more than studio lots."

I scoot into the slowly moving slice of shade that hangs over our table. "Either way, thanks for meeting me here."

"No problem. I'm ready to talk *Rocky Horror*." He pauses, the pep in his words fading. "About yesterday—I'm sorry Maeve was being like that. She's a third-year professor, and collecting enough accolades to get tenure gets harder and harder every year. She was having a bad day."

"You shouldn't apologize for her."

Ty shrugs. "We all have off days. I TA'd for Maeve last year and accidentally told the students one of the directors we were studying grew up poor when he didn't, screwed up a bunch of midterms. When I apologized to her, she forgave me without question. Another professor would've fired me. Stress can destroy the best of us."

I don't want to say it, but I'm thinking that Maeve must've been *stressed* the entire time I've known her. Even if I was the oblivious asshole when we started, she's kept being an asshole going longer.

"Maeve's pretty cool when you get to know her," Ty continues.

I cock my head. "Is she?"

"Yeah, and she's obsessed with California locals. She's asked you about it, hasn't she?"

What? Is perfect, poised Maeve actually really fucking weird? "Asked me about what exactly?"

Ty frowns. "Aren't you from Pasadena? Maeve's from Ohio, and she's so starstruck by LA. She used to take local students out to Study Hall with the TAs she was working with to, like, buy everyone drinks and make the one local student feel like someone special. It was kind of sweet, you know? And especially after she saw *Needlepoint* with me at the New Beverly, she was so excited . . ."

And Ty just trails off, like he realized he made a huge mistake and hasn't figured out how to remedy it. The fear filling his eyes is so intense that even I have to look away. Which, dude, calm down, I'm *confused*, but not because of him.

Is it possible that Maeve was so cold and stiff with me that first lecture in particular because she was trying not to fangirl over me? There's just no way. And I *swear* she mentioned seeing only *Goodbye, Richard!* when we first met. When did she and Ty see *Needlepoint*? And *Needlepoint*—my stomach tugs, and stays taut. It's official. Maeve has seen my sexy movie. Maeve has seen me naked. Maeve has seen me arch my back under a warm body, heard my fake orgasm, knows exactly what my body looks like beyond the slices of skin I expose in professional clothing.

Jamie's weird comment about how I feel about people masturbating to that movie comes back to me as a flush spreads across my skin. That, and the way Maeve was so concerned with not crossing professional boundaries. Because, honestly, I *do* think about what Jamie talked about. People I've slept with have mentioned *Needlepoint* in bed. Hell, *Luna* thought I was using my real orgasm sound in that movie when we were hooking up last year and was baffled when she learned I wasn't. Usually, the idea of my partners getting turned on by one of my films does little more than mildly flatter me. At best, it plays into the dom role I usually inhabit in bed. A little celebrity legend worship as a treat.

But Maeve has made it clear she doesn't worship me. It doesn't seem like she even respects me. The idea that Maeve thinks about me sexually is definitely not work appropriate. But I can't get over the fact that she's seen me naked on-screen and hasn't brought up *Needlepoint* once.

Is it possible that Maeve *did* feel something when she saw the movie? The idea of Maeve even *possibly* getting turned on by that movie, it's stirring something deep inside me . . .

"Valeria?" Ty says, his voice soft even as he prods. "Are you okay?"

I shake my head, returning to this moment on the Warner Bros. lot, grounding myself in the present. It's like eighty-five degrees. Ty and I are planning a lesson for *Rocky Horror Picture Show.* We are only two classes into the semester. I cannot be losing it now. As I continue to pursue this teaching thing, I may need Maeve—kill me—to put in a good word for me someday. Meanwhile, I still have Trish's obligations today. I have to meet with HBO after this and demand a gay sex clause in my contract if they want nudity for this limited series they're circling me for, the only project I have in that seems vaguely interesting.

I sigh. I'd never admit it, but the new responsibilities Maeve gave to me are a lot. Ty and I haven't even gotten to the minutia of lesson planning and my leg's bouncing hard enough that the table between us is actually shaking. I clutch my thigh to keep it down.

"Yeah, sorry," I say. "I imagine *Rocky* will mostly be a history lesson. How it got to be a cult classic. Talking about the shows."

"Have you been to a midnight showing?"

I laugh. It's supposed to be an actual laugh, but the sound chokes off at the end. "Ty, I'm gay."

"It'd be amazing if you or Maeve talked about the queer angle," he says, not skipping a beat. "Students love personal anecdotes."

Personal fucking anecdotes. The blood drains from my face.

Okay, so. Maeve's gay.

And has seen me simulate sex. And she's attracted to women. Which I am.

Wonder if Ty would notice if I left to go throw up in terror.

"Yeah, sure," I say.

What personal experiences do I have with *Rocky*? Maeve won't even be in class when I do this deep dive into queer culture. And I shouldn't care about that. I shouldn't be thinking about who she does and doesn't fuck at all. It doesn't matter. I wave a hand in front of my face, hoping a breeze can bring some feeling back to my skin.

"Do you have any ideas for *Little Shop*?" Ty asks.

Work. I'm talking work with Ty. I need said work to go extremely well so I never have to do a half-assed lesbian-representation shit movie and talk about my personal life with scumbags like Winston ever again.

"Well, an obvious talking point is that the original movie aligned more with the off-Broadway ending, but that was cut from the movie because of the audience's reaction in test screenings. So we can discuss what happens when you get too close to or too far from the source material. How movies often sanitize themes, especially anti-capitalist themes like the ones in *Little Shop*."

Ty smiles. "Okay, I think you got that one." He looks at his notes, and I wait to hear his suggestion. But Ty doesn't speak. He's just *looking* at me. "Seriously, are you okay?" he finally asks.

I have not interacted with Ty long enough to have come up with a canned answer.

"Yeah," I say. "Just a lot of meetings today. We should keep going."

"Okay, but I'm gonna talk to Maeve. She must be giving you some vibe."

God, did Ty Dhillon actually threaten to do something more embarrassing than the time my mother called Sandy King's mother and confronted her about Sandy making me eat sand in kindergarten?

"Please don't do that," I mutter.

He's gonna do it, though. I can just tell.

And now I know Maeve's seen me naked.

CHAPTER SEVEN

Even though I'm emotionally drained from the equivalent of a full high school day of meetings, less than an hour after I get home, Charlie drags me into my home gym. Eustace naps on my Pilates mat as Britney Spears croons her greatest hits from the speaker. Charlie sorts through the couple of medicine balls I own, picking the heaviest one. He chucked his shirt before stretching, and I'm in a sports bra, as if we're silently begging each other for validation. *You're so hot, babe. I'd hire you in a fucking action movie. In fact, if I swung the other way—*

"So how're the auditions going?" I ask him as we do our first exercise—obliques and core, passing each other the ball after each rep.

"Nothing much to report," Charlie replies, passing me the ball. "It's a ton of self-tape work. I thought I was done with that."

"I wouldn't get discouraged. We all have to do self-tapes sometimes."

Still, I can't imagine what I'm saying is much help. Right before *Star Trek,* he was on a pretty great roll. A lead in a moderately received adaptation of *Hadestown,* a part in the ensemble of a limited series that had a cult following—all the benchmarks of success a working actor strives for. And to lose that . . .

Charlie throws the ball back to me a little harder than I expect. "You just took like seven meetings on the Warner lot with producers begging you to be in their projects. No offense, Sulls, but don't pretend you can relate. And you don't have to try to empathize."

Shame cuts through me, but once that fades I just feel angry. "And you don't have to be a bitch to the only person who's been actively propping you up since this setback happened."

We get through another rep each before he answers. "That doesn't mean it feels any better knowing that you've been working consistently for over five years without so much as a lull. Don't forget I was scraping for yogurt commercials while you were in England thinking you were going to be a professor and being called a shallow idiot by Emily. And your career *still* took off before mine even got started. I don't mean to take a dig at you. I'm just telling you the facts. Your career has been perfect up until now."

I throw the ball back to him. He *nearly* loses abdominal control, but manages to stay upright. "Well, wonderful, Charlie. I don't know what pointing that out is doing to help either of us. I think it hurts you more than me, actually."

"It's—I'm just airing my thoughts. Honesty. That's always been our policy, hasn't it?"

"Yeah, well, it's not the right time. It's been a long day, and I need more than an hour to decompress, and it's been harder to do with—"

The words catch in my throat as the ball returns to Charlie's hands.

He stops exercising. "What? Are you saying you don't want me here anymore?"

When did this even turn into an argument? I just wanted to know how his auditions were going. Why am I so angry right now? Charlie's just complaining. Yeah, I do have privilege when it comes to my career. It's not something I have to get pissed about. Charlie has an easier time maintaining his body because he has a better metabolism and doesn't crave carbs; I have borderline wet dreams about Pizookies and will lose my abs within a week of laying off the routine. We both have cis and white privilege. The lists could go on forever.

Am I really letting this Maeve stuff turn me into a raging lunatic? I'm sure from Charlie's perspective, I should be grateful for this gig. I mean, what is it about Maeve that's getting to me right now? Is it feeling academically inferior, frustration over how fame is affecting my actual relationships, the fact that I can't get hot queer women despite the objective game I have? Hope?

"No," I say. I reach for my water bottle and take a long couple of swigs. "I just—I hate seeing you so directionless. This"—I motion vaguely to us—"isn't healthy for either of us."

Charlie grabs a set of dumbbells and starts doing bicep curls. I massage out my aching sides.

"I don't like that I'm couch crashing. But it's also fucking weird that you're, like, my landlord. How am I supposed to pull myself out of a funk if I can't even hook up with fellow losers off Raya without feeling like I'm violating your space?"

Back when Charlie and I lived together the first time, the walls were so thin that we were well aware of when the other was having sex. It was just something we had to deal with. We were both doing it and were too bad at communicating to really set boundaries. But now—yeah, I do appreciate that he hasn't brought a random Raya dude to my house. And not just because the idea of a stranger having my address is deeply uncomfortable. Maybe it's jealousy, even if I don't want to call it that right now. Yet it's not like Charlie has had many more boyfriends than I've had girlfriends. He was secretly dating another closeted gay actor for a few years, but they've been broken up for nearly a year. And it's not like I'm interested in anyone in particular. It's not like I'm disappointed that I can't have Maeve because I would never want someone so pretentious and judgmental in my life anyway. Especially not someone who's apparently rather kind but is choosing to withhold that side of their personality from me.

"Well, we can do something about the staying-with-me thing," I say. "Do you want to do, like, chores?"

Charlie sighs. "What exactly would I be doing that your housekeeper doesn't do?"

My phone rings, startling Eustace. "I will let you pay theoretical rent if you keep my team away from me and read my script options for me and tell me if they suck. No joke. And you can secretly inquire about any roles you want that you find through it. Just tell them I hired a personal assistant again."

Charlie squints at me. "Before I give you my answer, the job you described is literally less important than an intern's. But I'll do it." He grimaces as he says it.

"Look, if you can find some way to legitimately pay for a room in my house, I'll let you do whatever you want in there. I'll try to treat general common space more as common space."

There's a long pause as I wait for Charlie's reply. He exhales. "Okay. I'm sorry I snapped at you."

"I'm sorry for being a bitch too." I give him a tiny smile. "I'm sure I've been annoying you with my Maeve bullshit anyway."

"No, I live for that shit." Charlie grins back, rolling me a set of free weights. "What's going on there?"

I sigh. "I have to nail these next two classes to impress her, but I have no idea why I'm trying to impress her so hard when she's being such a dick."

Charlie shrugs. "Maybe she's *not* being a dick?"

I glare at him. "We're not arguing about that."

"Then, and hear me out on this, maybe your clit's the one running the show and it doesn't matter if she likes you as a person if she'll get naked for you."

"And how pathetic is that?"

"We respect horniness in this platonic living situation."

"Charlie," I say, looking him in the eye. "I'm not gonna sleep with her."

"You also said you weren't gonna sleep with your PA, so . . ." Charlie laughs as I turn red. "Look, fine, just say your most gay lizard brain thing, and I'll say my gay lizard brain response, and then we'll stop and finish this workout. Cool?"

I exhale. "Fine."

"Go."

It spills out like a badly rehearsed presentation in middle school. "Maeve's not only gay, but she's seen *Needlepoint*."

Charlie grins. "Spicy. Well, now you can freely touch yourself to her and know she's probably done the same."

"She might not even think I was hot in that." And she might not think I'm hot in her classroom.

He looks me up and down, a smirk on his lips. "Trust me, Val, there's no way."

And just like that, the conversation ends. We return to our workout. Leaving me with only my thoughts.

Thoughts that carry me up to my room, through a shower, into pajamas before dinner. My brain feels foggy, except for one thing: I want to watch *Needlepoint*. It's been years since I've seen it. I'm not one of those actors who can't watch their own performances, but that's just one of those movies I can't really watch with company. The tightness in my stomach returns as I shut and lock my bedroom door. Slide back onto my bed. Flick open my laptop and pull the movie up on a streaming service.

I don't even manage to click PLAY before I set the laptop to my side. All it takes is looking at the banner for the film. I inhale sharply as I stare at it. A moonlit silhouette of a woman arching her back in ecstasy. Me: a younger, lither, more tortured version of myself who watched movies where two girls kissed with that same arched-backed body. I slide my fingertips down shower-damp skin under my waistband, and the motion tugs at memories nearly as old as this banner.

Maeve watched this movie. Maeve sat in a luxury movie theater and watched me be kissed, be touched, be fucked. I can imagine it so clearly. Maeve thinking she's seen a billion erotic indie films that've been analyzed to death in her grad school career, but then this one is *different*. Maeve crossing and recrossing her legs, thinking she's fidgeting but really she's just trying to get pressure between her legs. She tells herself it's just the general eroticism of the film, but she's looking into *my* eyes through the silver screen. She thinks that the feeling will dissipate once she's in the car, but curiously, the feeling doesn't just go away. It sticks in her head until she's back behind a closed bedroom door. My heartbeat flutters as I tease circles on my skin. It's been so long since I did it like this. So long since I wanted *someone* and wasn't just chasing plastic-induced pleasure. My fingertips feed a sensation that almost feels new.

Does Maeve touch herself like this? Is she still proper and elegant in her most private moments, when she's set alight by thoughts and fantasy? She seems like she'd light candles. Bourbon-vanilla candles and her perfect red nails sliding around slick skin thinking of me. Fuck. My stomach jerks at the thought, winding a tighter and tighter grip on me as I think of it. Her wanting me. Her gaze, the way she *stares* at me in class. The way her eyes travel up my legs and across my necklines and over my lips. I'm trying not to pay attention, but her gaze is like hot wax.

God, I want that timbre of her voice in my ear. Her hands on my jaw, my neck as she leans in to speak. *I saw your movie, Val,* she'd say to me, hot breath making the fine hairs on my neck stand up. *Do you really sound like that?* My muscles clench as my circles grow faster, tighter, harder. My wrist cramps, but fuck it, the pain feels miles away. I want to be across from her again I want her to cross her legs I want her to let me run my fingers up her skirt I want to cradle her jaw *god* I want to kiss her. I want my lips on hers. I want to stop with the academic debates and I want us to just be *honest* and for her to tell me I drove her *crazy* in that movie.

Tighter and tighter I go, my breath catching in my throat. I arch my back, muscles taut and ready from my thighs to my abdomen. Everything's sore, I'm sweaty, I'm hot, everything's on fire. The breath knocks out of my chest as the pressure builds to a crescendo. *Tell me I drive you crazy,* and I'd say it right back. *I can't think straight knowing how much I need you, Maeve Arko—*

The pleasure rips through me like a bomb, and a high-pitched sound barely stops at my teeth. The feeling simmers on my nerves, and my muscles heave softly, weakly, from too much use too soon. My vision's even a little blurred around the edges, heart hammering, but my anxiety is gone. I just feel the electric buzz of euphoria. I even find myself grinning as I stare at my laptop's abstract screensaver and pull my sore fingers out of my shorts.

I manage another two minutes of happiness before the reality of what I just did hits me.

CHAPTER EIGHT

True to her word, Maeve isn't in class for the *Rocky Horror* lecture, and Ty takes over her office hours after mine. Being out from under her scrutiny should've made the *Rocky* class my best yet, but I found myself teaching as if she were in the room, giving me dirty looks whenever I went off on tangents. I'm still not great, but I'm feeling better at reacting on my feet when students chime in with questions and comments. It was a good class, but I missed the way Maeve fields student interaction to give me time to regain my spot in my notes, the ease with which she talks about film theory. I fucking hate admitting it, but not only was her critique of my lecturing style correct, but her presence makes the classes better.

Speaking of Maeve, I don't hear a word from her all week. Even reviewing our latest email chains (which I do daily now) have me burning like I have a fever, a feeling that only subsides after I delete my mail app off my phone and it doesn't go off again within the hour I allot for playing video games to try to take my mind off her while Charlie reads the HBO script.

It was a moment of weakness. Weakness, loneliness, horniness. It doesn't mean anything. It *can't* mean anything, yet the shame hasn't faded. In fact, it hasn't faded for the entire two weeks since it happened. And now I'm sweating through my antiperspirant on a mild September day, my heart lodged in my throat, as I wait for Maeve's return to the classroom.

True to her word, she's back for week four, the *Little Shop of Horrors* lecture. There are only two more classes before the midterm, and *I'm* tense wondering if all the students are learning enough to pass. I take a deep breath and set my stuff on the desk in the lecture hall. As per usual, I'm fifteen minutes early and only Cory is here, clicking away on her phone.

"Have you seen *Little Shop* before?" I ask her, hovering near her seat. Anything for a bit of distraction. She's been popping by office hours every week since week two, and we've begun chatting normally. Once you get past that initial layer of shyness, she's actually quite a sharp student, equally invested in her technical animation classes as her film students' electives. No offense to any of my costars, but it's refreshing talking to a young person who didn't take the California High School Proficiency Exam to escape high school early.

Cory puts away the phone. "My school did a performance in high school, so I'm familiar. Are you and Professor Arko focusing on a particular angle?"

So much for Cory distracting me. It makes my heart beat even harder to know she's thinking of this class as *Maeve and Me*. Like we're some comprehensive unit. Yeah, sure, if "Horny Weirdo Who Can't Keep Boundaries" and "Mrs. Professor Boundaries" are a unit.

"Anti-capitalism," I reply.

Cory nods. "Cool." She looks up at me, and I swear she senses my nerves. "Makes sense."

I have to just keep repeating it. *Maeve doesn't know what I did thinking of her.* It's just built up in my head because we haven't physically seen each other since I did it. She doesn't have psychic powers. There's no way it'll be brought up. Plus, sure, she's hot, but there's still the matter of her actively disliking me. Hell, she's not even my *type*. I don't get with academics, not after Emily. The fantasy was a fluke, something that will never gain another ounce of real-world fodder. Maybe Mason has a friend who wants to get laid who she can hook me up with. Just to let off some steam. Charlie and I have sushi with her once a month, and that's coming up soon; I'll ask her then.

Cory flashes a smile. "Is this lecture on the midterm?"

Well, assuming Maeve didn't rewrite everything. I smile back. "I'd pay attention."

The door hinge squeaks. I whip my head to see who's coming in, only for it to be a group of students. I move back to the podium to wait.

I have the PowerPoint set up when she enters with Ty. They laugh as they come in, and when I look up, I catch Maeve mid smile. Her eyes scrunch up when she laughs, and her smile is big enough to make dimples appear along her cheeks. It emphasizes the sharpness in her cheekbones. I feel a pit in my stomach waiting for that smile to disappear as soon as she sees me.

Her laughter fades as she leaves Ty and approaches her usual seat. "I like your watch," she says as she sits down.

No *hi*, no updates about class, just . . . complimenting my watch? My brow pinches as I look down at my wrist. I'm wearing a '68 Omega gold watch, the kind that's small enough to be mistaken for a bracelet. My grandma gave it to me for my eighteenth birthday. And since when does Maeve compliment my style?

But when I look at her, she's casually pulling out a notebook and pen, going through her usual prep for class. Students' eyes are starting to turn toward the front of the room. I swallow, centering myself. I can do this lecture without looking at her. It won't be that hard.

This time will be the worst, and it'll only get easier from here. In fact, for some reason, Maeve hasn't looked at me today like I am a waste of time. Maybe her good mood will last another couple of minutes.

"When most people think about *Little Shop of Horrors,* there are some very specific moments that stand out," I begin. "Audrey II, plant monstrosity and the bane of high school drama programs everywhere."

A couple of students laugh, and I exchange a knowing look with Cory.

"Song-wise, we remember love ballads like 'Suddenly Seymour' and twisted doo-wops like 'Dentist.' But I'd argue the seminal song, the song that contains the musical's heart and soul, slides in at the beginning and goes by without much fanfare. 'Skid Row,' also known as 'Downtown,' presents a simple thesis: class structure is rigid, and people long to escape it. Ultimately, though, those who've seen the off-Broadway show know that the dream of escaping capitalism dies as quiet and meaningless a death as Seymour at the jaws of Audrey II."

Jamie raises his hand. Whereas this kind of break would've thrown me off weeks ago, I mentally put a bookmark in my lecture and call on him.

"But, Professor Sullivan, Seymour survives in the movie," he says.

For the kid who was so caught up on my nudity in films, I'm surprised he noticed. I glance at Maeve, who's looking at her notebook, tapping her pen. She might hate me, but I have to admit whatever she said to Jamie straightened him out.

"And that's exactly where we begin our discussion: at the end. Why did Frank Oz make that change? Unlike other adaptations we've looked at, we can't blame societal changes. The musical hit stages in 1982, and Oz's film was released in 1986. So, what else can we look at to explain the difference?"

Hands raise into the air. Cory in particular leans forward as she waits. But, to keep things interesting, I let other students give their ideas.

"Budget."

I shake my head, catching Ty's gaze. He mouths something, but all I need to make out is the little smile on his lips. I'm doing okay.

"Studios."

"Timing."

As we go around, Cory squirms in her seat, raising her hand higher. Finally, I give her the floor.

"Audience expectations," she says. "People who go see stage plays and people who see big studio movies expect different things from a story."

"Bingo." I throw her finger guns. It feels almost too playful, but I'm slowly getting back into a groove. "Now, before we really get into this, let's give this clip a watch."

We kill the lights to put on the clip, and I find my seat again. My seat—my breath quickens—right next to Maeve. We make eye contact. Prolonged eye contact, on-purpose eye contact. Embarrassment floods my face, but the smile she gives me helps. It's not the full-face smile she gave Ty, but it's encouraging. It forms a stark contrast to the very depressing alternate ending to *Little Shop* the students are watching now. Unlikely as it seems, this is the first time I remember Maeve actually being encouraging in class. Who is this woman, and what did that conference do to my Maeve?

She leans over to me. My heart pounds. "You're doing a nice job involving the students."

I nod, pulling away as quickly as I can. "Quick to learn."

The clip ends far faster than I anticipated, and I don't really know what comes over me. It feels strangely like the buzz I get after a glass of wine, like my organs and words are a little slippery.

I sing a line from Seymour's part in "Skid Row," the melody easy in my ear and playful as it comes out between my lips.

Gwyn's the real singer in the family, sounds like a Disney princess. But I have a voice that Trish says is underused in Hollywood. I could do a musical if I wanted or perform a song as a strong addition to a drama. But god, I wouldn't have been able to sing in that moment if not for this groove I've found myself in.

Students are staring at me, entranced. It's the look fans get at signings, like they're under a spell.

I turn to Maeve as I sing the last line. " 'Someone gimme my shot or I'll rot here.' "

We hold the eye contact this time, and it's heavy. And god, my insides swoop.

She's got that entranced look too.

I blink a few times as I trail off after the last word, look away from Maeve. Out of the corner of my eye, I can see her rub her face, return her expression to neutral. What the hell has changed between the last time I saw her and now?

I click my tongue. "A little more ominous with that ending, eh?"

I look back at Maeve one more time. Her looks aren't scary anymore. In fact, I'm already starting to forget what she looked like when she wasn't looking at me like this, soft and enamored.

The hour-and-a-half lecture passes without a hitch. I recall big ideas with surprising clarity and ad-lib better versions of the one-liners I'd intended to infuse into the lecture. I keep the students engaged and get through most of the meat of the lecture. My blood's buzzing when the screening operator switches the movie on. I return to my seat and lean back, biting away a smile. I didn't think it was possible to feel that same euphoria that comes with a great take on a movie set anywhere else, but this sure feels similar. Like the best moments of directing *Oakley in Flames* last year.

Maeve grabs my shoulder, making my heart leap. She leans in to whisper in my ear. My stomach drops, and my brain buzzes. It's— No, this is a normal thing humans do. It's not similar to what I imagined that night.

"Hey, can we talk outside?"

I nod and get to my feet despite a rather unfortunate quaking in my legs. No big deal. I was shaking like this when I accepted an Oscar; surely I can fake it for Maeve.

We leave the singing chorus and blaring horns of *Little Shop of Horrors* for the quiet echo of SCI's hallway. Maeve takes a seat on one of the leather chairs right outside the door. I take the partner chair. She crosses her legs when she sits. It tightens my stomach just like it always does. I mimic her, crossing my own legs.

"Is something—?" I start to ask.

"I'm sorry." She tucks a piece of hair behind her ear. Her earrings are shaped like little stars. "I have been— Your lecture today was wonderful. It was honestly better than half the lectures I see tenured professors do. It was thorough, engaging, and you said something new about *Little Shop*. Ty says your *Rocky* lecture was excellent too. And I"—she sighs deeply—"have been unfairly dismissive of you since you started. You clearly care about this class and the students, and that's all I could've asked for in a co-professor."

Part of me is shriveling up inside from all of these nice compliments, leaving nothing but the idiot part of me behind. The idiot is flabbergasted. "Are you apologizing to me?"

Maeve's frown deepens, her eyes growing watery for just a moment. "I want you to know it's not you. I took on this job because I needed a stronger portfolio as I move through the final stages of a major research grant for my second book. I really only knew you from *Goodbye, Richard!* and your jokey interviews and videos."

Interesting that she still doesn't bring up *Needlepoint.*

"It didn't align with your dissertation and—shit."

Has Maeve sworn before?

"No. No, this isn't— I didn't give you a fair shot. I thought you were just doing this for the publicity and were lying about actually caring. I was wrong. You're very smart and charismatic, and I'm glad someone so capable is teaching with me."

She exhales, running her hands down her face. Shakes her head, looks back up at me. Her hair is back in her face. I hold my breath as I resist moving it.

"Um, this is really nice of you," I say. *Yeah, sorry you were being a jerk. I'm also sorry I touched myself thinking about you.* And fuck, she called me smart, charismatic, *and* capable? No one calls me *all* those things.

"Can we start over?" she asks.

Is she serious? Was it really just a good lecture that changed her mind? This is way too convenient, but I'm exhausted, so I'm not willing to look for a deeper meaning. "Like . . . reintroduce ourselves?"

And Maeve does it.

She laughs.

She laughs and gives me her squinty-eyed, full-face smile.

My insides might've been taut from our last encounter, but somehow that laugh is all it takes to melt them to mush at my feet.

"Not everything has to be like the movies," she says, biting away the smile. "But I have also been embarrassingly short with you outside of class." She finally pushes that hair out of her face. "In all honesty, I've been fitting you in between a ton of paper and chapter writing and student org work. I imagine you've got a lot going on too. But maybe we could meet here and grab food at Study Hall or somewhere downtown? Maybe next week? I feel like I have a lot of catching up to do."

I've been out for ten years, even if I was publicly back in the closet for three. Yet in all that time, I don't think my heart's fluttered as hard as it is now, hearing Maeve ask me to eat food with her. *Catching up* feels like a plea, a promise to be fulfilled. She's got none of that LA fake niceness I'm so used to. Hell, I've seen the proof of *that* up close and personal.

Maybe this is real; she's really holding out an olive branch. Even the *thought* is downright terrifying considering the way I've been feeling about her lately. Especially the way I've been feeling in private.

"Okay," I say.

CHAPTER NINE

Maeve and I settle on a Friday evening two weeks after the *Little Shop* class for our dinner. In the meantime, our *Beauty and the Beast* and *Chicago* lectures go well. Maeve still gives me pointed looks and takes the reins when she deems I've gone off track, but I also go off track way less. During the *Chicago* lecture, we get through the entirety of our talking points for the first time since the class started. Not to mention Maeve smiles at me every time I look at her. It's incredible how much faster the new energy makes time pass too. It's already October, and our class will consist of a truncated lecture and handing out the midterm I thought was so impossibly far away. We're nearly halfway done with the course, and I feel both like I've fully kicked myself out of my rut and like I've dug myself into a new hole of uncertainty. Yes, I do love teaching and want to do just that, but I'm guaranteed only nine more weeks. Then it's back to the pile of unread scripts and trying to salvage some joy out of the mess my career's become.

But my existential dread gets a break in favor of Maeve dread come Friday night. I'm quaking in my skin as Maeve and I enter what looks like a hundred-year-old wooden house with a red door and a blue sign that reads STUDY HALL. It's all disgustingly cute.

"So don't expect anything too fancy," Maeve says.

"You really don't need to impress me," I reply. Even though the honest response is *Fancy things don't impress me after half a decade immersed in celebrity opulence, so this is an ideal choice.* Hell, I just spent my thirtieth fucking birthday with five of my closest friends watching action movies in my living room and loved every second of it.

Maeve's in one of her floral blouse and pencil skirt outfits, leaving me feeling underdressed in shorts and a flowing top. I mean, I'm glad Charlie talked me out of wearing a crop top, but the vibe is still not *relaxed.* Or, okay, *I'm* not relaxed.

Inside, the restaurant is small, done in medium-colored wood. There's a handwritten menu, one of those white tablet card readers between Maeve and me, and a fresh-faced cashier with purple hair. The only things they serve here are bar-type appetizers, flatbreads, and burgers. Very classic comfort college food, and now my brain's ping-ponging between wanting to follow Maeve's lead and eat, like, normal food, and the Hollywood devil on my shoulder telling me to not even think about risking my body for a girl.

Maeve looks at the menu like she doesn't have a care in the world (maybe she's just saner than I am) and orders something called an Aloha burger, medium. She turns back to me, and I notice that her cut jawline is perfectly visible from this angle. "Do you wanna get a beer?"

Charlie and I drink exclusively white wine and Skinny Bitch (or whatever that brand is called) vodka, but alcohol is not a bad idea. Right now, in this moment, anyway. "Sure."

She gets a Lagunitas IPA, and I select the most alcoholic cider and pork belly sliders. I'm not supposed to have a single ingredient on them according to Charlie and my "lifestyle guidelines." But there isn't much time to focus on that. When I try to slap my credit card down to pay at least for my meal, Maeve stops me.

"Don't," she says. "I'm paying for my apology dinner."

She takes a single number for both our orders and leads me out to the outdoor patio. The sun's dropping below the horizon, bathing the patio in a pleasant almost fall-like crispness. It's also mercifully empty out here.

"Surprised there aren't more students here," I say as I run my fingertip along the condensation on my cider glass.

"It's early," Maeve says, picking up her drink. "They'll be piling in within a couple of hours." She leans her glass toward me. "To another successful class?"

It gets a smile back on my face. "Santé, mon invité."

My French is rusty, but Maeve smiles as we clink glasses. The cider I picked out tastes fine. Good enough that I don't wince drinking it. I know the alcohol isn't entering my system that quickly, but I pretend that it is, just to help shake off the nerves from being out in public with someone I don't know very well.

"So before you have the chance to interrogate me about being from LA, what's Ohio like?" I say, smiling sneakily.

Maeve smiles, just barely. "Ty told you about that? Well, I'm from this village in central Ohio called Gambier. The only worthwhile thing about it is that it's home to Kenyon College. Otherwise, it is completely surrounded by fields, and that's all you ever need to know about it."

I chuckle. "Now, see, as an avid *Stardew Valley* player, I'm very invested in village life."

Her eyes don't light up in recognition, but I can weather that blow. With another sip of alcohol, anyway.

"Seriously, what did you do growing up? What pushed you out?"

She shrugs. "There's really no secret to it. You drive around a lot, see movies, hang out in parking lots, get drunk in fields, trek out to Walmart to loiter. And the sad part about my journey is that I actually stayed there for much longer than I thought I would. I *went* to Kenyon. My parents are physics and philosophy professors at the college, so tuition was free." She takes a long sip of beer. "Now, please. I know it's become a cliché about me, but tell me about growing up here."

I draw circles on the table. "It's really not any more interesting than what you did. I lived in a suburb and had no friends. I went to the mall and was an indentured worker at the Huntington because my parents thought I was going to become an emo cam girl . . . despite the fact that I was the biggest virgin on the planet."

Wasn't anticipating saying the last part, but Maeve chuckles. Egging me on.

Just then, a waitress sets down our food. The smell emanating off the meat and fries makes my mouth water so fast it hurts, but I can't get my hands to move as fast or as naturally as Maeve's as she grabs the knife and the plate and cuts her burger in half. She shoots me a glance as I reach for a slider.

"You okay?" she asks. "I won't push if you don't want to talk about it, but if the food isn't right or anything . . ."

"No, no." I consider taking a bite to buy time, but I let the sauce slide onto my fingers instead. "I just don't go out much. I've had social anxiety for a long time, before the fame . . ."

Maeve frowns. "Val, I'm so sorry! If you need to leave, we can go somewhere else."

A single laugh escapes my lips. "I didn't tell you; you'd have no way of knowing. And it's really not a big deal. I just don't do crowded restaurants. This"—I motion to the empty patio—"is really fine."

"Are you sure?"

"Yeah, absolutely." It helps that I love the way she says my name. Not Valeria anymore. Val. Like she finally considers me familiar. This do-over is really happening.

I take a bite of the slider. Maybe I'm biased from going so long without, but everything about this thing is amazing—the meat is juicy, the pulled pork is the perfect balance of sweet and tangy, the coleslaw's crunch gives the necessary added texture. It takes all my willpower to not say *Fuck, oh my god* to Maeve, the acquaintance who I thought hated me two weeks ago.

"Okay, now I'm genuinely not sure if you're okay," Maeve says. "Blink twice if Hollywood hasn't been letting you eat."

I snort. "I refuse to disclose how correct that stereotype is." Another swig of cider. Both of our drinks are draining dangerously quickly. "But don't worry, I'd stab someone for my Urth order just like every other basic bitch in LA."

Maeve chuckles. "I feel like that'd be funnier if I knew what Urth was."

It's the alcohol, but I *do* gasp out loud. "Okay, so you want your cultural tour of LA by a native? Urth Caffe is a ridiculous organic, fits-LA-dietary-restrictions chain. There are like twenty locations around Los Angeles, so there's definitely one in your neighborhood. They're crowded as shit, but their coffee products are truly top-notch. My favorite brunch in town."

Maeve nods. "Well, I'd love to go sometime." She looks at me, really settles her gaze on me, and, god, I can't tell what part of my face she's looking at. Maybe the cider has already softened me up, but I swear the floating feeling I have right now is because she's look-ing at me like that. "What's your ideal way to have Urth, then? Do you sit there?" she asks.

I snort. "God, no. Take out. I spent way too much money on

a house with a panoramic view in Hollywood Hills, so on even a semi-nice day, I take the meal poolside." *You're welcome to come over sometime. Just ask.*

Maeve takes a swig of beer, grinning beneath the rim of her glass. "I can't believe how close you are to my shitty place in Mid-Wilshire."

I eye the last bit of gold still in my glass. Maeve's pretty much done. There's a tug in me, a little devil crooning that if I could just finish that drink, maybe I'd be loopy enough to invite her over. This friendship is so new, but there's something about her. It can't just be the alcohol. I didn't even tell Luna about my own struggles with anxiety until well after we *stopped* dating. And Maeve has asked me how I am multiple times. Maybe it's that she just feels so different from the type of person I've been associating with since moving back to LA from London. I feel like I don't know how Maeve is going to respond to my questions. She doesn't get my references, doesn't speak Los Angeleno, doesn't care to know Hollywood. It's thrilling.

Our food is almost gone. Tiny clumps of students start filling the tables, and their conversations carry through the air. Our night is fading away.

I want out, but I don't want to leave alone. I'm willing to accept whatever danger comes with that.

I chug the remainder of my cider and slam the glass on the sticky wood table. "Another round?" I give her my best crooked smile.

She bites her lip before saying, "Let's do it."

I know I'm not drunk. We literally had two and a half alcoholic beverages over the course of an hour's worth of conversations about roller coasters, our theories about who killed JonBenét Ramsey, and waxing poetic about nineties queer cinema before packing up as soon as every table around us started to fill up. But I still managed to convince Maeve we should walk tipsily through Exposition Park until we were both sober enough to drive responsibly. I'm relieved that bonding with Maeve is going so well. I'm starting to feel like I could ask her for a job recommendation and she'd say yes.

The second we walk into the park and are surrounded by the rose garden and the fountains and the Natural History Museum (or is it the Science Center; they're next to each other) on our left, everything smells nicer. I could just lie down and if Maeve wanted to lie down next to me that would be cool. Ideal, really.

So when Maeve stops to sit on one of the stone benches that flank the fountain plaza, specifically facing a nice bunch of flowers, I happily follow suit.

"I think it's finally happened—I've become so pathetic that I'm feeling it after two drinks."

Maeve snorts. "Well, if it helps, we're in the same boat." Given she's swaying a little, I believe it. She raises an eyebrow. A rare, coveted skill I had to *learn*. "So does that mean you're not a coke celebrity?"

"Ooh, no, I've only really done blow once."

She leans in a little, and that one curl she's always pulling behind her ear falls into her face.

"So it was a little while after winning the Oscar," I say. "Some wannabe actor I was hanging with gave me some, and I ended up buying a night with a stripper at some club, but through circumstances I've blocked from memory, I ended up at my sister's house—without said stripper or my pants—holding like five of those walking nylon animal balloons you buy at malls. There's a fifty-fifty chance I got bath salts instead of cocaine. So . . ." I break out a smile as Maeve doubles over laughing. "No, not my current pastime. And I'm not a big drinker, as you can tell."

She nods, that hair still in her face. "Right, I imagine you wouldn't go to bars or clubs."

"I need you to know that for every tale of debauchery, there are about five billion nights where I am at home doing photo shoots with my dog. I don't even have a good story about my broken engagement."

I lean over and push the hair out of her eyes. God, her skin is warm under my touch, and I can see the rose rising in her cheeks. Her hair fits perfectly behind the shell of her ear.

"Thanks."

I yank myself away, back to regular-people distance apart. But she's looking at me now, just *barely* biting her cheek. I can't tell if she knows I can see it. That small movement emphasizes her cheekbones. Movie star cheekbones. I don't know how else to put it. My fingers gravitate to my own cheeks. I guess I've always figured they were nice. Hollywood looks. That's what my team says. And then there was some guy on YouTube who once commented that my looks were wasted on a lesbian. Okay, dude.

"You were engaged?" she asks.

I drop my hand from my face. "Yeah. We were together for the last few years of undergrad and all of postgrad. She was an English academic thoroughbred who happened to be superhot, and we were both studying the Beatles. Dated four and a half years, engaged for a little under six months."

"I'm sorry that—"

I put my hand on her arm. "Please, don't be. She was a controlling asshole. Like, the kind of person who always had to be smarter than me, doing better work than me, but she also couldn't date someone dumb, so I was still expected to be, like, publishing papers and applying to conferences and whatever. I came home sobbing after my dissertation got rejected, and she told me a walk might be a good idea, but when I came home she'd packed up all my stuff and moved back in with her parents. She left the engagement ring I got her with a note saying, 'I think you're better off in America.'"

Maeve's hand slams down, clutching mine. I think the force launches my stomach into my throat. "Holy shit, Val."

"It's . . ." A lump is forming in my throat. No. What the fuck, I haven't cried over Emily in years. A year? I guess I cried about Emily with Luna after she ended up crying naked in my living room. "I always tell people I had my *Stroke* audition before Emily and I broke off the engagement and that that's why she left. The audition came soon after, thank god, because I needed something good, but she literally left our five-year relationship because my dissertation was denied."

"That's awful." Maeve holds on to me, running her thumb over my knuckles. "If it helps, I had a shitty relationship in college too."

"Man or woman?" Or nonbinary person. Why didn't I say that?

She sighs heavily. "Woman." She shrugs. "You clearly know how it is. I mostly dated girls in high school anyway. The first time I had sex was with a cis guy senior year, but then she came along in college, and it was like a whole new world had opened up to me." She licks her lips. "But she was so . . . particular. Constantly criticizing what I did, what I wore, how I acted around people. She was genuinely upset to hear I'd had sex with someone with a penis before her. Around graduation I just woke up and got out."

"Holy fuck, dude . . ."

I've had a ton of queer friends over the years, so I always knew abuse *happened* in the queer community, but seeing someone who experienced it. This woman. This soft, wonderful, wickedly smart woman.

She's still touching my hand.

"But the thing is"—she squeezes her eyes shut—"and I'm not proud of this, you know? But once I got into Berkeley for grad school, I just stopped being with women. I figured I wasn't queer enough for them. All through my PhD it was just nice man after nice man, and the relationships never got serious enough for me to say I was bi, and all my real focus went into my career."

Her hand slides off mine, and our bodies retreat back to neutral positions. My skin feels cold without her.

"God, Val, I'm"—she laughs—"I don't know why I'm telling you this. I still think about the good parts of my relationship with Fiona all the time. How we understood each other without having to say a word, how unabashedly queer we were together, how we'd giggle over celebrity crushes."

She glances at me, and *I swear,* she looks at my chest. Or my eyes? Fuck, those are in very different places.

"We—there's just an understanding. A shared experience. And being with her"—the softest moan escapes her lips, sending a shiver down to my bones—"the *sex,* Val. I dream about sleeping with a woman again. I— Fuck."

Hearing her swear, god, I never thought that would be my kryptonite.

She turns to me, full body facing mine. Looks me in the eyes. "I had this date like a month ago. With the job, I have time to go on a date maybe once a year. But you know how sometimes you wake up and you're inexplicably horny?"

What are we doing? My legs twitch with the urge to open them ever so slightly.

"So I figure this date I'll let him get lucky. If it's my rare outing, I'm gonna make it worth it. We go to a bar, down a few, start kissing at the bar, then continue in the Uber on the way back to my place, and I'm just thinking, *Yes, this is what I needed. I cannot wait for this.* We get in the door, and kissing turns into taking off our clothes, and I stick his hand down my panties."

She leans in as she speaks. *Fuck. This.* I am starting to sweat and I really hope she can't tell.

And she pulls back. Pulls back like a perfect tease, a crooked grin on her face.

"And he has *no idea* where the clit is. Grown man, doctor, *doesn't know where the clit is.* I show him at least three times, and he just gives up in a little huffy fit and reaches for his cock. I made him leave." She leans in again, not quite as close as before. "But god damn it, Val, I'm still horny, right? Angry and horny." That crooked smile shifts to just a regular amused grin. She makes eye contact. "So I just . . ." She pauses, lip back in between her teeth, slowly released. "Think about being with a woman and finish it myself."

Fuck. We are on Day One of Friendship and Maeve just told me how she masturbates. Which, fine, most people masturbate, but what the fuck am I supposed to do with this information? I mean, *I* masturbated to her. Did she even mean to tell me all this? What if I admit to what I did?

Still, I'm an actress, right? I smirk. "Sounds very unfortunate. Like you need a much better partner."

She sighs. "It's pervasive. I think about it all the time. Being back in a woman's arms."

She doesn't mean to be telling me all this. I can't keep playing along. This is like she just told me about her abusive relationship, I can't turn this into flirting. She's saying serious stuff; the least I can do is respond seriously.

"I mean, *bi*sexual means you shouldn't be ashamed of being with a girl again. There are people who aren't like your ex."

She pushes her hair back behind her ear again. "Are you?"

I tell myself it could be a general question, but my heart's hammering like it's not. "Nope. Honestly, if someone likes me as much as I like them, my partners can be whatever."

Maeve's smiling again. "Thank you. I seriously need queer friends out here."

I smile back. "You have one."

Then my phone alarm goes off, startling both of us.

The alarm is entitled "CALL TRISH" and there's no context, nothing. It's 8:47 p.m. on a Friday.

But it's enough to knock me out of this spell and analyze what's been happening a little more rationally.

Maeve has just spent two hours breaking down her barriers. I get a pang in my chest, thinking—knowing—I'll likely get a text tomorrow morning apologizing for being crass and oversharing.

"Take it from someone who's had her heart ripped out, chewed up, and spat back into my body by a woman and still dates them: next year, when you're on your annual date, go for someone you really want to be with," I say.

"And you have my number if you're ever dying for a woman's touch," I add with a wink.

CHAPTER TEN

I wake up the next morning in bed with Charlie.

It's not even the kind of scene all the hets who shipped us during our fake relationship would've swooned over. Like his elbow is in my back and I can feel his morning wood on my leg and even after only two and a half drinks, I can already feel a headache coming on.

"Ugh, Charlie, please tell me I'm remembering last night wrong," I say as I disentangle myself from his overheated body.

Charlie rolls over and grins, looking all cute with his bedhead, ready to start the day. "Well, you walked in, told me that Maeve is wonderful, and then you went to bed. The next thing I know you've climbed into bed with me like a psycho and you start calling me"—he grabs my face with both hands—"your *best friend* and you give me a couple little face kisses—"

Oh *god*.

"And snuggle into me and fall asleep."

"Jesus Christ," I say, thrashing out of his grip to avoid eye contact.

"So I assume you were a hundred percent sober, you needy bitch."

I sit up as slowly as an eighty-year-old. "I won't be sober ever again."

"Hey, one time and it's like a fun sleepover," he says. "More than once and I'll become paranoid you're trying to seduce me."

I smile. "In your dreams, Charles."

"Only the magic mushroom–induced ones I had when we were twenty-five. And I unpacked those for, like, three years with a therapist." He sits up, stretching like Eustace. "Do you still go to Rosalie, by the way?"

"Yeah, every other week."

I have an appointment on Monday, in fact. I told her about the little masturbation incident last week and I cannot imagine what we're going to do with what happened yesterday. I've been seeing Rosalie since I was eighteen. I left for London telling her I thought I liked girls and returned seven years later with a broken engagement, telling her that I was gonna try fucking a bunch of girls as an exclusive top since I hated bottoming for Emily.

"Well, now you have something to talk about that isn't Hollywood," Charlie says as he steps into the bathroom.

"We'll never finish talking about Hollywood."

My phone, which is somehow also in Charlie's room, starts ringing.

It's Maeve.

My stomach drops. Why would she be *calling* me? And at— I glance at the clock on Charlie's nightstand—9:00 a.m. on a Saturday?

I pick up. "Hey." Easy, breezy, I didn't wake up a minute ago.

"Hey," she sounds a bit more nervous. Her voice seems deeper, but I shake the thought away as best I can. "So weird question, but can you see if my wallet is in your car?"

Right. We walked back to our cars, and Maeve said the beer was hitting her harder than she expected. I—god dammit, I called Charlie, he Ubered from a photo shoot in Downtown LA, and drove us and my car back home. Maeve told me I had a middle-aged straight man's car, and she was very enthusiastic when Beyoncé came on my shuffle.

"Lemme check."

I put the phone on speaker and walk out to the garage. Eustace squeezes out the door to join me. I pick him up, kiss the top of his head, and search the back seat.

Yep, there's a wallet in the floor space. It's soft red leather and has an Italian label on it. I imagine she got it abroad. It feels very sophisticated. She's certainly put more effort into choosing it than I did. My wallet is one Gucci sent me for free after the *Goodbye, Richard!*'s premiere. I use it for convenience's sake. Eustace leans over from my arm and licks the wallet.

"Eustace, the fuck," I say, pulling the wallet away and wiping it on my pajama shorts.

I hope she's not allergic to dogs.

"Who's Eustace?" Maeve says, still on speakerphone.

"My dog," I say. "Don't worry, a strange man doesn't live in my garage."

Just in my guest room.

"I'm relieved," she replies. "I don't want to inconvenience you. I can Uber and come by to get it. Will you be busy in like twenty minutes?"

My chest flutters. All this time, I still can't believe she lived *twenty minutes from me.* "No, that works." I give her my address.

"Cool. I'll see you in twenty. Thank you so much."

As soon as we hang up, I get a text from Trish. Perhaps related to that "CALL TRISH" alarm I set for myself last night.

> **Trish:** Hey V - I'm in the middle of an emergency call with a client but once that's done, I'm gonna call you.

We have news and I want to hear what you think of the
scripts you've read.

Great. Love when managers say there's "news" and don't have the
decency to specify whether it's good or bad. And as for the scripts,
Charlie gave the HBO pilot a thumbs-up and has been reading the
animated feature for two days now because he had to stop to "collect
himself" halfway through. Once I'm back inside, I release Eustace
and prepare his breakfast. Maeve didn't specify what she looks like
right now, so what should I change into? Street clothes? Workout
clothes? Remembering how close Maeve was to me last night still
sets my heart hammering.

I go with workout clothes, back out of my bedroom as quickly
as I can. Charlie comes into the kitchen, and I sigh, feeling vaguely
guilty about being so needy the night before.

"What do you want for breakfast?" I ask.

"If you're scrambling eggs, that's fine with me."

I decide to add some sharp cheddar, my boy's favorite, into the
scramble as a flimsy apology. While I sauté in peppers and spices,
Charlie gets to work on a smoothie for us. God, we *are* ridiculous.
Charlie pours me a glass as I cut up avocado.

"Did I actually inconvenience you last night?" I ask.

I think we've slept in the same bed one other time. Maybe twice?
It's the type of thing that only happens in emergencies.

"Sully, shut up. You're my wife, even if the fake relationship is
over. Also who's coming over? I heard you on the phone."

My face gets hot. "Maeve. She forgot her wallet in my car."

Charlie looks down at his uncovered chest. "Well, fuck, man,
when's she—?"

And my doorbell rings. Eustace starts yapping. I take a deep breath, try to ignore my thrumming heart, and scoop him up. Open the door.

Maeve's in a T-shirt and shorts. Thank god, on level with what I have on.

Maeve smiles as she looks me up and down. "Stars really are just like us, huh?"

Charlie peeks in from the kitchen. "If you mean her clothes, she does half her Insta pictures looking like that!"

There's no way to properly capture the pure, unfiltered shock on Maeve's face as she makes eye contact with Charlie in all his shirtless glory. Her gaze flits between me and Charlie anxiously. She's probably processing a million things at once. And I shouldn't laugh . . .

"I have a live-in himbo," I blurt.

Charlie's mouth opens into a little insulted O, and Maeve bursts out laughing.

"I'm her *best friend* and a working actor," Charlie says. "And in case you were too drunk to remember, I drove you two home last night."

I hand Maeve her wallet. "His show got canceled, so we're doing some TLC. And also we fake dated for like three years to appease my old manager."

Charlie rolls his eyes. "She's sensationalizing it. We knew each other in high school."

Maeve still looks confused. "Oh. Okay, so he's not . . ."

Charlie and I exchange a look.

"Oh, no, I'm gay. We're totally platonic," he says. "We've only been naked together once."

All the blood in my body freezes. Maeve blinks a little more rapidly.

"No, like, we took a shower together once," Charlie says, which is really not helpful. "Because we had to. She was drunk and threw up on both of us."

His lease is ending. Right now.

"Thank you for driving us home, by the way," Maeve adds. "I wasn't that drunk last night. Like I—I recognize you. You just didn't mention you two lived together."

I turn to Maeve. I give up. I'm probably bright red right now. "Yeah, so if there isn't anything else you need . . ."

"No, wait!" Charlie says. "Val talks about you so much—"

CHARLIE!

"And I've been dying to actually talk to you." He looks down at his chest. "I can put a shirt on; hold on. Stay for breakfast."

Maeve looks between Charlie and me. Her gaze lingers on me, an eyebrow raised as if asking if he has any authority in this household.

"Yeah, why not," I say.

Charlie leans in to me as I brush past him. "I'll say I have a business call," he whispers.

We have breakfast out on the back patio. It's a high-visibility day, and I can show off the view I was bragging about last night. I catch Maeve's smirk as Charlie and I set down our health food.

"It's not vegan," I say.

Maeve is clearly not vegan; I watched her eat a burger last night.

Charlie lifts his smoothie glass. "The smoothie is, though."

Maeve isn't even paying attention to our banter. She puts the metal straw into her mouth without looking, gaze fixated on the view of LA. Those brown eyes are a little watery, her expression soft. Contemplative or in awe, I can't really decide. In movies, it's the kind of look we're supposed to give people we love.

The sun paints her features in its light. Her profile is silhouette-ready, and I can see the bumps of her knuckles as she holds up her chin, the blue of my pool reflecting in her eyes like a photo. And not that I *love* her, but I wouldn't mind spending a few hours capturing the way Maeve looks right now.

"Good?" I ask. It doesn't really matter what I mean.

Maeve shakes her head a little to break her trance. Her gaze turns to the smoothie, then back to the view. "Yeah, both are amazing."

Charlie looks between Maeve and me, grins at me, takes his plate, and leaves.

Maeve doesn't even notice. And as the screen door clicks shut, I'm alone with her again.

I wait maybe ten seconds, expecting Charlie to pop back up and save me. For Trish to call me. But it's silent out here other than the birds' chirping and the pool water lapping. Eustace pushes his way through the dog door and jumps onto Charlie's chair. Maeve notices, smiles, and holds out her hand for Eustace to sniff. He licks her without hesitation. It makes my insides melt more than I expected.

"He's really cute," she says. "What is he?"

"About last night," I say.

The smile my dog put on her face falls.

"I hope we didn't go too far off the rails. I was having so much fun just getting to know you, but I know we're coworkers. I respect your work so much. In fact, I . . ." I don't know if I've said this out loud. "I might want to teach more. Really, seriously make a career of it."

Eustace jumps into Maeve's lap, and she occupies her hands petting him. Homophobic prick. She smirks at me.

"I figured as much after I saw you after your first office hours. The other celeb guest professors never so much as look at papers. But that's quite the career change."

I flash back to last night, how Maeve described all the responsibilities she has years prior to achieving tenure. "I think it's the right move."

"Well, I'll keep my eyes open for you."

Oh my god. "Really? Even after last night?"

"If anything, *I* was inappropriate." She blushes. "You were perfectly wonderful, as usual. If you're fine with what happened, I think we can keep getting to know each other." She takes my hand. Under the table, like a secret even we aren't supposed to know about. "I can't thank you enough for what you said about dating bisexual folks."

Her hand is soft. It's so, so soft. She has moisturizer hands, elegant hands, and she's holding my hand tight. I feel like I'm having a holiday romance with a stranger, like the intimacy has built too fast because it's not supposed to last. It lies uneasy in my gut; I'm afraid someone's going to yell cut because this isn't real.

Turns out director me yells cut. I pull my hand away.

"Of course," I say. "But we can keep the topics a little lighter if you want. You have any passions outside of work and the state of California?"

Maeve's eyes pop open wide, and she seems to realize the same thing I have. Her hand retreats to my dog. "Music. I was in choir all through elementary and middle school. By high school, I worked through the stage fright enough to be involved in every musical my high school put on."

Somehow, I can picture little Maeve so easily in those velvet dresses on overcrowded school stages. I'd peg her for an alto and wonder if I'll ever find out. "Were you any good?"

She shrugs. "Good enough for small-town Ohio high school. I actually played Belle in our *Beauty and the Beast* production my junior year. So, I'm biased, but your animation lecture was my favorite so far."

She does have silly little opinions after all. "Any other fun facts?"

"Hmm." She taps the side of her glass a couple of times. "I was devastated to learn that you can't own hedgehogs in Cali because that was my childhood dream—the reward I planned to give myself for 'making it' in adulthood." She scratches under Eustace's chin. "But this boy is almost as good as a hedgehog."

"He's evil, and I don't know why he's being this sweet," I say. "Also, if you can sing, why the hell didn't you harmonize with me during *Little Shop*?"

She laughs. "If you want me to harmonize with you about the woes of the lower-middle class, just say the word."

"I'd rather hear you sing Belle's part."

"Only if you tell me what the hell *Stardew Valley* is."

I shake my head, a smile spreading across my face. "Nope. You have to commit to playing *SV* with me for two hours before I explain what it is."

"So you're a gamer, then?"

"Yes."

Eustace leaves Maeve and climbs into my lap. I take a sip of my smoothie.

"Are the children on your Instagram really your niece and nephew, or are they secretly your kids?"

I laugh. "My niece and nephew."

She leans back in her chair. "You don't strike me as the nurturing type."

I fake gasp and then gesture at Eustace. "Excuse me, what do you think this is?" And as I say that, some residue on my smoothie falls onto Eustace's white head. He startles and jumps out of my lap, and my only motherly response is "Fuck!"

Maeve full belly laughs as I scoop up my dog and wet a cloth napkin to get the stain out of his fur. And that's when my phone rings, Trish's name flashing on the screen.

"Shit, I have to take this," I say.

Maeve gets out of her seat. "I can blot your dog."

"You're the best."

I take the phone and scurry into the kitchen. Charlie is watching TV in the other room, food on his lap. We make eye contact, and I shoot him a thumbs-up.

"Hey," I say to Trish.

"Hey," Trish says. "So let's cut to the chase, yeah?"

My stomach clenches. "Um, okay."

"So Sundance got in contact with me. Gave me some confidential information much earlier than we'd get it otherwise, so that's a relief at least." She sighs, which gives me all the information I need. "*Oakley in Flames* didn't get picked."

She moves on from there. Says we're going to submit to Tribeca, South by Southwest, all the big European festivals on the circuit. Sundance isn't even that big of a deal. She says everything a manager has to say when they're doing damage control.

But I can't hear her anymore.

It's like I'm on autopilot. I put her on speakerphone and pull up the group chat. I have to tell Luna. She's the one who was so fucking excited about the opportunity to go to a festival. She's happy in her TV job, but this is *her* dream. I send the news into our group chat with Romy, Wyatt, and new addition Charlie, who doesn't know any of them but insisted he be included.

VS: We didn't get into Sundance.

The responses aren't general sadness. They're sorry for *me*, not the movie. Even Luna says, I'm so sorry, Val!! It should be comforting. But it feels more like pity.

I didn't want to go to Sundance anyway. This isn't something to feel bad about. It's good. My muscles are relaxing now. My throat's scratchy, but who cares. This is a relief. I didn't want this. I ranted to

Charlie about it for days. I hate Utah, I hate altitude, I hate schmoozing, and I hate festivals. Maeve just told me she's going to help me transition to academia. I'm doing what I said I'd do after that Winston interview.

I don't know what I say to Trish, but she ends the call before I have to figure it out.

Charlie's wrapped his arms around me before I even realize he got up. "I'm so sorry, Val. Sundance is being a dumbass."

He doesn't need to hug me. This isn't a bad thing.

I have more important things to deal with. My class. Maeve.

My heartbeat picks up. Maeve. Maeve who's outside trying to clean my dog.

I push Charlie off and head back outside.

She looks up at me and frowns. "Everything okay?"

And suddenly everything is crumbling down. That scratchy feeling in my throat is now a lump digging deeper inside me. Tears burn in my eyes, even as I try to blink them back. My muscles ache as if I've been standing for hours.

"Hey, uh, I gotta deal with something," I say. "Can we catch up on Tuesday?"

Maeve lets go of Eustace and gets to her feet. Approaches me, hovering about three or so feet away. Perhaps unsure if she can bridge that gap. "Yeah, of course."

Once Maeve leaves with her wallet, I let the tears fall. It's like knocking down a set of dominoes, and seconds later I'm burying my face in Charlie's chest, only able to say "I'm sorry" through the sobs.

He rubs my back, holding me tight. "It's okay. It's gonna be okay."

CHAPTER ELEVEN

There's no one in this world who I'm more willing to get showered and dressed up for than Rosalie. It started off as a coping mechanism after I returned from London to face the depression void of losing my PhD and Emily. I'd guilt myself into getting out of bed to go to weekly sessions, nudged to appease basic hygiene standards because she works in this cute office in Pasadena and you don't show up to cute Pasadena offices smelling like death and covered in ketchup stains.

After the Sundance news, I fall back on that compulsive need to look presentable for therapy. I'm still not entirely sure why I broke down with Charlie on Saturday, but Rosalie's office is as good a place as any to figure that out.

I look at my phone again. My heart leaps when I see I have one unread text.

Maeve and I haven't spoken since she left with her wallet. And maybe part of that is because I told her I'd talk to her on Tuesday, when we have class. But I spent part of Saturday giving Eustace a bath to wash the stain off him and I sent Maeve a picture of his clean self along with the caption *ONLY TOOK THREE HOURS* when we finished. There's no reason for her not to answer that text.

But the unopened text is from Charlie. He asks if we can go to Erewhon later today so he can cook a nice dinner for us. A very sweet offer, something to look forward to, but it doesn't put me at ease the way it should. I look back to my phone, to the picture of Eustace that is still the last thing in the chat between Maeve and me.

"Valeria?"

I look up at Rosalie standing in the doorway. She's always in jeans and a sweater, and today that sweater is a blue that contrasts perfectly with her pale skin. I slip past her, a couple of feet between us, an easy distance that speaks to our intimacy. I suppose it comes with growing up together, starting from when I was an eyeliner-smeared teen and she was in her first junior position in a private practice. Over the course of ten years, three babies, one Oscar, and one complete sexual journey, we're still doing our dance. She's one of the few people left from my pre-fame life, and she's also one of the few people who uses my full name interchangeably with my nickname.

I take a seat on her red couch and slip off my sneakers so I can tuck my legs up under me. She sits across from me. A hilariously cliché painting of Pasadena's annual Rose Parade hangs on the wall adjacent to us.

"How're you doing?" she asks. She leans forward, though, which tells me she knows my answer before the words form on my lips.

"*Oakley in Flames* didn't get into Sundance," I say. I'm technically supposed to start with an emotion, but after this long we've developed a bit of shorthand.

"Oh, Val, I'm so sorry," she says, bridging the gap between us to set her hand on mine.

We pull away at the same time, and she straightens out while

I hunch closer into myself. I wish I could lie down, but that's a depressed Valeria move. "What's coming up for you?" she asks.

I sigh. "Guilt."

"For what?"

"When Trish first said we'd be submitting to Sundance, I bitched about it to everyone who'd listen. I said that I hated Sundance, hated film festivals, hated talking to people, hated the way altitude exacerbates what my body already does when I'm stressed. I *genuinely* didn't want it to happen."

"Why didn't you want a film you worked on to get into a festival?"

"I—I mean, it didn't feel worth it. As soon as I started directing, it was clear that the important people in my career didn't want to support that aspect of my work. Why would I invest emotionally in something that'll ultimately disappoint me?" I motion to the air. "Case in point with Sundance. *Oakley* is good enough for it, but it was never gonna get in."

"You said you thought the film was good enough. So, okay, you saw this coming, but maybe there's some disappointment in there?"

My throat tightens. "Of course there's disappointment, but again, it doesn't matter. I'm switching my life trajectory. I don't regret—" *Not emotionally investing in directing.* The words catch in my throat. I can't force them out. Because I don't regret anything. I grasp for something else to say. "It's— I didn't expect to feel this heavy about letting down an entire team. I feel like I need to be comforting people who aren't me. And those same people keep saying, 'Oh, I'm so sorry, Val,' as if they didn't work on the film too and—" I sigh. "I just can't take on that energy right now. *Oakley* is in the past, and I'm trying to move on."

"Is there any way to tell the people bringing up *Oakley* this?"

I snort. "Without looking like a dick?"

Rosalie shrugs. "You're being honest. It's not like you saying 'I'm doing okay' is going to change the trajectory for the other festivals, right? It's okay to feel okay about something that would've upset you months ago."

Except it did upset me. I can't form the words, even in an open environment like therapy. It's not like I think Rosalie will judge me for my reaction. But saying that out loud, admitting that a piece of me is still emotionally invested in *Oakley*, feels like it could undermine everything I've put into Maeve and academia. Because if I admit directing is still whimpering along, or dare to admit that Maeve's insane schedule is terrifying and that I don't know if I can do it, I'm right back to that crisis in Trish's car in August. No, this is stupid. I'm sure of where I'm going, which means being sure of what's in the rearview mirror.

"Thanks." I pause. "Anyway, it's a sign. The day this happened, my coworker Maeve said she'd look out for open teaching positions for me. I have to finish up some projects next year, and then I'm done."

Rosalie's face lights up. "Congratulations, Valeria, that's wonderful. So everything turned out fine with Maeve?"

"Yeah." Except for the teeny, tiny crush, which I'm ignoring. It's nothing I haven't dealt with before. "We seem to be meshing well. I really like her and her whole world."

Getting so upset over Sundance was a fluke, which is proven by the weightlessness coming over me as I think about the weekend I spent with Maeve.

A text tone goes off. I check, muttering, "Sorry."

It's not Maeve.

"Luna's asking if I want to get dinner later this week," I say.

"How's Luna doing?"

"Good, I think. I mean, she has Romy and a camera job and told her parents that she's bi maybe six months ago. But she's an anxious baby, so . . ." She had also mentioned that her parents refuse to call her bisexual and that they tell their friends Luna is a lesbian, but *overall,* I suppose, things are good.

Rosalie laughs. "Two peas in a pod."

I hold up a finger. "Except I'm going to be honest about how I feel about Hollywood with her." I'll try, anyway. If it doesn't happen at a one-on-one dinner, maybe I'll have the courage to tell her a few drinks in at the monthly group hang with Mason and Charlie that I invited her to at Nobu.

Rosalie smiles. "Good. I'm proud of you for realizing what makes you happy and going for it. I know it's not easy to leave something that's been such a big part of your life for so long."

I smile back. "Thank you."

I sneak one more look at my phone when our session ends.

< Maeve liked *"ONLY TOOK THREE HOURS"*>

No actual words from her, though. The unease returns. She liked it, the way I like texts from people I feel bad ignoring but don't want to engage with.

Somehow, that's fucking worse than if she'd done nothing.

CHAPTER TWELVE

It's finally midterm week.

It's been nearly a decade since I took a midterm as a student, yet I still find myself tucking my shaking hands into my pants pockets as I walk into the lecture hall. Maeve and I haven't talked since I sent her the picture of Eustace four days ago. We're halfway through the semester, eight more classes left, and I'm just starting to feel like Maeve and I may finally be in sync. Have I already ruined it? Are we going back to a tense truce?

Maeve's sitting in her usual spot in the first row, laptop out, typing furiously.

I consider, for an embarrassing second, letting her go on typing. But no, I want to see the midterms before lecture starts, and she's the one who has them.

So I plop down next to her, setting my bag on the empty seat next to me.

"Good rest of your weekend?" I ask.

Maeve tucks a hair behind her ear, eyes on her screen. My muscles tense, ready, impossibly, for Old Maeve to reemerge. "I wish I could say that, but I pumped out a whole chapter on the monster bisexual and fell asleep on my couch. Sorry about not saying more about Eustace; he looked beautiful after his bath."

She closes her laptop and turns to me.

I unclench my jaw. "Oh, the life of the tortured genius."

She smiles. "Hardly." There's a long pause, her gaze on me, trying to figure me out.

"How was—?" she says right as I blurt out, "Can I see the midterm?"

Recognition flickers across Maeve's face. "Right. Ty has the hard copies and should be by any minute."

So we're back in our space alone, no business to get done until everyone arrives.

"It was really nice hanging out with you," I say. "Your dissertation made me so curious about you, and I feel like a lot connected. I love your lecture pieces, but it was nice just hearing you talk."

Maeve blushes maybe half as hard as I do, my heart suddenly thundering. "That's good to hear. I thought for sure I was just boring you rambling about Kimberly Peirce."

I laugh. "You can't bore me with fringe nineties movie talk."

She gives a half-hearted chuckle. "You'd be amazed at how many academics act like it's pulling teeth anytime you try to get them to talk about anything they're passionate about. I think I've scared off dozens of colleagues that way." She forms her mouth into a thin line. "They were a *little* too neurotypical, y'know?"

I glance at the door, thinking of how Ty talks about Maeve. I'll tuck the neurotypical comment away in my mental notes. "I thought you and Ty were friends."

She blows air out her lips. "We're around the same age, but it doesn't go beyond friendly colleagues. I think I forgot how to make friends after undergrad." She really seeks out my eye contact. "Not like you and Charlie."

After undergrad. As in, after she got out of that terrible relationship. My heart pangs. "If it's any consolation, I've made great friends in adulthood too. My director friend Mason and I connected because she wanted someone to go *Twilight Zone* mini golfing with her in Vegas, then we ended up talking about childhood experiences in Vegas, and then we went to this silly male strip act that was playing in the same building. You start with mutual interests, move into asking them about their feelings on life, repeat." I glance at the door, which is still miraculously shut. "Ask Ty to go to a screening for a film he's studying. Kinda professional, kinda friendly, shows you know and care about his life." I smirk. "Maybe go to the New Bev since that's the only proper way to watch movies?"

Maeve, thank god, laughs. "I wish that was just a pretentious thing. Try explaining to anyone you get sensory overload watching a movie in a theater with people talking and looking at their phones."

And right as I'm about to reply, the doors open and Ty comes running in with a stack of packets. "Got 'em! God, sorry, the copy machine was being a bitch!"

The students start filing in right after him, swarming Maeve like the intellectual celebrity she is. Meanwhile, I take a peek at the questions on the midterm.

> *1. Define diegesis and how it informs the narrative in any of the films discussed in the first half of the semester.*

> *2. When historical events are incorporated into the world of a musical, such as the Holocaust in* Cabaret, *does the inclusion of music act as an emotional buffer for the audience? Why or why not?*

3. Do musical numbers feel more natural within the context of animated films such as Beauty and the Beast? *Why or why not?*

4. Did the change to the more optimistic ending support or hinder Little Shop of Horrors' *anti-capitalist message?*

5. The Rocky Horror Picture Show *derives meaning from both the content of the film and the culture surrounding midnight showings. Select one to two scenes from the film and discuss an interpretation of the scene in a vacuum and then how selected audience callbacks change or inform that meaning.*

Maeve adjusted the wording, but she kept my question.

And she looks at me, *really* looks at me, as we go over the questions with the class.

Maybe something really did shift over the weekend. But what do I do with this?

I don't know. All I gather as the students file out after our shortened class is that I want to keep talking to her. To hear about her struggle making friends and about the chapter she's going to write in her book tonight. To go to a quiet movie theater with her. Me masturbating to her and her telling me she masturbates to women be damned. I'm almost feeling bold enough *to* ask if she'd see something like *The Handmaiden* with me, despite how inappropriate that would be.

I may not be able to ask Maeve to a movie, but we could at least grab coffee after this. Maybe redeem Literatea.

"So I'd err on writing more than less," I finish explaining to Cory as the last of the students head out.

"Thanks, Professor Sullivan," Cory says.

Before the semester ends, I'm going to need to offer her a one-on-one industry-coffee-type meeting. If she wants it, I'd love to help out such a bright soul in whatever way I can.

As soon as Cory leaves, I scan the room for Maeve so I can ask about that coffee. Without all the students, Ty, and the folks operating the projector, the huge classroom feels tiny. I know she's busy, but I want to keep up the momentum. I feel grounded when I'm with her, and I don't want it to stop. I want to see how much more I can learn about us, what she'll pull out of me. She's made it clear she feels the same way.

"Hey," I say, approaching her as she packs up. "Do you want to grab coffee after this?"

She looks up. "I would, but I gotta get ahead on my chapter tonight. See you next week, though?"

And with that, she leaves me alone. The last person in the lecture hall.

I'm an actress.

If I were going to be a real dickhead about it, I could add *Academy Award–winning* to qualify that, just like they do in trailers for my movies.

But today my profession has one purpose: getting me through this *Phantom of the Opera* lecture without staring at Maeve, without interpreting every last twitch of her lips, every single time she tucks a hair behind her ears.

After the midterm coffee rejection, I let Maeve be. We exchanged a few emails in the lead-up to this week, revising the lecture; she told me to take the lead, and here we are. It's only been seven days, but the cavern I feel like I somehow dug has made each hour feel like an eternity. And now I have to get through *Phantom of the Opera*—the quintessential tortured preteen theater girl movie—and not look at the woman who told me she touches herself thinking about women. Plus, as much as I'm feeling better about Sundance and I'm eager to keep working with Maeve on honing my teaching skills, I'm exhausted.

But once Maeve collects the students' midterms, she leaves the floor to me with a smile.

I'm an actress, so I act. I keep my recap of Andrew Lloyd Webber's life snarky and informative, involve the ever more eager students as much as possible, and explain cinematography and directing while leaving enough time for Maeve to discuss the history of opera. Maeve and I are in sync in the only language we know how to be in sync in, but the fact that I don't know if she'll scurry off again when lecture ends leaves a hollow feeling in my chest.

So as soon as class does end, I turn off. My heartbeat slows, but I still struggle to get breath into my lungs as students file out of the room. Thank god, none of the students—not even Jamie or Cory—stick around to ask questions or chat. In fact, the next class is already entering the room. I can envision the rest of the day—pajamas, a mind-numbing video game, then Nobu tonight, where I'll ask Mason to hook me up with a rando. I'll wash Maeve and the friendship that never was out of my brain even if it hurts.

And then Maeve's standing in front of me in a navy blazer and ankle pants (*Fuck you Charlie, these* were *on trend*). She's smiling again, which is curious.

"Do you have plans tonight?" she asks.

The answer is a clear-cut yes, but I can't get the words out. "Uh—"

She grabs my wrist, nearly knocking me out of my skin. "Because you don't now."

I swear Maeve's touch is like a shot of B$_{12}$. My skin's electrified, burning where her hand touched me over a generic black blazer I found in the back of my closet. And as Maeve gently tugs me out of the room, I desperately want my blazer to creep up. I want to feel that burning touch right on my skin. We leave the crowds of students in the building and head out into a punch of cold on this bizarrely chilly day, and then we're back inside, in her office.

"Should I ask what we're doing?" I say.

At this point, I've had three weeks of Nice Maeve, maybe five if I counted the weeks where she was awkwardly ignoring me as nice rather than mean. The nice shift has slowly overtaken the four weeks of Asshole Maeve, but I don't trust the change yet.

"Almost," Maeve says. She checks her phone and smiles.

She takes us up the elevator and stops dead in front of a Postmates guy.

"Maeve?" he asks, monotone.

Maeve gives him a quick smile of confirmation and plucks a take-out bag out of his hands. The Postmates guy stares at me as we walk back to her office. The sun's starting to go down, bathing the room in an orangey light. It's not quite late enough for us to turn on the lights, but it'll be that time soon enough.

Maeve sets her things down and places the bag onto her cleared desk. She unwraps whatever's inside like she's a magician. I bite my inner cheek.

"So," Maeve says, "I had to watch a *ton* of your interviews, but I finally figured out your favorite food." She pulls out three little circular tins. Plucks the lids off all of them. "Or at least something you like when you're not on a diet."

Skillet cookies.

A lump forms in my throat, and I struggle for breath as I cover my mouth with my hands. Why would she—?

"I knew you were upset on Saturday at your house, but I didn't think it was my place to push myself in," Maeve says. "But I've been thinking about it nonstop since then. I should've done this when you asked about coffee last week, but I . . ." She pauses. "I was nervous I'd cross some boundary like I did last time. But it must've looked like I hated you, which I don't. So . . . can I make up for it with a bit of kindness?" She pauses again, staring at me. Arms stiff at her sides. "Are you okay with hugging?"

It's not funny, but I find myself coughing out a laugh as I say, "Yes."

She hugs me tight, close. Our bodies bury into each other; I can feel her heartbeat through our suits. She fans her fingers out over my shoulder blades and for just a moment, I give up and rest my chin on her shoulder.

"My directorial debut didn't get into Sundance," I mutter. "That's all it was about."

My directorial debut, the first story that sunk into my bones, the project I put thousands of hours into, that genuinely filled me with a sense of hope because I finally saw a representation of myself reflected back on the screen.

"I'm so sorry. I can't imagine how much that stings," she says as she pulls away. She claps her hands together. "Well, then consider these Fuck Sundance cookies."

I smile. Around Maeve, smiling is starting to feel like the most natural thing in the world.

She unpacks the three cookies, speaking as she goes. "I got their trio deal: cookies and cream for you, salted caramel for me, and figured a chocolate chip would be a neutral third. But I'm not sick, and I'm happy to share."

I take a seat on the couch and accept a plastic spoon from Maeve. The first bite of the Oreo skillet cookie tastes insane. It's sweet, it's heavy as hell, and eating it feels like sitting by a fireplace in the winter with friends. It sparks visceral feelings of comfort and happiness. I catch Maeve as she takes her first bite of the salted caramel—she's careful, making sure to get ice cream on the spoon, dainty in how she eats. She goes back after swallowing to clean the spoon before scooping up another bite.

We don't really speak for a while. Then again, the cookies aren't that big. I switch over to the chocolate chip one before finishing my own. Our spoons clink as we each dig out a bit. Even that minuscule impact ricochets back at me and leaves my muscles tense.

"So, while I have your attention, there *was* another purpose to this," Maeve says.

She deliberately creates a moat around the middle of her salted caramel cookie. Strategy. I like it.

"We ought to grade a few midterms together to make sure we're consistent in our interpretations, and, I'll admit, I'd love you to talk me through a bit of your plan with *Rocketman*. I know that class isn't for a few weeks, but I'd like to adjust my lecture to match yours better. You're the expert on anything made after 2010, and I need to get a sense of what you're thinking."

I leave the core of my own cookie. "Well, it's prime traffic time anyway, so might as well stay late." The thought has my heart pounding. I'll keep an eye on the time for Nobu.

Maeve smiles. "Great." She looks back at her cookie, then flicks her gaze to me. "Do you want the last bite?"

She left me a core piece of her cookie? God, even that has my heart squeezing. I smile back. "Switch?"

But something makes me feel bold. I don't slide her cookie over to my side of the desk; I reach over into her space and dig up the last bite myself. She does the same almost at the same time, and then clinks her spoon with mine before retreating to her space. I know it's the cookie that tastes like salted caramel, but my insides shake a little imagining I'm tasting Maeve.

She tosses my empty tin into her trash and pulls out a stack of packets. She passes one to me, and I notice she's double-jointed: her pointer, middle, and ring fingers fold as she slides the packet my way. A pen lands on top.

"Let's grade maybe six or so, then decide what we'll give to Ty?" she says.

"Perfect."

I click my pen, and we get started.

CHAPTER THIRTEEN

Watching Maeve grade these midterms, it's clear how considerate she is, how much she cares about her students. It's rare for me to bump up against people who feel this much compassion for other humans. I follow her lead, and the marking goes remarkably quickly.

"So for *Rocketman*," I say as I pull up YouTube, "we're dealing with a very deliberate mix of diegetic and non-diegetic music, all of it attached to emotional moments rather than simply playing Elton John's songs in chronological order. The film relies on fantasy and a campy, heightened world to represent Elton's tumultuous emotions. To illustrate the point, I'll rely mostly on set pieces. We'll discuss the primary emotion being expressed in the scene and where the scene sits on a realism/fabulist scale."

Maeve nods as she watches my mouse move across the screen. She's on the couch with me, and the laptop sits on both our legs. Her thigh is pressed against mine, and I'm doing everything I can to ignore the heat that stretches from my kneecap to my stomach. "So what clips do you plan to use?"

"Hmm," I say. I click on *"Honky Cat."* "So here we have non-diegetic music, which uses a lack of cuts and long pans to represent time melting into itself. It's like being in love, which Elton is in this scene. Even within the movie's universe, movements, costumes, and facial expressions are more animated in this scene, especially Egerton's expressions, and especially compared to Madden's. You can see some darker themes haunt the whimsical scene—Madden eyeing the waiter is the biggest example."

Maeve leans in, closer to me. "And the visuals in the background too, right? It's never explicit, but you see it when Bernie breaks up with Heather."

I smile. "Exactly!"

"You *really* know your technical filmmaking. It's so impressive."

I flush. "Just a bit from the directing."

"I still need to see the TV episodes you directed. I bet they're great." Maeve takes her fingertip to the trackpad and clicks on *"Rocketman."* "This song employed a lot of heightened reality, didn't it?"

"Uh, yeah, it talks about your deepest pain coming to you in your darkest hours . . ."

I take a deep breath, hoping to steady the chills running through my body.

"But it's one of the few songs that pauses to return to reality," Maeve says, pausing the clip. "We exit his head to see how the real people around him are actually reacting to the suicide attempt."

I smile briefly, despite myself. "Yeah, it's a heavy scene. I know when I—"

Maeve sets the laptop aside, turns to face me. Our thighs pull apart, but she's pressing her knees hard into mine. "When you . . . ?"

I take a deep breath. "I've—I've just felt that devastated when it comes to mental health and fame. Winston wasn't even the worst interview I've done. This one guy—"

"John Henry."

Jesus, she saw *that one*? It was from my really early, Oscar-buzz days. Before I was out, he was one of the most aggressive interviewers asking about my dating life and the mystery surrounding it. She seems to read my mind.

"Yeah, it was one of the ones I watched to try to figure out what your favorite food was." She pauses, chewing on her cheek. "It was painful."

I look back to the paused frame of *Rocketman*. "That scene has always spoken to me. Being trapped in a world of pain people refuse to see because your purpose has become making others happy. The anger that comes with that. The vicious desire for everyone to see what pain they've caused you."

She slips her hand in mine. The butterflies flap inside me.

"You don't have to talk about that scene if it hurts too much," she says. "But your analysis is wonderful."

I break out in a tiny smile. "It's okay. It's just my first time seeing it in a while. It hits differently."

She looks back to the laptop. "So what's your favorite song in the movie?"

I shrug. "I really like the mix on 'Crocodile Rock.'"

"'Crocodile Rock,'" she says, her mouth wrapping around every syllable. My throat tightens watching her.

She pulls up 'Crocodile Rock' and places the laptop on one side of her desk.

"Why'd you move the laptop?" I ask.

She smiles. "Let's just enjoy it for a moment." She puts the song on, a smile forming on her beautiful lips when the first line hits. "I love this song!"

She giggles as the next couple of lines play.

Then she starts singing. As the piano picks up, she sings along, that dopey grin still on her face. And her voice is beautiful. Beautiful and lively and—fuck—I could listen to it all night. She beckons me up off the couch with one tug. And before I know it, I'm joining her, our hands clasped as we move to the upbeat tempo. I know this song and these lyrics so well, but it feels like I'm hearing them for the first time. Our hands are growing slick, yet they anchor us together as our bodies move to the music.

I grin as I execute Elton's signature foot-on-the-piano move by slamming the toe of my shoe onto Maeve's (mercifully low) desk like a fucking showgirl. Maeve squeals, laughing as she says, "My *god*, you're flexible!"

Flexible, sure, but not coordinated. I lose my footing as I yank my shoe off her desk and drop back to the coach. But because we're still holding hands, Maeve goes down with me.

I'll admit that the initial impact of her full body weight knocks the wind out of me. It leaves my head a little fuzzy when we finally make eye contact.

We're close. We're so close, close enough that I can see her individual eyelashes and the lick of lipstick still stuck to her lips. She breathes on me, her chest and stomach rising and falling on mine. Heat. She's so warm. So warm and so close and on the screen "Crocodile Rock" is in the time-stopping sequence, the crescendo of "la, la-la-la-la." We look right at each other, already mixing breath.

So I kiss her.

I kiss her forcefully yet as tender as I can manage. She kisses me back so fast I'm practically woozy. She pushes her lips to mine, dropping her body weight onto me as if she forgot about everything but our mouths connecting. We hold our breath as we hold each other, starving the rest of our senses. I'm dizzy. Yes, kissing her is *dizzying*.

I pull away, and Maeve drops to her knees in front of me.

"Are you sure about this?" I ask.

"Yes," she replies before climbing into my lap, kicking off her shoes.

Her hands go straight for my jaw, dig into my hair. And god, she holds me tight. Maeve, who I thought was so delicate and gentle, is pressing her fingers into my bones, pulling my hair by the roots. I'm sighing into her mouth before I've even settled my hands on her lower back. My own grip on her grows as urgent as hers is on me when my fingers trail under her blazer and blouse to finally feel that hot, soft skin. Her quickening breath digs into my insides.

We kiss like we're trying to devour each other. The way you'd hold on to someone you were determined to keep. It's a hunger with a beating heart that says *I'm only this ravenous for you.* Then thoughts start to poke through the veil as oxygen reenters my brain. Maeve could be kissing any woman like this if she just missed a woman's touch. But she's kissing *me* like this. She's kissing me like she's waited half her life to have my lips on hers. And even though as I can't fully admit it to myself, I feel the same way.

My brain's swimming, but clarity shoots out like a rocket when she suddenly pulls away. "I want you on top," she says, her words ragged.

And who am I to deny her?

I hold on to her as I climb into her lap. Lower myself until our hips align. But as I make adjustments, Maeve grabs for my blouse, swiftly pulling the buttons apart. The moment her finger pads leave my goose bump–covered flesh, her mouth is on my breasts. Kissing, licking, pushing my bra aside.

"Is this illegal?" I ask, barely keeping a moan at bay. I can't believe Maeve Arko is touching me like this.

Her lips and teeth pull at my skin. "Two teachers kissing?"

I glance around the office for just a moment. "On school property."

Maeve snorts a laugh. "No, it's a private school."

She pulls her hips up, bucking against me. And *god,* just that one tease, that one promise of what we could do to destroy each other.

My own breath picks up with hers, that knot of pleasure clenched, growing bigger by the second. I mount her, pressing all my weight and contorting my body in such a way that the pressure hits hardest between our hips. And as I grind against her, I muffle the sweet taste of her moans with my mouth on hers. She tastes like salted caramel and chocolate still, and I'm starved for her. Nothing's ever tasted better. Nothing's built this fast before. My heartbeat is throbbing in my lips, my fingertips grab her ass to pull us closer together, my stomach jumps, and the desire between my legs deepens as we dig into each other.

Her hands slide against the GG buckle on my red belt, and I feel like I'm nineteen in a dorm room, hooking up with a girl for the first time, her hands running along my waistband. I grin through our kiss, pulling away. I know this game. I know what I am, how I look, what to do with the hunger in Maeve's eyes as she watches me place one set of fingers on the end of the belt and the other on the clasp.

Charlie and I did one late-night interview together very shortly after I came out, before things went sideways. We'd decided beforehand on a bit where Charlie, me, and the middle-aged host would show off our abs to tease out a few whoops and laughs from the studio audience. I looked great then, plus Charlie had to be subjected to the same amount of objectification, so I didn't care. But my stylist had put me in high-waisted pants, cinched by a Hermès belt. I knew exactly how to control showing a late-night audience only my abs, but it still involved unbuckling my belt and sliding the front of my pants down. Charlie, lovely and hyperaware of the fact that my part was extra sexual, made some joke about how everyone in the audience should know this is just what I looked like on the toilet. It'd gotten its belly laugh from the audience; I'd gotten to finish the bit without feeling uncomfortable.

But the thing is, here with Maeve, I know Charlie wasn't right.

Pulling off this belt *is* the fucking sexiest thing in the world. Maeve is drinking in my movement, the crooked smile on my face, the tendons in my hands as they flex. It's been so long since I've felt like this. Like I'm *exactly* where I'm supposed to be.

Maeve grabs the clasp and zipper on my pants. God, just the pressure of her touch has me nearly ready to burst—

And someone knocks at the door.

I barely manage not to fall back on my ass in the space between the couch and Maeve's desk. Still, I'm on my back trying to zip, clip, and resecure my belt. Maeve runs a hand through her clearly makeout-tousled hair, but otherwise looks much less worse for wear than I do.

"Ty?" Maeve says to the other side of the door.

"Uh, yeah. I was gonna pick up the midterms."

Maeve looks down at me. My pants are now secure, but my blouse is buttoned a few buttons too low and our shoes are scattered around the room. She motions to the door, as if asking me if she should let him in. I roll back to my knees and stand up. Maeve moves to the door, grabbing the midterms as she goes.

Ty looks perfectly innocent as he steps into the office. Some Elton John mix is now playing from the laptop. I'm curious to see how many songs played during that makeout. "Hey, Val."

"Hey." My voice is hoarse. I clear it back to its signature dumb Valley girl range. "How are you?"

Maeve shoots me a look, but Ty doesn't notice. "Good, how are you?"

I press my lips together, the light pink lipstick I had on for lecture totally gone. "Not bad."

"These are our samples," Maeve says, her voice back in perfect professor mode. In fact, if I didn't still have the taste of her skin and mouth in mine, I wouldn't know she was about to stick her hand down my pants less than a minute ago. "Let's all aim for a week from today to get these marked, but if you have to give them back in sections next week, that's fine too."

"Okay, cool," he says as he accepts the papers. "Have a safe drive home!"

Ty steps out of the office and leaves the door open. My muscles are taut, but that ajar door feels more symbolic than it should. Maeve and I hold eye contact for a long moment.

She sighs. "I . . . think we should be heading out too. Traffic's down."

I glance at the laptop clock. Yeah, it's almost seven.

I take a deep breath, hoping the aching feeling will fade fast. "Yeah. Of course, traffic."

The mood's killed. I can accept that much.

She grabs my shoulder as I try to walk out with my stuff. Leans in so her breath is back on my ear. "But worth the risk."

My heart's speeding again, and I choose action over thought. I turn to her, tug our lips together quickly before she pulls away.

We separate for real this time.

Not even my long car ride can unwind the knot of desire from inside me.

CHAPTER FOURTEEN

As I make my way through LA after leaving Maeve at USC, an old memory overwhelms me. Back when I was a teenager forced to work at the Huntington, there were these scholars in residence—researchers, college professors, combinations of the two. Being the antisocial shit that I was, I had insisted that I take a gig that involved as little human interaction as possible. I spent my first year working in the office—copying, filing, delivering mail, standard stuff. But there was this one woman who worked in the library. She was a tenure-track professor at USC, actually, and one of the first people who said I had a brain for history and the humanities.

She was also one of the first women I ever had feelings for. Feelings I'd hash out with Rosalie week after week, oscillating between *It's just admiration* and *She's like an aunt to me* to *She's so beautiful* and *I keep dreaming about having sex with her.* Our relationship ended the way I'm sure most volunteers end relationships with people at work—she wrote me a recommendation for Oxford, hugged me hard when I got in, and we added each other on the now "Val Beverly" friends-and-family-only Facebook account I have that I created when I graduated high school. She stayed through my high-school-friend purge and still comments on big life events—my first movie role, the Oscar, coming out—with reasonable support.

It's got me smiling now, the coincidence that my first crush was a USC professor and now I've finally locked lips with one. It's like I've always had a type I was meant to go back to. Sure, I had fleeting crushes on Oxford professors, and obviously I dated Emily. But I've been exclusively pursuing fellow actresses and people who work in Hollywood for *so damn long.* Luna was a major departure from the actresses I dated before her, but even she spoke my language.

At the same time, though, I don't think my feelings have to do with *what Maeve is.* It's just—fuck, it's Maeve. *Maeve Arko,* this hugely successful, ridiculously smart, incredibly kind human being who kissed me like *that.* Wanted me like *that.*

And it must be written all over my damn face because Charlie is grinning like a fool. Despite getting stuck in traffic, I'm still basically on time for our monthly hang with Mason at Nobu. The general dining area ambiance here is already amazing, with wine cellar lighting, but the three of us have been dropping money for their private room for a while now. Charlie's the first one here, hair a little tousled, the red light spilling behind him, and—when I get up close—I can see it matches red lines in his eyes from what I can only assume was a joint break outside.

"You're late," he says.

I grab a seat across from him, taking a gulp from the water glasses already on the table. "Mason isn't even here yet."

Charlie grins again. "Why *are* you late?"

God, I haven't felt this *good* in so long. I'm addicted after the first hit. "Maeve and I kissed."

"Holy shit!" He covers his nose and mouth with his hands. "Holy— How did you pull that one off?"

I explain the situation as briefly as I can, knowing I'll have to repeat the story for Mason when she comes, and for Luna, Romy, and Wyatt after that. Mason is just late, but the youngens all have late shifts.

He leans forward when I finish. "Well, *did* you fuck?"

I shake my head. "We got to unzipping, but Ty showed up."

We've had conversations like this before. Despite having absolutely zero frame of reference for the other's sexual experiences, we used to dish out dirty details. I forgot how much I loved sharing with Charlie.

"Are you gonna see her again?" he asks. He squeezes his eyes shut. "I mean, *obviously* you have to see her again for class. But, is this like a one-time thing, or should I expect more updates?"

Somehow, in the month of lusting after Maeve, the couple of weeks of liking her, all I've thought about is the *what if*. Now that the thing I thought could never happen has, I don't even know what comes next. Do I want to kiss her again? Of course. There's a hell of a lot more I want to do with her. But the reason I was so hesitant to pursue Maeve is still looming over us. We're *coworkers*. She's supporting my academic ambitions, but any recommendation from her would be discounted if we're romantically involved.

I sit up and adjust my belt, straighten out a loop that I missed when I sloppily put it back on. "I dunno, man. I have to think—"

Right on time, Mason launches her way through the door, sliding into a seat between Charlie and me. She's in shorts and a patterned shirt, one of her two outfits that isn't a suit. "Don't film in Agoura Hills, boys," she says. "I already ordered an extra soju to pour directly into my eyes to combat the bullshit of today."

"But you already ordered the bottle of Junmai Daiginjo—?" I say, glancing at the menu.

"Of course I did," Mason replies, just as Charlie throws an arm around me and says, "Guess who doesn't need to pour soju in their eyes?"

Mason looks up from her menu, a smile playing on her lips. "Oh, and why's that?"

"This one got some *action*—" Charlie says.

"We kissed," I say quickly.

"With her co-teacher!"

Mason takes about a second to process. "The hot one?" She breaks into a joyous bark of laugher. "Why are you *so* bad at professional boundaries?"

I open my mouth to protest, but considering we now have Maeve, Luna, and Phoebe . . . "We don't have to talk about it. I still need her help at work, so it won't happen again."

Mason picks up a menu and flips through it. "Well, maybe you two can do an end-of-the-year, end-of-collab dinner and start dating after that."

I cringe; right, Mason doesn't know about my plan to leave Hollywood. I steal a glance at Charlie, who's pleasantly high and not picking up on my discomfort. I start looking at the menu. "Luna said she'd drop by sometime around nine, so we should order without her."

We'll do as we usually do and order a $250 bottle of sake we say is our monthly treat. I'm reminded yet again that as much as I want to be perceived as normal, I'm nowhere close.

I wonder if Maeve's thinking that at home right now, the taste of my lips still on hers.

"Oh!" Mason says, interrupting my daydream. "For you." She drops a graphic novel marked *Advanced Reader Copy* over my menu—*Goodbye, Richard! Vol. 3*.

My stomach flips.

"It's really fucking good. You never know if a writer will be able to sustain the plotline, but it would make a killer movie, and the studio's on deck for volume four too. With the buzz *GR2* is getting, I don't think it'll be a hard sell to the studio." She smiles. "And Aurora and Lacey are, like, *fucking* in this one. They can't write it out. Oh, and our second AC dropped out for *GR2*. I was gonna ask Luna since it films over the summer."

Right.

Sourness rises in my throat as I look through the panels. I haven't really thought about what my plan to leave Hollywood would look like logistically. Not taking on random people's projects is one thing, but *Goodbye, Richard!* is Mason's baby. And it looks like this baby's going to grow up over the course of one or two more movies. Maybe even more beyond that. Can I quit a franchise I'm starring in? We haven't contracted beyond *GR2*, but the idea of not signing on to the next one makes my skin crawl. And now Mason's talking about involving Luna? Isn't it bad enough that I'm failing Luna with *Oakley*? I can't let her down with this too. Plus, these films feature an on-screen sapphic couple. To have representation like that in a major franchise is a dream. A dream I never considered I'd have to miss out on.

Which means I've very grateful when a waiter brings in the sake. I take my first gulp a little too fast as I thank Mason for the copy.

"Charlie," Mason says, "go ask your reps about cons, okay? It's the quickest way to make a few bucks. Actors swear by it."

"What would I be doing?" Charlie asks. "A sad-person panel?"

"No, a righteous anger, fanbase-will-sustain-your-residuals panel," Mason replies. "Plus, you get press."

Charlie takes a long slug of sake. "I'd rather just look forward."

Mason shakes her head. "Okay, tiger. I'm just saying we can't all be relying on *Oakley*." She turns to me. "And you. You were nice to Leonard Ballard at HBO, right?"

I nod.

I tend to be nice to every producer I meet. "Yeah, Charlie says the detective show script he sent me is really good."

"He is a rare gem. He uplifts underrepresented voices." She swirls her drink. "And he's ours. He's on board to back *GR3* and he said he'd let me do what I need to do with it. So I'm not saying you *have* to take that show, but it would *really* help us if Leonard had multiple projects invested with you."

I think about it. It's a limited series, which would mean only one new shooting commitment. "Uh, yeah, I'll give it a read this weekend and talk to Trish."

When I look over at Charlie, he's doesn't exactly look happy. In fact, he's trying to hide a lot of his face in a menu. "Wait a minute . . . does the script suck?"

"No, it's great," Charlie says. "It just . . . films in France early next year."

France.

I take a deep breath as inconspicuously as I can. I know Leonard won't take it personally. Actresses have reasons they can't join projects all the time. But I— With Mason's relationship with him on the line, I don't know if I can take the gamble. Or . . . if I can take the gamble without strategizing with Trish first. Trish, who's been gunning for me to get at least one Emmy nomination ever since I started with her. Who respects my nudity wishes and gave me opportunities outside the standard Hollywood fare . . . like working with Maeve in the first place. Who's been so patient with everything going on with USC. There's no way Trish and my team will just accept that I want to turn down this major TV role because I don't want to be away from a woman I kissed once. Not with my blockbuster franchise on the line.

Yet I can't imagine a world where I kiss Maeve and then have to tell her I'll be in France for five months after our semester ends. It was just a kiss, but the spark in me is unlike anything I've ever felt before. Plus, the HBO show is false hope. There's a tiny buzz inside me eager to read the script now, but I push it down. Even if it's *great*, it doesn't mean my career is suddenly going to get better, that people will treat me differently. Shows, especially great sapphic shows, get canceled alarmingly fast. If I took it, I'd be resigning myself to going on another trip around the merry-go-round not even three months after I vowed to get off for good.

"Well, shit, have fun," Mason says.

There has to be a way to get out of this.

Luna shows up at Nobu at 9:00 p.m., just when she said she would, arriving in her cute little crew-regulated cameraperson outfit, her makeup smudged from what I assume is her eye-rubbing tick. I know she sent me a picture of her hair when she cut it, but it's my first time seeing the bisexual bob she got a few months ago in person. Despite how tired she looks, her happiness is palpable. It's great to see her.

"So how's life behind the camera?" Charlie asks as he sips his wine.

For a moment, Luna just stares at him. I catch her attention, enough to get her to shake her head and say, "We've met in person before, right?"

Now Charlie looks to me. I shrug.

"I think we must've." He holds out his hand. "If not, Charlie. Thanks for helping me look beautiful and tragic on *Oakley*."

She blushes. "Luna." More staring. "I still can't believe you were Val's friend and it never came up when *Oakley* was filming," Luna replies. "Romy has been obsessed with *Star Trek* for, like, years."

Charlie gives a polite smile. "Where is she?"

Luna's eyes brighten. "They—Romy's using she/they now—are actually in San Fran preparing to open her new play. It's a two-city tour, which is so amazing. I'm so proud of them." She shrugs. "And Wyatt's on a date."

Mason snorts. "Like the best way to date isn't to bring your date to a free dinner at Nobu with a bunch of celebrities."

"Maybe you'll meet some other time. I think one of his clients got a role in the thriller you're doing right now," Luna continues. "Some guy named Chance or something."

"Oh, the really, really tall guy," Mason says. "Yeah, great asset, that one."

I glance at my phone. The restaurant closes in an hour, Charlie's handing Luna a dessert menu, and I still haven't figured out what to do about the HBO show.

I need to get Mason out of here.

"Hey, Charlie, do you still have that joint?" I ask him quietly.

"Uh, yeah," he says, rummaging through his pockets. I meet his eyes and motion to Mason, and he nods. "Mase, wanna take a hit with me?"

"I drove," she replies.

"Yeah. Just . . . come with me."

Mason looks between me and Luna, probably doing a lot of confusing math about Luna's relationship status and the fact that I've been saying Luna and I weren't a good match for a year now. But she stands up to leave before saying, "Order me a carrot cake."

Once Charlie and Mason are gone, Luna looks to me with fear. "Is everything okay?"

"Did your old manager boss ever fire a client?" I ask.

Luna takes a sip of sake. "I don't think so. She certainly bad-mouthed clients every day. And she thought a lot of them made really stupid decisions." She grimaces. "Did you do something to Trish?"

"I . . ." I look away. "Need to decline a really good role to try to pursue this girl."

Luna's eyes light up like a freakin' Christmas tree. "Oh my god, who is she? Is she a costar?"

Even though I managed to adjust to Luna being with Romy pretty quickly after our breakup, she's been less inclined to bring up my dating life. A part of me thinks she doesn't actually want to know. Or, well, *didn't* want to know. She seems genuinely enthusiastic about this now.

"No, she's uh"—fuck, I just remembered Luna *went* to USC—"an SCA professor."

Luna gasps. "*Who?* I didn't even know SCA *had* queer professors!"

"Maeve Arko. She works in cinema and media studies."

Luna's eyes light up in recognition, and I'm almost embarrassed. Up until now, I've been convinced that I discovered Maeve. "Yeah, she taught New Queer Cinema our senior year! I didn't know she was gay. Romy was dying to get into that class but never had the chance. That's . . . a small world." She frowns. "Isn't it too early in your relationship for you to just decline a role like that?"

My sweet still-baby bisexual.

Of course, Maeve could not like me like I like her. She might not even want to do anything more than make out again. But if I don't risk it all for her, then I might as well not risk it for anyone else ever again. How can I explain that without sounding like I'm counting my chickens before they hatch? How can I explain that I've never met anyone as intelligent and compassionate, that her opinions on even the most mundane topics enthrall me, that she's noticed my pain in a way no one else ever has, that I can't stop thinking of having her under me?

"What's the best way to soften the blow, from a manager's perspective?"

"Does Trish believe in love?" Luna asks. "I mean, that's a legit excuse. You deserve to find happiness in your life . . ."

"I can't risk it. Too personal," I say. "These are still business relationships. Was there *ever* a time that Alice wasn't pissed when a client of hers declined a really good opportunity?"

"Honestly"—Luna leans back in her chair—"I think you just have to bargain with her. All she wants to do is keep your career alive. You're both on the same side, you just have different perspectives."

Right.

CHAPTER FIFTEEN

There's no way this is going to go well, but here I am, running my hand along the same red Gucci belt I nearly fucked Maeve in, as if this thing is good luck. I'm not sure what I'm doing. I didn't have to dress up for this meeting. But I'm here, sitting in the lobby of Trish's company in my *reading glasses,* as if that's not weird. Like Trish even cares whether I look professional. Maybe I should have slept last night. Maybe not buying a mediocre latte at the café here (the coffee is the one thing I miss about Slater Management and Steven) right after checking in would've been smart too.

I flip through the HBO script one last time. Charlie was right. It's exceptionally well written. I think I've read it five times in the last twenty-four hours, and four of those times were during the hours I should've been sleeping. It would truly be an incredible project to work on. I could even imagine it in that sleep-deprived haze—how it'd feel to learn the lines and bring that character to life, working with the intimacy coordinator to make the queer sex scenes realistic and affirming, drinking wine in the French Riviera on off days. If Maeve wasn't in the picture, I would've been tempted.

But Maeve is here. Maeve, who's become more of a sure thing in a few weeks than Hollywood has in over a year. I'm not gambling on that fantasy. So, here we go. With Luna's advice hanging over me, I'm starting to get a migraine.

Clarissa steps in from down the hall, smiling at me shyly as she approaches. "Hi, Valeria."

I get up and hug her. Clarissa is the second assistant Trish has had since she signed me, and so far so good. She's a bit less of a jokester than her predecessor, Hope, but I always respect someone who answers emails promptly and uses emojis. She was brand-new during the August emails debacle, and I honestly wish I could do more to show her I'm not usually that much of an ass. She leads me back down the hall, asking how my day is, complimenting my blouse, and then giving me a couple seconds of respectful silence. My kind of human.

Trish is at her desk when I enter. "I didn't know you wore glasses."

I push the glasses up onto the bridge of my nose and take a seat. Clarissa closes the door behind us. "Yeah, forgot my contacts."

Trish holds my gaze a moment longer than she needs to. "Well, I'll remember to put you forward for hot-librarian roles."

My fingertips practically go numb clenching my hands as I wait for the other shoe to drop, for her to realize exactly what I'm up to and give me a professional lashing.

I think for a moment about bullshitting Trish, buttering her up with small talk, but stop myself. I'm too smart for that and so is Trish. "So about the HBO pilot . . ."

Trish takes a deep breath. "I don't like the sound of that."

This is my one chance. If I don't explain myself, I'll never get Trish's blessing. I can't risk burning the bridge with Trish, even if I don't plan to come back.

So this better work. "I . . ." I swallow. "You said that if I wanted to transition into academia, I could. Maeve and I have been connecting more, and even she thinks I'd make a great professor. Since *Oakley* didn't get into Sundance, I want to keep going down this new path. I'll finish the *Goodbye, Richard!* movies and see out all my current obligations, but I don't want to do anything new."

And I cannot say just how painful it is to have Trish *stare* at me like I've just told her I believe the earth is flat *and* I'm voting Republican in the next election. Every ounce of confidence I had has completely slipped away. And Trish can tell. Her arms are crossed over her chest.

"Val, I don't think we heard the same things last we talked about your career. This HBO show isn't just a quality-acting role. Did they not tell you? You'd be directing several episodes. It's Emmy bait, a real next step in your directing career. It's about a fully formed character whose sexuality is second to her work. Exactly what you said you wanted when you first signed with me. And you want to turn that down?"

I pause, letting that sink in. *Emmy bait. Directing.* When I was having my breakdown, this was the kind of gig I thought I would never be able to get. That I'd need *Oakley* to win awards at festivals to get. It's a dream opportunity.

Possibly, anyway. What happens if I take this role? I leave Charlie to watch over my house, drown in French women for the next couple of months? Come back, do press, maybe get nominated for an Emmy, do *more* press, get more questions about being gay? Maeve will fade away. She has just as many obligations as I do, and long distance never works.

"Yes," I say. "I want to turn it down. I just need a way to make sure Leonard Ballard isn't upset. I don't want him to drop the funding for the new *Goodbye, Richard!*"

Trish shifts in her seat. "You need a good reason. Clearly it's not that you're taking on some other, better offer." She looks up at me, her gaze burning. "Why *are* you doing this?"

A tingling sensation creeps up my neck. "Academia is where I want to be now."

"Even when you were crying to me after that interview, it was about directing. You would never—" And then she realizes. "Is this about a girl?"

"Trish, I—I'm not trying to be ungrateful about this directing gig. I just can't leave town right now. I'll get back on track as soon as I have more time to try to—"

"Who is she?" Trish asks, cutting right through my impassioned plea.

God, I can't even lie. Trish *knows* Maeve and would know the moment things became serious. This was such a terrible idea. I look at the door, wondering if I could run to the bathroom and pretend I was having an IBS episode in order to leave the building.

"Maeve Arko."

Trish's earlier stare was nothing compared to the look she's giving me now.

"*Who?*"

I hunch into myself like a fucking child. "Maeve. We've really connected over the past couple of weeks. It turns out she's not an asshole. She's—" I take a deep breath, forcing myself to look Trish in the eye. If Maeve is worth fighting for, it's time to start fighting. "Things feel different with her. This gig will only last a semester, and my best chance to really explore this is here. I have to stick around LA for a little while longer. I know it's stupid, but—"

Trish replies before I can even finish my speech.

"You're taking her to the Oscars."

It hits me in stages. One, Trish is okay with this. I get to stay with Maeve with Trish's approval.

But then I get it.

What Trish is saying implies that Maeve is my *girlfriend*. And she definitely is not. My heartbeat picks up again.

"Trish, we're coworkers. I can't ask that of her now!"

"Look, you asked me how you'd turn down this role without angering Ballard. This is how. Could you imagine Ballard saying he's mad at this lesbian star for finding the love of her life and pursuing her own happiness over a Hollywood gig? You get the public on your side, and the execs can't openly argue with you. Plus, you get some articles written about you, making his other baby, *Goodbye, Richard!* the sequel, a gold mine."

"And the professionalism issue?"

"It's not illegal for professors to date each other. It might even be good publicity for her, help her make her own moves."

This is not good.

"What if she doesn't even want to date me?"

Trish smirks. "I don't think that will be a problem."

Why am I freaking out? This is what I wanted. I get to see Maeve tomorrow and I'm not going to be leaving her in a matter of months. I have a chance to see where this goes. If I do have to get her on board with the Oscars, it's in five months. That's five months I get to date her, pull out all the stops and get her to fall for me the way I feel I could fall for her. This is a win. I have to get it together.

"Fine, deal," I say, although the thought of seeing Maeve tomorrow now fills me with more terror than joy.

I know I taught today. I know I lectured on *Mamma Mia!* and the jukebox musical. I know Maeve gave particularly strong background information on seventeenth- and eighteenth-century vaudeville. It is moderately embarrassing how hard I have to work to hide my swoon when she goes into her professor zone.

I love women who can deconstruct big, pretentious words and make them accessible. I used to think I just liked intelligent women whose speech was peppered with SAT words. But being with Emily was like being in a continuous game I didn't sign up for, dodging snickers and snarky comments when I didn't understand academic language and procedures the way she did. It was a lot of *Sorry, I should know that.* But Maeve doesn't hoard language and knowledge. She's an incredible teacher. It gets me breathless.

That feeling gets worse when Maeve and I make eye contact after class. It's like I'm having a sapphic awakening all over again. And this time, she's not running away from me. I have to wonder whether she did any processing after what happened in her office. I'd ask, but part of me is satisfied already. Maeve's still here, still looking at me like that.

She walks toward me, and it feels like we're tied together by an invisible rope that tightens with every step she takes. This wanting, Jesus.

"Hey, can I talk to you about something?" Maeve asks.

Her words are like a kick in the gut. I'm suddenly terrified. Maybe she isn't dragging me back to her office to make out.

"Val, stay with me. It's just about work," Maeve says, catching the look in my eye. "Can we walk and talk? I need to work off some of the adrenaline from class today."

I take a deep breath as inconspicuously as I can. Okay, we're still in the neutral zone. "ABBA can really get a gal going, I know."

Maeve shakes her head, a tiny smile on her face. "Do you ever get nervous about getting up in front of people?"

Oh, the answer to that. "Not really."

When we walk out of class this time, there's a different feeling in the air. Less the searing electricity that forces us to glue our hands to our sides to avoid touching each other in public. But something's still there. An ease, maybe? Like Maeve doesn't care if we bump hands or shoulders as we weave through the crowds of students and make our way to the faculty parking lot.

"So, I doubt you've been keeping up with faculty gossip," Maeve begins, "but one of the other adjuncts dropped their course after getting a writers' room gig."

That is so intensely a USC problem. "Tragedy."

Maeve snorts with laugher. "Truly. But that means there's an open slot for a new class. The dean is scrambling to fill it, and it seemed like the perfect opportunity for me to try to pitch something. They've never even come close to hearing me out before, and this feels like the one time I have some leverage, you know?"

"Of course. You definitely should."

I suddenly realize why she's telling *me* this. And I swear to god Maeve is flustered, rubbing the back of her neck. "And I was hoping if you aren't already booked with projects, maybe *you'd* want to teach another course with me. Me filling in on the adjunct's course is just a temporary solution. But come May, if he doesn't get kicked out of his writers' room, an application will open for his job. You'd have a real chance, especially if you have two successful courses under your belt . . ."

The idea hits me with a jolt to the heart. I'd intended to keep seeing Maeve after the semester ended, but if we were still teaching together—god. Excitement shoots up my spine. More evenings tucked away in her office grading papers, the opportunity to start doing viewings with her, just the two of us, to discuss our syllabus movies, being able to see her in her professor attire for an additional eight hours a week? I never imagined a world where I'd get to keep teaching *now*; it feels like an invitation to step into a dream future early.

"I'd love to," I say. "When are you pitching this?"

She sighs. "Tomorrow."

I push my hair out of my face, smirking. "Well, then, bud, I guess we gotta get planning."

CHAPTER SIXTEEN

With less than twenty-four hours before we need to present our pitch to the dean, Maeve offered up her place for planning so we wouldn't disturb Charlie. I'm heading there now. This is the kind of high-pressure, *we gotta make some magic* environment I actually thrive in creatively, but I'm still trying to steady my racing heart as I stare down a wrought iron gate armed with nothing but a code Maeve texted me along with her address: 1341½.

The main house on the lot is nice—old Spanish style with a burnt-redbrick roof, a pouf of drought-resistant foliage outside, well-maintained sidewalks typical of a suburban offshoot in Mid-Wilshire. Overpriced, a little midcentury historical in the architecture, and very, very hip. The kind of place a creative would move to upon receiving their first big check, before being away from people and having space mattered. A long driveway leads to the back of the lot, and even though I figure that's what the ½ means, I fidget outside the main house.

Maeve leads me down the driveway. "Thanks for doing this."

The back house is in the same style as the front and is maybe showing a little less wear from the streets. I'll admit, it's a lot quieter back here, with some more foliage and a little patio set up in the backyard. The converted garage that Maeve calls home may even have been a two-car once judging by the size.

She puts her keys in the lock, but it takes some jiggling to get them to click and the door to open.

"Sorry if it's a mess," she says. "I tried to spruce it up, but my landlord gave me a fixer-upper for the great location."

The back house is pretty cute inside for what is indeed clearly a "fixer-upper." The whole place feels worn—old appliances are scrunched into the kitchen competing over minimal counter space, there's wall-to-wall faded maroon carpet everywhere, and the windows all have old-school white blinds. But there are lovely touches everywhere: a vintage cookie jar in the shape of a strawberry on the kitchen counter, monstera plants perking up the corners of rooms, vintage movie posters framed on the wall. Two doors lead off the main kitchen/living room, which is more than some folks can say they've got in LA.

"It's sweet," I say. There's even a swath of airy floral fabric and a sewing machine on the coffee table. "Is this yours?"

Maeve sighs. "It was, but I fucked up. Never try to make curtains when you can't sew."

I look over the raw materials. I used to unwind after hard shifts at the dental office by sewing with my maternal grandma. But I doubt Maeve wants advice on curtain-making now. "Who's your landlord, by the way? Does he live in the main house, or is he some ghoul?"

"He lives here with his wife," she says. "They're an artist couple who posted on Craigslist."

And I don't *want to*, but the words *Oh god* escape my lips. I'm an asshole.

But Maeve just laughs. "I reaped what I sowed. I make decent money, but I wanted something close to work that was cheap enough that I'd have extra to spend. They're my best bet for now."

I look her up and down. "I must use my money differently than you do."

We make eye contact, and she laughs. "No, I don't mean designer clothing."

I put my hands up, palms forward. "Some professors do."

"The ones who are paid half a million dollars for no explicit reason, maybe." She glances at a shelf nearby, covered in neatly arranged vinyls, CDs, VHSes. "Some collecting, weekend vacations around California, camping supplies, ski season passes, that kind of thing."

All great activities, but I can't help but wonder how they connect with her saying she doesn't make friends easily. Maybe she's a really good solo traveler, but that idea pangs in my chest for some reason. It's too early to offer it yet, but maybe I can treat her to a bougie ski trip someday. "Sounds fun."

"Do you want something to drink?" she asks.

I hold up the water bottle I bring everywhere I go. "I'm good."

"Let me grab my laptop. Hold on."

With that, she makes an unceremonious exit through one of the two doors. Leaving me to stew in the apartment she lives in. Where she's brought her one date a year back to, the place she came home to after watching *Needlepoint*. Maeve has been acting more flirtatious, but we haven't talked about what happened in her office. If we're going to co-teach again, *would* it be bad form if everyone knew we were together? We only have a month or so with this batch of students and a vast majority of them won't take our course in the spring. Maybe we don't have to be explicit about it. Let rumors fly, or just not tell USC people?

"Okay, so," Maeve says when she returns, dropping onto the couch next to me. "Here's the thing." She sighs. "I still get stage fright. I'm fine when I teach, but it's still there when I have to advocate for myself with anyone. When it comes to"—she shrugs, almost sarcastically—"all bosses ever, I clam up. I know what to say, but I've been up half the night trying to nail the delivery." She rubs her arm. "And I was hoping since you have so much experience with public speaking that you'd be able to help . . ."

I've collaborated with Maeve, I've faced her sharp tongue when I took her on, and I've kissed the fuck out of her. But Maeve wants my *help*? My heart flutters. Maeve could still reject me when she gets to know me better. At least I can cushion the blow by knowing I've shown her some kindness.

"Yeah, I can help." I make eye contact with her.

She's leaning forward—just a tad.

"Are there particular aspects of public speaking that are the hardest for you? Like, is starting out terrible but then you get into a flow? Or do you struggle when you start to get audience feedback?"

Maeve plays with a little gold bracelet hanging off her right wrist. "Both. I always have a hard time starting, and flow is more complicated. Sometimes it happens, sometimes it doesn't. Sometimes I can handle a boss's blank expression, but sometimes I can't."

"And this is just an informal pitch with the dean, right?"

"Yeah. No visual aids."

I exhale, looking around her apartment as if there's a clue hidden somewhere. "We want to showcase your poise and professionalism, right?"

She nods.

"So let me help you with the lead-in and then I'll be there to back you up if you don't get into the flow state. But it's such a short pitch; I'm sure you'll be great."

I reach over, taking Maeve's hand to stop her picking at her bracelet. My lips turn up as I see her twitch in surprise.

"Yeah," she says as I drop her hand back into her lap. "That's—I struggle with intros. I never know how much context to give before jumping into the meat of a pitch. I always end up rambling and forgetting my transitions."

It's a feeling I know all too well. Something that I conquered years ago. I lean in to her. We're not quite within kissing distance, but we're close enough that the thought enters my mind. "All you have to say is: 'I know the department is looking for a replacement course, and I asked Valeria if she'd be willing to teach with me again. She said yes, and I think it'd be a great addition to the spring roster.'"

Maeve takes a deep breath, her chest rising and falling. She's undone a button since I saw her in class, giving me quite the view of her pearly skin. "Should I say my name?"

I chuckle. "Maeve, they know you. I never intro with execs I've seen more than once. Walk through the world expecting people to remember you."

We make eye contact, and looking into her darkened eyes, listening to the sound of her slow breath, I consider bridging the gap, but instead I pull away.

There'll be another moment.

It's a strangely-cold-for-LA October day when Maeve and I walk into Dean Ashlee Gomez's spacious, classical office. Someone's blessing me today, because I *actually* recognize her from a photo I saw when I was researching USC's faculty a couple of weeks ago, so it feels less like I'm meeting with a complete stranger. I pull my sleeve, trying to resist complimenting Maeve on her periwinkle circular yoke sweater. I should've done it when I first saw her five minutes ago. Now she's shaking, and she has her hands stuffed into her pants pockets.

"Hi, Ashlee," she says. "Have you met Valeria yet?"

Ashlee holds out her hand toward me. "I talked only to your manager; it's so wonderful to formally meet you."

I flash my best professional smile. "Likewise."

After facing off with Trish, impressing Ashlee feels like a piece of cake.

Assuming Maeve gets into a flow. She's still got her hands deep in her pockets, and her smile is stiff. It looks like it's about to switch to a worried frown.

Once we take our seats, I lean in to Maeve. "I'm right here." I know I can't sneak a hand squeeze this close to the dean, but hopefully Maeve can psychically feel it.

Ashlee takes her seat, and her gaze falls on Maeve. She sets her clasped hands onto the thick wood of her desk.

"What's up, ladies?" she asks.

I look to Maeve and take a deep breath. She copies me and looks to Ashlee. "I know the department is searching for a new course now that Geoff is going to leave, and I"—she glances at me, and I notice that she still looks terrified—"asked Valeria if she'd be willing to teach with me again." Back to Ashlee.

Good, good.

"She said yes, and I think it'd be a great addition to the spring roster."

Ashlee, all big smiles before Maeve started talking, merely nods now. My chest tightens, and I hope Maeve doesn't notice as she moves into the rest of her speech.

"The numbers don't lie," Maeve says. "The course we're teaching together had a long wait list at registration, including students outside the department. It's already getting positive reviews from early course evals. Students who aren't in the class come to my office hours asking if they can sit in. An additional opportunity to take a class like this would be a fantastic surprise for the students who're already interested. And student excitement is what we're here for, right? More happy undergrads, more prospective students, more acclaim." She glances at me, and thank God above, her pupils have returned to a normal size. "Valeria and I already have ideas for mixing up the material so there could be repeat students—"

"Geoff's class was a professional course, though," Ashlee says.

Even I wince as Maeve stops short.

"And while your course is popular and fantastically run, it wouldn't incorporate the professional element students who now can't take Geoff's course are looking for."

If there's one thing our course doesn't do, it's give practical information for filmmakers. My veins have gone ice-cold, and I'm thrown right back into audition rooms with casting directors asking for an entirely different direction than I had prepared for. Taking a horror movie role and asking for a romantic lead.

And speaking of horror, Maeve is practically catatonic. The only part of her that's moving is her leg, which is bobbing like she's a kid high on sugar. It's noticeable. The flow is gone.

So I do what I promised I'd do.

"That should be easy," I say, my voice a little higher than normal, even, *airy*. Like this is *no big deal,* even as my heart hammers. "Movie musicals continue to be churned out and wait in development hell all the time. I'm currently testing for a musical adaptation. We could revise the syllabus to include more hands-on discussion of the industry. I also know a bunch of directors and producers who work in that space who can come do Q and A's. I'd be happy to share my resources for the same fee as last time." Which was pro bono.

Ashlee purses her lips.

"Okay," she says, and that one word launches my heart into space. "I like that." She straightens out, her hands dropping into her lap. "I really appreciate you jumping in to help out, Maeve. You're such a valuable member of the faculty."

For the first time since walking into the room, Maeve smiles. "Thank you."

"Of course. Send me the updated course description tonight, and I'll get you your schedule before the semester ends."

Like that, it's done. And god am I working off a high. Blood is pumping through my body, and my skin is so warm I could take off my sweater. I haven't felt this way since Mason and I exchanged that knowing glance after I auditioned for Aurora in *Goodbye, Richard!*

As we exit the building, I throw a smile at Maeve. "How're you feeling?"

The world goes fuzzy as I focus on her.

Maeve smirks. Maeve smirks and fucking *leans in,* gets so close her breath is in my ear. "Far too excited to celebrate in public. Your car here?"

Fuck. Every word zings into my brain like I'm a cartoon character. "Isn't that a little high school?"

"I can't wait."

It takes all my willpower not to grab Maeve's hand as we walk to the dank corner of the faculty parking lot where my Porsche sits.

"I can't thank you enough, by the way," Maeve says as I fumble for my car keys.

"Any time, colleague," I say, giving her a little salute.

She leans in, running a hand along the cherry red paint of my car. "You know what, despite how male midlife crisis your car is, I like it." She slides between me and the car door, inches from me. My heart lodges in my throat, and I can feel my heartbeat knocking off my teeth.

"I like you."

I've wanted to hear Maeve say these words for so long. It lights my body on fire. Sitting in that classroom, seeing her apartment, giving her tips about public speaking, I almost convinced myself that she was just another cool person in my life. But no. She isn't that, and she never was. She's heaven incarnate in a world where I'm not sure God exists.

I don't even care if she freaks out after I tell her about Trish's Oscars stipulation. I need her right now.

We drop into the back seat. Once those doors shut behind us, our hands are into each other's hair, digging into goose bumps–covered flesh. Breath hot, chests heaving, mouths on fire kissing. It's like my brain just deleted everything that happened in the last week and a half. We're back in her office, and separating was never an option. I feel myself kissing the lipstick off her. The sharp, floral scent of her perfume envelopes us. It's harder to breathe, but god, I don't want to breathe if it doesn't taste like her and make my head spin. It's tight in here, these Porsche seats aren't that comfortable, and parts of my body are starting to ache, but somehow even that feels good, feels right with Maeve in my arms.

But then she pulls us horizontal. Pulls us horizontal, her on top, her hand slipping right into the hot space between my pants and panties, rolling her thumb *exactly* the right way, and I'm moaning and I *need* this, but god I can't believe I'm saying this. If Maeve and I can be more than body-melting hot sex in the back of my car, I need to try. I can't fuck this up like I fucked up my chances with any of my costars, with Luna, with anyone who might have wanted me beyond my body. Even if I might strain a muscle bringing this to a halt.

"Maeve, stop," I say.

She pulls herself off me, rocketing back so we're both sitting up. I'm dizzy for a moment from the rush.

"Are you okay?" she asks. "I'm sorry, we hadn't . . . and I should've asked."

"No, no, I *want* to have sex with you, but not like—I mean it when I say I *like* you. I don't just want to have sex with you. I want— I want to take you on a date. Before we have sex. Maybe sex can be part of the date, but there's a date in there. And maybe instead of hooking up we go on dates that include sex."

Maeve eyes me for maybe three seconds, and that crushing fear of rejection is back.

"Okay," she finally says.

My heart sinks, despite her words. "Okay what?"

She smiles. "*Okay,* let's go on a date. Maybe even more than one date."

That whole thing about fireworks? I don't know exactly what happened when we kissed. But they're definitely going off now. I pull her mouth right back to mine, barely able to move my lips against hers I'm smiling so hard. And when I feel her smiling right back into the kiss—fuck. I'm so lost to her.

"I like spending time with you," I say.

"I like spending time with you too," she says. She looks up at me, biting back a grin. "Something feels right with you. Like I could never get enough of the way you think. And now we get to spend another semester together."

I nuzzle into her flower-scented neck, and I can feel that her heartbeat is still thumping from our kiss. "Concurrent with the dating?"

"For sure."

"But what about . . . the future. With me, here. Can we be public?"

I run my fingers up her neck. Her hairs stand on end.

"I think it depends. If we did go public—like, your public persona was seen dating me—I probably couldn't write a recommendation for you if you ever wanted one in the future."

I'm not ready to make a move like that.

"Let's stay quiet for now," I say. And I'll cross that bridge as we get closer to the Oscars.

She smiles. "Great."

"But we're still on for that date?" I ask, desperation dripping from my voice. I kiss her to make up for it.

She kisses my neck, tickling me. "Yes." Anxiety is still swirling inside me, but now it's mixed with elation, and the whole thing feels like the buzz you get from a good cheap cocktail. Maeve laughs, adding another spritz of sweet syrup to the mix.

"Teaching college film theory and dating. What are the next seven months going to be like?"

The next seven months.

But as the moments pass, as she lingers, kissing my skin, the dread quietly builds. More about my meeting with Trish floats to the surface.

I potentially have to get Maeve—grounded, not-impressed-by-Hollywood Maeve—to agree to go to the Oscars. If *Oakley in Flames* gets into Tribeca, South by Southwest, Cannes, or Berlin, I'll be at those festivals promoting it. When Maeve wants me to be teaching this class. How can I take this opportunity when I *know* what could come up?

Sundance, though. Thinking about it still stings. If my film can't get into Sundance, there's no way it'll get into Cannes or Berlin. Hell, I'm not even really sure it could get into slightly smaller festivals like

Tribeca or South by Southwest. It's most likely a lost cause. But this class with Maeve, that's real. That's possible.

This class is making Maeve so happy. There's no reason to bring up potential obstacles. Maeve and I are together, and the future is bright. This is my career, my life now. And I'm *happy* with it. I am.

Now I just have to keep it.

CHAPTER SEVENTEEN

Maeve and I select the first Monday in November to go on our date. It gave us two weeks' buffer from the meeting with Ashlee, fewer crowds than Veterans Day or Halloween weekend, and another buffer before Maeve has to fly back to Ohio for Thanksgiving. Enough of a gap for us to not feel desperate, but not so long that we'd end up compelled to rip each other's clothes off in the USC parking lot. Still, I feel like it's been too much time.

She asked me to pick the place, laughing a little when she said, "Make it weird." So, naturally, I spent all of my therapy session that morning agonizing over a location with Rosalie before texting Maeve *La Brea Tar Pits* maybe two hours prior to the date itself. Which, in the School of Dating Etiquette, is at a Little Dickish when it comes to lead time to getting ready. Not Full-Blown Dick like if I'd given her less than an hour, but the faux pas still makes my stomach ache as I drive to Mid-Wilshire.

To pick up Maeve. Like a proper date.

Thinking about it is not helping the stomach pain.

But at least I get an endorphin release when Maeve steps into my car. With the weather in the low sixties, she's got on a dusty-rose sweater, light jeans, and white slip-on sneakers. The sweater flows perfectly around the curve of her neck, and a delicate gold locket rests on her chest. I'm already itching to know what's inside, if anything. And given the way she smiles at me with her rose-painted lips, I'm not totally sure I'm not dreaming.

"Sorry about leaving you in suspense," I say as she clicks her seat belt in.

She chuckles. "You're driving. You didn't even have to tell me where we were going if you didn't want to." She stares at me; it feels like I'm a slide under a heated microscope. The corner of her mouth turns up. "I like your hoodie."

I steal a glance down, and the hotness instantly rises to my ears. I'm wearing a white pullover with a fucking *rainbow* on it. What had seemed like a fun pop of color in a casual outfit now seems cheesy. "Pretend I'm wearing something else, please."

Maeve laughs. "*No*, I love your gay hoodie for our first gay date. You're cute."

I'm sure I'm bright red by now, but the joy I feel hearing those simple two words, Jesus. I'm so far gone. We haven't even gotten to the tar pits yet and I may be in—

No. Fuck. I have to calm down.

Parking is actually bearable, probably due to the fact that we're going to a kid-friendly museum on a Monday night during the school year. But there's a crisp LA winter breeze in the air, which is the perfect excuse for me to throw my black leather jacket over the hoodie, and I realize I missed this. The tar pits, being on a date. All of it. I open the door for Maeve, which is easy enough, but as we step from the parking lot to the entrance to the tar pits, my fingers tingle. I'm not sure if holding her hand is the right thing to do. Both on a date-appropriateness level and just on a being-in-public-and-acting-gay level. I've never had any bad experiences with PDA, but it's always a concern in the back of my head.

"So, what made you pick this spot?" Maeve asks as we get in the one-person line for tickets. Ahead of us is a dude with a big beard, artsy camera, and a fedora. He's not exactly an odd specimen for LA, but I wonder what brought *him* to the tar pits on a Monday.

I tug on my jacket sleeve, covering the hoodie. "I always loved it here as a kid. Dinosaurs are great and everything, but Ice Age animals are underappreciated."

She smiles. "Can't argue with that." She stuffs the hand closest to me into her pants pocket. It makes my heart sink. "What's your favorite Ice Age animal, and were you obsessed with the movie *Ice Age*? Because if so, we have to stop dating."

Oh, I caught that jab. "Okay, first off, fuck you, *Ice Age* the original was *great,* and dire wolf."

Maeve's eyes widen. "Wait, shit, that's not something *Game of Thrones* made up?"

I make a mock surprised expression. "You don't know about the majestic and *very real* dire wolf, may it rest in peace?"

She laughs as the hipster guy takes his ticket from the attendant. "Well"—her hand launches out of her pocket and squeezes my shoulder—"you'll have to show me one."

I've been touched before. But I'm sure Maeve *thinks* I haven't when I stiffen abruptly like her touch is an electric current. I would've never clocked Maeve for an affectionate person. But here she is, in her casual wear, freely throwing me smiles and touching me lightly, and it's like the floodgates open. I want to grab her hand, I want to squeeze her in a hug, I want to take her lips in mine and know what that sweater feels like under my grip.

Hipster Guy catches my gaze as he passes. He stares a hair too long, the familiar look of someone having a celebrity recognition light bulb moment. My gut twists until he turns his head back toward the inside of the museum and raises his camera to photograph something that isn't me.

I grab Maeve's hand for *just* a second. A guiding touch. "Let's check out the tar pits themselves first."

Maeve follows along, watching the entrance to the museum as we walk. "Did you know that guy?" she asks as we approach the tar.

"No, he just recognized me," I reply.

"Right." She clears her throat. "I forget you're famous sometimes."

I wince. I think about what Trish said, what's expected of me. What may be expected of her. Maybe it's good practice for both of us. "That makes one of us."

My heart flutters as we approach the pits. This was more exciting as a kid. Right now, the tar pits are just, well, *tar pits*. Still, there's a shiny new railing around them, they sparkle in the sunlight, and it looks like the museum recently refurbished the illustrations of mammoths and other animals in distress dying in the tar. It's a little more morbid (and tar-smelling) than I was going for, but there's something charming about the setup nonetheless.

Maeve doesn't seem to mind either way. She leans on the railing and stares at the bubbling tar. "Does it ever get overwhelming? The way the success of your career is so linked to fame?"

I run a hand through my hair. It's really getting too long. I should cut it. I wonder if Maeve prefers it this length, though. "I think I used to care more. But as I move into doing more indie work, and build an audience there, I think it starts to matter less. And I'm not getting any younger, any shinier, or any newer. I try to think of it as a relief."

"You don't seem to enjoy it. Fame."

I don't know what's put this in Maeve's head, but I'd love it if the universe would stop prompting her to ask questions about fame, thank you.

"I mean, I don't think anyone but the clinical narcissists do."

Maeve smiles. "Aren't most actors raging narcissists, though?"

I wonder if Maeve thought I was one.

I chuckle. "Half are. The other half are dysfunctionally anxious."

Somehow, it was the right thing to say. The move is subtle, soft. She slides her hand over to mine on the railing. Puts a couple of fingers over my knuckles. I intertwine our fingers. A conversation that would otherwise send my heart racing is actually slowing it down.

"Do you ever think about leaving it? Forever?"

The opportunity is suspended in the air: I could tell her the truth. That I've been really, actively trying to leave Hollywood behind as I pursue this teaching thing. I haven't overtly said the leaving Hollywood part, and I'm sure she thinks I'd never give up the life I have.

But the words that come out of my mouth are "I don't know."

When I do know. Right? I just turned down a career-changing acting-and-directing role because teaching—and Maeve—are *all* I've been thinking about for months. It's like a part of me still wants to hide the truth away, to freeze time and pretend this is just a possibility me, Charlie, Trish, and Luna are talking about hypothetically.

"Well, for what it's worth, I think you're a really good teacher. You inspire the kids."

"*You* inspire them. I put on a show."

"You do so much more than putting on a show, and I'll never forgive myself for not pointing that out to you in the second class."

I bump my hip against hers. "Hey, I thought you were an asshole too."

She blushes. "I *was* an asshole, though!"

"Look, I walked in in designer heels, I get it. Plus I used to comfort myself by thinking you were the type of pretentious dickwad who, like, watches 1800s film for fun and lights scented candles when they masturbate. I was just as unbearable as you."

As Maeve's mouth forms a perfect O, I kind of more or less *really regret* letting that one slip.

"Oh my god, my favorite movie is the Keira Knightley *Pride and Prejudice*," she says.

I smile. "So that's a yes on the candles . . . ?"

She just gets redder. "You're horrible."

"And how *dare* your favorite movie not be *Portrait of a Lady on Fire*! I had you *pegged*."

Maeve shakes her head, a huge smile on her face. A smile that shows teeth, giving me a peek at a canine that's a little too sharp. "My favorite sapphic movie is *Carol*, although *Portrait of a Lady on Fire*'s close. You?"

"That sequel to *The Shining*, but only because of that erotic scene where Ewan McGregor gets chased by the hot demon lady with an ax."

She laughs. "Okay, but for real."

"*Y Tu Mamá También*, the ultimate movie in favor of lesbianism—"

Maeve just keeps laughing. "Val, *please*."

"Okay." I pause for dramatic effect. Maeve wipes tears out of her eyes.

"*Disobedience*, because I can turn on that spit-in-mouth scene and give myself full body shudders on command."

She grabs my shoulders, laughing into my chest. Laughing so hard she's starting to wheeze. "*Stop*."

With the way my heart's hammering, no way. "It's *Thelma and Louise*. You can stop choking now."

Maeve finally pulls away from me. She's still got this utterly beautiful smile on her face. The kind of smile that just radiates pure, unfiltered joy. Like I can *feel* that I'm making a positive impact on this person's life. My chest swells, and maybe it's time to move inside, because the pull to her is getting to be too much and—

And Maeve kisses me first.

She's kissing me and the metal railing is digging into my back, but I sigh into her mouth like she's given me oxygen. The kiss—it feels different from the other two we've had. It feels . . . tender, magnetic. Indulgent, even? The hunger's still there, it gnaws and tugs at my belly as we touch, but time seems to move slower. Like I can finally savor the slightly fruity taste of her lipstick and feel her long fingers gripping my neck. She holds just the slightest amount of her weight against me. Challenging me to keep her afloat, but not overburdening me. Our shared warmth is like holding hot coffee in the snow, *just* right—

But we're not alone anymore.

I know what I'm sensing. Someone has lifted a camera, and I'm in the frame.

I know I should be boiling with rage. My privacy has been violated. But the anger just doesn't come. All I feel is anxiety clawing at my insides, dragging the good feeling I just had into the abyss like those mammoths in the tar. Maeve's out, it's not like when I was with Luna and I worried about her being outed. But Maeve's reputation could be at risk, and this isn't even an Oscars publicity setup for Trish. This guy isn't going to do this to us on our first fucking date.

I wrap my arms around her and swoop her into a dip, covering her lips with mine. As she gasps into my mouth, I shove my middle finger into the air right where the photographer would be seeing the top of Maeve's head. He'll have to blur her out.

I pull away, just in time to see Hipster Guy lower his camera. He doesn't even make eye contact when he skitters away like a rat.

"Was that paparazzi?" Maeve asks, fiddling with her earring.

I shrug. "Probably, but I angled us so I'm the only recognizable one in the photo."

She takes my hand, jolting my heart. "Can we go find a dire wolf?" Her tone is . . . off.

I glance inside. It won't be any safer in there, but it somehow feels more inviting than the pits right now. "Are you okay?"

"Come on."

As we head inside, I can't help but notice she doesn't answer my question.

There are a few more people inside. Fewer than five. But when each person feels like an extra boot pushing down on your chest, it seems like fewer than five is still a hell of a lot of other humans. My phone is in my purse, which bounces against my hip, but I swear it burns through the thick material of my bag as Maeve and I stop in front of a model of a dire wolf (taxidermied? No? Not everything here has been frozen in ice, right?). Hipster Guy must have had the whole encounter planned out. I have no idea *how* someone could know I would be at the La Brea Tar Pits, but maybe he just has a general deal with a tabloid for whatever photos he gets. We're close enough to a celebrity hub for that not to be too outrageous of a theory. My stomach twists. I must've made his fucking day.

I squeeze my eyes shut as Maeve focuses hard on the wolf. Stress is mounting, and I feel bad right now. God knows how quickly my IBS could kick into gear, and we still have to eat at some point. I can't pass off having just broth as part of a required diet for a role, and, besides, Gwyn always says liquid diets are a terrible thing to do anyway. I need to calm the fuck down. That guy doesn't have a photo of Maeve.

But it was such a close one. We really shouldn't be hanging around here much longer.

"Have you thought about what movies we want to switch out next semester?" I ask.

She smiles. "I've yet to see your *Cats* lecture, so let's see."

"I have *Dear Evan Hansen* waiting in the wings."

"Don't remind me that movie exists."

We're not holding hands anymore. I dig mine into my jacket pockets. Finger a piece of lint I find inside. Take as inconspicuous of a deep breath as I can and focus on a model of a saber-toothed tiger. In my pockets, I tap my thumb against my fingertips. Count each tap.

"Val?" Maeve says. She sounds miles away.

She touches my shoulder. It breaks the film over me, at least.

"Sorry," I mutter. "I'm just— Do you wanna move the date somewhere else?"

Maeve goes still, but I can see the relief flash through her brown eyes. "I don't want to cut this short because of him, though. Maybe we do a quick look-through?"

"Okay."

We pass swiftly through the other exhibits, through prehistoric animal dioramas where I seem to genuinely impress Maeve with my obsessive elementary school–level knowledge. We then make our way through the gift shop, where I buy her a plushie of her favorite prehistoric animal so she has a fond memento from the date itself. But even though I've managed to turn our time in the museum around, into something positive, pressure releases from my organs the second I step out of the building. I take a deep breath once I'm back at the wheel and the car doors have shut Maeve and me away from the outside world.

"Better?" I ask.

"Yeah. That was so bizarre. Does that happen to you often?" Maeve glances out the window.

"Depends on the week."

Luckily, she purses her lips and changes the subject. "Is there an Urth on the way back to your place?"

She just invited herself back to my house. People only do that when the date, despite a paparazzi face-off, goes well. A twinkle of light flickers inside me.

"Yeah, there is," I say.

She smiles like this was what she wanted all along as well. "Good. I wanted you all to myself."

Mile by mile, the tension I've been feeling slips away. Slips away as Maeve digs for every opinion I have as to which items at Urth are the best and tosses out every option before we order over the phone. Slips away when Maeve's eyes light up at the little piece of foam art on her to-go chai latte. By the time Charlie texts to say he's gonna be away for the evening on a networking happy hour, I feel almost as good as I did during that kiss at the tar pits.

"Do you want to check?" Maeve asks as we set up our food in my backyard. The sky's as clear as it gets in LA, and it reminds me of the first morning Maeve spent here. I hope she'll get that look of awe again.

"Check what?" I ask as I drop into a seat.

Eustace jumps into one of the other three chairs. He's shaking, and I mentally try to locate where the sweaters I bought him are.

"The photo. I wanna see what you did."

The thought of finding the photo makes my chest tighten again, but I need to just rip off the bandage. "Are you worried?"

"I just want to see."

Maeve's phone chimes as I boot up my Safari. God, I *hate* googling myself. I've never gotten to the last page of search results, but I *know* it's weird male gaze porn. Like the kind where they photoshop your head onto pregnant or huge-titty anime girl bodies.

But I don't have to go further than the first page of results. I type in my name and click "News" and there it is.

GOODBYE, RICHARD! ACTRESS LOCKS LIPS WITH MYSTERY GIRL AT LA BREA TAR PITS

I hold my breath and click on the first article. Scroll down to see the picture.

It's me. Very clearly me in my gay outfit, my still gay haircut falling in my eyes, making out with someone. *Someone.* Because Maeve's shot from the back, and you can barely see more than her brown hair and her pink sweater and jeans. No distinguishing features, especially with my middle finger forcing a pixelated square over her head.

No one but Maeve and me would know it's Maeve.

Smugness washing over me.

Let people gossip and call me trashy for making out with someone at a dead animal museum. Maeve's free from the fire.

Still, I hope she's feeling what I'm feeling about this.

When I look up, Maeve's looking at me expectantly. "It's just me."

I hand her my phone, and our fingers brush, leaving my skin tingling. "Mystery Girl. They're not very creative, are they?" she says.

Whew.

I smile. "Not in the least. I'd at least call you Pink-Sweater Girl."

Then, in a move that shocks me, Maeve straight up *removes* her pink sweater. Guess she really trusts my giant hedges.

"Are you trying to prove me wrong?" I ask.

She doesn't answer, just smiles and wiggles out of her shoes, socks, and jeans. She turns fully toward me, her smile growing into a little smirk. "Like what you see?"

I . . . I mean, *yeah*, of course I do. Maeve isn't even in matching underwear—she's wearing a flesh-tone bra and red-and-white polka-dot panties—yet she looks more glamorous than a Victoria's Secret model. Seeing how the waves of her hair just barely brush her collarbone and knowing her exact curves is really, really nice.

And then, with a jolt, it occurs to me that I'm supposed to be stripping too.

"It's not gonna be warm," I say.

"Good, there's a little adversity for you to overcome."

I laugh as I remove my jacket and pullover. Her gaze burns on my skin as she watches me undress. Undress for the first time. I haven't seen Maeve like this before. She has—well, I guess she *has* seen me like this before. My chest pangs a little wondering if this is as special for her as it is for me.

I tug off my shoes/socks/jeans. She undoes her necklace and places it on the patio table.

If I can't make it a novel experience to *see* me like this, maybe I can at least make that first touch special.

I approach her more tentatively than I normally would. When I cross the last few feet separating us, I feel like I'm stepping into a different ecosystem. Heat seems to swirl around us, but the fine hairs on my arms and the back of my neck stand on end. My insides tighten, but there's no pain. Just the wind-up of anticipation. I brush her hair behind her shoulder.

"You're unreal," Maeve says, her voice vibrating in a low timbre.

I shiver.

Fuck. I'm hers. I'm all hers.

I grab her shoulders.

I'm hers, but I'm also terrible in intense moments.

I plunge us both into the pool.

CHAPTER EIGHTEEN

Yeah, it's cold. It's really fucking cold. Cold enough that I have to release Maeve to regain circulation.

"Oh, fuck!" I say as I dart across the water.

When I surface, Maeve's hair is wet, plastered to her neck, and she's hanging on to the side of the pool.

"How are you not reacting to this?" I ask, my voice quite a bit higher than usual.

Maeve laughs. "I'm from *Ohio*, remember? This water doesn't even have ice!"

She's gotta be kidding me. And yet the idea of having someone in my pool who's eons tougher than me is, uh, appealing. I push the stray pieces of my hair off my face. Once I can see, I swim over to Maeve.

"Is ice swimming your only vice or are you a more complicated rural daredevil?"

"You say that as if there are things to do in rural Ohio that are dangerous for a white person." She turns her body toward me. Her leg brushes against mine as she treads water. "But my first kiss with a girl was in this secluded little swimming hole about an hour outside of town. It felt like I was in a queer coming-of-age film—a quiet build-up of anticipation sitting alone in the car with a girl for the first time, just chatting about school and the movies we liked—nothing important." She puts her fingers on my tricep. "I looked away as we stripped down, but I glanced back a couple of times, and certain images seared their way into my mind—the curve of her calf, the shape of her hip bone, a mole on her back."

"The way skin feels slicker in the water," I say. I lean in. Just a hair. One of her eyebrows got a little messy during our swim, and I have to stop myself from smoothing it out.

"Yeah," she says. Then she pulls back. "I miss the seasons and Midwestern kindness, sometimes, despite how wrong the Midwest was for me in general."

As much as I'm tempted to veer back to flirtation, curiosity overtakes me.

"Are you close with your family?" I ask.

"Yeah," she says. She pulls a bra strap that's fallen down her shoulder back up. "It's just a huge hassle to go home. It's one of those *airport, airport, long drive on either end* type places. All my siblings stayed in Ohio but moved to major cities, so they prefer having family reunions back there."

"Do they . . . ?" I don't know how to ask if they're Republicans. I doubt it considering her professor parents, but . . . "Mesh well with you?"

She nods. "Oh, yeah, I mean, they're all liberal and feminist and well educated, but I'm definitely at the extreme end, being queer and in academia, y'know?"

Oh boy do I. "Yeah, for sure."

"You have a sister, right?" she asks. It occurs to me that I don't know if she knows that from reading about me or if I told her and forgot.

"Yeah. She's a gastroenterologist and married to a guy who works admin at Cedars, so they're very . . . bougie. A little less Pasadena-white-people version of left-of-center than my parents, but I definitely had to convert her."

Maeve's shoulders seem to relax. "So she's a good ally?"

"Gwyn? Oh, yeah, the best. She's been advocating against my parents' microaggressions and reading books and going to ally support groups for years. She's the only reason I'm not up at night sweating over my little nephew who wants long hair." I give her a weak smile. "Always worried we share the gay gene, you know?"

Maeve nods. "I think my brothers would step up to the plate, but yeah. It's hard being in a family if there's only one other queer person and the straight people just want to play 'I accept you but please don't make me live and breathe gay issues.'"

"Any of your siblings have kids yet?"

"Yeah, my older brother has a preschooler and an infant. My other two siblings are under twenty-six and barely have their lives together."

Barely have their lives together. Such a weird phrase. On paper, I seem like someone who does have their life together. Financially, career-wise, maybe in the eyes of my niblings. But for me, it feels like my life is this whirlpool of mental health cycles and aching for companionship and stability in a chaotic career. I tell people I thrive on that shit, but being in the moment with Maeve right now, learning about her family and her own niblings—I'm yearning for a future where I get to be present when one of her younger brothers gets married and has kids. The feeling settles warmly and gently under my skin.

"Do you feel like you have your life together?" I ask, my voice quieter than before.

She shrugs. "I don't think I'll be able to say I do until long after

I'm granted tenure, and I'm grateful to even potentially have that opportunity."

I hold eye contact with her, despite how difficult it is. "What about when it comes to love?"

There's a searing moment where I realize I said the l-word *on the first official fucking date.*

Then another searing moment.

And another.

Until Maeve smiles. "Something about that doesn't feel so scary when I'm with you."

When we come together to kiss this time, it feels like a promise.

There's something about gay people talking about the future that gets them unreasonably horny. I've learned to just accept it at this point. Before I know it, we're climbing out of the pool in each other's arms, barely toweling off on our way into the house because we just want to make each other feel really damn good. No babies, no consequences, not even a love that I'm afraid to say out loud. I manage to come up for air long enough to say, "My wood floors are fragile."

We climb up the stairs, holding on to the railing and each other with white knuckles to keep from slipping. We giggle as we swipe pool water off each other's faces and bodies, as it drips from our wet hair. We drop the towel and stumble into the shower.

But it's not *exactly* like the movies. Worth noting. As Maeve slips off her bra and panties, she does this half-gasp, half-laugh thing. "Oh my god, you're *bidet* rich?"

I had no idea that was a type of rich. I laugh as I turn on the water in the shower. It's steaming already. "Do you need to use that right now, or . . . ?"

Maeve blushes, presumably from my comment and not because I've thrown my own panties and underwear into a sopping pile on the floor. "No, just . . ." She grabs my hand. "I can't believe you're you but also a real-life rich person."

"I'll take that as a compliment."

I kiss her and lead her into the shower, shut us inside the steam. It's almost choking hot, though, so I turn on some cold.

"I'm clean, by the way," Maeve says.

I grab a bottle of bodywash, put a liberal glob of it in my hand, and turn to Maeve to give her some.

"STD-wise. I get checked after every new partner, and I was clean as of mid-August."

"Oh." Oh, she's a responsible adult. Not to mention she, what, has spent the entire time we've known each other not fucking other people? It's embarrassing to say how much that turns me on. "Yeah, I was clean as of a year ago." I'm blushing now too. "I haven't been with anyone since then. I swear I'm not skipping out or anything."

Maeve smiles, grabbing some of the bodywash off my hands. Her touch sends a jolt of energy through me. Hot energy. "I trust you. You seem starved enough for this, anyway." *That* ignites me.

I smash our lips together, bodies together. The bodywash is still on my hands, though, so I rub it up and down her skin. Her soft fucking skin. Her hands move to my hair, dig into it, tug as the kiss deepens. A moan escapes my lips, into her mouth. I swear she smiles. She holds me tighter.

She holds me tighter, and I can't take it anymore. Cradling her head, I pin her to the side of the shower, pressing us together lips, tits, and hips. Grind up against her, coaxing the most beautiful little yelp out of her.

"You hungry for this too?" I ask, my voice hoarse.

"This?" she chuckles. "I've been dreaming about this for years."

She leans in, her breath brushing against my ear. "Specifically you since I saw *Needlepoint*."

Fuck.

Holy fucking shit, she just—

All this time shaming myself for enjoying the idea that she might find me attractive. All this time and she *actually was* fantasizing about me after seeing *Needlepoint*? It swells in my heart, makes me even prouder of that movie. A bro high five to Past Me—*Thanks for doing such a good job pretending to get nailed by a dude because now we're going to have sex with the most wonderful lady we've ever met.*

God, Maeve liked me. Maeve *likes* me. Maeve is right in front of me, and we're both naked and want each other.

I can't play around anymore. I shut the water off. As it dribbles to a stop, I pull us out of the shower, wrap a towel around us both. Still kissing Maeve, I walk my way back to the bedroom using nothing but tactile memory. Nothing to see, nothing to hear, nothing to experience but her lips, her skin, her sighs, her body.

Dropping onto the bed feels like the drop on a roller coaster. Butterflies flap viciously in my stomach, but I'm loving it. I want the extreme sensation, the extreme pressure in my chest, my gut, between my legs. That *ache* for something that's suddenly possible. That's suddenly so goddamn possible I could cry.

I push her down to the bed, and she looks up at me as I straddle her. "Let me know if there's anything you like or don't like," I say. "Or anything you want to try. I'm open."

Well, *open* relatively speaking. Still a top, but Maeve isn't protesting about being under me. So . . . fingers crossed.

She grabs me by the hips, pulling me down so our pelvises rub. I bite my lip to hold back the moan as we meet. It's so simple. It's so fucking simple, but as we grind against each other, my body fully on top of her, my weight supported with strength I'm proud to have, my heart is hammering and I've never felt this good. She squirms under me, her breath getting faster. *So* fast, like this is a quick release for her. It's amazing the way that connection tugs at my own body, makes my mouth moisten with each movement. I forgot how good it feels to make these motions, to feel that skin, to have my lips on her neck as her back arches. If she lets me, I can't wait to fuck her.

These sensations are familiar, yet what I'm tasting—Maeve's breath, the salt of the sweat on her skin, the flowery scent of my bodywash—is in its own league. A custom-made flavor only I can experience in this exact moment. I memorize the topography of freckles, moles, and scars on Maeve's body as I explore her neck, her shoulders, her back as we move against each other. Every partner I have is a thrill—I'm always eager to learn every fact, every trick, every twitch and sound the person in my arms makes.

The first thing I learn about Maeve: god does she *shudder* when I kiss the nape of her neck as we come one after another. It's a trick I learned from a torrid one-night stand with an Oxford grad student (not my department) back before Emily, and it's like it was *made* for Maeve. When she goes so far as to bury her face in my chest as the pleasure is still rippling through me, I feel so much *joy* at making this woman happy. She drapes herself over me, like she can't get enough of our skin touching. It's the kind of affection I had to beg for when I was with Emily.

"So I require performance reviews after every go," I say. "Out of five stars . . . ?"

Maeve chuckles, her chest knocking softly against my stomach. "Leave it to a gay girl to make grinding that hot."

I run a hand through her hair. "Wait until I fuck you."

Maeve takes my hand, sliding my fingers slowly down the length of her torso. My own breath catches as her stomach muscles contract under my fingers. "You sure those fingers can do more than look pretty?"

She lets go of my hand as I reach between her legs. It's one of those questions that doesn't need a verbal response. I just put on my best smirk and rub a couple circles around her clit. She doesn't make a sound, but the crunching of her abs speaks volumes.

"I dunno, babe," I say. "It'd be a shame if they're just for show, though." I slide my finger around her opening, lubing up. "This okay?"

"Yeah."

I slip it inside her. She's soaked.

I slip another finger in. It's such a deep, primal feeling, a breathlessness that washes over me as I explore her. I never thought I'd miss the feeling of being inside someone so badly. My fingers curl around, pressing against that sweet G-spot. The little buck I get makes me smile.

"You good?" I ask. "Can I go deeper?"

"Yes." It comes out as a sigh.

My heart races.

Am I showing off? Okay, a little. But hey, it's to get that squeak of pleasure as I feel my knuckles knocking against her pelvis, pulsing to the quickening of her breath. And with all my attention on her, I can gauge her every reaction. The way her cheeks get pink, the way she holds me as I rub circles around her nipple. For a while, I just soak it all in. Memorize the feeling inside her, how hot her breath comes on my skin, how hard she slams her hips against my hand as I pulse.

"Up to your standards?" I tease.

"Absolutely," she replies. She lets out a breath. "But one request?"

I stop. "What?"

She grins. "Can I ride you?"

My stomach gives a little flip. Fuck, no one has asked me for that before. Back in my baby gay days, Emily *would* just ride me, but there were no questions. She also wasn't too good at checking in about fingering either, but—

No. Focus. Maeve wants me under her. Which is fine. She still needs my fingers. I'll give it a shot.

I pull out and drop back onto the sheets. The spot is hot from Maeve's body. I rest my right arm by my chest as Maeve straddles me. Shit, I have to just sit with that a moment—*Maeve* straddling *me*. She smirks a little as she eyes my hand. Honestly, I should've seen this coming once she yanked my belt off in her office, but here we go. My heart is slamming in my chest as I slide back inside her. Same come-hither, same up the knuckles. But she's the one pulsing. Fucking me? I don't even know what to call it. But it's thrilling in a way I never expected. And with this view, I have Maeve on full display. I may think of myself as an actress, but she's putting on a little cheeky show for me too. Chewing on her lip, throwing her head back to expose her neck, reaching down and teasing my breasts.

By the end of her performance I go back to pulsing as eagerly as she rides me. We're in perfect synchronization, and I can see that it knocks her to the bone. And for all that the ease in her posture and face are fucking killing me, she *collapses* into me as she comes, and the way she says "God, Val" is music to my ears.

"Let's make you come too," Maeve says as we hold each other. "What do you like?"

"Anything but penetration," I say. "Not my style."

She kisses my neck. "I can work with that."

"Great. Gimme a minute to catch my breath, though," I reply.

I kiss her forehead and wash my hands off. My forearm aches, my fingers are settling into that characteristic stiffness that comes after a good fuck, but it's an ache I strive for. I'm aching because I made the woman in my bed happy. No better reason to hurt.

I flop back into bed. Maeve's turned to me, but her desire seems to have cooled a bit. She's looking at my crotch, though, so what do I know?

"Does this scar have a story too?" she asks, reaching down and—

And, well, running her finger along the scar on my upper thigh. My chest twinges.

So she wasn't looking at my crotch. She's also the first partner I've ever had who even *noticed* the scar. (Not that Luna or the others really had the chance; I kept all the focus on them.)

But looking into her eyes, as much as I don't want the pain to flow back in, there's a different kind of pressure building inside me to the one I had moments ago. Sex is great. Sex with Maeve is already like a dream. But the tugging in my heart can't be solved by coming.

It might make the coming better, though.

"It's not a fun story." I laugh.

She takes my hand. It electrifies me more than if her hand was between my legs. "That's okay. I'm here to learn about more than just what your body can do."

I sigh. "It was . . . maybe five years ago? Charlie and I went cliff diving, and I hit a rock. The real twist, though, was that my old manager, Steven, came to visit me in the hospital. He said I needed to have a scar revision. Couldn't let it risk my appeal for future roles."

Maeve runs her finger along the scar. "What the fuck? Why would anyone—?"

"That's Hollywood."

"That's bullshit. It's just a scar." She sighs, long and hard. She plants a soft kiss on my lips. "I just . . . I need you to know how much I want you to feel okay." She kisses the spot between my throat and collarbone. "To feel respected." Between my breasts. "Seen." Right on my leg scar. "Loved."

My stomach's back to fluttering under her touch.

"Thank you," I whisper back.

She kisses between my hip bones. "Is this okay?"

I take a deep breath and nod. If Maeve wants to see me, I owe it to myself to let her see me. I let the tears fall. Wipe them away as Maeve continues to work her way down.

And when her mouth touches me, lord above, this woman was made to be gay.

CHAPTER NINETEEN

Maybe it's arrogance because I'm finally having sex again, but I'm feeling amazing. Cloud nine, *holy shit is this real life* incredible. Maeve and I are in full synch the rest of November, gliding through our *Rocketman, Sing Street,* and *Les Misérables* lectures, sneaking makeout sessions behind her locked office door before she had to move to her next class. I'd squeeze in any opportunity to see her, sleepy hookups at her place after attending her QuASA and film club events. We kept the promise of anonymity, avoiding anywhere I could be photographed again. Honestly, I didn't mind—all the best spaces to be with her were private. As soon as we both said goodbye to the students for Thanksgiving break, what had started out as a date to see a double feature at Alamo Drafthouse ended in sex at my place that had Maeve coyly texting me all Thanksgiving break about how sore she was.

Now it's the day of our last class of the semester before the take-home finals are distributed, and it starts out after Maeve's first sleepover. She's looking amazing in one of my Zara suits. I don't remember the last time I was this happy. So much so that I've slipped on a 2008-era studded belt and cat ears, and I only feel slightly like a dumbass.

"Do you know what day it is?" I ask, biting back a smile as I peer into the kitchen. It's past 8:00 a.m. and Maeve Arko is sitting at my kitchen table holding out a mug so Charlie can pour her a cup of coffee as he looks over a script.

Charlie doesn't look at me as he squints at one of my walls. "Tuesday?"

"Nope!"

I turn on Alexa to the Original Broadway Cast Recording of "The Rum Tum Tugger." Maybe it's because I come from an upper-middle class white family, but I fuck with *Cats*. And I spent too many hours in college learning how to pelvis-first masc stripper dance to *Rocky Horror* and later *Magic Mike,* so I know I fucking *own* this song. I sing to Maeve and Charlie the first couple of verses, my hands sliding to the center of my belt, my tongue out, my hips gyrating *perfectly.* And even though Maeve is bright red watching me, probably from secondhand embarrassment, I see a flicker in her eyes that tells me that she's into it.

"Why are you like this?" Charlie asks, covering his face to laugh.

"Hope you're ready, Dr. Arko," I say as I slide behind her chair and grab her shoulders.

"Is *this* why you wanted to do *Cats* so badly?"

I slip into my chair next to her and pull off my cat ears. "No."

"You never did theater in high school, yet you're still the worst kind of theater kid imaginable," Charlie comments as he takes my cat ears from me and puts them on.

Maeve crosses her arms and studies me. I could get used to the sight of Maeve in my clothing. I don't think I've dated anyone my size before.

"No," I repeat, throwing Maeve a small smile. "Gotta provide balance. I make a clown of myself, then Maeve delivers some stellar T. S. Eliot knowledge and a perfect history of camp. That's why together we make the ideal team."

That gets Maeve to beam. Her cheeks flush a light pink, and her big ole smile makes my heart melt. "Can you believe today is our last lecture?" she asks.

Nope. Yes, this week marks the start of December, but with next semester looming it doesn't really feel like much is going to end. In fact, I'm looking forward to making this scene in my kitchen a more frequent occurrence, and to our next class together in January. "End of one thing, beginning of another."

She knocks her foot against my leg. "I gotta get going soon, but you're welcome to hang in my office so we can meet up after my class."

I happen to glance at Charlie. As much as I *do* want to sit in Maeve's office and stare at her couch and think about fucking her on it, I'm needed elsewhere.

"Charlie, wanna work on campus?" I ask him.

Unlike me, Charlie does kind of like going out in public. He scratches his temple and looks at his pajamas. "Uh, didn't Maeve just say you guys had to get going?"

I glance at Maeve. "You can have until I get out of this lazy cat costume."

Charlie nods and runs back to his room. Once his booming footsteps have faded, Maeve looks back to me.

She tugs on the blazer. "Thanks for letting me borrow your suit. I promise I'll have it laundered—"

I hold up a hand. "*I'll* have it laundered. Please."

For a moment, a hardness falls over Maeve. My heart jerks in my chest, but then her features soften once more.

She squeezes my hand. "Thanks, babe."

I know it's only been a month since our first kiss. But sitting in the kitchen with her early in the morning, watching her have breakfast with Charlie, is doing something to me. Something too powerful to deal with before 9:00 a.m. I'm about to leave a room to go change for maybe five minutes, for god's sake, yet I want to kiss her goodbye. I'm going to see her again in a matter of seconds and I can already anticipate the ache of being away from her.

But I lean over and give her a peck anyway. Just the way my parents did every day before work, despite the fact that they worked in the same office.

"See ya in the car," I say.

She blushes. "What was that for?"

"I guess I like you." I even *nail* a wink as I walk out of the room.

The high lasts for a while afterward.

It lasts through the car ride, where Charlie blasts his Lady Gaga and All Time Low mix. It lasts through a contactless goodbye with Maeve in her office as she exchanges us for some binders and rushes off somewhere. And it's still there even after she leaves, when Charlie plops onto the couch Maeve and I almost had sex on and smirks.

"Zero to one hundred, huh?" he says.

My face gets hot. "We're not married."

"Yet you're already lining the floor she walks on in money, and you're following her around like a puppy. You're pretty smitten. It may even be time to take her out somewhere other than the movies."

Then there's a pause. A pause where Charlie should say *And she's crazy about you too.*

Charlie's not saying anything, and now there's this gross thought growing in my head. One I'm definitely supposed to identify as irrational and kick away. Here with Charlie—away from Maeve—I have some perspective, and I realize that this bit of dating is the easy part.

That I have been deliberately choosing dates that have low chances of another paparazzi encounter. I have no idea if she'll get more comfortable with the idea of me being famous, or if her reaction at the tar pits is indicative of a bigger issue, one that won't be easy to handle no matter how good I am in bed. I bite my lip.

"That's not entirely up to me," I admit.

He looks up from his script. "What do you mean?"

"You know how we got photographed together on our first date? We haven't really talked about it."

"So talk about it. The last thing you need is to make this a bigger issue than it is."

I rub my forearms. The room is a comfortable temperature, but the hair on my arms is standing on end. "When we're at the house or here at school, I have her wrapped around my finger. But the second we cross that line again and go out in public and we have to dodge paparazzi and rumors and my public persona, I'm one bad day from losing her."

"Do you think maybe you should tell her this?"

The words lurch out of me. "I signed on to teach another semester, and Trish is riding me about what my commitments will be if *Oakley* gets into any spring festivals. Maeve has no idea, and I don't know how to bring it up now."

"Is that what this is really about?" Charlie takes a deep breath, then places a hand on my shoulder. The gesture, coming from *Charlie,* means I know I've done fucked up. "The semester hasn't even started. Just tell Maeve you got too excited and—"

There's a knock on the door that nearly startles me out of my skin and leaves me staring pleadingly at Charlie like he's the one out of the two of us who has more of their shit together.

But, to his credit, he nods at me and then gently pushes me by the small of my back in the direction of the door.

Ty wears his expressions on his face, and he goes from wide-eyed surprise at seeing me in Maeve's office to bright eyes and a wide smile.

"Ty, this is Charlie Durst," I intro. "Charlie, this is Ty. He's a PhD candidate in the Film Studies Department."

They shake hands, Ty confidently meeting Charlie's Hollywood-trained grip.

"Nice to meet you," Charlie says.

"Same."

It warms my heart to see Charlie beam for the first time in a while.

"Super-gay *Star Trek* was a revelation."

Charlie only beams harder. "Gotta start somewhere, right?"

I've been scouring the internet for weeks about *Star Trek*'s status, but there haven't really been any articles mentioning the cancellation other than those written by fans lamenting the loss of rep. Ty's reaction cements that. I wonder if Trish knows anyone powerful who might be able to pen an op-ed or something that would pressure other networks to bring the show back. Or—okay, at least dig out a great follow-up role for Charlie.

But then Ty turns to me. "So rare to see you without Maeve these days," he teases.

I flush. "Sorry to steal your movie buddy."

"Maeve and I graduated to museum buddies now, so go ahead." He smirks. "Wouldn't want to keep you from your dates."

I visibly blush then, making Charlie laugh. "I . . . guess we haven't been hiding it well."

Ty shakes his head, a smile on his face. "No, not really." He stares at me a moment. "Maeve's teaching right now, isn't she?"

"Yeah," I reply. *In my clothing.*

"Cool. Dean Gomez was looking for you both to give you an update. Student evaluations continue to be stellar."

Which is kind of a huge deal.

"Good evals feel more Maeve than me," I say.

"You've done right by her. The way she's going, Maeve's a shoo-in for the SCA Media Studies Grant."

Holy shit. It's coming back to me, the name SCA Media Studies Grant popping up in bold in a list of things Maeve was working on. That's the award she needs to finish her second book, the one about monstrosity in modern queer cinema. She still hasn't gotten that locked in yet. Ty's words cause my throat to tighten.

"Yeah, Maeve's at the final stage. Just an observation period for one of her courses and she's locked in," Ty continues.

My heart drops. "They observe a class? When?"

"Next semester. It's low-key. They evaluate how she is in the presence of students, co-professors, and guests. It's so amazing that you're staying another semester. It may just help make Maeve's career."

I keep my smile plastered on. "Happy to help."

He turns to Charlie. "Great to meet you, Charlie."

Charlie, who looks as shocked as I am, manages to say, "Same to you, man!"

Ty leaves, the door clicking behind him.

Charlie turns to me, slow and overdramatically, which fits perfectly with the way my stomach is roiling. "So . . . maybe don't quit on Maeve right now . . ."

"Holy fuck, Charlie" is all I can say. I try to massage my stomach, but the pain is like a fisherman's hook in my guts. I still have to teach a class in a few hours, so my body needs to chill *now*.

He shrugs. "Maybe *Oakley* won't get into any festivals anyway?"

Maeve keeps herbal tea in her desk somewhere. I scoot over, start rifling through. Peppermint, chamomile, I'll even try fucking essential oils to get through this lecture. No tea, but she does have a little bottle of lavender. I squeeze some out and dab it on my face.

"You okay, Sulls?" Charlie asks.

The lavender isn't working. My heart's still racing, and the pain is intensifying. Fuck, I haven't had a full-blown panic attack since—

"I'll be right back," I say.

It's feels like *Oakley in Flames* keeps doing the exact opposite of what I want.

So watch it get into every spring festival.

CHAPTER TWENTY

If there's one thing having a publicist has taught me, it's that the average attention span is six seconds. The more optimistic, Rosalie-advice-flavored spin is that people are made to adapt to uncomfortable situations by turning them into our new normal.

I, like most people, have adjusted to the new normal in which I'm a raging fucking dumbass and haven't told Maeve that my directorial debut could be picked up by a festival, forcing me to leave her in the dust during possibly the most important semester of her teaching career. Possibly. If *Oakley* gets in anywhere. Which it won't. But it's still a possibility. Even as my name falls faster and faster on the IMDb STARmeter and *Oakley in Flames* dies with me, the prospect still simmers in the back of my mind. Not to mention Trish's Oscars idea . . .

I taught the *Cats* lecture with my body in full collapse post–panic attack mode, yet I somehow convinced Maeve and the students I was fine. I skipped end-of-the-semester celebratory drinks with Maeve and Ty by claiming to have food poisoning, just like I used to do with ill-timed press events.

The flare-up died by the next morning, as they tend to. But the worrying thoughts set in by the afternoon.

December passes in a surprisingly uniform pattern:

> 1) Maeve and I hang out. Maeve talks about academia or studying at Berkeley and asks me about what courses I taught at Oxford and King's College. Sometimes we discuss movies, music, family, or politics. We have really good sex.

> 2) I remember that I still haven't told Maeve about potentially causing her to lose a huge grant and the career-making prestige of it.

> 3) The cramps come back.

> 4) I take dairy, spice, red meat, alcohol, caffeine, and heavy fiber out of my diet, concurrent to 3.

> 5) I deliberately refuse to go to public places with Maeve. I tell her it's because of tabloids, and she seems to accept that.

> 6) Go back to 1.

Somehow, I've managed to make it to January fourth. Maeve's lying in my bed in the Cosabella pajama set I got her for Hanukkah, humming along to the German Beatles covers I put on as a joke as I finish up reading her latest paper on her laptop.

"Done," I announce.

She bounces up and takes her laptop back from me gingerly. I have a bolt of realization: I'm dating a noncelebrity for the first time in years. Maybe that's part of the reason I'm amazed by how gentle she is with every expensive thing she owns. I almost feel bad about getting her an expensive Hanukkah present; she's asked me like ten times how to properly wash these pajamas. And she hand-painted me ceramic bowls, which takes way more effort than driving to Bloomingdale's.

"The abstract sounds great," I say.

She asked for my opinion, but considering the proposal is due tomorrow, I know she doesn't *really* want it. Still, I'm not lying when I tell her I like it. I look over her shoulder and see she's still working on a new paper.

She gives me a tiny smile, scooting an inch closer to me on the bed as she sets the laptop back on her stomach. "Thanks for reading this. I'm sure it's eye-bleedingly boring for you."

I shake my head. "Nothing you write is boring."

And I genuinely mean it. Reading drafts of Maeve's latest conference entry, a study of *I Killed My Mother* and Xavier Dolan's early work, has brought a joy back into my life I haven't felt since Oxford. Back when I'd read Emily's papers for her, I'd write little jokes and questions in the margins that I always made her answer in the paper to appeal to the lowest common denominator in any academic audience. She got tired of the comments by the end of our relationship, but the light in Maeve's eyes as she reads my margin notes is something I wish I could etch into my heart forever. Maeve and I haven't *exactly* had the girlfriend talk yet, but I think our status is clear in the little things, like Maeve saying she can't wait to see my comments on her next paper, Maeve and I watching sapphic TV in small doses while we form theories together about future episodes, Maeve video chatting with me when she was home for Hanukkah with her family, letting me talk to her little brothers.

I get a pang of regret. I can't keep putting off telling her I'll potentially have to bail on her this semester. What we have is too perfect for me to be this dumb. Yet I can't shake that raw fear from the Emily days, that I'm one wrong move from losing her. I barely handled it last time; I can't go through it again, I just can't. And what I might risk is so much bigger than Maeve's ego.

"So what's your dream paper?" I ask.

Maeve purses her lips. "I'd love to do a paper on queer representation in modern genre film." She shrugs. "Just wish there were, you know, *actual films*."

I laugh. "Mason Wu and I are *working on it*."

Mason kind of kept me from spiraling into a deep depressive episode when we met. She went from being the only director in Hollywood who knew I was gay to one of my best friends. Before I came out, she was the only person I could do press with who'd make me act, well, like *myself*. I'm almost looking forward to doing press for *Goodbye, Richard! 2* just because I'll have to hang out with her again for extended periods of time. She may be the only force in Hollywood who can save me from the gay pigeonholing. She also responds to my every Maeve update in under thirty seconds. So far, she hasn't said anything about Leonard complaining to her about my turning down the HBO role, but I'm waiting for it, certain the news will hit me when I'm least expecting it. I wish there was a world where I only ever had to work with her, but it's a fantasy, a numbing cream on an open wound more than any real solution.

"What's on her slate? I'd *genuinely* write a paper on it."

"She has this really cool semi-autobiographical coming-of-age indie filming this year. It's based on her experience being a Chinese American literary magazine gay in high school in OC. It's set in that nebulous time when you know you're gay but you still haven't figured out enough about yourself to try to date. The script is hilarious."

"Who would you play?"

I narrow my eyes as I think. "I wanna say we decided I'd play her white therapist who she had a crush on, but I was also up for white biology teacher who ran off to Florida with the Spanish teacher she also had a crush on."

Maeve laughs. "Oh my god, is Mason a Libra?"

I gasp. "*I'm* a Libra!"

"Yes, I *know*. I still like you very much." She touches my nose. Maeve's a Cancer/Leo cusp, and yes, I was *very* relieved to learn we were still somehow compatible on Co–Star.

"She's a Gemini."

"This explains *so much* about *Goodbye, Richard!*" She studies me a moment. "Is your character gay?"

I smile back at her. Mason and I have been bouncing this question around for a year now doing press for the film, and finally having the opportunity to answer it honestly is like throwing a nineties kid into Chuck E. Cheese. "Yes. So the reason I got Aurora is because I whispered in Mason's ear during an audition that I was gay. She trusted me to put out what we called 'gay signs for idiots.' The studio heads were super nervous about canonical gay characters for a comic franchise, but Mason and I just *knew* Aurora was gay. We figured we'd just act like she was and have her do everything but say the word and kiss ladies. The way I walked, talked, looked at women, listened to men, *everything* was deliberate."

"Is anything changing for *Goodbye, Richard! 2*?"

"Mason is fighting for Aurora and Lacey to have a sex scene."

Maeve raises her brows. "Oh, *okay*."

I'd forgotten how good it feels to talk about this franchise. The playfulness of the film has always spilled into the way we talk about it, the way everyone on set treated one another—it's like telling someone about your favorite year at summer camp.

I laugh. "I mean, a PG-thirteen one. There's gonna be a scene where Lacey and Aurora check into a hotel, and then there's another scene—a major one—where they talk in bed. We know we can have them snuggling in pajamas, but Mason is hoping we can have a scene in the middle where they have one of those silent, bedroom-eyes, bodies-thrown-against-the-door-kiss-to-implied-sex scenes."

"Oh."

It occurs to me for the first time that, assuming we get through the yet-to-be-discussed Oscar situation, I could bring Maeve to *GR2*'s set. As my girlfriend. And then she'd have to watch me slam another girl against a wall and mouth-fuck her, since we can't show the gays fuck-fucking.

Which maybe isn't actually fun to watch. Another part of the Hollywood thing Maeve might bristle at.

"Trust me, it's not sexy as an actor," I say. "They keep the room super cold and, despite the crew's best efforts, you're mostly just standing there hoping the men on set aren't staring at your pasty-covered nipples," I say. "Not to mention your lips start to hurt after about three takes, and you usually have to do more like fifteen."

I notice that Maeve still has a dent between her brows.

"Besides, Phoebe Wittmore is straight."

I lean into Maeve, teasingly close. My heart flutters as I look at her lips. "I'd never get to kiss her the way I get to kiss you. You'll be what I'm thinking of the whole time."

Butterflies flap up a storm inside me. I lean into Maeve and plant a firm kiss on her lips. "I can't do *this* with her." Then I barely brush my lips against hers, which leaves my own tingling. "Or that." I shrug. "You can't even use tongue on-screen unless you practically stick your tongue out into their mouth."

Maeve sets her laptop aside and, taking a firm grip of my waist, pulls me on top of her. Her worry has seemingly melted away. My muscles twitch under her touch.

"Oh? How do you like it with me?" she purrs.

I dip in for the kiss at the *exact* moment my phone goes off on the nightstand. I look to Maeve—*Can I take this?*—and she nods. It's Gwyn. I put it on speaker.

"Morning, sunshine," I say.

"Morning, Val," she says, in a very not-sunshine manner. "Hey, are you with Maeve?"

I raise a brow at Maeve. She smiles, a little red in the cheeks.

"Hey, Gwyn," Maeve says.

Maeve's been around long enough to have had a couple of quick conversations with Gwyn when she calls me, but they haven't met yet. In fact, no one in my family has met Maeve yet. Besides Charlie, Luna, and Mason, the only person who even knows we're dating is Ty.

"So my kids are having their fourth birthday this upcoming weekend, and I was wondering if you wanted to come?" Gwyn asks. "I figure if you're still with my sister by now, it must be serious."

Maeve's blushing even harder now. "Yeah." She pulls some hair behind her ear, but it falls forward again. I tuck it back for her, our hands brushing against each other. "Is there a theme or anything?"

Gwyn laughs. "No, it's just a dinner with our parents. Val will get a present, so don't worry about that."

I shake my head. "Hey, bitch, am I even invited?"

Gwyn sighs. "Oh my god, *no, you're not.* Don't you dare come."

Maeve stifles a laugh. My chest's fluttering. "Do they still love *Frozen*?"

"Dinosaurs now. I'll send you a text with the info."

Maeve's going to my niblings' birthday party in less than a week. I've never introduced *anyone* I've dated, not even my ex-fiancée, to my family. Two seconds after hanging up the phone, and my heart's already pounding. Maeve is going to meet my parents. Maeve is going to meet my parents, and I haven't told her about the film festivals. We're going to start the semester next week, and I *haven't talked to her about the film festivals.*

Maeve grabs my hand. "Hey, it's okay. I'm great with parents."

I look away. "No, I don't think— You're not what I'm worried about."

My stomach twists. I just need to tell Maeve. Even if there's no good way to transition to the topic. She can't meet my parents without knowing about my obligations for *Oakley* and how they could affect her. If she'd leave me over this like Emily would've, at least it can all happen before everyone knows and I get humiliated all over again.

Maeve's soft expression fades. She drops her hand from mine, scooting so she's fully sitting up. "Can we talk?"

I *know* there's no way anyone told her, but the thought lodges in my mind. Maybe it was Trish. Or Trish's assistant. Or Charlie, even though he swore he wouldn't tell her before I did. Maybe she saw a flash of the *Oakley in Flames* group chat with Luna and Romy where we were talking about festivals.

I haven't spoken yet. "Yeah. What's up?"

She bites her lip. "You're happy with how this is going, right?"

"Yeah, absolutely—"

"Because I am. You—I mean, you know. I've . . . always had such a hard time finding people who kept me engaged, pushed me to grow. Met me on that special brain level, you know?"

I find myself laughing. "So, like, you're happy I comment on your papers?"

She flusters. "No, I—I mean, yes, but I'm talking about connection in a broader sense. You have this incredible wealth of knowledge, like I learn from you every time I see you. Even among academics, that kind of passion is rare. It's important to me in a match and I'm, like, giddy that I've found that with you. I'm so glad you chose to guest-teach and we met and—" She exhales. "I really like you."

Something in me lights up, despite the tension I still feel. I reach my hand out to stroke her arm, just to feel that connection. "I like you too."

"And now I'm going to meet your family and I still don't even know what to call you."

I let my heart leap and forget about my anxiety for just a *moment.* Just long enough to say, "How about girlfriend?"

Maeve grins. "That's what I was hoping you'd say."

She pulls me in for a kiss.

Dr. Maeve Arko pulls me in for a kiss.

Dr. Maeve Arko, my *girlfriend,* pulls me in for a kiss.

We kiss. We weave our fingers into each other's hair, draw them along the lines of our clothing and tuck them under waistbands and onto hot skin. We kiss as girlfriends, with the ease that comes from weeks of experience and trust and something bubbling up that looks like love with just the *L* and the *O* set in stone for now.

All that, and I haven't told her about the film festivals.

I pull away before Maeve's hand drops into my pajama bottoms. "Wanna go with me when I buy my niblings a birthday present? We can make sex a nice treat for being real adults?"

Maeve sits there and stares at me for a moment before lightly pushing me away. "You're my girlfriend."

My heart's buzzing harder and harder every time she says it. It overshadows the anxiety. I *need* her to keep saying it. "I am."

She giggles. "Oh god, my girlfriend's a—"

"Academy Award–winning actress?"

"*Libra.*"

And I let myself collapse on her and laugh. I let the anxiety melt away. It may be poking the bear more and more each time I avoid bringing things up, but for now that bear is stuck in its cave.

There's literally an indie store called the Dinosaur Farm in Old Pasadena, so I figure that warrants a little trek east. Not that Maeve seems to mind much. Conversation fills the air, blending perfectly with the playlist she's curating from my Spotify. It hits me in little waves. Maeve is my *girlfriend.* I haven't had a girlfriend in five years. I haven't had a girlfriend since I started acting. The last time *girlfriend* meant anything to me, I was in England TA'ing Irish–African American Relations at King's College, coming back to a dorm room planning my marriage proposal. Maeve is my girlfriend, I'm teaching again, and do I dare toy with the possibility that Maeve and I could be marriage serious? I haven't made plans more than two years in advance since I got accepted into my PhD program. Hollywood just isn't built for that.

Yet as I take Maeve's hand to walk her down the Old Pasadena streets, I let myself run the film of our future. I imagine holding on to this hand for decades to come, seeing a ring on her left hand. Embarrassment creeps up my neck and, well, there are more than a few butterflies fluttering again.

"So this is your hometown?" Maeve asks as I open the door to the Dinosaur Farm for her.

I consider keeping my sunglasses on, but that's more conspicuous. Besides, I've been back to Pasadena more than a few times since becoming famous, and people tend to leave me alone. Some of them even remember me pre-fame and will ask how my parents' dental practice is going. I glance over at the cashier, the only employee currently in my line of vision. She's somewhere between teenage and early twenties, with short black hair and a nose stud.

"It's too cute, isn't it?" I reply.

Because this store truly is adorable. There's a light green jungle facade on the walls, and the shelves are lined with dinosaur-themed children's books and puzzles. A breakout section is stuffed to the gills with dinosaur toys—cars, plastic tchotchkes, stuffed animals, *Jurassic Park*–type LEGO playsets. I head to this toy section first. Part of me wants to pick the most obnoxious one to mess with Gwyn, but I can't tell if Maeve *quite* shares my jokingly petty/childish streak when it comes to my sister.

"I can't picture you growing up here," Maeve says. "It's so quiet. Your hypothetical children"—she visibly hesitates—"would be too edgy to live here even when they're in diapers."

In order to keep my cool, I try to focus on the bit of pink that raises to Maeve's cheeks at the mention of my future progeny as she picks up a dinosaur set that reads 3+. She can see me having *kids*? I know Gwyn's always joking when she says I shouldn't have kids, but no one has gone so far as to say that they could actually see me having them. I've always loved the idea of being a parent. I've been in love with tiny humans since Oz and Lily were born. Sometimes, on the hard nights when I was closeted, my only self-soothing tool was to imagine my future family. *One day you'll have your own world that's full of gay love. You'll have a wife and raise kids who'll never go through what you're going through now.*

Of course, my phone dings with a text right in the middle of that little euphoria moment. It's from the group chat.

LR: VAL are you reading this????? It came out like
5 minutes ago.
<Romy loved "VAL are you">
<Charlie loved "VAL are you">

She attaches a link.

My stomach sinks as I click the link. Please be Mason confirming to the press that *Goodbye, Richard! 2* will contain gay sex.

FIVE FILMS WE'RE WATCHING FOR SXSW

I force a deep breath, then stow my phone and continue looking for toys. Maybe I should just get the kids marginally similar-looking stuffed brontosauruses. Should I assume they've seen *Land Before Time* and its fifty direct-to-video sequels? Almost certainly, except I'm not sure if they're all streaming. Picture books are a good alternative. But no matter how hard I try to concentrate on my niblings' gifts, I can't escape the twisting in my guts.

That article is just speculation. People are excited for *Oakley in Flames*. As an A-lister making my directorial debut, there's bound to be some hype. It doesn't mean it'll get into South by Southwest. No need to throw myself into another anxiety episode for one article.

Then my phone starts ringing.

Trish.

My chest caves around my heart. Trish calls only with huge news. Usually, good news.

"Are you good at picking out picture books?" I ask Maeve. "No price limit."

Maeve mouth goes into a thin line. "Oh, uh, yeah."

"Be there in a sec." I fumble my AirPods in and accept the call. "Hey."

"Hey," Trish says. "Short and sweet . . ."

God, no, please. But no, maybe this is a blessing. Maybe if I *know* the dates, I can just tell Maeve, and SXSW is in March anyway. Not during, like, crunch time. We could make it work. I'll tell Maeve the reason I hadn't brought it up before is that I didn't want to talk to her about it unless it actually happened. This is a *good thing*.

"*Oakley* is on the short list for features in South by Southwest. It doesn't mean it's *in,* but we're getting amazing feedback. Fuck Sundance, you know?" Trish says, launching right in.

Okay. I put a hand to my chest, force a deep breath. I'm not *in* at South by Southwest, so there's no need to tell Maeve what Trish is reporting. I glance at the book section. Maeve is on her knees, staring intently at a shelf of picture books. She pulls one off the shelf and gingerly turns the pages.

"Val?" Trish says.

I shake my head. "Yeah."

"Reaction?"

Shit. "Uh, that's great!" I act for a living, and that was possibly my weakest performance yet.

"Yeah, I know, South by Southwest isn't *quite* prestigious enough, but it's a huge start. And there's still Tribeca, TIFF, some more, you know, up-our-alley festivals. This might put some pressure on them, you know?"

I swallow as I make my way over to Maeve. "Yeah, totally."

My heart pounding, I lean in. She's looking at a book about a dinosaur who's going to school.

"Find anything?"

"I think this is cute," she says. "Coordinate it with dinosaur toys that look like the main character, and . . ."

I have no clue how she finishes that sentence because suddenly

I hear Trish in my ear saying, "Is that your new girl?" Trish says through the phone.

My heart nearly stops. I look at Maeve. If Trish can hear Maeve, does that mean Maeve can hear Trish? I'm losing it. "Uh, yeah . . ."

"Did you invite her to the Oscars yet? I'm not dealing with dating rumors about you anymore. Especially if they're *true*."

I settle my gaze on Maeve. She's looking at picture books again. Completely oblivious to the clusterfuck I've created around her. "I haven't asked her yet."

"Yeah, well, she's going. Let her know."

"Trish, I need more time to come up with a lead-in. She's up for this really prestigious grant, and I don't want this to interfere—"

"Then get your shit together and figure out what's going to have to give."

I exhale. I *did* make a deal with her. And the Oscars isn't as big of a deal as the festival thing. Maybe we can even use it as a good stepping stone for the conversation about festivals. "Who am I presenting with?"

Maeve looks up then. She studies me for a moment before pulling another picture book off the shelf. I'm too far away to see the title, so I just focus on her neutral expression as she watches me. Neutral for now.

"Charlie, like you requested. That guy's gonna owe you his career when he's back on set."

My chest aches; Charlie's the one who got me the *Needlepoint* audition back before *Stroke* got all the award-season buzz. "I already owe him mine."

We end the call, and my screen returns to the group chat with Luna and Romy. Guilt gnaws at my chest a little more. I shouldn't keep what Trish said from Luna considering her stake in the movie. I send the information through to the group and stow my phone.

"You wouldn't happen to know their favorite dinosaur, would you?" Maeve asks.

I don't, and how dare my sister not tell us on the phone. I'm now getting a stabbing pain in my stomach, so strong it's hard to focus on speaking or using fine motor skills. I need to focus.

I text Gwyn, swiping out of a surprisingly quiet group chat to do it.

She replies almost instantaneously. Oz loves . . . eerr they're like water t-rexes? Lil loves stegos.

"What's the water carnivore dinosaur called?" I ask Maeve.

Maeve shrugs. But we very easily locate oversize stegosaurus and whatever-the-water-ones-are-called stuffed animals to go with a handful of picture books. I pull out my credit card as we reach the cashier. I need to stop driving myself up a wall about the film festivals. I don't have to screw Maeve over if we plan ahead. She might not be that mad about my not telling her earlier. It could all be okay.

"It's called a plesiosaur," the cashier says with a smile.

Well, thank god it wasn't a dinosaur I *should've* known. I smile back. "Thank you. That would've bugged me all day."

She hands back my credit card. "You two are really cute together, by the way."

No recognizing me. No weird looks. Just a normal person looking at my normal person relationship and thinking it's cute. Maybe I don't hate Pasadena all that much after all. In fact, as we walk back to the car, I consider asking Maeve if she wants to go to another shop around here—a local coffee shop or the soda fountain down the block. But I don't have time to say it out loud before we reach the parking lot.

I get into the car. Strap in. Set my phone in the charging dock, confirm Maeve's strapped in. Turn the engine on. Going to a coffee shop is just a distraction. I need to tell Maeve about the Oscars, and I know I won't do that unless we're alone.

Then my phone starts chiming with notifications.

Maeve looks at it. "Here, I can read . . ."

No. No, no, no—

"No, it's okay," I say. The words come out like a plea for help. Too little too late.

"Luna Roth is asking when you'll get more news," Maeve says.

Luna wasn't specific. Holy shit, Luna, *thank you.* "Thanks."

She sets the phone back, eyes bright. "Anything worth sharing?"

Okay, this is my window. "Just Oscars stuff. Charlie and I are presenting." No one would turn down the Oscars. I've had dozens of women beg me to bring them to the Oscars. "You're welcome to come as my plus one, by the way."

I wait, mentally begging for a yes.

I wait, but there's only silence. My stomach tightens as I focus harder on the road. Grip tighter on the steering wheel.

"That's . . . very public," Maeve says. "It's not that I don't want to go, but I'd— They'd write articles, right? Use my name?"

All concerns I should've considered before agreeing to get her to go. The pressure only increases. "Only if you wanted. There's a different red carpet normal people go down if they don't want to be on the main one with the celebs. The cameras will focus on me." I pry a hand off the wheel to rub the back of my neck. "My manager would love for you to go down the red carpet with me, but it's totally optional."

Maeve sighs. "I . . . don't know how that'd look with us working together. Is this something you want, or is your manager pushing it?"

"My manager." I say it quickly, even though I'm feeling a twinge of hurt at her answer.

"Well, look, I'll ask around the department about optics. But you can always tell your manager I agreed to go and then got sick the night of, right? I don't want her to keep bugging you waiting for me."

"Yeah, for sure."

My fingers twitch to text Mason, to fess up and then ask how big the fallout with Leonard would *really* be if Maeve and I didn't go extremely public. Trish and I could weather the blow. And hey, maybe Maeve will even come around and eventually say yes. In the scheme of things, mine aren't the worst headaches Trish's clients have given her. But I'm still on edge as we drive home.

If this is how Maeve reacts to one night out with me as a celebrity, is there any hope for she'll be understanding when she finds out I might have to go to festivals? What happens when she sees that I won't, *can't* choose her over my career if I have to be at a festival on the date of her observation class? My not having Maeve at the Oscars is a blow to what's left of my professional reputation, but my not being there for Maeve during the most important class of her career could make her lose that grant. The thing she said about seeing me as her intellectual match rings in my head. She said she really liked me, but are there caveats to that? Would she join me in future appearances, stuff I'm genuinely proud of, like Mason's indie or any future *Goodbye, Richard!* films? Maybe even join me late if *Oakley* gets into a festival, come to a future premiere? I've never had to think about bringing a significant other around these flashbulbs of joy in my career. Thinking of Maeve not being there stings.

My knuckles go white on the steering wheel as I drive us back to Hollywood Hills.

CHAPTER TWENTY-ONE

I don't think I've been this nervous to see the twins since they were born.

Which—fine, it's not really the twins. In fact, Oz and Lily are probably the ones who are going to warm up to Maeve the fastest. They're supposed to be the focus tonight, but I can't get the others out of my head. I also can't even get the fact that Maeve hasn't given me a definite reply about going to the Oscars yet out of my head, which isn't helping things.

But just like we'd talked about, when Maeve arrives at my place to head over to the party, she's ready to go. And even though I'd been planning to ask her if she'd made a decision about the Oscars the moment she got into my car, the time I spend prying my jaw off the car floor admiring her hot-but-family-appropriate black dress gives Maeve an opening, and she starts asking about my family before I can bring it up. And once someone gets me talking about the time back in middle school that I was fully convinced my dad was a serial killer because he was a dentist and I'd watched *Little Shop* one too many times, there's no getting me off the subject. Maeve's laugh is liquid gold, so it's not like I'm going to risk losing that to talk about the Oscars.

Not yet, anyway.

"I'm gonna say the presents are from both of us so they'll like you," I say as I steady the twins' rather large gifts in my arms.

Maeve shakes her head as she rings the doorbell of Gwyn's bougie Pasadena home. It has beautiful LA views, and, in fact, we once determined that she looked so far into the city that she could see Hollywood Hills. It's not quite as modern flashy as my house, but Maeve's getting a good idea of how far the wealth extends in my family. I can only hope it isn't deterring her.

"You have so little faith in my ability to win kids over," Maeve says.

"Well, from a four-year-old's perspective, you are the most boring person ever. You don't even get my *SpongeBob* references."

"My parents were no-TV parents, I'm *sorry.*"

It's around then that Gwyn answers the door, standing eye level with me thanks to her at least four-inch heels and my slip-on sneakers. Gwyn's brown eyes light up as she makes eye contact with Maeve.

"Thank you so much for coming," she says, flashing the sparkly white teeth she gets through being a responsible teeth owner rather than incessant badgering from her publicity team. "I feel like I'm meeting a legend at this point."

Maeve blushes, tucking a hair that isn't out of place behind her ear. "That's a gross overestimation of my impact on the larger world, but thank you."

I love that she starts using bigger words and more complicated phrases when she's nervous.

"Well, I'm thrilled you're here." Gwyn looks to me and grins. "I haven't seen Val smile like this in quite a while." She pats my back as we walk in, leaning in to whisper in my ear: "She's cute."

I fiddle with my jacket sleeve. "I showed you her photo last week."

But before Gwyn can justify her sudden crush on my girlfriend, Oz and Lily, dressed in adorable color-coordinated overalls, squeal as they rush into the room.

"Aunt Val!" they say in near perfect unison, grinning ear to ear.

The little monsters straight up jump onto me, forcing me to drop their presents in order to catch the two of them. Thank god for the minimal training Charlie and I have been doing, because they're starting to get a little heavy. But I nuzzle them into me and spin them around.

"Happy birthday to my favorite people on the planet!" I say through my own dopey grin. "How old are my peanuts?"

Lily says, "Four!" as Oz shoves four fingers into my face.

"That's amazing," I say as I give them each a kiss. I adjust them to keep them in my arms. At their age, I know it won't be long before they're squirming like beached flounders. "Before we get started, though, I want to introduce you two to someone very special." I turn all three of us to Maeve. "This is my girlfriend."

Lily takes the sunglasses off my head and puts them on as Oz studies Maeve.

"Hi, guys," Maeve says, making easy eye contact with the toddlers. "My name's Maeve. What's yours?"

"Ozzie," Oz says. He points to his sister. "That's Lily."

Lily gives a little wave, burrowing into me. Maeve smiles and gives a little wave back. My heart flutters at the sight.

"Presents?" Oz asks me.

I raise a brow. "I *think* that part comes after dinner and cake, doesn't it?"

Oz grins. "Not with you!"

Of course, Gwyn manages to catch only that part of the conversation as she, Dave, and my parents enter the room. With Lily starting to squirm, I let the twins run off. While Gwyn shoots me a brief *What the fuck is my son talking about?* look, I cycle through hugging my family. A quick *Hey, Dave* to my brother-in-law, a hug with a squeeze from my mom, and a hug-and-grab-my-jaw-to-evaluate-my-teeth combo from my dad.

"Dad, what the hell? Now?" I say as I wrestle out of his grasp. Like, in front of *Maeve*?

Dad belly laughs. "Can't let your new girlfriend worship you too much." He shakes Maeve's hand in that aggressive-white-man way of his. I squint at him; has he started *dyeing* his hair blond? He stopped being a natural blond when I was a kid. "So, are you from Val's fan club?"

Oh god *no*. "Dad!"

Gwyn and I lock eyes, and she rolls hers. "Dad, they work together at USC."

Maeve still manages a genuine smile. "I'm Maeve. It's a pleasure to meet you, sir."

After dry introductions in which Dave makes a point to say that every adult in the room is a doctor, Gwyn serves dinner. It's, naturally, kid-food central—sloppy joes, homemade cheesy tater tots, roasted broccoli. Food that simultaneously makes my mouth water and my chest tighten with the dread that comes before a panic attack. Red meat, grease, fried food, dairy, and cruciferous vegetables. All things I've been actively avoiding for—oh, a month. Just fuck me.

I feel Gwyn's gaze as Mom nods toward me. "I made you a kale salad, sweetie."

I give her a brief smile as I pass the broccoli to Maeve. Deep in conversation about Berkeley with Dave, she doesn't seem concerned in the least about the kid food. I'm between Maeve and Oz and Lily, which leaves me perfectly exposed for prolonged eye contact with Gwyn, Mom, and Dad. And I vowed to not drink tonight.

"Thanks," I say.

Gwyn is still eyeing me. "When's *Goodbye, Richard! 2* filming? Wouldn't expect Mason Wu to need you back in shape now."

I shrug as I try to serve myself enough kale to hide the fact that I've taken very little of anything else on the table. "It's never a bad idea to maintain."

Maeve nudges me with her shoulder. "Oh, come on, babe, you don't take nearly enough cheat days for how great you look right now."

It should make me feel better. Usually, Maeve's unwavering assurance that she'll find me attractive whether I have a six-pack or a belly is semi–world shattering. Still, I'm avoiding most of the food for IBS reasons; the salad, unfortunately, is my safest option.

"So, Maeve, Arko's a very Jewish last name," Mom says.

And like we're in a fucking slapstick comedy, I choke on the bite I was working on. I'm like full-on weak coughing, going red-faced at the table. Oz pats my shoulder.

"Yeah, my parents are from Boston and New York and moved to Ohio to teach," Maeve answers fluidly. She glances at me, head subtly tilted.

I scrape my dignity off the floor without missing another beat. "Mom, what if she *wasn't* Jewish?"

Mom grins. "I'm just so thrilled to see my Valeria with a grounded, smart young woman."

I want to say calling a thirty-two-year-old a young woman is weird, but I'm still kind of thinking about that Jewish comment.

"We were losing hope that it was going to happen for her."

Okay, Jewish comment officially forgotten for the gay comment.

I turn to the birthday kids, who really *should* be the focus right now anyway. "Oz, Lil, are you doing anything extra special this weekend? Your mom told me maybe you were going to LEGOLAND?" Their eyes light up when I say the magic words.

But before these poor children can answer, their *mom* has to butt into the other conversation.

"Jesus, Mom, can we leave out the gay remarks on my kids' birthday?" Gwyn comments.

Maeve exchanges a glance with me—*Guess your sister is a badass*—while my mom gets a little flustered.

"I meant her *celebrity*, Guinevere."

Gwyn goes right back to staring at me. I rip a piece of the white bread off my sloppy joe.

"Mama, we going to LEGOLAND?" Oz asks.

Gwyn shoots me a glare—they clearly weren't—before looking to the kids. "Sure, and maybe it can be a special thing with just you guys and Daddy."

Dave shoots Gwyn the same glare. "Or maybe *Aunt Val.*"

But Mom is not off her shit yet. She now turns to Maeve herself. "Jewish-parent curse, you know. Can't stop worrying about our babies."

When she really could be worrying about her *grandbabies* on their *birthday*.

Maeve just chuckles, though, diffusing the whole damn thing. "I get it. My parents didn't think it was going to happen for me either."

Dad puts an arm around Mom. "No, honestly, it wasn't even about Val. We knew she liked women too much to never *not* find someone. This is the girl who committed to watching every single episode of *X-Files* every night"—he *winks*—"because she absolutely worshipped Gillian Anderson."

What. The. Fuck.

"No, we just thought she'd end up with a complete idiot like Phoebe Wittmore."

Which, okay, I'm a *little* too embarrassed about the *X-Files* thing to focus on how brutally my father just dunked on my *Goodbye,*

Richard! costar. But—I repeat—what the fuck? They roasted me less at my own birthday dinner in October. Maybe it's time to legally separate from the family.

Maeve looks to me, an amused-as-shit smile plastered on her face. "Did Phoebe Wittmore hurt you?"

She starts to laugh as I go tomato red. "Isn't this a children's birthday dinner?" I mumble.

"Phoebe's nothing compared to some of the girls she's told us about over the years," Dad says.

"Finn!" Mom snaps, finally on my level.

A long beat of silence follows. Maeve knocks her foot against mine under the table. Reassuring, I think. If only I could be properly reassured that my parents wouldn't talk about my Hollywood exes anymore. Lily asks me for one of my tots, and I give her two. ·

Dave looks between Gwyn, who's still mildly pissed at me for the LEGOLAND thing, and me, who looks like I was choking two minutes ago. "So, Maeve, it must be weird, though, right? Being with someone as famous as Val?"

Just the conversation I need to lower my anxiety. Thanks, Dave.

Now Maeve's the one shifting her food around her plate. My stomach tightens, hard enough that I don't even think I can eat the kale.

"It's . . . strange, I suppose," Maeve says. "I've never dated anyone who's had more than three hundred Instagram followers, let alone a *platform*." Maeve looks at me. "There's a lot I don't know if I'll ever understand about it. I wish I could have her more to myself." She takes my hand. "But it's not like, a huge deal for me. I try not to think about it. I've just never really had any investment in celebrity culture."

She looks me in the eye, which I think is supposed to make me feel better about what she's saying, but my insides just go tighter, like an invisible rope is ripping through my flesh. "I see you for you," she says to me. Then she looks back at my family, who seem like they know *exactly* what Maeve means. "I wasn't like, a superfan of hers or anything before. I wasn't seduced by the glamor or fame or any of that. Just Val herself."

I know what she's trying to say. I believe she's telling the truth.

I just also know the subtext of what she's saying. She's saying that there are very specific parts of me she likes. Hell, even if she *loves* those parts, there's a lot she could do without. Including fame. Also known as the thing I can't just work away with therapy.

Dave coughs a laugh. "Guess Val isn't taking you to the Oscars to impress you, then."

Fucking *Dave*!

Another bout of silence fills the room as the adults look to Maeve. Like we've already decided what we're doing and they're waiting for her to tell them.

But she isn't speaking.

She isn't speaking and it's saying volumes.

"I'll be right back," I say.

I used to obsessively read reviews of *Stroke,* as though I was begging any- and everyone with an internet connection to explain to me why the hell I won an Oscar for my first role when it seemed so unfair. One of the reviews had described the *subtlety* in my performance, how emotion came across in the smallest movements of my body and face. How grounded my performance felt. How real confrontations weren't about screaming and flipping tables.

I guess I follow my own school of acting as my "storm out" looks exactly like I got up to go to the bathroom—there's no outward expression of how crushed I am other than how quietly and swiftly I leave.

I manage to sit in the powder room for about twenty seconds, trying to breathe in the diffuser they put in there, until Gwyn ever-so-quietly knocks on the door. I open it a crack, just enough for her to slip in.

"To keep this from becoming a huge deal, I told them I'm checking on the cake. Let's make this quick and effective, yeah?" Gwyn says after she shuts the door behind her.

I take a seat on the floor. Gwyn joins me. "First of all, are you feeling okay, physically? I noticed you picking at your food. Are you having a flare-up?"

I can't help but smile as I blush. "Sort of."

Gwyn frowns. "When's the last time you had life-inconveniencing symptoms?"

"December."

Gwyn puts a hand on my shoulder. "Val, it's the second week of January. Please go back to your normal diet and tell Rosalie about this."

I take a deep breath, and the claws of anxiety start to slip off. "Okay."

"I'm following up on that, by the way." She exhales. "Can I guess what stress is inducing your symptoms?"

I hold my gaze heavy on the bathmat. "I just— I really do think Maeve likes me and it's been so, I don't know, *healthy* for me to be dating someone who isn't in the industry. But there was this slight with a *Goodbye, Richard!* producer that Trish is gunning for me to remedy by getting Maeve to go to the Oscars with me. But look at her. Sometimes I just think she only likes my personality and looks or whatever but is compartmentalizing the fact that I'm famous and actively hates that. I mean, at least people like Phoebe understood what fame is like and wouldn't think twice about this posturing I have to do." I pause, the words heavy on my tongue. "I've been thinking of quitting acting for a while, but to do that, I have to finish fulfilling my obligations to Mason, and I thought—I thought I could do that and commit to Maeve and academia."

Gwyn takes a deep breath. "I really like Maeve. I think she's quick-witted and intelligent enough for you not to get bored quickly, yet grounded, and she has a calming energy that balances you." She frowns. "But if she can't handle your fame, I don't think she likes you enough."

A chill runs down my spine.

"Look, none of us are thrilled about how fame affects you. The amazing acting and humanitarian career you've set up, yes, we love that. But I don't *really* like the way people try to control what you say, how you look, your work-life balance. I don't really like having to be concerned that my kids will be photographed by strangers when they're spending normal bonding time with their aunt. But you know what? This shit is ten times harder on you, and I love you so much and want you to be okay. So I'll go to your tedious award shows whenever you need me." She takes my hand. "And if Maeve doesn't realize that she has to support you unequivocally, even if it's temporary, through the truckloads of bullshit, then I don't think she's right for you."

I take a deep, slow breath as I hold back tears. "Gwyn, I like her so much . . ."

Gwyn gets to her feet. "Just be careful, okay? But I'll try to give her the benefit of the doubt. Your fame shit is insane."

I hug her. "Thanks."

"Put the twins to bed tonight and we'll be even," she says, winking.

I massage the tension out of my shoulders as I return to the table.

Maeve smiles up at me when I sit back down, seemingly oblivious to the fact that anything happened. Dinner continues with a few less awkward conversations: more basic information about Maeve's family, Ohio, her PhD journey, and then she asks Dave *far* more questions about hospital administration than I've asked the guy in the six years I've known him. The twins tear into the homemade birthday cake and rip through presents as Gwyn dutifully photographs their every micro expression.

By the time Gwyn's lovingly demanded that they get in their pajamas, brush teeth, and head into their room for bedtime, I'm starting to think Gwyn's still annoyed about LEGOLAND and put me in charge of bedtime as a punishment. Yeah, *of course* I'll be able to get two sugar-high toddlers to bed.

"Read dino book?" Lily asks as the two of them run back into the living room, where my dad's handing out coffee. She holds out the stack of picture books Maeve and I picked out.

"Aunt Maeve too?" Oz asks, joining her.

My heart does a big leap on that one. It throws me a little off-balance, but when I look at Maeve she's smiling.

She gets down into a squat to make proper eye contact with my nephew. "I'd love to."

So *Maeve* and I take on the task of putting two sugar-high toddlers to bed. And she's amazing with them, doing voices to read the book and letting the kids snuggle into her as she reads. Any doubts I was having about our relationship are washed away.

Oz eventually falls asleep in his bed with me beside him, Lily in Maeve's arms. The bed creaks when I get out of it, and Maeve bites back a laugh, putting a finger to her lips. We pad our way outside to Lily's room, where Maeve tucks Lily into bed, and we both make our way back into the main hallway.

And I can't stop thinking of the image of Maeve holding Lily.

Maybe it's the fucking estrogen in my hormonal body, but I'm pretty sure men don't get as head-over-heels with adoration/desire/*fuck me I love this person* seeing a woman with a baby, but ooh boy.

I sure as shit do. I'm suddenly drowning in the feel-good chemicals, making it difficult to move, to fully take in what I'm seeing, to hear anything around us. It's just Maeve. Maeve, whom I so deeply want to be my future. I feel more strongly about her than I've felt about anyone ever, even Emily. It's suddenly so clear, how naive I was back then. How I thought any good feeling I had would stay forever because I had it in the moment. Even when I don't feel good with Maeve—which, frankly, I'm still anxious about the Oscars— I still care about her. Every step she takes makes my heart flip.

"Thanks," I say.

"Of course. They're really sweet kids."

As we head back into the hallway, back into the adult world, that air of serenity seems to diffuse. Maeve's easy smile fades. Her gaze is heavy on me, but she doesn't say anything for what feels like forever.

"So do I have to buy a dress for the Oscars?" Maeve asks.

My heartbeat all but stops.

Moments pass. My heartbeat returns, quicker, frantic. "What changed your mind?"

"Well, I guess I should slow down," Maeve says. "I did ask around the department, and the general consensus is that we can date; that's fine. I'm sorry it took so long, but I was trying to be thorough with who I asked."

In that moment, thinking about Maeve going with me to the Oscars, thinking about Trish not being mad at me and my not having to ask Mason if I pissed anyone important off, I can't feel the sting of losing a potential rec letter. I can't quite grapple with what that means yet, but I know my answer. "No, that's fine. I'd still love for you to go with me. I— Thank you."

"There isn't a huge time commitment prior to the event, right?"

Was that why she was so hesitant? "No, as a presenter, I go to like one rehearsal."

She exhales. "Okay. With the new semester starting this week, I know it's selfish but I was . . . a bit concerned."

I brush her hand. "Don't be." I'll be enough of that for both of us.

Maeve gives a tiny smile and nudges me with her shoulder. "So, the dress?"

"Uh, no. You—they dress me in custom dresses by designers usually. They'd make you one too. So we'd, uh, match."

Maeve nods slowly. "Okay."

"It's ridiculous, I know, but—"

Concern floods Maeve's features as she grabs my hand. "No, I'm just"—she laughs, lighting up my heart—"nervous about wearing something that expensive."

I let my gaze fall away from Maeve, where I make eye contact with Gwyn. She's shamelessly eavesdropping like we're kids again, and I should be annoyed, but her beaming smile spreads right to me. My breathing and my heart rate slow, and the stomach pains are finally gone.

I squeeze Maeve's hand. "Charlie literally picked me two feet off the ground at last year's Oscars and my gown didn't rip. You're going to be fine."

She smiles. "Can't wait to see you in your original element."

It's going to go perfectly. There's no other choice.

Because if I have it my way, it'll be the first event out of many.

CHAPTER TWENTY-TWO

The rest of January and February pass by in a blur. Rosalie recommends some nonprescription antianxiety supplement that dampens my anxiety enough. The new semester starts, and our class is free from problem students, and Maeve and I are a perfectly oiled two-women show. I take a wide-eyed Maeve to fittings in boutiques where we're the only ones inside to be offered champagne. I teach her how to pose for a camera until she's on the floor laughing because *apparently* the juxtaposition of me in full femme glitz mode while wearing a flannel, a T-shirt I'd just gotten a coffee stain on, and jeans is *too much.* She's a great sport, even seems to be a little swept up in the glamor, and it's such a relief after the hiccup of the initial ask.

Meanwhile *Oakley in Flames* doesn't come up once. Mason calls and says she's 55 percent sure that the studio execs will let us have a gay kiss in *Goodbye, Richard! 2,* and she still doesn't mention Leonard. Once Charlie's name is announced as an Oscars presenter, he starts leaving the house for more auditions.

Good. Everything is *good* as Charlie, Maeve, and I get into a tinted-window Escalade. Of course Charlie looks sharp in his suit, and I did tell him he looked great to boost his self-esteem, but god I can't keep my eyes off Maeve. She's in a deep-red satin gown, which is tight around her waist and chest without exposing any tit and has this gorgeous sequined black-rose design that covers the top and then spreads lightly downward, exposing more of the red at the bottom of the dress. Someone was getting really cheeky putting me in a black sequin gown with a halter neckline and a thigh-high slit. She wears a diamond necklace, and I wear a bracelet and earrings from the same set, so we're basically high-end coordinated for prom. And lord, she can't keep the smile off her face as she runs her fingers along the fabric of the dress.

"I still can't believe this is happening," she says. Charlie's sitting up front chatting with the driver, Jordan, leaving Maeve and me in our own little world in the middle row.

I smile. "You look stunning."

"You look like you're actually supposed to be on TV tonight."

I run my hand through my newly cut hair. It was stuck somewhere between an undercut and a bob, and my stylist opted for giving me a clean undercut that emphasizes the length on top. I like it; it leaves that gorgeous Grace Kelly bob style for Maeve.

"Are you nervous?" I ask.

She tries to give a blasé shrug, but her dress accentuates the fact that she's shaking. "I'm still not sure what to do with all the cameras."

I chew on my inner cheek; can't wreck the lipstick. "Did you go to prom?"

"Yeah."

I take her hand. "Then think of this like prom but with a bunch of rich theater kids."

Maeve laughs, her breath gradually slowing down. "I'll try." Her hand drops back to her lap.

But it turns out the red carpet isn't even the most stressful part of the night. That's picking up Romy and Luna from their apartment.

They're both in suits, and it's honestly adorable, but I really didn't anticipate having a physical reaction to seeing Luna all dressed up. My chest tightens trying to figure out how to greet your ex appropriately with your new girlfriend sitting in the car. Luckily, makeup limits us to those air-cheek-kisses.

"Hey, thank you so much for this," Luna says, gesturing to the tickets I got her, as we pull out of our hug. Romy's already given me a courteous fist bump and climbed into the back row.

"No problem," I say, flashing a more charming smile than I intended. I guess I haven't gotten those out of my system with her.

Maeve looks back to chat with Romy as everyone puts their seat belts back on.

"So did you take over QuASA for Leland at SC?" Romy asks.

Maeve nods. "Yeah, I think like two years ago? Took long enough; the guy still thought *queer* was a slur."

"Romy," Luna says. "Enough with the inquisition. We haven't even introduced ourselves."

Romy laughs. "Maeve seems cool." Romy holds their hand out, and she and Maeve shake. "I'm Romy, Luna's partner and the only person in this car validating Val's belief that Mothman is real."

Maeve gives me a look. "Mothman?"

"Those kids saw Mothman *twice*," is all I have to say about that.

"I'm Luna," Luna says without offering Maeve her hand. "I'm Valeria—Val's—"

She's gonna try to just say *friend*. "Ex," I say. Better to break the tension now. "Friend now."

"Friend always," Charlie says emphatically. "We gotta start feeding that narrative instead of the cradle robber one, Sully."

"She was twenty-four!" I say at the same time as Luna says, "I was twenty-four!"

Maeve just watches, an amused smile on her face. "You two have strangely similar energy."

Romy throws their hands up. "Exactly! A Libra and Gemini *can't function together!*"

Okay, for all that this is becoming a roast, I'm relieved. Maeve doesn't seem threatened by Luna. Good. Now I just need to let Charlie shine during our award presentation and this night will be a success—

"Okay, let's just get it all out there," Maeve says. "What's the craziest thing you two have done?"

The car feels twenty degrees hotter, and I'm stuck to the seat. I don't dare look back at Luna. "Uh . . ." Fuck, does her crying naked on my living room floor count? "I gave her a hand job in an Uber."

As Jordan stiffens from the rearview mirror, Romy and Charlie laugh. Maeve stares at me, blinking. She's clearly stunned. And now I'm suddenly not so sure she meant sex when she said "craziest thing."

"Was it at least an Uber Black?" Charlie asks.

"X," I reply.

"Cheapskate!"

"It wasn't *necessary.*" Embarrassment has created a gunk that's blocking my arteries, and my blood has to slog through it.

"Also that's fucking *wrong*," Romy says. "How can you not say the time you coated Luna's lips in ghost pepper sauce during the hot wing thing?"

"It was Trinidad scorpion sauce!" Luna says, surprisingly indignant.

Charlie keeps going. "Oh my god, Luna, do you know what happened to Val *after that*?"

That piece of shit—

"They don't need to know that!" I interject.

"Have you ever seen a person after they survive a rare river parasite? When their intestines are just *decimated*," Charlie continues.

"Oh my god, I'm so sorry," Luna says, genuinely apologetic.

"Get out of the fucking car, Charlie!" I snap.

But Maeve's laughing right along with Romy and Charlie. She makes eye contact with me, and I see joy in her eyes, not jealousy. "Why would you *do* that?" she asks.

I shake my head. "I don't wanna talk about it."

But I have to admit, as she gives my hand a squeeze, I do feel better that she brought it up. It's good to know she's not the jealous type. I feel a relief like no other. It affects the rest of the car ride, bringing about a warm, joking mood. We all exchange Hollywood stories and supernatural theories, and Charlie and I give the others our best Oscars survival tips.

By the time we arrive on the red carpet, I almost can't hear the roar of cameras, reporters, and whatever the hell else is going on outside. I start my deep breathing as Luna, Romy, and Charlie exit the car. Charlie gives me a particularly long smile and a thumbs-up.

Then it's just Maeve and me.

Maeve, who I know is completely out of her element but is doing this for me. Maeve, who, despite the fact that she's visibly shaking, takes my hand and squeezes it.

"Ready, babe?" I ask.

Maeve nods. Still, she's gone from shaking to rapid breathing. Not so ready.

"Focus on my breathing," I say, keeping my voice calm, gentle. "Try to copy what I'm doing." I take her hand and put it over my chest.

And as her breathing gradually slows to match mine, all I can do is stare at her in awe.

Maeve put both me and my ex at ease for my sake. Maeve ran Queer and Ally Student Assembly and thinks my being a paranormal conspiracy theorist is the most entertaining thing she didn't know about me. Maeve looks absolutely incredible in a dress that matches mine. Maeve's ready to go out there and be paraded around for me despite how terrifying this clearly is for her. She's ready to tell the world that she's mine, that I'm hers. In public. In *public-public*. After everything she's done for me, I'm going to be there for her. For everything.

I take one last deep breath, my heart hammering. "I love you."

She's in shock for a second. One, two, my stomach dropping, three—

Then she smiles. Full grin, cheeks pink, I've-never-seen-her-this-elated smile. "I love you too."

Hearing those four words gives me more courage than any alcohol, drug, or the hundreds of strangers outside cheering could do. I know there's pandemonium around us. I do. I avoid the bumps in the red carpet and blink back the dots in my vision after each camera flash. But it doesn't matter. For the first time ever, when I step onto this red carpet, I can't see the crowds and chaos around me. It's just Maeve, who follows my lead as I gently hold her hand. We arrived late enough that the reporters are distracted by others and aren't dogpiling trying to get to me. We move to the fork where celebrities separate from their normie guests for photos. I let go of Maeve's hand.

"Whatever you feel comfortable with," I say.

She takes my hand back. "Let's go."

I mean, hell, she looks gorgeous enough that people are gonna ask if she's from some movie they don't remember.

The choruses of "Valeria!" start, making my name not sound like my name anymore. The requests for a shot of "just me" come pretty fast. I glance at Maeve; she nods back. Even though it's the last thing

I want to do, I step a few feet from her. A clean shot for the dozens of cameras.

I go through the motions, adjust the way I stand, where I put my hands, how I angle my chin, and how I screw my face up to give my neutral glamor look. Give a few practiced smiles. Accidentally throw up a peace sign.

"Valeria, who's the girl?" Shayne, one of the reporters I actually recognize and kind of like, says.

"My girlfriend."

Out of the corner of my eye, I note how Maeve remains relaxed as I say the word out loud. So far, so good.

"Can we get some photos?"

I look to Maeve again; she nods. But she's shaking again as I put my arm around her. "If you're worried about your face, kiss my cheek. You always look good that way."

"Lipstick?" she asks.

"It's transfer-proof."

She puts her arm around me, slowly relaxing into familiar territory. She looks to me, and copies what I do. No smiles at first, but neither of us can keep from them long. She kisses my cheek once, very quickly, though, clearly not in the full mood for hamming it up for the camera. Some of the photographers whoop.

I look over at Shayne, who smirks and asks, "Can we get a full kiss? For the gays." A little joke between us that yes, I'm fully aware she's gay too. "And name?"

I turn to Maeve, heart in my throat. It's such a simple gesture, one we've done so many times, but I still feel like I'm on the downward slope of a roller coaster as I swoop in to kiss her. Closed mouth, my hands on her cheeks as she leaves hers around my waist. Her lips are so soft, and I feel so secure in her arms. It makes my heartbeat thrum and I get into it, kiss her a little longer than I probably should.

The photographers all look to Maeve. Her grip on me tightens. She opens her mouth, but her voice just cracks.

"Maeve Arko," I say as we pull away.

But I don't look at the photographers. I focus on Maeve, searching her features for any distress. Is this too much too soon, was that too long a kiss, anything. But she looks relieved. More than that. She's got a smile plastered on her face, and she's looking at me like I'm the only person in this crowded venue.

She leans in to whisper to me. "I've never had someone cheer for my PDA."

I giggle, my hand naturally falling to her arm even though we're separated now.

And it hits me.

I'm on the red carpet with a woman. I'm on the red carpet and I don't have to pretend I'm dating Charlie or that I just wanted to bring my family. I'm on the red carpet with my *girlfriend*. We love each other, and we just kissed and the people around us cheered. Me, a girl, kissed my *girlfriend* on the red carpet, and nothing bad is happening.

Three years of agony, three years that nearly took everything from me, and it's over. I never have to do that again. After so long thinking I'd never make it to the next day, let alone get to the other side, a place where I was happy. And now I'm there. I'm on that other side. I can finally be *myself* up here and everything is okay. It's a spark of good in those months where I wondered if the invasive questions made coming out worth it at all.

I know it right then and there. It was all worth it.

I'm trying to blink back the tears, but they're slipping down my cheeks.

"Aw, Val," Maeve says. She reaches over and blots my tears. I hope I didn't wreck my makeup.

The camera clicks snap around us, but it's over so fast. The tears are gone, I've checked my makeup in a compact and it's fine, and Maeve and I are walking toward the entrance to the Dolby hand in hand.

I can't believe this is my life now.

I think Maeve's enjoying herself. I hope she is. So far she's gotten through the first half of the infamously long program. I get a camera recording some of my too-honest facial reactions to the usual weird shit they always pull. I'm actually in a decent mood but, as usual, by the time Charlie and I go up to present Best Supporting Actress, I'm starving (fuck when they stopped having late-night hosts try to out-perform each other by delivering us food mid-show) and I'm ready to book it. In fact, if Maeve doesn't want to go to an after-party, I think we'll just go get food and head home.

Even though I've been doing public speaking for a long time now, being in front of this audience, knowing any flub I make *will* be part of a BuzzFeed article in two seconds, I'll admit my heart's racing a little. There's a teleprompter I can still sort of see without my glasses, but the nerves are present and accounted for. I slide my glasses on. I can *just* see out of the corner of my eye Charlie leaning toward the mic.

"Just for some behind-the-scenes trivia, this is all scripted and she's only wearing those to look hot," Charlie says, easily improving as usual.

I shoot him a look as everyone laughs. I'm intending to jokingly slap his wrist away, but I end up making the *fucking envelope* uncer-emoniously tumble to the ground. The crowd's laughter only gets louder as I put my hands over my face, half in shock and half to hide any changes to my complexion.

"Jesus Christ," Charlie says as I bend down and *slip forward*, spending one heart-stopping moment where I'm convinced I'm falling off the stage—

Until Charlie catches me, securing me with one arm while he swoops the envelope into his hand with the other. "I swear you will be back in your girlfriend's loving arms in a minute. No need to swan-dive off the stage."

At that moment, it's like my body reboots. My heart slows a bit. I'm alive, and I feel weirdly secure in Charlie's arms, despite where we are. Everyone bursts into laughter, including, fuck, *me*. I'm still laughing as I look from Maeve in the audience to the teleprompter to Charlie's joyful fucking face. And I too feel some form of joy coursing through my veins—and, okay, maybe it's really horror-filled adrenaline disguised as joy—but it *feels* good. I compose myself, look to the very boring opening for Best Supporting Actress, and pull myself together long enough to say, "And the nominees for Best Supporting Actress are . . ." and list off the names.

And the moment is actually really nice. To my utter delight, my on-screen child in *Stroke* wins her first Oscar, at age twelve, and she, Charlie, and I are able to share a little hug mid-moment. Maeve's grinning when I return to my seat. I hand her a napkin full of cheese and carrot sticks I found backstage, and she hands me her phone.

"You and Charlie are trending," she says.

My stomach pinches as I pull up the first article. But it reads, "10 Best Parts of the Oscars So Far . . ." and it talks about how charming Charlie is and how we have great chemistry. They mention Charlie's gay comment along with a link to another article.

This one talks about Maeve and me on the red carpet. How heartwarming it was to see me burst into tears of joy with Maeve.

I grab Maeve's hand as I give her phone back. "Thanks for coming with me," I whisper, and kiss her cheek.

The awards wrap up, and Maeve and I decide not to go to an after-party. With our hands *just* touching thighs, teasing, her head resting on my shoulder, our designer heels knocking against one another, we know no bottle-popping after-party can compare to what we can do together.

Luna and Romy are overjoyed to get my tickets to the *Goodbye, Richard!*'s studio's after-party, and tell me they plan to meet Wyatt and one of his coworkers there. Even *I'm* a little overjoyed seeing them practically skip toward the venue hand in hand in their matching suits, so clearly in their own world. When Mason texts me asking if I'll be there and I say I'm ducking out early, she just responds with a bunch of taco emojis. Charlie asks if he can bring someone home, and I think I say something along the lines of "I'm not your mom; you decide" as Maeve and I step into our Escalade.

Once we're inside, we put our seat belts on like everything's normal. We each managed one free glass of champagne on practically empty stomachs, but I feel loopy with her around. I almost repeat history and unbuckle my seat belt to reach under her dress, but I'm too sober for *that*. I settle for grabbing her hand.

"Did you have fun?" I ask.

She smiles. "Honestly?"

I nod.

"It was a lot more boring than I remember it being when I watched it on TV. But you and Charlie made it completely worth it."

"I'm glad you came."

"I am too. Thank you for, you know, giving me the opportunity of a lifetime."

"Eh, you'll be forced to come back next year." I feel like I've released a kite that's caught the wind right away. It's more a wisp of a fantasy, but I doubt Maeve will remember when we're both teaching in a year, Hollywood in the past.

When the drive ends, Maeve and I move effortlessly to my house, up my stairs, into the serenity of my bedroom. We kick off our shoes, but then the momentum screeches to a dead halt.

"Val, how the hell do we get these dresses off?" Maeve asks.

I smirk. "Very carefully."

"I'm not touching yours."

I chuckle. "Fine." I locate the zipper on mine easily, step out of it carefully, and hang it up on the hanger the designer gave us. Then, in nothing but some pasties and a black thong, I move to Maeve. I grab her shoulders and run my fingers down the lengths of her arms. "It's back here."

I plant a firm kiss on the nape of her neck. My own heart thumps as her hairs stand on end. Slowly, *achingly* slowly, I kiss down her spine. With each brush of my lips, she sighs. With my body pressed to hers, our heartbeats reverberate off each other's skin. Finally, when her skin is hot, her breath quick under me, I unzip her dress. I slip the dress off her as gently as she handles everything in her possession and hang it up. She tears the pasties off delicately as I remove my own, throw them into a nearby trash can. She turns to me, and it's like a fucking movie. I've never seen anyone more gorgeous in my life, and I never *want* to see anyone else.

I smile. "Now that *that's* over with . . ."

I slam her into the nearest wall. Her sighs turn to moans as we kiss, lick, and bite, as we all but rip the panties off each other. As we fall onto the bed, hands migrating to legs, asses, the supple skin between our legs, the moans only increase. We rip open my drawer. Yank out the harness underwear, the strap, a bullet vibrator. I slide the harness on, stuff the vibe and dildo in, and smile down at Maeve as she opens up for me.

"I love you," she says as I enter her.

"I love you too."

I can't wait to say that later tonight, tomorrow morning, maybe even for the rest of our lives.

It plays like a chorus in my head, provides a tune for my every movement, the way our hands clasp together, the way our lips come together and don't separate as we moan into each other's mouths. We clutch each other, scratching nails against soft skin and pushing bruises into shoulders and waists as we come together hard, arching into each other. Like there's no peace until we're as close to each other as possible.

We could have every inch of skin touching and I swear we wouldn't be close enough. Being inside her isn't close enough. Telling her my every secret and asking her to cradle my most vulnerable self doesn't feel like enough.

In that moment as I catch my breath, I realize that I haven't taken the fullest extent of her touch.

"Hey, Maeve?" I say as I pull off the strap.

"Yeah?"

I put my hand over my heart. But maybe it's time to embrace its racing. "I want you inside me." The words taste like honey on my lips. I can't fucking believe I'm saying them.

She raises her eyebrows. "Really?"

I take her hand. "Yeah." I bite my lip. "I probably can't take much, but . . ."

"Yeah. I mean, sure, of course." She smiles, leans in so her breath is tickling my ear. "It'd be my pleasure," she says, her voice turning into that growl I've fantasized about since I met her.

I roll onto my back. "Can I see you, though?" I ask.

She leans over to kiss my nose. "Of course." She scoots back, sitting on her feet in front of my legs. "Let me know if you want me to go slower, faster, pull out. It's no big deal if you're not feeling it."

I exhale. "Okay."

She slides a single finger down the middle of my body, from my throat, between my tits, past my scar, curling into a circle around my clit. My breath catches in my throat as I buck against her touch.

She barely grazes the skin inside. I tighten up instinctually, force myself to take another breath and relax. Maeve gives me a little smile and slides her whole finger in.

"This okay?" she asks.

The weird thing is, *yeah,* it is. It's—I don't know if I'd say pleasurable yet. But she's inside me, nothing hurts, and—and, well, that's it. Maeve's *inside me.* Another girl hasn't been inside me since Emily, and every session with her was far more grit-my-teeth-and-wait-for-it-to-end than good. Maeve draws gentle circles inside me as her other fingers circle around my clit.

"Yeah, it's fine." My breath hitches again as she hits a particularly sensitive spot. "It's nice."

"I'm glad," she says, her voice soft, gentle even.

My muscles strain around her finger, my breath quickening. It feels familiar in a way, but . . . more. Like my skin is tingling more than it usually does, my muscles are growing more taut with Maeve's touch. It feels similar to what usually happens, but there's something else there. I wish I could remember if the G-spot is just an extension of the clit or something else entirely. I'm pretty sure the former. And I'm—Jesus, Maeve curls her fingers in and presses them against my wall, and my brain shuts the fuck up. Because that, combined with whatever magic's she's doing outside, that really *is* amazing.

"God, you're wet," she says. "Do you want another finger?"

I exhale. "Yes."

Another goes in. I never thought it'd actually feel good.

She leans down to kiss me. Tender, heavy, wanting.

"I love you," she says.

"I love you too," I echo as she goes back inside me.

It's okay. Bearable.

And she goes back to the pulsing motion she was doing before. And that bearable turns to good turns to *fucking great*.

"I'm crazy for you, you know," I swallow. "I've wanted to tell you that I love you for months. So much before tonight."

"I did too," she says. "I can't believe I get to do this."

And then sex turns into the kind of frenzy I so rarely find myself in.

And when I do come, it's like a fucking hurricane. Lightning bolts through me, my upper half crunches all the way up. The pleasure rips from between my legs, into my belly, down to my toes. I grab on to Maeve's arms, bury my face into her chest. And when the pleasure moves from a storm to a patter of rain, I savor the sound of her heart racing in her chest.

I flop onto the bed, pulling Maeve into me as the feeling wanes.

"Better?" Maeve asks.

I grin. "The best I've ever had," I take her hand, "I wouldn't have wanted it with anyone else."

"I'm so glad," Maeve says.

I kiss the back of her neck one last time.

I hold her and savor the moment for a bit. The sharp floral scent of her perfume mixed with the subtle smell of sweat. How soft her skin is. How her hair is a little stiff from the hair spray my stylist used on her, but how it also smells like flowers as I dig my face into it.

Somewhere in the background, my phone's ringing. But I don't feel any particular need to answer it.

CHAPTER TWENTY-THREE

An alarm wakes me up at a time that I just know in my bones is *much* earlier than I want it to be. And true to form, my nervous system's immediate response to such a surprise is to startle like a fish out of water. Complete with a sound that doesn't quite form the word *what* as I move smack into Maeve. Our heads hit. Hopefully hers hurts less than mine does, but it's not *exactly* what I was going for after the night we had.

I rub my forehead.

"I'm sorry! I forgot to turn off my alarm from yesterday," she says as she turns to silence it. She rolls back over and surveys me. Then she starts laughing. "Babe, are you okay?"

I laugh. "You hit my ego harder."

She pulls me in to a hug, nuzzling into the crook of my neck. "Your ego's too big, so consider it a blessing."

I kiss the crown of her head. "Says the fucking academic." I glance over at the clock on my nightstand—7:00 a.m. "What were you doing at seven?"

We scoot back apart to talk. But I take her hand, running my thumb over the soft skin between each of her knuckles.

"I try to run and get some writing done before nine most mornings."

I smile. "I learn something new about you every day. We should go running sometime."

"Do you usually get up this early, though?"

"To see your face, I would wake up at any hour." I pull her hand to my mouth and kiss it. My heart speeds up as she blushes. I make Maeve Arko blush. It still blows my mind every time it happens.

She scoots in a little closer, raising her free hand to run her thumb along my jawline. "Thank you for last night."

I chuckle. The comment, despite everything, makes *me* blush. "I think I'm the one who should be thanking you."

Then she frowns. The smallest micro change in her expression and my chest tightens. "No, it's—" She sighs. "It was one of the things Fiona did to me. I always leaned toward switch, went more back and forth with the girls I dated in high school. But when I tried to tell Fiona I didn't want to bottom all the time, she'd just laugh and say bottoming was what I liked doing with men anyway."

The ache tugs from deep inside me, pressing my heart against my ribs. The type of pain she's describing can't be soothed by massaging it the way you would with most parts of the body. It's trapped behind her rib cage, deep in her heart. I settle for squeezing her hand tighter. "Maeve, I'm sorry—"

Maeve cocks her head at me. "What're you apologizing for?" She pauses a moment. "You know, I'm not the only one who has some relationship trauma. If there's ever anything I can do to make you feel better, please know I want to."

"No, there's—" I exhale. "Emily was a lot like Fiona. It wasn't about sexuality, but there was a right and wrong way to be. I avoided bottoming for so long because when she would do it to me, it would be more about her doing something to me than me actually enjoying it. But you make me want to try new things again. I felt safe in what you were doing."

"That's awful that she let sex be something so selfish. You're so generous in so much of your life. The least I can do is make you feel heard."

There's a moment of silence between us. "Do you hate that I'm a celebrity?"

She sits up, really staring at me a moment, the sleepiness gone from her eyes. "No, of course not. It goes hand in hand with the work you do. Work that is, by the way, incredible. I do, though, worry about the mental toll it must take on you. Anyone, really."

"My loved ones?"

She kisses me on the forehead. "I'll be fine," she mutters, burying her face in my skin.

"I love you," I say. "I love that you're bisexual. I love that you're a switch, that you have a PhD, that you're Jewish and kind of tall and have really pretentious movie opinions."

She nuzzles into me. "Val . . ."

"Nope, I love it. I love every infuriating thing about you too."

"I love you." She sighs, her body rising and falling against me. I swear I can feel her smile against my skin. "I love your charisma, the way you light up every room you're in. Your suaveness, the nerdy way you share your passions. Your PhD, your mixed faith, your gayness. The friendship I see you give, how cute your dog is, how athletic you are, and . . ." She pauses. "How you understand the bad stuff in our pasts."

I understand. God, it's like the ten-thousand-pound weight that's been on me for years is gone, those words have carried it away. Tears well and fall from my eyes. There's a twist of embarrassment, but I can hardly feel it. It's just me and Maeve, making heavy, intense, borderline religious-experience eye contact. A moment of perfect empathy.

I don't know if the moment passes so much as at some point during our silent meditation, my stomach growls so loudly that we start giggling and decide it's time to get out of bed.

"Wait, so are you off your celebrity diet?" Maeve asks as we head downstairs.

The smell of coffee has permeated the first floor. I wonder which beefcake Charlie has taken home this year. That's the nice thing about Charlie—he picks out these really airheaded pretty boys for hookups, so conversation is always easy and amusing the morning after. Personally, I hope Charlie eventually marries someone with more substance, but I'm glad he hasn't had to deal with the pain and anguish I've gone through with some of my partners.

"Yeah," I reply. "And I'm kinda mad I gave you fridge leftovers between rounds instead of properly wining and dining you."

She shrugs, smirking. "We were busy." She licks her lips. "But assuming you didn't throw away any of the groceries we bought last week, I can make us something special if you want."

Seeing that playful smile on her face has mine lighting up. "Like what?"

"Bananas foster French toast is my specialty."

I can't thank Jewish God enough for giving me this woman who can make me orgasm in two distinctly different ways. "Please."

Maeve goes into hyperfocus mode, gathering her cooking ingredients as I size up Charlie and Mr. Wonderful. Mr. Wonderful, who turns out to be . . . Jordan from last night. His light brown skin and perfect teeth glow in what I can only assume is happiness after a great night with my best friend. But one look at me and his joy turns to horror. He's full-on avoiding eye contact with me as he squeaks out a greeting.

"Hey, Val," he says.

"Hey, Jordan," I reply. Well, *this* is a pleasant surprise. The last time I rode with Jordan, about a year ago, he told me he was driving rich people around while working on a master's in social work. Definitely more substance than a Hollywood beefcake. I move my gaze to Charlie, who just seems . . . lighter. So much lighter than I've seen him in a long time. "How was the after-party?" I ask him.

He shrugs. "Eh, like any after-party. Trish and I talked for a while."

My heart leaps. "Is she thinking of poaching you?"

Technically, managers and agents aren't supposed to start promising clients jobs until after they've formally left their other representation, but the industry is pretty cutthroat.

Charlie shrugs. "She seems more interested than she has before. She was genuinely angry that *Star Trek* got canceled too. She says there's a slowly growing market for queer male lead roles in sci-fi, but that the reboot was the best there was."

I frown. "Still, if she could get you on one of the new shows. Where they don't dick around for two seasons before letting you kiss Casey . . ."

But it is interesting that Trish is angry about *Star Trek*. She doesn't get angry about anything getting canceled or dying in development hell. It's all business to her.

"Thank god there's even an option for you to take a role like that," Maeve says as she combines a bunch of spices, sugars, and rum into a pan. It sizzles and smells fucking amazing. I swallow as my mouth waters.

Charlie groans. "Ugh, tell me about it." He turns to me. "Did you talk to Trish last night?"

My heartbeat speeds up. I vaguely remember my phone ringing, but without any follow-up, I figured it wasn't a big deal. Was it? "No, why?"

"She just seemed eager to talk to you. I dunno, maybe call her back after breakfast?"

I clear my throat. "Do you think I fucked up the Oscars?"

Maeve sets down her wooden spoon to look at her phone. "According to the internet, you put Charlie back on the map and are now the savior of the gays."

Charlie and Jordan laugh.

I glance at Maeve and smile. "Hardly," I say.

"Well, you're the savior of"—he puts his *arm around Jordan; oh my* god—"these gays." He motions to Maeve with his chin. "Because whatever she's cooking smells amazing."

"Bananas foster French toast," Maeve replies.

Charlie's jaw falls open. "Oh my god, I haven't had that since I was little. Bless you, Maeve Arko."

This is sweet and all, but now I'm worried about what Trish wanted. I check my phone; one missed call from her but no message. I don't know what to think.

Jordan laughs. "Where are you from?"

"My family lives in Ohio and is from New York," Maeve says. "I only learned how to make Southernish food from a cohort member in grad school who was from Louisiana."

I glow with that comment. After this morning, I'm so grateful for every good person who entered Maeve's life after her abusive ex. I'm grateful that I get to (hopefully) be one of those people too. Maeve sticks several slices of egg-and-cinnamon-covered brioche onto my griddle. She's humming to herself, and her body language tells me she's completely at ease. Even though I'm currently trying to keep my fingers from drumming on the table worrying about Trish, joy still zings through me.

"You're amazing," I say to Maeve as she cooks.

"Wait until you taste this," Maeve teases.

Sure enough, when I eat the French toast, I can't tell what tastes better: Maeve's cooking or her.

I could go on, and fully planned to wax poetic about Maeve's culinary genius to Charlie and Jordan. But as I'm midway through trying to be cute by feeding Maeve, my phone rings.

There Trish is.

I look at Maeve. Charlie huffs. "Val, pick up the damn phone before she shows up here!"

"Go," Maeve says, smiling. Like she knows what Trish is going to say.

I sigh, swipe my phone, and head to my backyard to take the call.

"Hey," I say.

"The lady of the hour finally emerges," Trish says.

I blush but steal a glance inside at Maeve. She's laughing at something Charlie's saying. "Hardly. I nearly died at the Oscars."

"Well, I don't want to bore you with the PR update. You're doing amazing, people loved Maeve, your flub was the most entertaining part of the show, et cetera. Great." She pauses. "And . . . *Oakley in Flames* has been accepted to compete at Cannes!"

I know I hear her words. But it's like they dig their way into my brain and knock themselves around like a pinball game, like they're more a physical manifestation of pain in the shape of words than sounds that have actual meaning. Cannes. *The* Cannes. I don't even remember Trish taking European festivals seriously considering the genre of the movie. My movie. *Oakley in Flames*. Got in. They don't make sense together.

"Val?" Trish says.

Until they do. Until they *really* do.

My stomach churns; I swallow on instinct. "Yeah?" I say.

"You there? You hear what I said?"

"Yeah." I swallow again. The sweetness in the back of my throat has turned bitter, acidic. "Hey, uh, when is Cannes?"

"First week of May."

Fuck. No. No, no, no, no. The last week of classes. Right when finals prep begins and Maeve has her evaluation for the grant. You can't just fly across the world for the weekend. Between the schmoozing, press, and screenings, I'd have to be there for two weeks minimum. The time difference is an entire day and some.

My head's spinning. Sound cuts in and out, and when I can hear there's a ringing that won't stop. The sun's suddenly too hot on the back of my neck.

Because maybe I *can't*. I knew about this possibility in December, and it's *March*. I've lied about this for *months,* and she just made it clear how much she trusts me, and look what I've done. I could ruin her whole career. I can't just *get out of* Cannes. I can't just—

My stomach lurches.

"Great, thank you, we'll talk later," I say as the acrid taste of partially digested French toast hits my throat.

I hang up seconds before *just* managing to not puke my guts into a planter in my backyard.

Once I stop shaking, I slide back into the kitchen, into the warmth and laughter and sweet smells that I can miraculously stomach.

"What'd Trish want?" Charlie asks.

"Just some positive leads on a couple of projects I wanted her to chase after for the next Oscar role," I reply. I straighten out of the hunched position I sat down in. Sourness still tinges the back of my throat.

"I can't believe you manufacture it like that," Maeve comments.

"Welcome to Hollywood," Charlie replies.

I manage a weak smile. Guess the lies will just keep coming.

CHAPTER TWENTY-FOUR

By the time Maeve leaves to get ready for work after a relaxed start to her day, I've come down at least enough to understand that I was overreacting when Trish called. I know I've been lying by omission to Maeve, but the festival is still a little over two months away. There's no difference between telling her a month ahead of time and telling her four months ahead of time. Besides, she went with me to the Oscars; she even said she understands how chaotic Hollywood makes my life. We'll make a solid lesson plan for the week I'm gone and I'll throw in tickets for her to come down to Cannes on the weekend. She's a cinema historian; it'd be incredible to go to a festival like Cannes. It's a sweet deal.

This can be fine. I just have to stop—stop, I don't even know? Letting this fester inside me? Being completely irrational?

Out of the corner of my eye, I see Charlie saying goodbye to Jordan. I massage my temples as I sip ginger tea at the table, my weak attempt to soothe my stomach. Not that I even *really* need it. God, I can't even remember the last time anxiety wasn't the source of my physical illness. It should be a relief, the way the feeling disappears as soon as the trigger leaves (I just called my girlfriend a *trigger*), but all I can focus on is how quickly it comes on. I was lucky that this time it happened in my home, out of sight of anyone—

"You've got your anxiety face on," Charlie says, plopping back into his seat at the kitchen table. "And you never drink tea unless you're sick."

I exhale. "*Oakley* got into Cannes."

I expect Charlie to light up in that firecracker way he always does when he gets excited, get a sparkle in his blue eyes, a grin that's so big it looks like he's going to break his face, start jumping up and hugging the nearest human in the vicinity and squeezing all his excitement into them.

But he doesn't do that. His hand twitches as if he's hesitant to reach out to me. "You haven't told Maeve yet, have you?"

A lump clings to my throat. "I thought I'd at least wait until I knew if I'd be booked."

Charlie nods. "So now you know. Cannes is usually in the last week of May, isn't it?"

"Early May this year."

"That's two months from now."

I don't need to be this anxious; I need to problem solve. I grab the kava from my supplement cabinet, and down a dose. If this shit gets me through press, it can get me through having this conversation. Even if I have to pretend at first. I return to Charlie.

"So the dean says that they're evaluating Maeve on her ability to collaborate as part of this grant process. But this class has an additional professional angle. I was going to talk about the audition process and on set interest points for movie musicals, but honestly, I'm going off brief interactions with that world. Most of my musical knowledge is, as you know"—I grimace—"academic."

Charlie nods. "So you need a guest who's done musical movie stuff, basically."

"Yeah." I study Charlie, suddenly remembering the entirely of *his* filmography. Remembering *Hadestown*. "Someone like you."

It's like a siren has gone off in my head. Of course. *Of course* this is the solution. Maeve's comfortable with Charlie, so it'd be a natural fit. My breath catches in my throat as I wait for his answer.

"So, like, I do a Q and A before heading to France?" he asks.

"Yeah. I can write you a ten-minute lecture. The kids will come prepared with questions, so you won't have to fill space. I'll cover all the events for us that day in Cannes. They'll expect me to be fronting the promo being the director, anyway."

"And this would be assuming class falls anytime other than the premiere itself."

"The class this semester meets Wednesdays and the premiere is on a Friday. You don't have to go to anything before the premiere anyway. Even with the long flight, you'd have a handle on the jet lag before—" I pause. "I mean, unless you had something you really wanted to see. I'm asking you for a huge favor right now. No, forget it. The timing is awful."

He pulls his lips into a thin line. "I guess it's something to add to the résumé. And, yeah, you get more jet-lagged than me."

Before I even really know what I'm doing, I throw my arms around Charlie in a hug. "Thank you so, so much. I'll get everything to you within the week."

We pull away. "When should I talk to Maeve about this?" he asks.

Cold bolts through me. "When Ashlee confirms the evaluation date. There's no point giving Maeve time to freak out if the timing works out."

Charlie frowns. "Val, come on. Just tell Maeve now." He shakes his head. "I don't even understand why you think this is such a big deal. This is fucking *Cannes*. People should be bending over back-

ward for you to have the smoothest ride possible to a dream opportunity. And now you have a solid backup plan in place. It's not like
you're throwing an assistant into a press event to answer all your
questions for you because you 'got food poisoning.'"

Despite everything, a pang of mortification still hits me from *that*
memory. Poor Nicole. At least she's a junior executive at a Disney
affiliate now.

"Charlie, it's just—" I exhale. My heart's speeding up again. "I
committed to this. I've already majorly dropped the ball for my class
responsibilities in August. I just— I can't shake the feeling that deep
down, Maeve's still waiting for another reason to believe the first
impression she had of me is the real me. That I really am this vapid,
selfish asshole who only considers academia a distraction until my
career gets back on track. That— What if she thinks I think *she's* just
a shiny object to make me seem more interesting?"

Charlie grabs my hand. Heat prickles in my chest, but it doesn't
move to my whole body the way it usually does when he com-
forts me. "You know that's not true. What you and Maeve have is so
much more than that. You have to trust her and believe that she feels
the same way you do."

I swallow hard, trying to get rid of the goddamn lump in my
throat. But my eyes are starting to burn with tears. Charlie and I are
honest with each other.

"Okay."

Then he frowns. My stomach flips.

"I don't want to overstep, but have you, you know, talked to Rosalie about medication lately?" Charlie knows all about my mental
health struggles, from the huge stuff to the way everyday life has
become unbearable for me at times, the way each outing when the
anxiety is particularly bad feels like cutting wires on a bomb. He

knows, but we talk about it so rarely. And when my sweet, goofy best friend is saying it, it sounds so grave. It sounds *real.*

"I started nonprescription antianxiety meds at the beginning of the year. They're—"

"Clearly not strong enough. There are prescription medications. And maybe it's just that this one is not the right fit, but your anxiety has gotten worse lately. You shouldn't be this freaked over the class thing. And Cannes will be the busiest press schedule you've ever had, with more expected of you. I want you to be as prepared as you can be."

"There's just been more—"

"But, Val, there's *always* going to be more! You want to keep acting and producing and directing and there's *always* going to be more press, more filming, more public appearances. People aren't going to stop recognizing you and unless you become fully nocturnal, you're going to have to go outside—that's not going to change. Even if you left Hollywood behind completely and went back to your roots and taught and lived a cute little academic life with Maeve, it wouldn't make the anxiety go—"

Charlie's eyes widen.

My insides curdle.

"Is that why you're trying so hard to leave Hollywood?"

"What?"

But the realization hits me hard and fast, and all the color drains from my face. It makes so much sense, it's such an easy explanation, but to reckon with it. Fuck. Tears prickle in my eyes, falling as I try to steady the trembling in my throat.

Charlie's expression softens. Softens so much that I *swear* I see tears in his eyes too. "I really think you should talk to Rosalie about medication. I hate seeing you like this, and I don't want it to have a negative effect on the amazing things you've brought into your life. Both when it comes to Hollywood and with Maeve. I'll do you a solid this time, but more conflicts are going to come up in the future."

There has to be another explanation. This teaching job has brought on *more* stress than I've experienced in a while. Sure, it feels more manageable than the stress I get during press tours and photo shoots and film shoots, but it's still there. I never had *that* much of an ulterior motive to taking the teaching job. I *like* teaching. It's something I'm good at. And, besides, if I'm trying to escape my anxiety by doing this job, what the hell does that imply with Maeve? That I'm only with her because she represents an anxiety-free future I can never have?

Is that why I like her?

No. God, just the thought turns into a stabbing pain. My head starts spinning. "Charlie, stop."

"I'm just trying—"

I flex my fist in anger; I can see a scenario play out in front of me. I snap at him, tell him to fuck off, tell him he has no idea what he's talking about. I make him leave my space so it doesn't feel like it's closing in on me.

But I can't do that.

"Please," I say. "I'll—I'll think about prescription meds. I'll tell Maeve about Cannes. I don't want to have any more secrets."

My body feels like it's turned to ice as I watch Charlie's face, brittle and ready to break if I say the wrong thing. I wait with breath caught in my throat for his next move, for him to deliver the verbal lashing I've deserved for months.

Charlie sighs, though.

Then he gets sad again. "Would you be mad if I was keeping a secret from you?"

What secret could Charlie be keeping from me? "No, I wouldn't. But I'd want to know if I could help you."

"I didn't tell you the whole truth about *Star Trek*." His voice is soft, pulsing with vulnerability I haven't heard from him since he moved in. "I know why it was canceled."

A jolt goes through my heart. He'd told me it was canceled in such a straightforward way, but he *had* seemed extra upset about it. I can't believe I didn't ask more questions.

"Despite the great reviews, the majority of our fandom supporting Casey and my character's pairing and the producers being cool with it, there was still this huge vocal minority of viewers who hated it," Charlie explains. "They got loud enough that executives decided developing the romantic relationship was too risky. They asked me and Casey if we'd be comfortable backing down and returning to a storyline that focused more on unspoken longing. Basically they wanted to redact the gay plotline."

There's an ache I get when I hear stories like this. An ache that's so hard to describe to anyone who isn't queer. It's the feeling you get when people you were vulnerable enough to trust betray you, a sting of self-hatred that comes from a piece of you deep in your psyche that believes what you are is *wrong* after all.

"Casey was willing to try the compromise, told me that our clearly homophobic showrunner would be out in a season, and we could get back on track. But I refused. I couldn't do that to the queer people watching this show who were feeling so validated and seen and valued. I put my foot down, despite my team's insistence that I take it. I said I'd quit the show and expose what they were doing." He squeezes his eyes shut. "So they just canceled. All those people lost their jobs, *Casey* lost his first huge role just as he was blowing up. Because of me. Because I was too stubborn."

I can't blink back the tears anymore. I let them fall as I move over to Charlie and pull him into a hug. The kind of hug he normally gives me, tight, with my hands fanned out so he knows I'm here with him right now. He takes a deep breath, his body shuddering against me.

"That was so unbelievably brave," I tell Charlie. "I'm so proud of you, and I'm sure if everyone on that set knew what you did and why you did it, they'd feel the same way. I'm sure Casey does. That's—" The burn of anger is back, but it suddenly feels much more relevant. "That's fucking infuriating that they put you in that position. Fuck your team for betraying you and what you stand for like that. Charlie, I—" I exhale. "I think you *should* expose this. The gay storyline was so popular, and if fans and other networks knew why it ended, what if someone else picks it up?"

He shakes his head. "I can't do that. I can't— I could hardly tell *you* about this. Telling the whole world? For what? For some pity articles to gradually die out and have nothing concrete happen? I can't do that to myself. I'm not strong enough for it. I've been living at your house for *six months* because I'm such a loser. I can't—"

It stings to see a shame I'm so familiar with reflected in him. When all I want to say is that I wouldn't have gotten through the last six months without him. Yes, I have been kind of annoyed that he's seemingly overstayed his welcome at times. But I love and value him, and I am so proud of him.

"You can. And I'll help you."

"Val . . ."

"You've done so much for me. It's time I return the favor."

There's a long pause.

Then he nods, shooting me a friendly head shake. "Because obviously getting a film I'm starring in into *Cannes* isn't enough."

We spend the last Tuesday of March focusing on Charlie. We compose a statement for him to release on his social media platforms and then we post it Monday night. By Wednesday morning, we're flooded with an outpouring of support. Major Hollywood publications are asking Charlie to write a larger article for them, and by the time I step into lecture with Maeve, I've already signed, like, five petitions to have *Star Trek* moved to a streaming service. His team has been silent, but Trish texted me saying Charlie's a bold one. The closest, I suspect, she'll get to asking me if he's fired his manager yet.

It should leave me feeling good as I enter Maeve's office prior to lecture. But I just can't shake the feeling that I'm not following through on my promise to Charlie. In therapy on Monday, I told Rosalie about Cannes and the fact that I'm going to have to tell Maeve what's going on, but I failed to ask about medication. I'd gone in *planning to,* but the words got stuck in my throat and couldn't be coaxed out. It's left me feeling uneasy, like I've forgotten something important even though this time I know what I "forgot."

It's basically not a good time to put me on the spot. I force a deep breath as Maeve sits at her desk, Ty and I taking the couch.

"Hey, can you show me your notes from the jukebox musical lecture?" Maeve asks me.

"Do you want the couch?" Ty teases.

The answer to Maeve's question falls out of my brain. But Maeve herself just gives him a *Really?* look. "I think I can contain myself." But she flashes a smile.

I have to admit, there's a lot of stress going on around me, but it's made me really happy to see Maeve grow closer to Ty. Not to mention the relief that comes from Ty not being weird about us dating since he found out. I tried to give them their space to do their own thing, but they've even started to invite me to some of their screenings and museum visits. As they joke around, I send Maeve the notes.

"Thanks." Maeve leans forward as she scans my email. "If we get to do this class for a third semester, we need another older musical."

"Do *Tommy*," Ty suggests. "It fits jukebox, satire, and adaptation."

Maeve raises a finger. "Noting that one."

I motion to Ty. "That's way better than me suggesting one of the Beatles' films."

"Ha!" Ty says, jumping up to face Maeve. "You owe me fifty."

I may rescind that I-like-this-friendship thing. "You made a bet on me?"

Maeve's smiling again. "It was . . ." She pauses. "I thought you wouldn't want any Beatles on the course syllabus because that was your first attempted dissertation topic, not the dissertation you actually finished with. I figured it was an academic sore spot, but Ty thought differently."

"Wait, did you read *both* my dissertations?"

Maeve nods. "They're very thought-provoking."

"All good, I hope."

"Very good." Even at this professional distance, she makes my heart flutter.

"And then you'll tell me why you're so fucking obsessed with *La Vie d'Adèle*."

Maeve exchanges a look with Ty.

"The question is why you're *not* obsessed with it!" Ty says.

I just brought up queer cinema. *Oakley in Flames* is queer cinema. It's the perfect opportunity to bring up Cannes. With Charlie on board, all we have to figure out are flights for Maeve. Once the class is taken care of, we can do the fun stuff—I'll walk her through the first-class plane ticket, the luxury hotel accommodation, get her some more nice dresses for the red carpet. It'll be like the Oscars, but better. We can rip off the Band-Aid and I can start being an actual functioning human being. I can do this. The natural antianxiety medication works.

But even turning to meet Maeve's gaze is making my heart hammer, my stomach twist up. "I know the newest book is about 2000s queer cinema, but do you keep up with what's coming out now?"

Maeve rubs the back of her neck. "I did up until maybe three months ago, but it's been difficult with my schedule lately. I need to get a schedule going again."

It feels like my ribs are pressing against my lungs, digging into them. I don't dare take a breath for fear they pop like balloons. "I could get you tickets to festivals featuring the newest queer cinema, just so you know." *And* Oakley in Flames *got into Cannes . . .*

She smiles. "That'd be amazing." That smile, the one that filled my heart, holds me in a chokehold. I genuinely can't breathe.

"Yeah, uh"—I rub the back of my neck—"there's tons of amazing work out there right now."

Maeve's lips twitch downward. "Babe, are you okay?"

I force a breath, but it's like I'm trying to fill a pool with a bucket. The room starts to blur around the edges. And why the hell did I start this conversation with Ty in the room looking even more confused than Maeve?

"I'm—I—" Oakley in Flames *got into Cannes. This is the biggest career win I've had since my Oscar nomination. It could change my life, and I want you there if you'll ever forgive me for leaving for two weeks at crunch time in the most important semester of your career.*

There's a knock on the door.

It's Ashlee.

"Hey, everyone," she says, chipper and completely oblivious to what just transpired. "I'm so sorry it's been so long since we last spoke. Maeve, if you don't mind, I'm going to sit in on the last class of the semester. That'll be okay, right?"

The same week as my Cannes premiere.

I look at Ashlee and speak with the desperation of someone begging for their life. "I don't mean to be this way, but I actually have something planned that week. Could we do before or after?"

Ashlee frowns. "I'm so sorry, Valeria, but that's the only time we can fit it in. We're already pushing up on the grant decision date."

I'll make this work. I can't let Maeve down. "I should be able to move my conflict. Don't worry about it."

Maeve looks to me, head cocked. I give a soft dismissive wave.

"Sounds great to me," she says to Ashlee. "Get it out of the way before my conference in late May."

Ashlee smiles. "Perfect."

Maybe I'm too exhausted. I must be. There's no feeling in my body. Only the sensation that I'm a little too far away, a little too distant to feel the texture of Maeve's couch or the cold punch of the air-conditioning or the heat of Maeve's gaze on me.

"What do you have planned for that week?" she asks.

I can just say it right now. Oakley *got into Cannes*. Waiting for Ashlee to confirm the date was just an excuse, anyway.

"Nothing that can't be moved," I reply.

I wasn't able to get the confession out. I hate myself for it, but I can't.

Not that it can matter right now. I have a class to keep teaching.

CHAPTER TWENTY-FIVE

Despite knowing Charlie can swap in for me during the lecture Ashlee's observing, I still find myself spinning my wheels the first two weeks of April, doing the same thing I did that day in Maeve's office. It's like it's impossible to get the words out. It's to the point of utter embarrassment, something that keeps me up night after night, turning over every mistake I've ever made.

If I were still with Emily, telling *her* I've been putting off bailing on her, she would dump me instantly. Even thinking of how we ended things has me in cold sweat as I lie awake. But the days are passing me by, and I'm not dating Emily. I'm dating Maeve, who hasn't tried to break up with me. We haven't even so much as had a fight.

But if I wait another week, if I let it get to be less than ten days before I leave for *France,* that may not be the case.

I need to tell her after the "Oscar bait" lecture today. Two weeks before her evaluation.

She gives me a little smile as I step up to begin my lecture for this week. I tug at the collar of my shirt, despite the fact that it's freezing in here. I need to focus on the air-conditioning. It's not hot, I'm not feeling faint, Maeve and I have been great. She loves me. I'm going to remind her of why that is right now. I lay my hand on my diaphragm as I open my PowerPoint and force my breath to steady. My head's clear—clear enough—by the time I turn to the class.

"According to a 2014 study conducted by UCLA sociologists, the IMDb keywords most commonly associated with *Oscar bait* taken from films between 1985 and 2009 were"—I hold up a finger as the students, a new crop, but with about the same dynamic as last semester, lean forward—"*Family tragedy . . .*"

They laugh, just like I expected them to.

"*Whistleblower, Pulitzer Prize source . . .*"

The laughing only increases. I glance over at Maeve, who's smiling.

"*Physical therapy, domestic servant,* and *Watergate.*" I pause. "Sound right to anyone?"

Several students nod. "Well, the Oscar-bait phenomenon has actually been around almost since the Oscars' inception. Its first usage in the press dates to around 1948." I find myself smiling. "But today we're going to discuss the results of this blatant practice using two examples. One is of a movie musical that happened to hit every Oscar-bait button, seemingly unintentionally, and succeeded in sweeping awards season, and one is a movie musical that *tried* to hit all the buttons and failed miserably. *La La Land* and *Les Misérables . . .*" I pause for dramatic effect. "Respectively."

I switch to the next slide, watch as students type away, transcribing everything, seemingly even my jokes. I know this lecture so well, though, that I can let my mind wander for a second. Charlie will do great. Maeve will have the perfect last piece for her grant evaluation—

I can't concentrate on that now. I dig a nail into my palm, refocusing.

"People are singing in these musicals, and it doesn't *really* make sense. Musicals, by definition, are bombastic. They exist in a heightened reality that involves a sort of audience participation. When you're in the audience for a play, it doesn't matter that you know the actors are wearing mics, that the sets aren't real, or that people sing instead of speak. But with movies, particularly movies made in the 2010s, realism was a constant pressure. Real emotions, real gritty sets, real events, real people. Which, coincidentally, is also what the *Oscars* value."

A student named Paul raises his hand. "Wait, is that why they had the actors actually sing live in *Les Mis*? For the *Oscars*?"

The class and I and—I glance at her—Maeve all laugh at that. Maeve more than me, even. She *hates* Tom Hooper so hilariously much.

I give him a finger gun. "Bingo! Hooper wanted more room for natural acting *and* singing. Which is nice in theory, but the result is, well, I'll just say we're not watching all of *Les Mis* in this class, so . . ."

I put on Russell Crowe and Hugh Jackman's "The Confrontation" sequence, and then, while the students are watching, take the opportunity to sit next to Maeve and drink some water. Maeve smiles at me, and ever so subtly moves her hand to mine. Links our pinkies like *we're* in a movie. It makes me melt. But the clip is over both far earlier and far later (this fucking musical) than I want it to be.

I accidentally make eye contact with Maeve, and she's covering her mouth trying not to laugh. I know *exactly* what she's thinking about—we were watching *Les Mis* to create this lecture and Maeve said that the clinking of the swords while Jackman and Crowe were singing was the equivalent of singing 'Wishing You Were Somehow Here Again' while doing dishes, and she proceeded to actually deliver the most beautiful rendition of the song while loudly cleaning only to drop and shatter one of my clay bowls. I was too busy crying on the floor laughing to even notice.

God, I love this woman.

I'm going to make sure she gets this grant. Despite my idiocy over the last several months, I'm going to do it.

And okay, I do barely hold back a laugh. The class starts laughing too. "I'm sorry," I manage to bark out. "The fucking clinking of the swords being louder than the singing gets me every time." I exhale, fan myself a little to get my face back to normal. "But *La La Land* takes a different approach . . ."

I get through the rest of the lecture. It goes as smoothly as I could hope for. Students are laughing and asking questions and engaging with what I have to say. I get through all the material I want. No one grills me on my biased position within the Oscar system. Maeve doesn't stop smiling at me the entire time.

By the time I'm returning to my seat so Maeve can close the lecture, my heartbeat's steady and my step is light. I can hardly believe I was so upset a few hours ago. Charlie's question was wrong; I'm not doing this because I feel like I need to escape anything. I just *love* it here. I love how every class validates an existence Emily was so set on tearing down.

Paul raises his hand. "Not a question."

"Go ahead," I say, now nearly thirty classes in and feeling at ease with the students. Finally.

"I just got the alert from *Deadline* and—holy shit—congrats, Professor Sullivan, on your film getting into Cannes!" Paul says.

Congrats, Professor Sullivan, on your film getting into Cannes.

I haven't told her yet.

I haven't told her yet and it's on *Deadline*. I haven't told her yet, and I could've told her two days ago, a month ago, four months ago.

All that time I could've done it, and now it's just been snatched from me.

The class is clapping. Students are asking questions. But it's like they're not speaking English, or like the volume is too low and I'm straining to hear them. Nothing makes sense, and even their faces are starting to blur so they're splotches of color rather than humans I just spent the last hour interacting with. I can't feel my feet on the ground, this room isn't familiar, yet I *know* where I am. I *know* what was just said. I know, I know, yet I—

I touch my face, drag it down to my throat. My heartbeat is slamming against my fingertips, racing like a hummingbird. I must look shell-shocked. I can't look this shell-shocked in front of the students. I swallow, but there's no bile taste in my mouth this time. The anxiety is so fucking intense that it's ascended to a new level that doesn't affect my body at all.

"Congrats, Val," Maeve says.

I hear her.

I hear the way she sounds confused, the way her voice cracks a little like I've hurt her. It feels like I cracked one of her bones. A wall of guilt descends on me.

I have to speak. I've been silent for too long.

"Thanks, guys," I say, looking at the students rather than Maeve. "I can't answer any questions about it, but I'll keep you updated."

I need my bag. I need my bag, and I need to get out of this room, and if I can just do that, everything will be okay. Maeve will be okay. I'll be okay.

I laser focus on the bag. Grab it even as Maeve enters my peripheral vision. The lights go down as the *La La Land* screening starts. I dart toward the door, bumping into an empty seat in the audience, all but stumbling my way out. I know I'm awake, but I feel like I'm dreaming.

The doors are heavy, but I force them open. My eyes sting as the light of day burrows into my vision. The clack of heels follows behind me.

Then her hand's on my shoulder. It burns. It's the hand of the woman I love, the woman I've hurt. "Val, what's going on?"

I force myself to turn to face her. Her lips are turned downward, and there's a deep furrow between her brows. She drops her hand.

"I thought you only had your movie submitted for Sundance." A twisted, confused smile plays on her lips. Like she wants to make light of this but can't do it. "Why didn't you tell me about Cannes?"

I have to say it. I have to say it I have to say I have to fucking say it. "I'll have to be in the South of France the same day Ashlee is going to be watching your class for the grant. I'll be there during study days and final grading too."

She blanches, stopping dead in the empty courtyard. "I— Why didn't you speak up when Ashlee said that week if you knew—you— there's no way *Deadline* knew before you did."

"I don't know." That's not the right thing to say.

"Val, I'm"—she pinches her nose—"I'm so confused. How long have you known you had a potential conflict with class? Why didn't you tell me?"

I never thought she'd be hurt by my lie. Angry, yes, but this—in the strangest sense, this isn't what I expected to feel from her response either. It's not worth hurting her. Not by a long shot. How could I have done this to her? "I don't know."

Her mouth hardens. Her frown shifts to a scowl. *"How long have you known?"*

I force a breath. "I knew about the possibility since December."

"Since . . . ?" Her hands rise as if to touch her ear, but she yanks them back tightly to her sides. "You've been lying to me since before we had this class planned? *Why?*"

"I don't know . . ." I need to say something else.

"Were you—were you even planning on telling me?"

As much as it pains me to admit it, if Paul hadn't said anything, I might not have told her. It sounds so fucking absurd, and I can't justify it and never will be able to. "I was going to have someone come in to sub for me—an alternate. I'd help with the lecture still. I wanted that squared away so you wouldn't have to panic."

She throws up her hands, leans into me. I thought I knew the cold, angry look in Maeve's eyes from back when we met, but no, *this* is true anger. Icy gaze, lips practically curled into a snarl. She's getting right into my personal bubble when I want that bubble to be five fucking feet wide. My girlfriend, whom I want in every aspect of my life, is too close. I can't breathe. "But why wouldn't you tell me you were submitting to more festivals? I could've supported you through that. And the good news—I just don't get it. We're a team. Why wouldn't you—?"

"I'm sorry." I need a second to breathe. I'm not ready for the way her hurt oscillates into an anger on the verge of tears. Any good, rational response slips out of my grasp. My mind is blank, I'm scrambling for something, anything to say—

And I make a mistake.

I make a big fucking mistake.

"I didn't think you'd be this upset."

Which isn't true. It isn't true, and I need to take it back, but it's in the air now.

Maeve turns a whole new shade of red. "Are you *kidding me*? I'm your *girlfriend*! I should be there to celebrate your little victories, let alone something as huge as getting into *one of the biggest film festivals in the world*!"

She starts blinking rapidly. My chest twists. She can't start crying now.

"Although I can't say what kind of girlfriend I am if you want to parade me around at the Oscars but won't let me know about important milestones in your career."

I want to reach my hand out to her, but it feels like I'd be touching an open flame. "It was— I never meant for you to be slighted. I was just so nervous—"

"Nervous about what? That I'd be *upset* you got into Cannes?"

"It's not like you were thrilled with the Oscars. I can never tell if any aspect of my life is going to be too much for you, and—"

"I *told you* that I was going to figure out the celebrity-girlfriend thing. You didn't even give me the chance to prove myself."

I squeeze my eyes shut. "I wasn't thinking about that, though." My voice cracks. "I didn't want you to think I was abandoning you," I say, and every word in that last sentence feels small.

She takes a few long seconds to stare at me, her eyes wide and her mouth twisted. "Abandoning me?"

"I'm not trying to fuck up your grant. I know how—"

"And your bright idea about how *not* to abandon me was to lie to me and give me two weeks—at most, because god knows when you would've *actually* told me if a *student* didn't beat you to it—instead of two months to prepare. And prepare for what—a week? Two weeks without you?"

"Two."

"I just—" She takes a deep breath. "How can you be *so smart* yet so oblivious?"

"I told you I was a mess, but I'm trying out different antianxiety pills. It's just hard finding the right one and—"

She takes a step back, as if my words have knocked the wind out of her. She cocks her head at me, still wearing that angry expression. I crunch in on myself. "That isn't enough. It isn't enough, and you know that. You think— You know, Valeria, I thought I wouldn't ever have to tell you this, but news flash about what it's like to be one of the regular people you want to be so badly." She's stopped calling me Val. "I can't just forget my priorities and not communicate vital information to my coworkers. I can't just drastically change plans and say I'm a mess and it'll all be okay. This isn't something that someone on your team can just snap their fingers and fix. I needed you for this one little thing, and you didn't even have the courtesy to tell me you had a conflict—which didn't have to be that big a deal, by the way—until someone else did it for you. And now I have to deal with all this while you galivant off to sell your movie for millions of dollars and expect me to what"—she laughs—"come as your arm candy after doing both our jobs?"

It's like a punch to the gut, over and over again. Tears burn in my eyes. "Maeve, it's not like that at all. I'm sorry about not telling you—" I reach my hand out. "I love you," I say. "I didn't mean to hurt you. You're everything to me. That's why I didn't tell you—I just knew you'd hate me for putting it off for so long, and I was scared."

"Val, for god's sake, I don't *hate* you, but it really didn't have to fucking be like this." Maeve turns away from me. "If you loved me, you would've told me the truth. If you really thought I'd bring you down for something as huge as this, maybe we're missing something."

The tears fall but she doesn't even see them. "Maeve . . ."

"Just go. I'll talk to your manager's assistant. I need a break."

That's it. That's how I ruin the best part of my life. "So we're breaking up?"

She just *stares at me,* wary like I've dropped ten years of stress on her. "I *just said* I needed a break." She takes my wrist. "Look at me, Val. You aren't listening! Will you please just listen to what I just said?"

For a moment, the first one since Paul spilled the news, the world slows to a stop. My brain frees up just enough to process the last thing Maeve said to me, word by word and dissect it like we've done with films all year.

Less than five minutes ago, Maeve said she wanted space. She didn't ask to break up. Emily would've asked to break up, though. Emily would've been pissed, but Maeve is disappointed. Emily would've broken up with me, but Maeve wants a *break*.

But what's a break but a delay in the inevitable? If I agree to this, I'm just subjecting myself to weeks more of uncertainty. I can't do this right now. I need to just know, but—

"I'm gonna go check on the screening," Maeve says. "I'll talk to you later."

What do I do with this space?

"Okay," I say, pushing through the sting of panic that the worst will still be true.

CHAPTER TWENTY-SIX

I know this pain.

The knowing surprises me, but also brings me a measure of comfort, though that doesn't make it feel any better when Maeve truly doesn't initiate conversation aside from a single message asking for next week's lecture notes. There are no sweet PSes, no flirty asides, she doesn't even write my name on the email. It's as if I've fallen down the ridiculously long chute in Chutes and Ladders after being three steps from winning the damn game.

I thought I'd be more discombobulated, more weepy, more angry over the whole thing. Like I was with Emily. But there's just . . . nothing. A giant hole in my heart, and I know I'll never fill it again if I can't be who Maeve needs me to be. I want to fix it so badly, I do, but how do I fix who I am?

I don't know. So, I spend the majority of the next week in bed, familiarizing myself with the Cannes lineup and obsessively following the blowup over Charlie's *Star Trek* homophobia scandal. Gwyn asks if I want her to come over, and I say no. She leaves a pan of lasagna for me to heat up throughout the week on my doorstep anyway.

Usually, I can feign productivity for most of the day. Charlie's on auditions and living his life, so he's often out late. I hate to admit how much of a comfort his presence is when he is at home, though, hanging on my living room couch, forcing me out of bed to work near him. We don't talk much. I fear talking is just going to make me spiral. I'm trying to postpone the realization that Wednesday's going to be here before I know it, and I'll have to actually face the fact that I haven't magically become a person worthy of Maeve. I was the worst version of me—selfish and insecure and disrespectful. I'm terrified that on Wednesday, that one last bit of hope I have, that she'll realize I can be forgiven, will be extinguished once and for all.

Sunday night, though, less than seventy-two hours before I have to face Maeve again, I'm paralyzed. Paralyzed by anger at myself for promising this time would be different even as I fell back into hiding the way I used to with Emily. And I'm paralyzed by the thought of having to show up at Cannes and seem not only intelligent, charming, and worldly, but also *fucking happy* about being there. That I'll have to swallow my pain *and* deflect any questions about why Maeve isn't with me. Something that should make me so happy is making me feel like I've been dunked under water and I'm unable to breathe.

"Hey," Charlie says, my door whining as he opens it. "You decent?"

That sort of silly commentary would usually make me laugh. I pull up the covers, further burying me and Eustace. "Yeah."

He pads his way over to me and jumps into bed. "So . . . can I sleep here tonight?"

My heart jolts a little. He's up to something, clearly, but I don't have the energy to find out what it is. "Sure."

"Cool, 'cause, uh, I was in my room and I heard those creepy loud footsteps you're always talking about. I—yeah, I really do think your house infested by a demon."

Amazingly, this fills me with both body-wracking fear and excitement. I'd been—I'd been trying to convince Maeve that the haunting was real for months, even though she said believing in ghosts was like believing in fairies. But she'd always listen to my theories and stories anyway. "Cool."

"It's not cool," Charlie says, his voice getting higher. "It's fucking freaky, but I feel safer with you here, you lump, so thank you."

"No problem."

He wraps his arms around me, pushing up against me so we share body heat. It relaxes my shoulders. "I think you should talk to Maeve."

I wince like Charlie's carving Maeve's name into me instead of rubbing my back. "Don't go there, Charlie."

"I mean I don't think *she* even knows why she's asking for this break." It's unlike him to be this bold. But I can't summon the energy to leave this conversation. "I mean, all this over a scheduling conflict and you two touched each other's nerves. It's nothing a conversation can't fix."

As if I don't know that. As if I haven't tried to rationalize it that way all week. "Yet she's been radio silent for days. If she wanted to resolve things, she would've reached out."

"Okay, so she's taken her sweet time to cool off. That doesn't mean—"

I whip around, tears burning in my eyes. "Just drop it, okay? There's nothing I can do to fix this. Let me mourn this relationship in peace. I have to get ready to go to Cannes and build upon the one aspect of my life that's going well."

"What even happened in your fight? Like, where exactly did you two leave off?"

My heartbeat picks up just thinking about it. "I thought she was pissed, and she was, but it was—it was like she was disappointed in me. Like I'm one of her fucking students. She said that I—that I wasn't listening to her."

"About what?"

"Her, I don't know. Being sad that I didn't tell her about Cannes."

Charlie stares at me, long and hard. "Okay. That seems very normal."

"She's been against the celebrity thing since we met. Then with the Oscars—"

"Which she went to and told both of us she enjoyed."

"She just . . ." I pause, taking a deep breath. "She won't forgive me. What's space going to do? She'll end it just like Emily did."

Charlie takes his own deep breath. "Val, you're not going to want to hear this, but look at me." His blue eyes have never seemed brighter. "You need to be honest with her. But more than that, you need to face your fears. *Maeve isn't Emily.* Emily was an asshole who never respected you and was looking for any excuse to get out of a relationship with you and look like the victim doing it. But you're not in England right now. Years have passed, and Maeve is a new person. You're not in a relationship where you know the ending. You get to learn another person's whole set of flaws and methods. And, if Maeve's also a good girlfriend, she'll do the same for you. And it seems like she is trying to do that! She literally told you what hurt her about what you did. Yes, this could've been resolved without her needing a break, but that's her own shit. So tell her you're sorry and try to bridge the gap."

"We can't resolve this. Telling her what was going through my head while I was lying to her doesn't matter. The effect is what it is."

I expect Charlie to bat the spike right back at me. But he doesn't. He just lies there, eyes on Eustace as he frowns, brings his face back to neutral, and then frowns again. "You're self-sabotaging."

I snort. "And that means what exactly?"

I shouldn't be acting this bitchy to him. He's done nothing wrong, has supported me through so much. We're supposed to be such deep friends, yet he couldn't even rely on me enough to be honest with me about *Star Trek*. And that's probably my fault too, for not making him feel safe, not letting him know I would shoulder his worries. I've failed him just like I failed Maeve.

He reaches over. I bristle on instinct, but he's going to Eustace, not me. My ears go hot as he strokes my dog's soft back. "You're the reason I might have a job. You've successfully directed a film, juggled dozens of projects, and gotten a PhD. Your first film got into, and I cannot emphasize this enough, *fucking Cannes*. You can see how Emily is fucking up this relationship, right?"

I can see it in the facts, from comparing and contrasting Emily's and Maeve's reactions like a student. But that doesn't mean I can escape the drowning feeling at the thought of talking to Maeve again. "It doesn't change how it makes me feel."

"That's what therapy is for. Go pick yourself back up and figure out how to be a good girlfriend. I know *that's* the real you. Not this."

I'm not like Charlie. I'm not *good* like Charlie. Charlie never let anyone down, Charlie didn't prioritize his anxiety over the livelihood of someone he loved. Charlie didn't roll over and say that his mistake was an inherent character flaw rather than owning up to it. Charlie hasn't spent years cycling through one-night stands like disposable razors because emotion was too difficult. So I believe in Charlie more than I've ever believed in myself. I *believe* he deserves his *Star Trek* job back.

I don't believe I deserve Maeve back. Not right now.

"Can we talk about the demon?" I ask.

Charlie sighs deeply, his body pressing against mine. "Yeah. Dude, you need an exorcist. Or at least to get featured on one of those celebrity haunting shows."

And maybe the laughter releases something in me, or maybe

Charlie's words made more of an impression than I was willing to believe, but I realize something.

I can do more than I'm doing.

For the first time in years, when Rosalie asks me about my week during our session nearly two weeks after Maeve's and my break, I don't know where to start. Her concern is palpable—I notice it in her subtle facial movements. The way her lips are slightly downturned, the tiny line between her brows. And I *know why*; I fucking walked into the office in sweats and a hoodie and am currently curled on her couch in the fetal position. I know I have to tell her what happened, or she'll spend the whole session badgering me.

"*Oakley in Flames* got into Cannes, and Maeve and I are on a break," I say. Just to get it out. Just so maybe Rosalie can pick the most important topic.

And her bug-eyed expression tells me all I need to know: I've brought some serious shit into her office. She's maybe given me that look, like, twice, in a decade of dealing with my bullshit.

"That sounds overwhelming," she says. "Do you have any idea what you'd like to focus on for the session?"

Fuck. Well, so much for the Rosalie Guide Me plan. As if I even *know* what I want out of this session. I can't be a better person while my brain's like this. "I want to feel happy again."

The words surprise me as much as they do Rosalie. It's like a wake-up shot at a juice bar, my heart is suddenly beating really fast, my blood is buzzing. *Happy.*

"What does that look like for you?" Rosalie asks, recrossing her legs and regaining her signature composure.

"What do you mean?"

Rosalie chews on her inner cheek for a moment. "What's the first thing that comes to mind when you hear the word *happiness*?"

The answers ping-pong through my brain. Spending time with Maeve. Seeing the positive reactions to Charlie's letter. Celebrating Oz and Lily's birthday. Coming out publicly. Having Luna listen to me as I rambled on about kitsch in a Burger King at 2:00 a.m. The twins' birth.

"I'm not— It's so weird," I say. "Nothing is career-related."

"How does that make you feel?"

"I'm . . ." I rub my forearms. "I guess that surprises me. Because I—I don't know. I think I *was* happy when I won the Oscar, when I worked with Mason on *Goodbye, Richard!*, when *Oakley in Flames* got into Cannes. I mean, those things *should* make me happy, shouldn't they?"

"In theory, yes, but that doesn't mean on-paper accomplishments *really* brought you joy. Maybe you respond more to a different type of happiness."

As she says it, though, I find myself fixating on a specific memory. Mason and I, after I came out, did a sort of what we called *Goodbye, Richard!* redux press series. The movie had gotten an extended release in theaters, and Mason basically said now that I was out, we could be completely open about what the movie was really about. We must've gone on half a dozen late-night shows, done smaller interviews, even BuzzFeed-style Q&A's. I remember feeling euphoric throughout the entire process. Like every inhibition and anxious thought I usually had when I do press was just *gone*. I was just joking around with Mason and talking about queer cinema and representation and artistry as if the two of us were alone. The audiences energized me rather than stole from me.

"I remember this one interview with Mason in particular," I say, not even bothering to give Rosalie the context. "Writers Interview Actors. They just put me and Mason in a room together and said to just ask each other whatever. We knew each other so well that at first we were just idiots and asked each other what we were making for dinner that night and our Tupac death theories. But as the interview went on, we started talking about queer representation and what stories meant to us and what it means to tell a liberation story through violence and it just— I felt like I had a moment where I knew everything had been worth it, that I was exactly where I was supposed to be. That I was the real me."

Rosalie exhales slowly. "And you feel like you haven't had that since?"

"No." I'm back to rubbing my arm. "I—I think I got close. When I took this TV directing job and we had hope that *Oakley* would get picked up. I had this whole vision for my career where I could be more than someone else's mouthpiece for a message that didn't resonate with me. Directing was going to give me an outlet to really say something, to take on projects that were more cerebral and vulnerable, like *Stroke*. I wanted to be taken seriously, but then the interviews started going south and the thing with Winston happened and everything fell apart."

Rosalie pauses. Really pauses, like she might be uncertain about how I'll react to what she's about to say. "*Did* everything fall apart that night? What changed in your mind?"

"I realized that my ideas weren't going to be taken seriously. The last time I'd felt my ideas validated was in academia, so I thought it was destiny to go back in that direction."

"Did you find what you were looking for in academia?"

The answer comes so quick that I almost feel knocked out of my own body. "No." I think about the students who still ask me about Hollywood, about all the hoops Maeve has to go through just to get to teach her own class, what my future would look like as an adjunct. It wouldn't be better, even with my celebrity privilege. "It was just different."

"When you think about having to do another interview for your new film, what comes to mind? What impact did the interview with Winston have on you? What would've happened if you'd just done the guest-teaching gig and gone back to your career in Hollywood?"

All this time, and I don't think I've revisited that car ride with Trish after the interview. Everything felt so out of control, so awful, that I took the first balm available to me. It happened to be this guest-teaching gig. But I'm starting to wonder if the wound would've healed regardless. What *would've* happened if I'd kept pursuing directing? Would Maeve and I have still dated? Would I have taken that HBO gig and . . . actually felt good about it? It was such a good script, and there was directing potential.

But it also would've meant going back on the late-night circuit earlier than this week. Returning to that awful gay question cycle.

"All I can feel is this—this overwhelming fear and anxiety that I just can't shut down." My head aches. "I don't—I don't know how I did it before. Looking back, I can't think of a time I didn't feel this way. Like I had to fight through tar to get anywhere I wanted to go. I guess there must have been times that were easier than others, where I saw my path clearly and knew what to say and how to conjure my best self for people. I wanted to be the best version of myself for this class. But I also went into the teaching with an expectation. I just keep thinking, *If I get this, then the anxiety will go away. It'll get easier.* I'll be able to deal with things like what happened with Winston without it bringing me to my knees. But it—"

But it's like Charlie said.

There will always be more.

There will always be social anxiety, there will always be my health conditions, there will always be this fear that my parents were right, that I chose a path for myself that has no value and prevents me from living a fulfilling life. Fame is never going to get easier. I'm never going to be able to just make art and escape into a corner and not be bothered.

"Never will." I finish. "I just have to learn how to deal with it better. No matter whether I switch jobs or not. And I really love directing." Something buzzes in me, from my fingertips to my brain. "And I'm *really excited* for what's coming next." A smile spreads on my face. "After thinking I had no talent in directing, the board at one of the most prestigious film festivals in the *world* said I did. That's—" I put my face in my hands, feeling like a giddy child again. "That's *unbelievable.*"

I'm so excited for what's coming next, yet I ran from it. Even with the elation from the Cannes news finally able to be, there's still that twist of anxiety as I sit in Rosalie's office. And maybe more than that. It's pain. Pure, virulent pain. It all comes back to my coming out. After years holding myself afloat thinking maybe the world I loved could embrace the real me, they could only take me in a specific package. Put a bow on it, but it was rejection. Letting go of that fantasy as I went through the press circuit fucking sucked. I told myself I couldn't take it and so I abandoned a career I fucking *love*.

I never stopped caring about my acting and directing. I *wanted Oakley* to get into Cannes.

And it did. That film is wholly, nerves-exposingly mine and everything I ever wanted to say about my sexuality, and it's going to compete at Cannes. I'm tired of pushing away my wishes for it. I *want* it to perform well. I want to do everything I can to make sure that happens. This is a once-in-a-lifetime opportunity, and I've already wasted two months pushing it down and telling myself it meant nothing. I should be celebrating it.

My dream came true two months ago, and I didn't tell the person I love. *Of course* Maeve was upset about it. Of course she'd need a break after I couldn't even process that. I should be at my career high; Maeve should be able to look at me and be proud, like I'll be when she gets that grant. Charlie was right. I'm done sabotaging myself. I'm going to fight for *Oakley,* for my creative future, and I'm going to fight for Maeve.

I never want her to feel left out of my life again.

Still, I can't just psych myself up for Cannes and expect that happiness will come to me because I want it to. I can't just wait for the divine intervention of love to pull me up by my bootstraps and win Maeve back for me. But I can help make my life easier.

I take a deep breath. "Can we talk about medication again?"

Rosalie's expression softens. She picks up her clipboard and writes something down. "Of course. You know I can't prescribe it, but your GP should be able to, and I can help you monitor it from a mental health standpoint. You can get a psychiatrist as needed."

And for once in my life, hearing the word *medication* doesn't spin my heart into a frenzy. In fact, it slows my heart down. The only thing buzzing is my brain, but it's the kind of buzzing I get before sitting down and watching a movie I love. It's—it's hope.

It's been so long since I had hope.

CHAPTER TWENTY-SEVEN

My first week on Klonopin is not exactly a dream. In fact, it could be argued that I almost cease sleeping and become *very* convinced that the joke demon infestation in my house is a much bigger issue than it actually is. But the weird thing is, it's not *anxiety* that keeps me awake. Am I paranoid? Sure. Uncomfortable? Definitely. Battling vertigo I've never had before? Yes. But those incessant thoughts that make me afraid to go outside and see people, that have been making me panic about having to go to the South of France, are all fading into the background. They feel about as important to me as making sure my flight, hotel, and Cannes schedule information is correct. Things that, yes, do matter, but don't feel life shatteringly important; if things don't go exactly according to plan, I know I'll be fine.

And okay, it still stings when Maeve keeps her distance during our lectures. But that's easy enough to cope with when I tell myself I have a plan with a timeline. Maeve is qualified for that grant and deserves it a million times over. She'll earn it with the work we did together and everything that came before it. But as someone trying to be worthy of being her girlfriend, I need to do my all to support her. There's one last thing I need to do before I leave for Europe tomorrow. Even if Charlie's right and Maeve has her own shit to work out, I can do this.

Sitting in Ashlee's office, I drum my fingers against the side of the first belt Maeve touched. I fly out to France tomorrow morning. Mandatory Cannes schmoozing starts the second I arrive delirious and jet-lagged Wednesday, *Oakley in Flames* premieres Friday night, and then schmoozing continues through the next week and a half. Then it's other premiere invites, interviews, lunches and dinners, billionaire yacht parties, and spending some time with Gwyn and my parents, who agreed to come for emotional support. I have not packed yet. But nothing is more important than sitting at this desk, looking Ashlee in the eye, and fighting for someone I believe in. Charlie officially signed with Trish earlier this week, and he said talking to me about *Star Trek* was what got him to finally drop his old team. I *know* I can help make an impact.

In Hollywood, anyway. I'm not sure about academia yet.

Ashlee takes a seat across from me and smiles. "What can I do for you, Valeria?"

I stop my fingers from drumming and feel my heart beat faster. "I wanted to talk to you about Maeve before you review her next week."

Ashlee's fingers knit together on the surface of her desk. "Of course. We're so excited to see you and Maeve in action."

Even after everything that's happened, god how my heart warms thinking about Maeve. She could do anything to me, and I'd still be drawn to her like a moth to a flame. "This should actually be in your inbox already, but Maeve set up a fail-safe in case my professional obligations had to take priority over the class. We've arranged for a guest speaker—someone who can speak to the class about professional opportunities. You know Charlie Durst, right?"

Ashlee nods, her expression unreadable. I tug at my jacket.

"He's done a lot of movie musicals and is going to talk about what being on set is like on those kinds of projects. I thought it'd be helpful for you to see her work with a different kind of collaborator. She's the reason our class has run so smoothly, and I wanted her to have a space to shine."

And finally, Ashlee nods. "She does work well on her feet."

"Yeah, she's totally disaster prepared." I take a deep breath. "I know it doesn't seem like I have any academic clout or experience, but I've seen a lot of professors. I'm talking Oxbridge-educated, Ivy-educated trailblazers in the humanities. And Maeve— It's so rare to see a professor who has such a clear grasp of the material they're presenting, someone who keeps up with the current conversations in the field yet has thoroughly excavated the history as well. Someone who also connects with people, who's eager and takes genuine joy in finding ways to share her information with the next generation. Maeve's fucking incredible."

Okay, I was going for professional, but I guess one *fuck* is acceptable. I glance at Ashlee, who's just listening to me, leaning forward.

"I think your division is so lucky to have gotten Maeve, and I'd hate to see you lose her if she doesn't grow within the department. I know I've never done anything with grants, and I can imagine how difficult it is to allocate funds with so many qualified candidates." I take a breath. "But you'd be making the biggest mistake of your career if you decide not to give Maeve that grant, if you don't eventually give her tenure. And that's my professional opinion, not my opinion as her girlfriend . . ." Or whatever we are.

And even though I was ready to give a huge mic drop ending, my speech trails off. I fall into silence, with nothing but Ashlee's eyes on me and my own heartbeat vibrating through my eardrums.

Then Ashlee smiles. "You really believe in her, don't you?"

My heart flutters. "Yeah. And I also admire her so much." I rub the back of my neck. It won't do much to fix the thrumming in my ears, but oh, right, I wasn't done yet. "And she wants it so badly. If she hasn't already, she's going to blow you away. Supporting her work isn't just keeping an incredible professor. I stayed on to teach another semester because I believe in her, and you've seen the numbers and attention our class has drawn. I'd sign a contract right now to teach classes with her for the next five years because of how good she is. And I'm not going to be the last high-profile lecturer she brings in. The financial impact she'll have on this department is as unparalleled as her educational impact. I guarantee the return investment you'll get with her is leagues away from what you would get with some Columbia bigwig."

The wait before Ashlee speaks again feels like being in a doctor's office awaiting test results. Guess not *all* my anxiety is gone. I return to drumming, this time on the cushion of the chair.

"I agree," Ashlee says, plain and simple.

But I don't dare get my hopes up yet.

"Maeve is an incredible scholar and professor." She smiles again. "I'll be happy to add your testimony to our application for the grant. I'm sure it'll help her in our evaluation."

A big, goofy smile spreads across my face. I take in Ashlee's every word, let them fill me with air and metaphorically lift me off the ground. Maeve's second book might be funded within weeks. She can keep building a robust portfolio for tenure. I'm not the only one who thinks Maeve is incredible.

Even if she never loves me again, even if she never so much as looks my way from this moment on, I can leave this experience knowing I crossed paths with someone so special. Someone who will continue to influence the lives around her and be admired and acknowledged for years to come. I was given the blessing of being able to love and be loved by someone as incredible as her. I'll have to accept that for all the work I've done and will do for her, that may be all I'm getting.

The idea makes my chest ache, but even that ache is starting to feel okay.

I don't know if it's a sign, but Maeve has not confiscated my key to her office. So, once I'm finished meeting with Ashlee, I use that key to enter the room where Maeve's and my story started. She doesn't have class today, yet my chest still tightens as I slowly open her office door. But she's not here. I force a breath and step inside.

Same short desk, same brown couch, same Kenyon and Berkeley degrees hanging on the wall. I inhale, hoping to catch a whiff of her floral perfume, the soft one she uses for work. The one I associate with small smiles in lecture, hand touches grading papers, her brightened eyes as she climbs out of a rut in her academic writing when we're here working late. It's not here, though.

Once this semester ends, I may never return to this office. But it fills my heart to imagine that the nameplate on this desk might read ASSOCIATE PROFESSOR MAEVE ARKO sooner rather than later. God willing, maybe just "professor" one day.

I drop a single laminated pass and plane ticket on Maeve's desk. Probably should've written a sappy note to go with it, but it feels self-explanatory, right? I glance at her desk drawers, contemplating whether this would feel *that* much different with a note. I don't want there to be any confusion about my intentions. I rub my temples as an ache starts up; maybe there's a reason I don't do grand gestures. As if this is even *grand*. Hell, it was so simple that *I* made all the calls to get the pass and plane ticket for after her lecture—

The door whines open.

My muscles seize, and I'm right back to being a kid caught looking at Christmas/Hanukkah presents stowed in my mom's closet.

"Valeria?"

It's a low voice. Not Maeve. Ty.

I force an exhale. It's just Ty.

"Hey," I say, slowly turning to him. Hopefully slow enough to get the red in my cheeks to fade. "Did you get my email about discussion this week?"

"Yeah." He smiles. "And discussion for the week after that. I think the wording was 'just in case you want to get ahead' along with an emoji smiley face."

The urge to flee the room remains, but my heart is miraculously calm. "Yeah, figured it'd help take the load off you and Maeve."

Has she asked about me?

The words sit on my tongue like a bitter pill that's not dissolving fast enough. I can't say them, though. I can't break the professionalism code, even if Ty very obviously knows Maeve and I dated. It's not his job to get involved in our personal lives. Even though Maeve's been cold, she's been professional. The lectures have remained high-quality and office hours have been efficient. Ty's life, effectively, hasn't changed since Maeve and I broke up. Which is as it should be.

"I appreciate it," Ty says. "Maeve does too."

The words ache in my chest. "You don't have to placate me."

Ty doesn't answer right away. His gaze falls to the desk, to the pass, keys, and ticket. I watch his eyes dart as he processes what he's seeing. As he looks back up at me.

"Good luck in France," he finally says.

And just like that, it's time to go. I have no place in this office anymore. I've done everything I can. I force another breath. Cannes. Even my academic colleagues are telling me to focus on Cannes. On my directorial debut, an unabashedly queer film, premiering world-wide and possibly finding a home that will bring it to thousands of theaters across the country and maybe the world. This is huge, this is a lifetime accomplishment, and ready or not, I have to face it. I'm ready to fight for my little movie.

I force a smile. "Thanks."

It's time to get out of here. Leave the rest up to Maeve.

"Good luck with your movie too," Ty says with a smile.

CHAPTER TWENTY-EIGHT

I'm sure Cannes, France, is gorgeous in May, but I'm not given a single chance to find out for myself. Like, I'm talking airport → car → hotel → car → Cannes social function → hotel → Cannes-adjacent party → hotel for all of Wednesday going into Thursday morning. Whirlwind, sure, exhausting, yes, but god the Klonopin is a fucking miracle drug. I have nerves and butterflies when I take a last look in my hotel room mirror before I head out for my final junket before *Oakley*'s premiere tomorrow night, but it feels like everything is going exactly the way it needs to go and things are just *okay*. No, not okay. Honestly, this is *fun*. I've forgotten about the rush I get from all the cameras and the elation of walking down red carpets and laughing my ass off with Mason sneaking pissaladière and wine into our hotel. Suddenly it feels ridiculous and heartbreaking that I was so nervous to be at a festival again. Now I actually feel ready.

Or, well, I would if Maeve were here.

I try not to linger on the pain of Maeve not seeing me this way, happy and shining.

I sit at yet another makeup chair getting touch-ups, this time for Natalie Rockwell, an interviewer who writes for a smaller outlet. Her program is a bit longer, a bit more intellectual, and airs exclusively on a popular YouTube channel. When she reached out to Trish after my Winston interview to say how awful it was that he had treated me that way, I knew I wanted to talk to her someday.

Trish, dressed to the nines in a purple suit, grabs me as soon as I'm mic'd.

"How ya feeling?" she asks me.

I told Trish I had switched to meds out of, like, a concern about health and safety. I dunno, managers like knowing more about your medical history than actual doctors do for liability reasons. Still, I rub the back of my neck, thinking about it.

"Pretty good. Way more mellow than the last premiere. I think the new meds are doing the trick."

She smiles a genuine smile. "Love to hear it."

I turn to her, warmth spreading through my chest. "Thanks for poaching me a year ago."

She pats my hand. "Best decision I made."

The warmth hasn't faded yet. My film's about to premiere at Cannes, and I feel as open and relaxed as I do midway through a therapy session. "I'm sorry for causing you so much stress over the last several months."

"Your apology is noted." She smiles again.

"Promise, I know what I want now. I'm not done yet." I pause, trying not to laugh as Trish eyes me. "But I also appreciate you letting me try something new."

"I'm a romantic at heart," she says, giving me a few pats on the shoulder before I'm called out.

Natalie greets me with a handshake. The two of us are sitting in seventies art deco–type chairs in a room with huge windows, no audience in sight. Out beyond us, the cerulean ocean sparkles in the May sun. Natalie gives me a big smile when we sit down.

"You have no idea how excited I am to have you here," she says, a hint of blush creeping up her cheeks.

"Honestly, I don't think anyone else would want to talk to me the way you do, so it's mutual," I say.

Natalie smiles. "Well, we all know you're here for Cannes with your directorial debut, and we'll get to that, but I believe that's not the only thing you've been doing."

I smile, electric pride sparking in my chest. "No. I've also been teaching a couple of courses at USC. On music and movies, adjacent to my dissertation."

"So, no one except for the students in your classes gets to see that side of you, Valeria the professor. When my producers and I were talking through discussion topics, we thought maybe it'd be fun to do something a little different and ask you to give a little intro lecture."

I nod, my blood pumping. "Just for you." I laugh a little. "Promise, it'll come around to relate to *Oakley in Flames*."

By the time I finish recording my mini lecture and the rest of the interview, it's 3:00 p.m. in France. Maeve is probably still on her morning run. The timing isn't exactly as romantic as I would've wanted, but time zones are a bitch. I sit outside a Cannes venue knowing Mason, other producers, and Important Hollywood People are waiting for me. But as I dial Maeve's number, I'm hoping that she makes me very late for this party.

One ring.

Two.

Three.

"Hello?"

I heard her voice only a few days ago, but somehow she sounds softer. A subtle change that feels monumental now. She sounds softer, and I'm starting to wonder if she was always this soft-sounding and gentle and I let my anxiety fill in the gaps and turn her into something closer to Emily.

"Hey. Can you check your email when you get home? I made some filler for today's class."

"When did you make filler? What does that even mean?"

Her breath is quickening, and I assume she's trying to get back to her apartment faster.

"I made an introduction for the lecture as part of this interview I did at Cannes. I know you love having an extra ten minutes to get psyched up, and I know today's class is so important. Plus, the interviewer was nice."

"Wait. You recorded for *lecture* at a Hollywood interview? Your people must be—"

I find myself chuckling. "Annoyed? Maybe, but who cares. You're still my number one on your important day."

"Jesus." She pauses. "Is that what you called about? To tell me to queue a video five hours before class?"

I swallow, my throat suddenly thick. "No. I called because I know you like to be informed of things in advance. Charlie's still ready to do the lecture, but he's also on standby to head to Cannes." I pause. "I can do the lecture here over Zoom. We had incredible feedback on this class last semester and it's perfect to showcase you. I couldn't miss being your supporting act. The switch might cost *Goodbye, Richard! 2* a few financiers, but Mason tells me the movie will stand on its own if it's meant to be made."

"Wait, are you—?"

"Giving you the choice. Who you want to do the lecture with. Either option is cleared with Ashlee."

Another pause. "Val . . ."

Val. Not Valeria.

It might be nothing, but it gives me the hope I need.

She sighs. "Yeah, I'd love to have you there."

CHAPTER TWENTY-NINE

I'm riding high after Maeve's and my Zoom class—she absolutely killed it, and I *know* she'll get this grant. I'm riding so high, in fact, that the party I attend that night as I track Charlie's flight feels *amazing*. I even manage to charm and be charmed by some billionaire when he pauses the bullshit to tell me about his gay daughter and how much movies like this meant to her. Charlie, brave soldier he is, arrives at our hotel a little past noon on Friday, our premiere less than ten hours from then. I apologize to him for the crunch, but he shrugs it off and starts caffeinating.

And once Charlie is in France, everything becomes very real. I wish they'd given us more of a break before the screening, but at least I'm not having a panic attack when I walk into the theater where *Oakley in Flames* will make its world premiere at eight forty-five that night. I feel present. I can smell the expensive perfume and champagne and really soak it in—*my movie got into a prestigious festival. It might get bought this week.*

On top of it, I feel so *me*. My hair is looking tousled and bad boy, plus blonder because Charlie and I did the stupid lemon bleach on our tips when he was supposed to be taking a nap this afternoon. Combined with heavy makeup that emphasizes the angle of my cheekbones, dark rose lipstick that hugs the curves of my lips, and eclectic silver necklaces, bracelets, and rings accessorizing an otherwise figure-cutting black suit, I look incredible. Hell, with my lacy black bra in full view and my black pumps, I've never felt happier with a look nor looked hotter. It's perfect.

And as much as I want to fixate on Maeve, on the fact that she didn't say anything to me after the lecture, the fact that I don't know if Ashlee and the department are going to give her that grant, I push it away. I push it away and head on to the red carpet alone. Take pictures alone. Ignore the questions about where my professor girlfriend is. It's going to be okay.

One last breath and I step into the theater. I beeline right to Charlie, Mason, and my family, who are conveniently clustered in an area near the front of the stage where we'll do a Q&A later. Mason stuns in a shiny silver suit, her black hair cut into a sharp bob. Charlie went for a standard black suit like me.

Gwyn springs into action first, pulling me into a hug before even Mason gets the chance. And Mason likes to hug.

"Are there any graphic sex scenes in this?" Gwyn whispers to me.

I laugh. "Sensuality, no sex."

Mason throws an arm around me. "I have a cameo, and our characters fuck," she says, straight-faced.

Charlie just opens his mouth slightly. "I—I'm pretty sure you guys are invalidating my sex scene . . ."

I turn to Gwyn, who's just been staring in horror at us. "It's about sex workers, but no, no on-screen sex. Promise." I swear, for all that Gwyn is an LGBT+ champion ally, she's as prudish about my work as my parents are. Still there to support every second but doesn't want to see her sister simulate sex. Like, I get it, but also weak.

Charlie squeezes my shoulders as Mason and my family take their seats. "How you feeling?"

That pang does hit. Something about Charlie knowing everything just gets me. "Trying to focus on the positive."

"The film's incredible, and I'm not just saying that because I'm second-billed."

I smile and kiss his cheek. "I can't wait for people to fall in love with you again."

He smiles back. "I love you, Sulls."

"I love you too."

Minutes slip away. Charlie and I take our seats, him offering me a worn box of Sour Patch Kids I can only assume he kept from the airport. I decline, but after I give my brief introduction, having a piece of candy to suck on while I wait for my heart to slow down turns out to be lifesaving.

I lean my head on Charlie's shoulder as the movie plays. Try to zone out and not focus on the laughs or gasps I hear as it plays. In fact, I do a pretty bang-up job not looking at *myself* as I watch, especially considering I'm already semi-self-consciously worried that being my own director made me the film's weakest link. I focus on Charlie, on the other wonderful queer people who weave this film's fabric. I even think about Luna, how infectious her energy was on set. How it reflected what she was going through, how she was discovering her own sexuality as we made this film together. We've never really spoken about it, but I'm tempted to get her thoughts during the after-party tonight. We hugged on the way in, and she, Romy, and Wyatt picked seats somewhere toward the back.

Shit. I did this. I found this incredible, poignant, funny, fresh script. I had a vision in my head and turned that vision into a reality. It's a real feature-length film that was deemed good enough for Cannes. A full house of industry people and movie lovers from all over the world are watching it right now. If all goes well, I can look up at a billboard while driving along the 405 and see the movie *I made* advertised to local moviegoers. My unabashedly queer, unabashedly anti-police, unabashedly rebellious movie. Watching it is like falling in love with my own work, falling in love with *myself* all over again.

And when the credits roll, the room bursts into applause. I force myself to rip my eyes off the screen and look at the audience around me. People on the edges of the front row are standing up. My family stands. Mason stands. Charlie stands, forcing me to my feet as he slams his hands together. He looks me right in the eye too, mouthing, *You're amazing,* as the applause plays to a crescendo around us. My insides gets looser, but it doesn't *quite* bite the edge off the nerves that are still wriggling inside me in anticipation of the Q&A.

"And we welcome back to the stage, executive producer, director, and star of *Oakley in Flames,* Valeria Sullivan!" the emcee says.

Charlie lets go of me, I take one last deep breath, and step into the lights.

I take my seat in one of the little director's chairs they have set out. Three in total, quickly filled by Charlie and Mason, costar and EP who made this movie happen. It feels strangely like the three of us have sat down in my living room late at night/early in the morning after some other fancy Hollywood event. If we just had margaritas, it truly *would* be just another riff session between the three of us. But no, I'm looking out at the audience, past my family and the smattering of familiar faces. There are so many faces I don't recognize. Faces who came to see my film and enjoyed it without knowing me. It's kind of incredible.

No, it *is* incredible.

"Congratulations to all of you," Victoria, the French butch lesbian emcee, says.

Another round of applause swells around us. There's only one mic (always a technical glitch), but it doesn't even faze me.

"This movie is so fun, isn't it?"

Mason takes the mic. "In the worst way possible, of course."

The audience chuckles.

"Let's talk about that. This film has an undercurrent of something very sinister and dark from queer history. Queer sex workers in this story, like Charlie's character, really exist. Disappearances like Eddie's are ripped from the headlines. What drew you to the subject matter, and then how did you choose to speak on it?"

I take the mic. My heart is beating hard, but for a moment, I feel like I'm back in a college classroom. Talking up here, it's a giddy sort of déjà vu. Big themes and creative vision flow so seamlessly from my thoughts to my lips. Everyone in this audience paid to hear me talk and I'm finally confident enough to give them their money's worth.

"I think the tragic part about what queer sex workers go through is that it's *not* ripped from the headlines. No one in the general public really knows about these people's vulnerability. I wanted to do my part to bring that to light. And with this script in particular, I was drawn to the bond of solidarity that formed between my character and the character of Leon. This idea that these male strip clubs heavily discriminate based on cis-ness and race and are horribly sexist, yet when one of these 'privileged' white cis gay men goes missing, only a queer woman and a trans man love him enough to find him? I loved the focus on the marginalized within an already marginalized community through our protagonists, and I loved that the film showed the kind of love and connection that can exist within these fraught spaces. Especially because these characters are facing an external enemy that kind of hates them all in the same way."

"Plus, you know, mysteries are fun," Mason says, taking the mic from me.

I laugh along with the audience. "It was also fun. The dialogue was whip-smart. Getting those deadpan deliveries has been the most fun thing I've done as a director so far."

"I like the idea that you'll never actually improve and that will remain your best moment," Mason teases. I give her the lightest push on the arm.

"Thanks for believing in me," I return.

"I have to say," Victoria says. "The queer perspective here was pitch-perfect."

I blush. "Thank you."

"Obviously this is personal for you, but did you do any research to make sure you were portraying things as accurately as possible?"

I look to Charlie and Mason. Mason shrugs.

"I did try to find lesbian gaze film theory, but Mason told me to just not zoom in on breasts."

"Just my tits," Charlie says.

"Even *you* didn't have a body close-up," I say. "No, honestly, I just wasn't ever interested in body parts. I always loved watching bodies and figures move through space, so I tried to keep the shots wide as much as possible. And hey, it's a team effort. Mason's input is in the shots, my incredible DP Brendan Kim translated my vision so perfectly, and even camera assistants like the lovely Luna Roth, who's somewhere in the audience, would give me their own take on the non-cis male gaze."

I wonder if Maeve would agree with what I'm saying. If she were ever forced to write a paper on me, what she'd say about this film. What she'd say about the films I hope to make in the future. My chest aches hoping this film is good enough for her. Even though I might never know if she saw it.

"But we did have to rein you in," Charlie teases. "You *did* want to just randomly have 'Pinball Wizard' in this movie."

The audience laughs. They're being way too nice to me. "It would've added to the trippiness of the scene."

"It"—Mason puts a hand on my shoulder—"has never made sense outside of *Tommy*."

Maeve made that comment once. That it only kind of worked in *Rocketman*.

The Q&A wraps up. I return to my seat, looking back as people exit the theater. I'm— I hate to say it, but I'm on fire. My answers were insightful and witty, I nailed exactly what I wanted to convey about the film. After whether consciously or not treating teaching like a distraction, it turns out it was exactly what I needed. Every minute in the classroom adjusting to a new audience and expressing new thoughts has improved my communication. Taking every bit of Maeve's constructive criticism and praise has sharpened my thoughts themselves. I feel on top of the world. I feel like my thoughts matter. I feel *capable*. I feel like I deserved to make this movie and to take up this space. All because of a confidence Maeve gave me. I feel—

I feel like my heart's dropped to my shoes.

I'm standing in a theater in Cannes, my shoes digging into the movie theater carpet, and my tongue's coated in sugar, and my blood's buzzing from a Q&A, and I'm staring at Maeve.

CHAPTER THIRTY

Maeve Arko is standing at the other end of the movie theater, holding a bouquet of red, pink, and white roses. She tucks a hair behind her ear, fidgety. Dare I say nervous? She's really here. I keep blinking, waiting for the curtain to rise or to bolt awake from an altitude-altered dream and find out I'm still on the plane to the South of France. But I'm here. I'm here, Maeve's here, and she's—she's *here*.

I scrape my beaten and bruised heart up off the floor and make my way over to her. It feels like my body is moving on its own; I'm watching a movie where I bridge the distance between us. My chest swells, but there's no warmth. Not yet.

"Maeve . . ." I say, when what I'd fully intended to say was *What are you doing here?*

"Can we talk outside for a second?" she asks.

Maeve's in France. Maeve traveled thousands of miles and bought flowers and is in a lovely black dress all for me. This is . . . for me, right?

"Yeah, of course."

It feels like I'm seeing her for the first time in months. Maybe it's in the way she's standing. A little looser, like everything—down to her facial muscles—is a little more relaxed. She leads me just outside the door, stands next to a napkin dispenser and a popcorn butter container. There's a napkin that's not pulled out properly, and fixing that feels far more urgent than looking Maeve in the eye.

"You made it," I say.

"I did," Maeve says. "I can't thank you enough for the amazing lecture yesterday. And Ashlee mentioned what you did to recommend me for the grant." She exhales. "It means so much to me."

"Maeve, I—I'm so sorry." My lips tremble. "It was wrong of me to try to deflect when you were just trying to communicate about what was bothering you." I exhale, long and hard. A tremble goes through me as I glance around us; no one's looking, but I feel like I should be making a bigger gesture. "I'm glad the class went well, and that Ashlee and the department could see how wonderful you are."

She shakes her head. "I don't think I fully deserve 'wonderful.'" She sighs. "When I asked for that break, I was intending to get back in touch with you earlier. But you were acting so distant that I let my own doubts get the better of me," she says.

She takes my hand.

She takes my hand and it's like everything around us falls away. My stomach flips at the familiar feeling. I'm an addict whose craving has been satisfied once more. "But I could've and should've gotten past that feeling to reach out. You didn't need the extra stress added to your plate, especially given how new and monumental and probably scary this has all been for you. The scheduling conflict wasn't a huge deal, and I left you in the lurch. I'm so sorry."

I can't believe Maeve jumped on that plane thinking *she* was even this much a part of the problem with that fight. Still, there's the strangest sense of relief that she didn't go through with talking to me earlier. I don't know what would've happened if Rosalie and I hadn't finally breeched the medication conversation. Hell, I might've been a wreck tonight if Maeve hadn't waited.

The strangest smile spreads across my face as I run my thumb over her knuckles. "You don't have to apologize for reading the room. Truthfully, I think we needed all that space." Maeve looks up at me, her gaze soft if not a bit confused. I continue. "I wasn't listening to you. The truth is, Emily would've been so pissed at me for what I did to you. She would've broken up with me right then and there. I hadn't escaped *my* trauma enough to be in the moment and process your reaction, listen to your needs, work to fix the issue in front of us. But I think if we had that same fight now it'd be different. I'm ready to be with you. To try again and see each other as we are now."

Silence fills the tiny space between us. Too long, her expression unreadable as she processes. I let go of her hand out of necessity, yanking a couple of scratchy brown napkins out of the butter station and crumbling them in my hands as I wait for Maeve to say something, to move.

She smiles and hands me the flowers. "Then let's try again. If you'll have me."

I'm not used to having someone who would go through this effort to lie down and admit she was wrong even in a small way. It's so far removed from anything I could've imagined Emily doing. Fights used to make me feel unsteady, but right now I feel rock-solid in my resolve. We'll do better by each other next time. And I'll stop blaming Maeve for Emily's mistakes.

"You really want to?" I ask.

My heart explodes in a million colored pieces as she pulls me into a hug. "Yes," she says, a whisper caressing my skin. "A million times yes."

She squeezes me tight; droplets of wetness fall onto my shoulder. She mumbles into me, but I can't hear her. "What's that, love?" I ask. A jolt of embarrassment passes through me, but then I remember. I can call her that again. I intend to call her that for a long, long time.

"Can I kiss you here?" she asks.

My heart leaps like I'm a teenager again. "Yes."

We kiss. We share a single, tender kiss that makes me want to reach out to that devastated teenager, that devastated adult, that little kid who never quite fit in and tell them that everything is going to be okay. That everything is going to be *great*.

"Is that Maeve Arko?" Charlie asks.

I bolt away from Maeve. I don't *quite* love her enough to be obnoxious.

Charlie's grinning.

In fact, Charlie, Mason, Romy, Luna, *and* my family are grinning.

"Whatever are you doing in Cannes?" Charlie continues, rocking on his heels. "I'm so glad you coincidentally made it out to France and coincidentally took my fleuriste recommendation."

I look around at my parents, at Gwyn and Dave, at Luna and Romy and Wyatt, and at Charlie as he and Maeve hug hello.

"Charlie, did you know about this?" I demand, my voice cracking.

Charlie puts his arm around Maeve. "I like her a lot. Wasn't gonna let you two give up on that."

Mason even throws in a smile. "Yeah, if Val gets dumped, it can only be in a slapstick misunderstanding, we-leaked-a-fake-cheating-scandal-to-the-tabloids-for-fun-and-someone-believed-it way."

I realize, in the moment that Maeve turns to Mason and her eyes go wide, that I . . . might have not introduced them before. I laugh. "Maeve, this is Mason Wu. She directed *Goodbye, Richard!*"

Maeve just keeps staring at Mason with that dumb expression. Nearly eight months knowing her and I've *never* seen her with this little control and dignity. She looks so *human.* "You know, you kept mentioning a Mason, and I *knew* you meant a director, but it's hitting me that you meant, like, *the* Mason Wu, who trail-blazed twenty-first-century queer indie cinema."

Mason points to Maeve. "And you're the girl Val abandoned me for at the Oscars to go properly bottom for the first time!" Mason, always the maverick torturing me in front of my parents, has done it again. Luna's buried herself into Romy's shoulder as my parents and Gwyn exchange a *God, Mason* look. And Maeve, newest member of the party, goes *bright red.* Bright red, but still dumbfounded, still in utter awe to be in Mason's presence.

"Come in for a hug, my dude," Mason says to Maeve.

Mason envelopes a board-stiff Maeve in an embrace.

"Mason Wu knows about my sex life," Maeve not-so-quietly whispers to me.

"Welcome to the club," Luna mutters, just low enough that only Romy laughs.

Gwyn and Charlie, of all people, exchange looks. Charlie puts a hand on Mason's shoulder.

"Well, we'll leave you two to go catch up before the after-party tonight," Charlie says. He shoots Gwyn and my parents a glance. "I believe the Sullivans invited me out to L'Affable to celebrate my movie premiering at Cannes."

I can't help but notice him wink as they walk off.

With only about three hours between the screening and the after-party, I tell myself I'll be subtle. Easygoing. Not ridiculous. But I still manage to drag Maeve to the most expensive, best-reviewed casual French restaurant in Cannes. We're both hesitant at first, but soon conversation flows as we find our natural easy rhythm. Within an hour and a half, I'm taking Maeve's hand, both of us wine-tipsy and scallop- and cassoulet-stuffed and leading her back to my suite. I kiss every patch of skin I can in the elevator. Her shoulder, her collarbone, her neck, her jawline, her forehead, remembering the scent and taste of her skin.

We open the hotel room door and fall onto the chaise by the bed, kicking off our shoes.

"So now that you have this research grant . . ." I say, smiling at her.

She smiles back, shaking her head. "I don't know I have it."

"But like"—I narrow my eyes—"you pretty much do. You prepping for your conference next?"

She drops her head onto my shoulder. "That and a research trip. The grind never ends, does it?"

I brush a hand through her hair. It's especially soft, the way hair only feels right after it's been washed. "Nope. We just get better and better at bouncing back into it."

"You were amazing up there, by the way," Maeve says. "Did you have to plan out what you were going to say, or did you just speak from the heart?"

I think back to being up on that stage, seeing the film with an audience, the euphoria I felt throughout the experience. "It's the same way I approach our lectures, honestly. I know my main talking points, but the best answers come from passion. I love that movie. I hope they let me do more like it."

She runs a thumb over my inner wrist. It sends shivers through me. "How will you know if you can?"

"Depends on if this one sells. We'll know in a couple of weeks."

"You know, I always thought you were an exceptionally good teacher. I thought I was helping you find your passion by encouraging you to teach more and move away from movies. But seeing you up there, all the pieces of you finally fit together. The way you analyze film composition, the depth that you engage with theme and content, that passionate way you talk about making movies and TV. You were radiant at that screening. It would be such a crime for you to ever abandon that for anything." She brushes the back of her hand against mine. "Including me. You have the kind of talent I'd spend years studying to write about."

It's amazing how much loftier it sounds when she says it.

A lump rises in my throat. "Thank you."

"So . . ." She sighs. "Don't quit, okay."

I smile. "There's more to be done here, I think."

"Good." She shakes her head. "God, I'm going to be grading finals in the French Riviera because of you. You're a dream."

I run a finger along her jawline. "I *literally* dreamed of dating a professor since I was like seventeen and you're even better than my fantasy. So I think that honor belongs to you."

I look at her lips. It still doesn't feel like the right moment, though. It would be too easy to just fall back into our pattern. And yes, I'm medicated now and know what not to do. But I can't shake the feeling that I have to try my damnedest to make sure we don't fall into our old ways, seeing the other person through the lens of an ex.

Maeve smiles, though, tempting me. "What?"

I guess a new, better relationship starts with communication.

"What do we do this time? To keep each other as happy as possible, make this relationship as healthy as we can?" I say.

Maeve leans back, her head resting on the pillowy comforter behind us, her wavy hair forming a halo around her. I turn on my side and lay beside her. Watch as she looks up at the ceiling.

"What do you want from this, in the end?" she asks.

We're sitting in a luxury hotel room over six thousand miles away from our houses. The comforter is overstuffed, and the lighting is a little too bright, and one open window allows the rushing of the harbor waves to seep in. Yet my heart beats softly; my head's clear. I feel like I'm home. I'm home with Maeve. All I feel is pride at what Maeve has seen of me, what she will see, what I'll see from her when I go with her to her conference in a few months. I imagine us cuddling after the after-party tonight in ratty pajamas, taking turns showering tomorrow because the shower is too small, Maeve using her superior-to-mine French at a patisserie in the morning.

"I want each of us to be each other's solace amid the insanity of the careers and lives we've chosen," I say.

She inches closer to me. Close enough that I can hear her breathing. "I'll feel that way if you tell me when a worry comes up, if you ask me for help when you feel yourself spiraling. If you'd do the same for me. If you'd steady my breathing like you did at the Oscars during your more overwhelming public commitments and if you'd keep picking weird-ass date spots like the tar pits." She leans in closer still, kissing the tip of my nose. "What do you need from me?"

I exhale. "I'll feel at home if you remind me to take my meds even when I'm consistent, if you let me just cuddle with you after I go through grueling press tours. If you tell me when I'm picking shitty projects, if you befriend Dave so I don't have to. If you bring me cookies when I get huge rejections, and if you move out of your backhouse. Just . . . if you're gonna love me, love me for me. And I'll love you for you."

When I lean over to kiss her, I plant it on her lips. Soft at first, firm, then downright begging, digging my fingers into her hair and into the fabric of her shirt. Our bodies collapse into each other like a sigh of relief. She tastes like wine; she tastes like laughter; she tastes like home.

"I love you," I say against her lips.

"I love you too," she says back.

We hold each other, somewhere between peace and semi-consciousness, until Maeve finally passes out from jet lag and I have to get ready for the after-party. I don't mind that she's missing this one. I know she'll be around for plenty of other ones.

CHAPTER THIRTY-ONE

ONE YEAR LATER

On the morning of the one-year anniversary of our getting back together, Maeve tells me to meet her at Literatea and to wear my favorite outfit. I've already made a reservation at one of our favorite bougie restaurants, so I don't know why she wants to go somewhere else to eat beforehand. But I do as my girlfriend says and show up to the little coffee shop in a brown patterned blazer, the softest white T-shirt I own, jeans, and booties.

Maeve's smiling as I approach, two iced drinks in her hands. "All designer, or are you not fully disconnected from the hoi polloi yet?"

I roll my eyes. She says stuff like that, but Maeve's actually slotted into my world remarkably well. Besides moving her out of her back-house to come live with me, she's been happy to come visit me on set when I'm filming in LA, laughed at the free products people send me, tagged me in photos on social media despite the influx of my fans to her page. Plus, she knows as well as I do that *she* requested a Burberry winter coat on her past birthday. "I will not be seen in my previous workplace in a hoodie."

She kisses my cheek as she hands me my coffee. "I'm glad." Our fingers brush as I take the drink. "Exactly as you like it."

As in, a splash of oat milk and decaf because it's 4:00 p.m. I take a sip, relishing in my favorite on-campus coffee spot. Ty, Maeve, and I came a bunch last fall, and I've really fallen in love with the place. "Thank you."

"So," she says, tugging at her earlobe, "this isn't going to be as nice as what we're doing tonight."

Despite my bougiefication of Maeve's life, she's remained as grounded as ever. In fact, thank god none of the celebrity has bled into her work. She's now teaching two 400-level seminars she designed on top of the intro courses she has, and she's been using her grant money to take trips to Europe to do research for her upcoming book. The paparazzi don't bother her, although the fact that I no longer teach here and only occasionally visit her on campus might play a part in that.

"I wasn't rich less than ten years ago," I say. "I'm sure whatever you have planned is perfect."

"Then let's walk."

We walk the couple of hundred yards from the edge of USC's campus and head over to Exposition Park. It's the same stroll we took when we first had our truce dinner, but, unsurprisingly given the hour, now the park is much more crowded. We wait in a sea of people—students in their USC apparel, professors and administrators in their business casual, families with screaming little kids headed over to the museums. A year and a half ago, I wouldn't have been able to stare straight ahead without disassociating or feeling faint. A year into taking medication, though, I remain stable, neutrally aware of my surroundings. The smell of the asphalt, the hum of dozens of voices speaking at once, the rumble of the metro as it leaves the station, I feel a part of it. I don't really want to be here—

I'm holding my breath hoping there's a break in the crowd—but I'm okay.

I take Maeve's hand, jumping back into society like a kid riding a bike. The familiar ridges of her knuckles fit perfectly under my thumb. Sometimes I can't believe these hands have been mine for over a year.

I have no idea where Maeve is taking me. We've thoroughly explored LA in the year we've been together, everything from its best beaches to shopping spots, hikes, and museums. In fact, we've been inside each of the museums in Exposition Park already, and at this point the area feels nearly as familiar as USC's campus. Plus, it's not like now is a particularly practical time to be dragging each other out of our scheduled days—between Maeve's increased course load, paper and book writing, and conference attendance, and my acting and directing commitments, we rarely drag each other to the other's side of town, finding it more convenient to meet somewhere in the middle. The only explanation I can think of is that we're closer to the airport. Maybe we're going to pick up Maeve's parents? I knew they were getting in today for a conference, but I thought Maeve had decided to let them Uber.

"Did you decide to pick your parents up from the airport?" I ask. "I thought you were religiously opposed to LAX pickup."

Maeve laughs. "I am." She studies me. "Are you trying to figure out what we're doing?"

I hug her from behind, rocking her in my arms. My shoes have a little lift, and I'm relishing being tall enough to rest my chin on her head. "You're never this cryptic."

The light changes, and Maeve leads me across the street by the hand. She's moving even slower as we head toward the rose garden near the Natural History Museum. The crowds disperse around us.

"I decided this is one of my favorite spots in LA," she says as we stop in front of the fountain where the bench we sat after our first outing is. We've ended up back here a few times since then, sober enough to really appreciate it. "Nothing compares to color in cities built to be devoid of it."

I get it. Maeve's facing one of the grass walkways, and bursts of yellow, pink, and red roses surround us like low-hanging clouds. The air's tinged with the scent of the flowers.

"You know you never told me what Charlie did to piss off Gwyn," Maeve says.

I laugh. Far more than I need to. "Charlie took Gwyn's seat during a party drinking game on the Fourth of July because G went to the bathroom. Dave was drunk and didn't realize, so he turns to kiss his wife and it's actually Charlie. Charlie thought it was so funny that he kissed him back just as Gwyn returned from the bathroom. She's been annoyed ever since."

There's a pause.

Then Maeve starts laughing. That perfect, eye-crinkling, dimple-showing laugh that I've loved since day one. The butterflies flap inside me. The urges come in a quick succession. I want to hold her hand, I want to skip down the street with her, dip her and kiss her, never let her go.

"Dave is *weak*," Maeve says as she wipes tears from her eyes. "Jesus, bless your niece and nephew."

"I like to think they're stronger than him, but watch, they're gonna be doctors too."

Maeve shrugs. "It's a respectable position."

"I figure they'll be vets. Just to shake it up a little. Although I *really* want them to become, like, mob vets."

Maeve's lips turn up. "What?"

"You know, the ones who treat all the illegal lions in California."

"Val, that's not a mob vet. That's just a vet who can go to jail for treating animals for *idiots*."

I point to Maeve. "A *good* profession."

She shakes her head. "God, I love you so much."

I relish the flush as it climbs up my neck. "A thousand times back at you."

We stop by a particularly full bushel of light pink roses. We're now pretty far off the path. Maeve takes my hand. "Hey, so, can we add an extra dinner with my parents this weekend?"

I met Maeve's parents last summer, about a couple of months into us getting back together. I still don't know if asking me to go to Ohio for Fourth of July weekend was meant to be trial by fire, but it'd set her parents and me up pretty well. They had strong East Coast accents, talked fast, used lots of Yiddishisms I had to stealth google in real time, and went right from "good to meet you" to telling me about Socrates and string theory. I had their blessing by the end of the first night when I was the last one on the back porch with them, talking.

In fact, it was only the second day of knowing them that I learned that they had no idea why I was famous. That they haven't watched a new movie since 1995. That Maeve had sent them a photo of us and the interview where I answered K through 12 homework questions on BuzzFeed.

"Is this a trick question?"

Maeve chuckles. "No. Do you have time?"

I motion to the roses sprawled around us, Downtown LA beyond that. Besides our anniversary tonight, I'm free. We could have every dinner with her parents for all I care. I pull her into my arms. "Your time is my time."

She traces a line on my forearm. "They want to meet your parents too."

My heart picks up, as if sensing something before I can. "Why would they want to meet *my parents*?"

Maeve tries to bite back a smile. "Well, they want to meet family."

I open my mouth to voice my question, but Maeve's too quick.

She answers by getting down on one knee.

Maeve pulls a velvet box out of her jacket pocket and opens up the case to reveal a diamond ring.

My maternal grandma's ring.

This can't be real.

"Val, will you marry me?" Maeve asks, tears brimming in her eyes.

I'm thrust back to a conversation I had with Luna. We were driving to an advanced movie screening I'd gotten us tickets to sometime after filming *Oakley in Flames*. She'd asked me when I first fully understood I was gay and whether I associated that moment with a positive or negative feeling. The first thing I'd come up with was when I was eighteen, a few months from graduating and heading off to Oxford. I'd brushed every romantic and sexual feeling for my Huntington coworker to the side, yet there I was, sitting in AP Government as my teacher explained something painfully obvious about the judicial branch, and Riley Cooper leaned over to me and asked for a piece of paper. She smelled like strawberry shampoo, and I remember sitting there with my chest tight thinking it would be so nice to fall asleep being able to smell that shampoo every night.

It'd been a bad feeling back then, that soul-squeezing fear of being fundamentally different. I remember telling Luna that and watching her expression fall. She grew red when I asked her what her answer would be, only to remember another memory.

One of the first sleepovers I went to was one of those invite-all-your-classmates in first grade. I was six or seven, the friend in question, Jane, had a new little brother that she'd write about in the projects we had to do. She'd draw family portraits with two parents, one with short hair and pants and one with long hair and a dress. I'd been trying to find a bathroom to remove a Fanta stain from my white shirt and had accidentally witnessed Jane's mom breastfeeding her infant brother. Her *other* mom.

I'd brought up the encounter to my mom on the way home, and she'd fumbled through an explanation. She said some women married and had kids with men and some did the same with other women. I remember smiling and thinking to myself that if everyone in the world got to choose, I wanted to marry Jane. I corrected my answer for Luna, said that my first queer memory actually *had* been happy.

All these years later, tears brim in my eyes thinking about what I would tell that little girl in the back of Mom's car who wanted to marry Jane.

"Yes," I say. Maeve slips the ring on my finger.

I pull her up to her feet, hold her in an embrace as I kiss her. We kiss long and hard, pressed so close to each other that I can feel her heartbeat slam in her chest. There's noise around us, a swell of it. I'm vaguely aware that the sound is positive. But I can't move from this woman, from the feeling of her leather jacket against me, her weight pulling me down as she clutches the sides of my blazer. I've memorized the feeling of her lips on mine, yet nothing gets my heart to flutter faster than the thought of being able to taste them over and over again for the rest of our lives.

Then I hear the click. I hear the click and my heart sinks and I turn around and—

And it's Charlie. Charlie with a professional camera, grinning his bigmouthed face off.

"I got it!" Charlie cheers from across the pathway. "Fucking syn-chro-*nized*!"

"What are you doing here?"

"Documenting the greatest moment of your life so far."

I whip around to Maeve, who has the easy smile of someone who's in on a joke. "Uh, what's going on?"

Maeve nods toward Charlie. "Your best friend and I were kind of busy over the last few days."

What Maeve did for me—it really starts to hit. Like bricks coming together, building a beautiful tower that I thought I'd spent so long knocking down. I let the tears flow down my cheeks. "I can't believe you gay-proposed to me in the park you confessed you were obsessed with women in." I pull her into an embrace, burying my face into her soft hair. "I love you so much."

"I love you too," Maeve says through a squeak of a laugh.

"I love you also!" Charlie yells from across the way.

I smile. "Charlie, get over here!"

The moment Charlie comes bounding up, I pull him into our hug.

I'd never thought about what I would have wanted from a proposal before, but somehow my best friend being here has made it perfect.

In fact, everything is perfect. I have a future with Maeve. I have a future making movies that change lives, a future where the people around me are thriving. A future full of hope.

Acknowledgments

There truly is no joy quite like being able to sit down to write a third set of acknowledgments knowing that someone out there has let me publish as many books. *Director's Cut* came from a more intimate, close-knit place in my brain, written as an escape before *Sizzle Reel* was even a prospect for publication among the worst of the pandemic in 2020. But the world's changed and started to open up, and a tremendous group of people have been able to have such an impact on this story. It astounds me and warms my heart.

Caitlin Landuyt, I knew we had something special with *Sizzle Reel*, but with the trials and rethinking and digging we did with this book, I'm even more convinced that you're a genius and I couldn't be happier to be working with someone who wants to get as nitty-gritty with character psychology and subtext as I do. This book started as a flight of fancy, but you saw something more grown-up, more melancholy yet fun and hopeful in the work, and I couldn't be happier with what it turned into. Val and Maeve have a permanent place in my heart because of the love you put into them and their story, and I can never thank you enough for that.

To my entire Vintage team, I wish I could thank you again for the wonderful work done on *Sizzle Reel* and I shall give the biggest thank-you now for everything done on *Director's Cut*. Thank you to Kayla Overbey and Erica Ferguson for making sure my words made sense. Thank you, Steven Walker, for the gorgeous interior. Thank you to magicians Maddie Partner and Leni Kauffman for a cover that's blown me out of the water and brought such an extra layer of bounce and beauty to the work (and thank you for letting me give my alma mater a free advertisement via book cover; all my USC friends and I have been screaming about it for months). To my incredible marketing and publicity teams, Emily Murphy and Anna Noone, thank you for believing in this book and doing everything in your power to help it reach its audience.

A monumental thank-you, as always, to my dream agent, Janine Kamouh. Your dedication to this book, including reading far more of it than we ever needed for a book two sample to send to Vintage. Thank you for your unfettered enthusiasm, your wise notes, for taking this leap into romance wholeheartedly with me. I'm having so much fun and am so glad we made the jump together. Thank you to the incredible Gaby Caballero for the romance book club we've all formed, your discerning eye, and your hard work and love for my work. WME assistant pod, I adore you and forever will. And thank you to my wonderful and tireless extended WME team, including Caitlin Mahoney, Suzannah Ball, and Olivia Burgher.

It may be a cliché, but the best part of this publishing journey truly has been the wonderful authors in the romance community I've been able to call friends and colleagues. Thank you Courtney Kae, Rachel Lynn Solomon, Annette Christie, Alicia Thompson, Ruby Barrett, and Ashley Herring Blake for your kind words about my debut and your welcome into the community. There truly is no way to name every kind and talented soul I've befriended, but

Mazey Eddings, Alison Cochrun, Anita Kelly, Meryl Wilsner, Fallon Ballard, Justine Pucella Winans, Alex Brown, Shelly Page, Hailey Harlow, Courtney Summers, Emma R. Alban—I cherish knowing you. And to my Day Ones, Auriane Desombre, Marisa Kanter, Susan Lee, Courtney Kae, Carolina Flórez-Cerchiaro, Robin Wasley, and Kelsey Rodkey—I couldn't keep doing this without you.

Thank you to my beloved friends and CPs. This book was written in a four-person vacuum, a product of the writing group of Gay Introverts with Hip Problems and Anxiety Who Hate Boot-Cut and Low-Rise Jeans, aka Taylor Heady, Kate Koenig, and Will Miller. This book literally wouldn't exist without you. I'm sorry Val became *less* of a disaster over the course of revision. And to my beloved friends who read the countless drafts after that, Kade Dishmon, Rachel Lynn Solomon, and Kelsey Rodkey, I love and value you deeply. And thank you to the additional friends who supported me through the publication process—August Ryan, Shelly Grinshpun, Nisha Malhotra, Eva Molina, Charlotte Arangua, Page Powars, Sabrina Batchler, Sophia Lopez, and Emily Miner.

The biggest thank-you to the incredible writers who blurbed this book, Becky Chalsen, Rebekah Faubion, Erin La Rosa, Emma R. Alban, TJ Alexander, Susie Dumond, Mallory Marlowe, Emily Wibberley, Austin Siegemund-Broka, and Jenny L. Howe.

Thank you to my beloved Cake/Electric Postcard team, Dhonielle Clayton, Clay Morrell, Haneen Oriqat, Kristen Pettit, and Eve Peña, who have supported this dream and all the random midday meetings I've had to take.

An always shout-out to my family extended and immediate who have supported me through this wacky, a bit unexpected but hopefully inevitable journey. Including, of course, Phoebe, cookies 'n' cream dreamsicle of a rescue pup who didn't exist when I wrote Eustace but who I'm now going to claim is the influence for Eustace.

And lastly, to everyone who picked up *Sizzle Reel*, who took gorgeous photos with it, who reviewed it, who reached out to me saying it spoke to you in ways I could only dream of, thank you! I wouldn't be here without you, and I hope Val's story is everything you could've dreamed of. And to my new readers, welcome to my sapphic little universe; I hope you get all the feels.

ALSO BY

CARLYN GREENWALD

SIZZLE REEL

For aspiring cinematographer Luna Roth, coming out as bisexual at twenty-four is proving more difficult than she anticipated. Sure, her best friend and fellow queer Romy is thrilled for her—but Luna has no interest in coming out to her backward parents, she wouldn't know how to flirt with a girl if one fell at her feet, and she has no sexual history to build off. Not to mention she really needs to focus her energy on escaping her emotionally abusive talent manager boss and actually get working under a real director of photography. When she meets A-list actress Valeria Sullivan around the office, Luna thinks she's found her solution. She'll use Valeria's interest in her cinematography to get a PA job on the set of Valeria's directorial debut—and if Valeria is as gay as Luna suspects . . . well, that's just an added bonus. Enlisting Romy's help, Luna starts the juggling act of her life—impress Valeria's DP to get another job after this one, get as close to Valeria as possible, and help Romy with her own career moves. But when Valeria begins to reciprocate romantic interest in Luna, the act begins to crumble—straining her relationship with Romy and leaving her job prospects precarious. Now Luna has to figure out if she can fulfill her dreams as a filmmaker, keep her best friend, and get the girl . . . or if she's destined to end up on the cutting-room floor.

Fiction

VINTAGE BOOKS
Available wherever books are sold.
vintagebooks.com